BOOK THREE OF
The Spellmason Chronicles

Incarnate

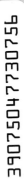

ANTON STROUT

ACE BOOKS, NEW YORK

THE BERKLEY PUBLISHING GROUP
Published by the Penguin Group
Penguin Group (USA) LLC
375 Hudson Street, New York, New York 10014

USA • Canada • UK • Ireland • Australia • New Zealand • India • South Africa • China

penguin.com

A Penguin Random House Company

INCARNATE

An Ace Book / published by arrangement with the author

Ace Books are published by The Berkley Publishing Group.
ACE and the "A" design are trademarks of Penguin Group (USA) LLC.

For information, address: The Berkley Publishing Group,
a division of Penguin Group (USA) LLC,
375 Hudson Street, New York, New York 10014.

ISBN: 978-0-425-27355-5

PUBLISHING HISTORY
Ace mass-market edition / October 2014

PRINTED IN THE UNITED STATES OF AMERICA

10 9 8 7 6 5 4 3 2 1

Cover illustration by Blake Morrow; texture © Allgusak/Shutterstock.
Cover design by Diana Kolsky.

To—
my beloved Clan Strout, who put up with much of my
madness as I experienced new horizons in balancing
writing time while raising two newborns and contending
with my book deadline (which is its own strange
birth process, I suppose),
and
a special shout-out to
Laurell K. Hamilton for much-Twittered confidence
boosting in this the year of the Twinpocalypse

Acknowledgments

Welcome once more, little word nerdlings, to the third and final book of The Spellmason Chronicles. I've missed you. Have you missed me?

Incarnate exists only due to the efforts (sometimes Herculean) of many supportive and/or talented people:

Every last Random Penguin (I'll never use Penguin Random House—NEVER!) that waddles in flightless waterfowl fashion through their hallowed halls, especially my friends (and coworkers) in the paperback sales department; my editor and the person I swap baby photos with all day long, Jessica Wade; editorial assistant Isabel Farhi; managing editor Michelle Kasper, assistant production editor Julia Quinlan, and copy editor Valle Hansen; Judith Murello, Diana Kolsky, and Blake Morrow for a gorgeously creepy cover; Erica Martirano and her marketing and promo team; my publicity superstars, Alexis Nixon and Nita Basu; my social media guru, convention coordinator Colleen Lindsay, an all-around structural support beam in the construct that is Castle Anton; my agent, Kristine Dahl, and Laura Neely at ICM; the League of Reluctant Adults for continued support and stocking of the bar; and my family—the always-elusive Orlycorn, the ever-analytical baby geenyus Julia, and my happy-go-lucky Benjers. And as always, dear reader, thanks to all of you, especially those who have stuck with Lexi and Stanis these three books to find out their ultimate fates.

Pity I kill them all in the end. Or *do* I? Stay tuned, gargoyle lovers . . . It's going to be a bumpy flight!

What is good? Whatever augments the feeling of power, the will to power, power itself, in man. What is evil? Whatever springs from weakness. What is happiness? The feeling that power increases—that resistance is overcome.

—FRIEDRICH NIETZSCHE, *THE ANTICHRIST*

One

☾

Alexandra

"You know, online, the visitors' guide said 'Fort Tryon Park on Manhattan's Upper West Side was a sight worth taking in,'" Aurora "Rory" Torres said as she trudged up the slippery slope of the dark, tree-covered hill, soaked to the bone from the rain. "I gotta say I'm not feeling it."

Rory brushed her wet blue bangs off her forehead and back underneath the lip of her coat's hood, revealing her hesitant eyes. Mercifully, Rory was sans glasses tonight, having wisely chosen to go with contacts instead. I didn't need my backup stopping to wipe her specs clean every five seconds.

I searched ahead for any sign of movement as we worked our way up, making sure there was no activity before answering her.

"I doubt they were writing about gargoyle hunting at three a.m.," I said, checking the time again on my phone. "Speaking of which, where the hell is *our* gargoyle? Stanis always monitors the police scanner. He would have caught the reports of gargoyle activity up here near the park."

"How could he pass up a fun night like this!" Rory said, spinning around in the rain.

"Especially during one of the worst October weather fronts in years," I added. "Still, a little bit of timeliness would be appreciated. He's probably off flying around with *her*."

Rory sighed. "Are we talking about Emily again?" she asked. "Really? I think it's perfectly reasonable for Stanis to seek companionship among the gargoyle community he's fighting to establish."

"Still not happy with him no longer watching over the Belarus family exclusively," I said, conceding the point despite my green-eyed misgivings over his time with Emily. "Less so when he's late, when it's already late."

"And on top of that, it's Monday," Rory added. "Never a good workday, whether it's my dance classes at the conservatory or hunting New York City for rogue monsters."

I couldn't argue with my oldest friend.

The wind and rain whipped though the creeptastic graveyard we found ourselves approaching at the top of the park. Even the weatherproofing on my Burberry trench was no match for the storm tonight, the rain coming into my hood sideways as the wind whipped at my face.

I wiped the rain away from my eyes, my fingers coming away smeared with mascara like a Rorschach image.

"Great," I said, holding my hand out to show the only one brave enough to weather the weather with me tonight. "Tell me I don't look like a panda."

"You don't look like a panda," she said with zero conviction in her voice, then muttered, "Ling-Ling."

There was something to be said about having a best friend since grade school. It meant I felt only a little bad about forcing her out on a night like tonight.

I rubbed the makeup off on the thigh of my already-soaked-through jeans. "Waterproof mascara, my ass."

I shivered. The heat of summer had already gone with the passing of the Equinox weeks ago, but the chill in my bones had me once more longing for the dog days of summer. Hunting in this weather was miserable work at best. At worst it might be death by pneumonia for the two of us.

"You okay?" Rory asked, her voice full of concern.

I shook my head. "It's been, what? Six months since we took down Stanis's father and his stone cronies . . . ? If I'm not cleaning up the mess I made chasing down gargoyles, it's the witches and warlocks of New York trying to take me down for making regular people aware of the existence of the arcane."

Rory gave a weak smile. "On the plus side, no one's tried to kill you in at least a week," she said, ever the optimist. "That's got to count for something."

I wondered how long that would last, but I kept my mouth shut. Even I got sick of my misery these days. I centered myself, willing my body to stop shaking, and after a moment I was composed once more. "I'm fine," I said. "Just wet, hungry, exhausted . . ."

Rory laid her hand on my shoulder, giving it a comforting squeeze. "So let's call it a night, then."

"No!" I growled, shrugging her hand off me so hard that I even surprised myself. "We *can't*."

Rory gave an exasperated sigh, drops of rain flying from her lips. "Yeah, Lexi, actually, *we can*. Go home, get some rest, have a hearty breakfast in the morning with milk and juice to make it complete . . . then we can pick this up tomorrow."

"You go," I said, snapping in my drowned-rat misery. "I'm staying. There's one of them here. Police scanners said their helicopters spotted one earlier."

Rory stood her ground, making no move to leave. After a long silence stretched between us, I turned from her, heading farther up the wooded path toward the lights of the Cloisters above. Sadly we weren't on a mission to visit the abbey-turned-museum for its fine collection of art, tapestries, and artifacts. At best I might get to keep them from danger, and a skirmish might not prove the best time to try and take the sights in.

Even though Manhattan looked relatively flat, the burn in my legs climbing to the highest natural point in our fair city told a different story. As we approached the top of the hill, the tree line gave way to an open clearing where the main building of the Cloisters rose up in all its European medieval glory. This late in the evening, the parking lot off to the right of it was dead empty.

"Visiting hours are most definitely over," Rory said, stopping at my side.

"Shh," I hissed in a low whisper, even though I doubted anything could possibly hear us through the beating of this rain. "Nocturnal creatures don't care about what passes for business hours. Besides, my guess is we're tracking a Griever tonight."

"Which kind is a Griever? Oh, should I look it up on Marshall's cheat sheet?"

"Shh!" I said, grabbing Rory and dragging her back toward the safety of the shadowy tree line. "This one's not rocket science. Look around; what do you see?"

Rory slipped her phone back into her pocket and stared off into the center of the clearing where the building stood. "I'm assuming the Cloisters."

I rolled my eyes at her. "What *else*?"

She craned her head up to the one tall tower that rose above the rectangular abbey, but I pointed down.

"There's a graveyard," she said.

"Where people—or in this case a *grotesque*—might go to grieve," I said. "Hence, Grievers. Trust me, that's what we're going to find here. I've spent more time than I care for in graveyards these past few months. Grievers can't seem to get enough of their precious final human resting places."

"Okay, fine," she said, "but—"

I slapped my hand over her mouth to silence her, pointing to a dense cluster of tombstones along the side of the building. One of the shapes moved, and I followed it with the pointer of my free hand.

I studied the figure as close as I could from where we stood. What looked like one of the massive tombstones carved to resemble an angel was definitely moving. Its wings were spread to an impressive span, their finely detailed carving easily recognizable as the work of my great-great-grandfather, the last of the old-world Spellmasons, Alexander Belarus.

Rory dropped to her knees when she spied the figure, pulling off the art tube she always wore across her back. The three pieces of her *glaive guisarme* slid out of it, and Rory set about assembling the pieces, first connecting the two shafts and then attaching the bladed end piece of the pole arm.

By the time she stood and strapped the tube across her back again, I was advancing forward, pulling off my backpack to release the heavy stone book from within. Once free, I pressed my hand to the book's carved cover and spoke the Slavic word for *release*, the book beneath my fingers transforming to one of ink and paper.

The bond between the arcane stone of the book and me was a strong one. Strong enough, apparently, that the stone angel felt it as well and rose up from the grave it stood before.

With its wings fluttering in agitation, the angel reached out to a nearby tombstone, tugged at it, and lifted it like it was made of papier-mâché.

"Incoming!" I shouted.

As it launched the grave marker in our direction, Rory dove to her right and I dropped right where I was to huddle protectively over my spell book.

The tombstone flew overhead and didn't stop until I heard the snap of branches and tree trunks from somewhere off behind us.

"So much for immobilizing him first," I said, scrambling to my feet.

"We've got a runner!" Rory shouted as she stood and the angel spread his wings, taking to the air. "I mean flyer!"

"Looks like we're going with Plan B, then," I said, picking up my backpack.

Rory just looked at me from under her wet, blue bangs. "We have a Plan B?!"

Ignoring her, I shoved my book back into my bag. "I'm sick of these things making a run for it," I said, searching around until my fingers found what they were looking for. I pulled free a curved stone hook and a coil of rope with a steel-core cable running down the center of it, looping it through the eye of the hook before knotting it tight. I took the other end of the coil of rope and wrapped it around my waist twice before tying it securely.

"I might not have the lasso skills of a cowgirl," I continued, forcing my arcane will into the stone of the hook, "but I *can* control masonry well enough."

Rory's eyes went wide as the realization of what I was about to do hit her. "Lexi, don't!" she called out. "You'll get yourself killed!"

"Better me than another innocent," I said.

By then the gargoyle was rising up past the old abbey, gaining speed. Wrapping one hand around the stone hook and sliding the loose coil of rope into my other, I wound up like a pitcher and threw the hook with as much strength as I could.

I held my arcane will to that of the stone of the hook, all the while my eyes continuing to track the gargoyle. At the bending of my will, the hook corrected its course to catch up with the fleeing creature.

Thankfully, it seemed that since I had accidentally awakened this particular grotesque six months ago, it hadn't spent much time practicing flight. The stone angel wobbled in the air unsteadily as it attempted to escape, allowing the speed of my hook to easily outpace it.

Still, I didn't let my sense of pride in my mastery of it go to my head. Until I could actually ground the creature, the victory wasn't mine.

I guided the stone hook past the angelic figure and then forced it into a sharp turn across the front of the creature's legs, forming a midair trip wire. I snapped my wrist on the hand holding the rope, managing to loop the line securely around its legs. The thrill of pulling off what felt like such a genuine cowgirl move overcame me, and only then did I allow myself the tiniest amount of pride for the fanciness of rope skills.

Which, naturally, was my undoing.

The force of the fleeing creature—as bad a flyer as it was—was *still* substantial. The line in my hand tightened quick as a whip and before I could release it, my feet were already off the ground. Pain shot across my midsection as the rope encircling me went taut, and I flew into the air as Rory's stunned face—and the ground—faded away below.

"Lexi!" Rory shouted, but already her voice was fading off far behind me.

My overall fatigue and this fresh series of aches filled me with the kind of wild fear that only an airborne magical creature dragging me across the night sky could. If it weren't for the growing sensation that I was going to die, I almost would have enjoyed the perverse and deadly pleasure of the madcap carnival-quality ride.

Rain whipped across my face as I flew through the night sky, my vision clouding as its sting filled my eyes. My arms burned from my death-grip hold on the rope—falling wasn't something I could afford to do with so many mistakes left to atone for.

I needed to gain control of this situation before this creature flew me out over the river or decided to smash me into the side of a building. The only thing going for me was my added weight throwing off the gargoyle's flight, twisting the creature in a spiral as it adjusted to my being tethered to it.

Hoping to use that to my advantage, I swung myself like the world's biggest pendulum, using my momentum to drive the creature away from the Hudson River and back toward the Cloisters itself.

My best bet was to aim for the high tower, driving the gargoyle toward it. I might be able to land myself on the lower roof of the surrounding abbey or drop down into its courtyard. If *that* didn't work, my extended hope would be to land in one of the trees of the surrounding forest. At least then I could try to wrap the line around the trunk of a tree and use the leverage to ground the gargoyle.

The tower was coming up fast, and the creature noticed it and tried to steer away from the stone walls. It managed to spread its wings as far and wide as it could, which slowed its descent, allowing it time to readjust its course. Like an airplane doing a rollover, the gargoyle spun until it was on its side, one wing reaching straight to the heavens while the other one pointed down to the ground below.

What the hell was it doing? I wondered. The maneuver still put him on course to smash into the building . . . a panicked second of calculating its trajectory, and my heart sunk when I realized what was about to happen.

Three vertical stained glass windows were set into the side of the tower, coming up insanely fast. The creature smashed through the center panel first, the panes of glass exploding into the building, leaving plenty of jagged chunks that I was about to get dragged through as the rope pulled me after him.

I curled myself into a ball as small as I could and braced myself as I flew through the broken window, the jagged panes of glass catching my clothes. The snags and tears slowed my momentum some and I fell through the opening onto the interior of the tower's floor, rolling until I was a tangled ball of flesh, blood, and rope, stopping only when I hit one of the transept walls of what looked like the nave of a church.

I wriggled myself out of the twist of rope and pushed myself up onto my hands and knees. The warm flow of fresh blood trickled harder down my left arm through one of the slashes in the sleeve of my coat. I poked at the spot, examining how serious the wound was while also, vainly, letting a moment of silence pass for my poor coat. I had loved my Burberry . . .

Before I could fully assess the damage to my body, the rope at my feet twitched to life and began to slip away from me. The now-grounded gargoyle writhed on the floor near the altar, the tangle of rope around him coming looser and looser with each thrash of his struggle to free himself.

When I tried to stand and chase after the rope, my knees buckled. I must have taken my landing harder than I realized. If I didn't get the line back in my hands soon, this gargoyle was going to free himself. I'd be fighting this whirlwind of wings and stone in an enclosed space where the confinement was likely to put me in harm's way, and that was the last thing I wanted.

The tinkling of glass behind me caught my attention and I turned. Rory stood in the frame of what had once been the stained glass window. Holding her bladed pole arm overhead, she dropped down into the room, the last remaining pieces of glass from the frame raining down behind her in a sparkling rainbow waterfall.

Back in front of me, the rope was quickly snaking farther away from me and I lunged for the line, barely catching the end of it with my left hand. The rope jerked with a burn across the skin on my fingers. I wrapped my legs around one of the columns within the old monastery, hoping to brace myself, but it was no use. They came free of the column and the line dragged me across the glass-covered stone of the floor toward the gargoyle, my body screaming with pain, but I refused to let go.

Luckily, not every spell I knew required free hands. I rushed out a power word for *control* toward the stone of the altar's pulpit, managing to topple it over onto the creature with a press of my arcane will.

I finally ground to a halt on the floor of the nave, coming to rest with a final crunch of glass sounding beneath me. Rolling over with the rope still in my hand, I carefully placed my hands on clear sections of the floor and took my time as I righted my aching body. I stood up slowly, then took a deep breath before limping toward the altar.

Rory ran past me and pulled the rope free of my hand. She slammed one of her Doc Martens on the stones of what still remained of the pulpit and steadied herself as she leaned back to tug on the rope, throwing all her dancer's strength into her flexed arms.

The slack in the line went taut. The gargoyle stirred, awakening, and a contest of strength began between the two of them. Rory held strong and advanced on the creature, securing the rope around him with several additional loops of it.

"Thanks," I said, brushing glass and debris off of my bloody coat.

"My pleasure," she said, handing me the rope before going back across the room to reclaim her pole arm. "He's all yours."

I walked to the gargoyle that lay on the floor, still struggling against the ropes.

I had to talk fast. Even restrained, it would take only a minute or two until the gargoyle would eventually figure out it could break its bonds using its preternatural strength.

"Easy, now," I said, following it by the whisper of an arcane Slavic word that reached out to the stone of his angelic form. Now that he was actually grounded and captive, it was easier to make that influencing connection, and I felt my will wash over him. I pressed one of my boots down on his chest. At the same time, I reached out with my power and raised one of the heavy broken blocks of the pulpit, hovering it over the creature's head.

"If you've got anything more than rocks in your brain, you'll stay down," I continued, finally taking in the damage to my torn and bloody coat. My face filled with a grim and manic smile. "You might look like an angel, but after what you've done to my jacket? You're about to bring out the devil in me."

Two

Stanis

As I flew over the wooded land along this Manhattan section of the Hudson River, my ears filled with a gentle laughter that reminded me of the chimes humans often left outside to catch the wind.

"Have you never been to the Cloisters?" my female companion in flight said.

I arced up into the air as we approached the ancient abbey, ceasing my flight as I set my batlike wings into short, rapid strokes allowing me to hover in place.

"I have been here much longer than the structure below us, Emily," I said.

My fellow *grotesque* attempted the same maneuver I had just completed, but instead turned too sharply and collided with me. The serpentine features of her face—half human and half snake, with yellow marble skin—were a stark contrast to the gray of my chiseled stone and demonic features. I held her until her own wings—far more dragonlike than mine—fell into the same rhythm as my bat ones before holding her out away from me at arm's length.

"I'm sorry," she said, her face full of embarrassment.

"I do have several centuries of practice on you," I said with a smile. "For a *grotesque* with only six months' practice, you have excellent prowess with it."

Keeping her hands in mine, I began our descent. This seemed to release her from her embarrassment and she looked down to the building below.

"You're older than this monastery?" she asked.

I nodded. "Yes," I said, "but in truth, I do not believe it actually *is* a monastery."

"Oh, no?"

"For the first century of my existence, the lush park you see surrounding the building went untouched. However, in my subsequent centuries of watching over Manhattan, I have come to learn that change is inevitable. The area I had come to know as Fort Tryon Park was not immune to this way of the city. Nearly a century ago I watched human workers laboring late into the night as five of the greatest cloistered abbeys of Europe were reconstructed here stone by stone. But I do not believe it was ever intended to be of monastic use, but to serve as a museum dedicated to medieval Europe."

Emily smiled, her fangs showing. "For someone who spent centuries with very little human interaction, you are remarkably well versed in such matters," she said.

"I am a good listener," I said, "and have long had a fascination with the place as an architectural wonder of Manhattan. For years, I did not know why, but since discovering who I am and where I come from, I can see why. I missed my home."

"But aren't medieval times well *before* your time?" she asked.

"Not by much," I said. "In my time, Europe was already old and the world slower to change. This building reminds me of my father's Belarusian kingdom in Kobryn. It belonged to Lithuania back then, but despite the iron fist my father, Kejetan, ruled with—Kejetan the Accursed, they called him—despite that, I can still recall the architecture of my human boyhood with some fondness. There was still innocence in me, long before my father accidentally struck me down when he took the crude but immortal stone form he forced from Alexander Belarus in his mad quest for power . . ."

The pain of the day he broke my human form flooded my stone body and I fell silent. Emily squeezed my hand in hers.

"But you are here today," she said. "With me, helping others . . ."

"I have Alexander Belarus to thank for that," I said. "Teaching me had been his one true joy when my father forced him into servitude. It would have killed Alexander to see me die in such a way. His arcane knowledge set me to this stone form, and I am forever grateful for it, if only for the sake of being able to contend with the likes of my father and his kind. May they rest, but not in peace."

Descending, the two of us passed down along the side of the tower, the figures of Alexandra Belarus and the blue-haired Aurora Torres catching my eye over by the entrance to the building. Behind them, ropes ran back through the doors leading in, the two of them straining with the effort of pulling something out of the building.

When Emily and I landed, we walked to them and I grabbed the ropes.

"Allow me," I said, giving one hard pull. Alexandra and Aurora stumbled out of the way as the burden they had been dragging shot out the doors, a writhing winged figure coming to rest at my feet.

"An angel," Emily said, leaning over to look at the figure.

The rope had pinned the figure's wings to its back, but there was no mistaking the iconic look or art style of one of Alexander Belarus's statues come to life.

"You couldn't have gotten here a little faster?" Alexandra said, the sharpness of her tone catching me off guard as she looked first to me and then to Emily. "Good to have the gargoyle—sorry, *grotesque*—back up, though."

Alexandra went out of her way in my presence to use the archaic French term I preferred when referring to my kind, but to hear her first use the vulgar form threw me. I stood there, unsure of how to respond for a moment. "Despite the police scanner you had Marshall install at Sanctuary, this island of Manhattan is a larger area to cover than you think,"

I reminded her. "And it would be easier on me if you would perhaps be a little less . . . diligent in your pursuits."

"I'm sorry," Alexandra said. "Am I wearing *you* out?"

"We cannot be worn out, save by the transformative light of day," I reminded her. "We do not require sleep."

This answer did not seem to satisfy Alexandra, as she shook her head and smiled, but unsure as I was how to respond, I looked to Aurora for guidance.

"Hello, Stanis," the blue-haired woman said. "Don't mind her. Someone's just a little overly ambitious, sleep deprived, and a wee bit sensitive."

Alexandra did not respond with words, but the glare in her eyes at her oldest friend was enough to silence Aurora.

"Then forgive our lateness," I said. "I will handle this creature."

Alexandra and Aurora stepped out of the way, and I turned my attention to the prone figure at my feet. The angel looked more like a statue right now as it lay there unmoving. I tugged at the ropes to rouse it.

I waited for the creature's snarl, the gnash of its teeth or an attempted swipe of its claws, but I was not prepared for the look of fear and confusion in its face.

"Do not hurt me," a male voice cried out from the angel's lips.

"Hurt *you*?" Alexandra said, laughing. "You've been the hostile one! *You* threw a gravestone at *us*, remember?"

The creature looked from her to Aurora, gesturing with the little movement he had in his bound hands toward the pole arm she held. "She showed up brandishing one of those . . . those . . . *things*."

His wings twitched, an involuntary telltale sign of nerves that I spent much of my time trying to suppress in my own.

I allowed myself to relax, turning to my human friends. "This creature was not going to rip you apart," I said, then turned back to the angel. "Neither my friends nor I are here to hurt you."

"I don't think you *can* hurt me," he said. His words came out full of fury and confusion despite the angel being prone.

Emily cocked her head at him. "What do you mean?" she asked.

"Look at me," he snarled, a sadness in his words. He pulled one of his arms free from the ropes and slammed his stone fist against his chest.

"Don't be *too* sure about not being able to die," Aurora said, sounding both offended and a bit prideful. She tapped the bladed end of her pole arm against the angel's chest. "We're pretty resourceful."

The *grotesque*'s face seemed uncertain, but he turned his attention to me instead, some of the fight going out of him. "What *are* you? What am *I*?"

"We will get to that," I said, kneeling down close to his face and lowering my voice, "but for now why do not you tell me who you are and what you remember."

"I do not understand," he said. "This . . . this isn't *right*. I saw my own gravestone. I *should* be dead. I should be in Heaven, not here as some cruel mockery of a Heavenly creature!"

I looked up at Alexandra, raising my voice once more. "Have you not done as we agreed?" I asked her.

She shook her head.

"You scold me for the lateness of our arrival," I said, "yet you have not taken care of your end of dealing with those you find of my kind who are in need of Sanctuary . . ."

"He threw a gravestone at us," she growled back at me. "With that kind of behavior I didn't think he was a likely candidate, okay? I chalked him up as one of the bad ones."

"So it would appear," I said, standing. "Do feel free to do your part now."

Alexandra sighed, but knelt down next to the angelic form.

"Easy," she said, laying her hand on his chest. "What's your name?"

"Jonathan," he said, calming a bit.

"Listen, Jonathan, I can appreciate your frustration here . . ."

"I doubt you can," he said with some bitterness to his words. "You're human still."

"I *can*," she insisted, trying to keep her composure. "I'm just dealing with a whole city full of your kind right now. It's a bit much."

"I don't care about those others," he said. "What I care about is how I've been forsaken after pledging myself to His service."

"What were you in life?" I asked him.

"He came here to grieve," Alexandra said. "And he threw what I think was his tombstone at us, so I'm guessing there's a connection to the Cloisters."

"Stanis," Emily said. "I thought you said they moved several abbeys here. They moved the graves as well?"

"I can answer," Alexandra said after I had been silent for a moment too long. "New York architecture is kinda my thing. Some of the spiritual ties to the abbeys used for this project were strong. It was a sign of reverence and respect for the deceased who were chosen to rest here." She turned back to the angel. "Go ahead. Who were you?"

Off in the distance the sounds of sirens cried out into the night, growing louder with each passing moment.

"I served the Lord," Jonathan said. "I was a man of God. A monk. I remember dying long ago. What a joke it is that I am now stuck in this form which so viciously reminds me that while I may look like an angel, I am no closer to His Kingdom than I was in life."

Alexandra fell silent beside him, her head lowering and her eyes slowly falling shut. "I'm sorry," she whispered. "I'm to blame for that."

The angel looked up at her, confused. "What?"

"I'm to blame," she repeated, with conviction and hatred in her words this time.

"How is that possible?" he asked. "Who are you?"

Alexandra took a deep breath. "I am Alexandra Belarus," she said. "And I am your maker. I'm responsible for this. Thanks to the magic practiced by older generations of my family—Spellmasonry—I accidentally drew you and others like you into these forms. Now Manhattan's got so much *grotesque* activity, it's made the news every night since my spell went awry. All of this running around is me trying to clean up a situation that's already gone way too public."

The angel's face filled with horror. "So you drew me out of Heaven and trapped me here?" he asked in shock.

"I do not believe so," I answered. "After talking with many of our stone kind, I believe we are inhabited by disquieted spirits that have been unable for reasons I do not know to pass on to the afterlife."

Red and blue lights flashed through the forest all around the Cloisters from the roads leading up to it.

Alexandra stood back up and looked to me.

"That's the CliffsNotes version," she said. "Satisfied? Now, Stanis, if you'll do your part. Rory and I have to go. Like, now."

"You're hurt," Emily said, pointing to the large amount of blood I had failed to notice along Alexandra's left arm.

"I'm fine," Alexandra said. "Not your problem."

"We really should be going," Aurora said, grabbing Alexandra by her good arm and starting for the forest.

I watched the two of them run for the tree line through intermittent flashes of red and blue light.

"We can discuss the alarming rate at which you are handing over these newly captured *grotesques* to me at a later date," I called out after her. "Unlike your . . . CliffsNotes version, you called it? The way of the *grotesque* takes time when we bring an initiate to our ways."

"Your ways?" the angel asked, looking up at me from the ground where he still lay.

"You will learn soon enough," I said, "but trust me now when I say the time it takes is both for your protection and that of those around you."

The bright white of headlights lit up the three of us as a male and female officer jumped free of the car, running toward us.

"Maron!" the female officer called out, her red hair pulled back and swaying wildly as she ran. "By the doors!"

"I see them, Rowland," the man said, pulling a gun free from the jacket of his suit as he ran toward us.

"NYPD!" the woman shouted, pulling a gun of her own. "Freeze or we will open fire."

The man slowed and raised his gun, waiting for the woman to join him. "Think guns will actually work?" he asked her, uncertain.

Emily and I did not want to be around to find out. I handed one of the ropes to Emily and secured the other in mine, leaping into the air. The added weight of the still-tied angel made it difficult to fly, but with Emily and I splitting the load, we still managed to shoot up past the tower and into the night sky before the two detectives could open fire.

"I do not understand," I said to Emily once we were in full flight with our newly acquired *grotesque* in tow.

"What exactly?" she asked.

"That is not the Alexandra Belarus I know," I said, troubled. "With my father and his men vanquished . . . with his threat eliminated, I would expect the Spellmason to be more at peace . . . yet to see her like this . . ."

"We all have our issues that lie beneath the surface of what others see," Emily said. "I can only imagine hers run deep."

Was it seeing me with Emily that had put Alexandra in such a mood? It was the only thing I could imagine, although Alexandra had no right to judge whom I chose as my companion. After all, the Spellmason had made her choice when she had chosen the alchemist Caleb Kennedy. Or rather, when I had stepped back to allow the like companionship that his human form offered her.

Tonight was full of questions, not all of them mine.

"Where are we going?" the angel asked, confusion thick in his voice as he dangled between the two of us high above the Manhattan streets.

"Sanctuary," I said, and fell silent as I flew on and tried to make sense in my head of the woman I had once been sworn to protect and had watched over my whole life.

Three

◖

Alexandra

While Rory and I had been playing the Winchester sisters all evening skulking after the gargoyle population of Manhattan, her roommate and my friend Marshall Black-moore had been working, too, but as we approached his store, Roll for Initiative, it became clear who had fared better.

In the reflection of the store's display windows, the two of us looked worse than the zombie action figures posed just on the other side of the glass. With her blue hair plastered to her head despite the hood she had been wearing, Rory looked like a drowned Cookie Monster. My eyes were sunk far enough into my head from exhaustion that I almost wished someone would shoot me in the head after mistaking me for the first sign of the zombie apocalypse.

Marshall, comparatively, just looked busy behind the cash desk at the front of his store. The worst thing he probably endured tonight was a paper cut from flipping through the pile of books he had spread out before him. Still, he had his hands full there. For this late at night there were a consider-able number of customers wandering the store.

Not surprisingly, when we entered the store as wet as two

drowned rats, we turned a few heads among Marshall's nerd herd.

Marshall looked up and did a double take when he saw us staggering in.

"You two look like hell," he said, nervously running his fingers through his mop of black hair. "You okay?" His eyes darted to the back of the store, then back to us.

"We're okay," I said. "*Ish*. Are *you*?"

His kind brown eyes came quickly back to us, and he nodded.

"We could have used you," Rory said, reaching into her pocket and fishing out the crumple of notes from the evening.

Marshall turned his eyes back to his books on the counter. "There's only so much time in my day," he said, tapping the books in front of him. "I can't stay up all night chasing *grotesques* down. Someone's got to catalog them, and I'm lucky I have the time to do *that*, on top of running my store . . ."

"Well, you *really* should have come with tonight," Rory said. "You know how hard it was for me to take notes by moonlight, in the rain, in the middle of Fort Tryon Park?"

"I appreciate the effort," he said, "but I just couldn't get away."

I looked back through the store's racks and shelves, further examining the crowd I had only given a cursory glance to upon entering. Each of them looked a bit like the types of people I saw dressed up on their way over to the Javits Center for the annual Comic Con.

"I'm sorry; are we keeping you from something?" I asked.

Rory took note of the crowd. "Is this one of your live action role-playing thingies?"

Marshall blushed, holding his hand out to Rory.

"Something like that," he said. "I'm sure you two did fine without me. I've just got a lot going on with the store."

"Who knew gaming could be such work?" Rory asked. She stepped up to the counter and threw down the notes she had been taking at the Cloisters earlier. "This should make your night. Tagged another Griever. Released it to Sanctuary."

"Thanks," he said absently as he pulled the notes over, already looking down at his books again. Marshall pulled open a large binder, flipped to a tabbed section labeled "Grotesques," and began transcribing Rory's notes onto a blank page there. A few lines in, he pulled his hand up to find a wet smear of ink on his hand and the page.

"Sorry about the pages . . ." Rory said. "It was raining."

"And the blood, too," I added. "I was . . . well, bleeding."

"You okay?" he asked, for the first time looking at us as if he was genuinely concerned.

"I'll be fine," I said, even though as I finally took the time to assess myself, I felt far less than it.

"She could have died tonight," Rory said. "You weren't there for us and she could have bled out."

"It's no big deal," I assured him even though I felt blood dripping off my left hand onto the floor of his store. "Just crashing through a stained glass window, is all."

"Jesus, let me look at that," Marshall said, shutting his book and coming around the counter.

I shrugged my jacket off my shoulder, a wad of notebook paper pressed against the wound still sticking in place. What had once been your typical white-lined paper was now a crimson brown.

Rory's eyes went wide upon seeing the papers. "We need to get you to a hospital," she said.

The sight of my own blood did make me feel queasy, but I shook my head. "No time," I said. "If I can get back out there and hunt, I can at least bag another gargoyle tonight."

Marshall pulled away the clump of blood-soaked notepaper. "Not if you look like one of Dracula's victims," he said. "This looks pretty bad, Lexi."

"Listen to the man," Rory said, nodding in agreement with him. "You're no good to your cause if you don't take care of yourself first. Let's just hit Beth Israel's emergency room and call it a night."

"No," I insisted, harsher this time. "I *need* to be out there in the streets. I need to find more of these *grotesques*."

"Lexi—" Rory started, but Marshall cut her off.

"I can fix this," he said, which caused both of us to turn to him.

"Oh, really, *Doctor* Blackmoore?" Rory asked. "Funny, I failed to notice any medical degrees hanging on the walls of our apartment. Do you keep them here, covered over by that Settlers of Catan poster, perhaps?"

I wrinkled up my face in uncertainty. "No offense," I said, "but won't your 'help' just end up putting me in the hospital with something worse?"

Marshall ignored both of us and hurried back to his counter, disappearing for a second as he dropped behind it.

"Keep it up, ladies," he said. "If you prefer, I can just let you stand there until you lose enough blood and collapse . . . ?"

Curiosity—or maybe it was light-headedness—got the better of me.

"All right," I said. "How?"

Marshall stood, but continued searching beneath the counter as he spoke. "Just because I've been busy with the store doesn't mean I've stopped experimenting with the alchemy your boy toy Caleb got me started on," he said. His hand came out from under the counter with a dark plastic vial in it, the only marking being a piece of duct tape down its side with the letters *CLW* on it. "Ah, here we go."

"CLW?" I asked.

"Cure Light Wounds," he said, coming back around to me once more.

Rory eyed him with skepticism as she finally pulled off the hood of her coat and fluffed out her wet blue hair. "This is one of your gaming things, isn't it?"

Marshall looked down his nose at her. "When *isn't* it? It's from Dungeons and—"

"That's more than I need to know, Marsh," she said with a grin.

Marshall rolled his eyes, shrugged, and fished in his pocket, pulling out one of those thick Sharpie markers.

"Here," he said, handing it to me. "Bite down on this."

With some reluctance I took it from his hand. "For real?" I asked, unable to hide the hesitation in my voice.

He nodded.

"For real," he repeated. "It's bad enough you're dripping blood all over the entrance to my store. I don't need you biting off your tongue while I'm applying this and have it flap all over my floor."

The imagery left me feeling even *more* light-headed, but I was determined to stay standing and caught myself before it had me staggering. Without another word I lifted the Sharpie to my lips and slid it across my mouth the same way a dog would a bone.

Marshall pulled the vial's stopper free and lifted it to the bloody slash on my arm. A black, tarlike substance oozed from the vial, and the second it touched the wound, there was instantaneous pain. Intense, burning-like-Hellfire pain.

My lips snapped shut involuntarily around the marker, my teeth biting down hard on the cold plastic. The sounds I heard coming from my own lips reminded me of a wounded animal. It drew looks from the people at the back of the game store, but I was so busy trying to pull away from Marshall that I didn't care who heard. I wanted to wipe the liquid away, but Rory's fighter reflexes were quicker than mine. Her hands flashed out and gripped tight around my wrist, holding me in place.

My skin crawling back together to close the wound sent a shiver down my spine. When it was over and the pain subsided, the only signs that there had ever been a wound were a few flakes of dried blood and a faint pink line where the cut had been.

"How's that feel?" Marshall asked, stoppering his vial.

I pulled the pen from my mouth, my teeth having left deep impressions in the plastic.

"Good," I said, flexing my arm, then smiled. "Great, actually."

Marshall raised his eyebrows. "Nothing that feels like your flesh might be being eaten from the inside out, right . . . ?"

"No," I said, drawing the word out. "Why are you even asking that?"

"No reason, no reason," he said as quick as he could, then turned his eyes away from me, hurrying back behind the counter. He held up the now-empty vial. "Let's just say there's a good reason I've started making sure that I label these well."

Despite the wound being gone, I blanched at the idea of being a test subject of some kind. "I don't want to be your guinea pig, Marsh," I said.

"You're not!" he insisted.

"Me, either," Rory added with warning in her voice.

"Don't worry," he said to her. "You don't get hurt *nearly* as much as Lexi does." His eyes turned to me and his face went serious. "You're getting reckless, Alexandra."

I started to argue, but decided against it. There was no malice in what Marshall said, only the fact-based concern of a true friend. I gave him a genuine smile.

"Thank you," I said. "You work miracles."

He dropped the vial behind the counter and leaned forward on top of it. "Just promise Rory and me that you're not going back out tonight."

It was my turn to avert my eyes in avoidance, busying myself as I pulled my blood-covered Burberry jacket back on.

"I can't make that promise," I said. "I just . . . can't. Too much to do . . ."

"You need rest," Rory insisted.

"I can sleep during the day," I countered, heading for the door, "when they're inactive."

Rory sighed behind me.

"Ten bucks says she doesn't make it to the weekend without another injury," Marshall said.

"Wait," I said with a growing sense of doom. "What day of the week *is* it again . . . ?"

"Monday," Rory said, shaking her head at me.

"Crap on a crap cracker!" I said with dawning realization.

"What's the problem?" Marshall asked.

"You'll both be happy to hear that I *am* going home," I said.

"What's the matter?" Rory asked. "Has getting knocked about enough finally beaten some sense into you?"

"Worse," I said, spinning back around to the door and walking out into the night, thankful that at least the rain had subsided. "I've got to be social."

Four

Alexandra

Entering the familiar comfort of my building on Saint Mark's Place always calmed my soul and reminded me of my great-great-grandfather's guildhall beneath all of its new construction. It reminded me of how far I had come as the only practicing Spellmason in the past year since discovering the location. The only thing that outdid my own transformation was Caleb Kennedy going from the alchemist who had attacked Rory and me there, to becoming actual dating material.

I wasn't sure reformed alchemical freelancers were typically considered the best boyfriend stock, but given how little time I had for things like practicing my artistic endeavors or just a life right now, someone who shared my arcane interests was as good as it got as a distraction from all the crazy.

As I climbed the stairs up to my main living area and dining room, my heart raced a little in anticipation of what our planned date night might have in store for me. Much to my surprise, however, I found the dining room untouched.

"Awesome," I said to the empty space. I pulled off my backpack and laid it on the table, disappointed. Only then did

I notice the plain white note card sticking out from under it, and that was because a piece of string snaked off the table from it and ran across the room.

I pulled the note card free.

The presence of your company is required for an
evening under the stars.

A small smile crept to my lips, and with curiosity getting the better of me, I followed the string across the room where it led out the doorway and continued up the stairs. It snaked around the banister the entire way, other cards dangling from it as I followed.

Closer.
Almost there.
Getting hungry yet?

Pushing open the rooftop access door, I stepped out into the familiar sight of Gramercy Park, recreated painstakingly on my rooftop. Much of the rain had dried up from earlier, and the string trailed off down one of the cobblestone paths. I turned and pushed the door shut behind me, watching it vanish as its false stone facade matched itself back into the column concealing it.

The string continued along the path next to the running brook, and the farther I moved into the park, the more sounds of activity within there were.

In the clearing at the center were two tables lit only by the minimal light of the moon and a few scattered candles. One of the tables was set with a dark red tablecloth, flowers, and place settings. On either side of the gold chargers were more forks and spoons than I was used to seeing. Caleb worked over a mix of food, test tubes, and vials at the other table, the moonlight catching in his muss of dirty blond hair.

The string led to one of the chairs and I went over to it, finally drawing Caleb's notice.

"Sorry I'm late," I said, as sheepishly as I could. "I . . . umm, almost forgot."

"Forgot?" he said, looking up from the table he was work-ing at. "Or were you working too hard?"

"Not you, too," I said. "Did Rory and Marshall call you?"

"No," he said. "Let's just say I have mad pattern recogni-tion skills."

"It's busy out there," I said in my defense. "Halloween's coming, and I'd like as many gargoyles off the street as pos-sible before costume confusion sets in. I don't want someone getting crushed because they mistook a *grotesque* for some-one on their way to a Halloween party."

"Relax," he said, coming over to pull my chair out for me. "You're home now."

"Thanks," I said, remaining standing. I leaned against the back of the chair.

Caleb held a small white spoon with a raw slice of beef in it. He pulled a vial from within his jacket of a thousand pock-ets and poured whatever mixture was in it over the spoon. The piece of meat sizzled, and I detected not only the aroma of the meat from the spoon but the hint of buttery potatoes, corn, and what smelled like apple pie.

"What is it?" I asked when he offered me the spoon, taking it with a bit of reluctance.

"Taste it," he said. "It's something new I'm trying. Alchem-ical cooking."

I pulled the spoon away from my mouth. "I'm really not an experimental alchemical-potions-imbibing kind of gal," I said.

Caleb took my hand in his and eased it back to my lips. "Try it," he said. "It's safe. I promise. Alchemist's honor."

Given his checkered past, I wondered how honorable that actually was, but held my tongue. There was a comfort and trust in the way he asked, and I put the spoon in my mouth. An explosion of the flavors I thought I had smelled erupted in my mouth, so intense I couldn't quite process all of them.

"What exactly am I tasting?"

"It's your complete dinner," he said. "All in one spoon. There's steak and potatoes, creamed spinach and corn, topped off with both a blueberry and apple pie. But that's just the beginning of dinner. That amuse-bouche is the essence of the arc of the meal I've prepared tonight for you."

I sat there for a moment, moving it around in my mouth, letting the various flavors hit me. Hearing what Caleb was going for helped me to pin down each of them.

"Well . . . ?" he asked, his eyes desperately seeking approval.

I smiled. "The snozzberries taste like snozzberries, Wonka."

His face lit up. He walked back to his prep table.

"So, honey," he asked in a singsong voice. "How was your day?"

"Day?" I repeated. "During the day, I was asleep. My night, on the other hand . . ."

"Busy?"

"You might say that," I said, pulling off my coat. I poked my finger through the gash in the upper part of the left sleeve of my shirt, the blood there now a dried brown stain.

Caleb's eyes widened and he stepped back over to me, examining the jagged hole.

Under the moonlight the hint of a scar was barely visible. I reminded myself to get something fancy for Marshall from that ThinkGeek site he was always showing Rory and me.

"Don't worry," I said. "I'm okay. Now, anyway."

I wasn't about to tell Caleb the full extent of my wounds from earlier. There had been enough lectures about it at the game store this evening. My late-night dinner date with Caleb might go easier if I kept quiet on the subject.

"You really should take it easy," Caleb said.

I couldn't hold back a sigh as I sat down in the chair.

"What?" he asked. "Is it so wrong that I don't want you getting yourself killed, especially on date night?"

"Maybe if I had some help," I shot back, half kidding but also half serious. "You *are* partially responsible for the recent resurgence in gargoyle activity, after all."

"Through no fault of my own," Caleb added with lightning speed. He walked back to his prep table and continued on with his cooking.

"No fault . . . ?!" I repeated, shocked. "You're joking,

right? My *intended* spell was meant to work on *one* statue, not all of Alexander's across Manhattan."

"You and I have different recollections of that evening, then," he said, throwing me a sidelong smile.

"Do we, now?" I asked, slumping back in the chair, arms folded across my chest.

"Yes, we do," he said, walking back over to the dining table and sliding a plate across it to me. "By my accounting of it, I was trying to save you and your friends."

"You were trying to save *yourself*," I said, pointing a finger at him.

He considered it for a moment. "Those are *not* mutually exclusive."

"Fine," I conceded. "Continue."

"I *had* a plan," he said, going back to his prep table. "Kejetan's evil little gargoyles would have had to contend with the *other* gargoyles I created by way of amplifying your spell. Had *my* plan worked, I would have added, what? Maybe several dozen stoners out there, tops, not the whole city's worth." He pointed at me with a fork. "That's on you and your friends for interfering with what I was trying to accomplish."

Caleb finished filling his plate before dropping it across the table, joining me.

"And that doesn't bother you?" I asked. "Knowing what you've brought down on this city?"

He sighed and looked up from his plate, his attitude blasé. "If I got upset with every arcane twist or turn that's happened in my freelancing career as an alchemist, I'd be the most morose person out there. Magic is a pseudoscience on a *good* day, which means it's at best often unpredictable." He shrugged. "I roll with the eldritch punches."

"I couldn't do that," I said. "Jesus, I can barely sleep for all the guilt I bear over my involvement in it."

"Of course you can't sleep," he said, going back to eating. "You're a product of arcane privilege."

"Excuse me . . . ?" I asked. "What the hell is that?"

"Don't be so offended," he said. "You can't help it. You were born into it. You've never had to hustle on the street to

make a living selling spells or potions or taking odd alchemical jobs to make ends meet. *That's* arcane privilege."

"I work hard at what I do," I protested.

"Sure you do," he said. "But it's not like it's a job."

"Not everyone is motivated by profit," I said.

Caleb laughed at that, enjoying the good-natured ribbing
and verbal jousting as much as I did, maybe more since just
then I was actually a little offended by his accusation.

"Do you even hear yourself?" he said with a laugh. "Ever
hear the maxim 'Money makes the world go round'?"

"Some people do things because they have a love for it,"
I said. "A talent for it. Maybe a family legacy to excel at it."

He held his hands up. "Fine, fine," he said. "Look. I didn't
come here for an argument. I came to celebrate."

It was too late. I was riled now. "I'm out there every night
trying to get control of this situation . . . a situation you and
I created! Anything bad that happens while those stone creatures are out there is on us. With great power comes—"

Caleb shook his head at me. "Don't give me that Spider-
Man crap," he said, then reached across the table to take my
hand, squeezing it. "Lexi, I love your altruism, but I just don't
think the best solution is to try to personally hunt down every
last one of these creatures." He tapped his forehead. "You
know, work smarter, not harder and all that."

"Well, what are you actively doing to help the cause?" I
asked. "Because right now it looks like you're doing two
things: jack and shit."

He smiled at that.

"I've got my connections," he said. "My feelers are out
there. The arcane community—what spastic factions there
are of it, anyway—is already trying to contend with this sudden influx of gargoyles in their own way."

"How?"

"Well, for one, I've done a lot of groundwork making sure
no one knows who actually caused said influx of gargoyles."

I shook my head with a grimace. "Again, protecting yourself," I said.

"And you," he said, his face turning serious. "You don't

understand these people, Alexandra. They see this awakening, as they call it, as a hostile move by some grand sorcerer supreme out there. Some of the local factions in the boroughs are out for blood. It takes a lot of effort to keep you and me out of their sights."

"Wonderful," I said. "I'm a child of arcane privilege *and* a Magical's Most Wanted now."

"Back to that, are we?" he said. "You've just never had to scramble for it, that's all. It's not a judgment call."

"You don't have to scramble anymore for it, either," I reminded him. "You can come work for Team Belarus. I'll put you on retainer."

Caleb raised one eyebrow. "Tempting," he said, "but I think I'll pass."

"What?" I asked. "My money's not good enough?"

"You know what high esteem I hold financial gain in, but it would be . . . well, odd. Let's not bring money into our relationship. My favorite part of being a freelancer is the being free part."

"You, sir, have commitment issues," I said, my mood a solid mix of flirtation and frustration by then.

His eyes met mine from across the table and he smiled. "I'm here, aren't I?"

His words bordered on being far too suave, almost cheesy, but I couldn't help smiling back.

"I tried to resist you," I told him as I raised a glass. "I really did, but you just *had* to go be all adorable by blowing yourself up on our enemies' boat to save me and my friends, didn't you?"

"Years of downing alchemical concoctions will make a fellow nigh invulnerable like that," he said with a shrug like it was an everyday thing for him.

I reached across the table and took his hand, squeezing it. "You act like blowing yourself up was nothing," I said, "but back then *you* didn't know you were going to prove near indestructible, which only makes your intended sacrifice all the more noble."

And Lord, did I have a soft spot in my heart for nobility, I thought, allowing myself to finally relax into my evening and try to enjoy the moment.

Or I *would* have. A flurry of activity dropped down out of
the sky into the shadows to the left side of our table, the rooftop
shaking with the impact. Caleb and I were both up and out of
our seats before either of us could process what was going on,
reacting out of pure instinct. Caleb's hands were already reaching into his coat for one of his alchemical concoctions, and I
had snapped my connection out to pavement stone pathways
all around us.

A lone figure stepped out of the shadows, but even before
it fully came into our circle of candlelight, I recognized its
gigantic bat-winged form.

"Stanis," I said, letting go of my connection to the pavers,
settling them back into the pathways. "You startled us."

"Forgive me," he said.

Strangely, I already had. After a long evening of hard words
with friends and arguing up on the roof with Caleb, it was Stanis
I realized that I felt the worst about having been unkind to
earlier. If anyone should be asking for forgiveness, it was me.

Caleb, on the other hand, appeared wary still, his hand
remaining inside his coat.

"Easy," I said, waiting until Caleb's hand dropped back to
his side before turning back to Stanis.

The *grotesque* looked around the space and took in everything Caleb had arranged up here tonight.

"I am perhaps interrupting something," Stanis said.

"Ya think?" Caleb asked, already exasperated as he settled
down.

I laid my hand on Caleb's arm, silencing him. "Did you
happen to get a chance to take care of that Fort Tryon *grotesque* Rory and I had to contend with earlier?"

"Given your agitation at the Cloisters, I came by to reas-
sure you that Jonathan would be taken care of. He is off with
Emily now. She has a natural way with the induction of her
fellow initiates into their newfound lives."

"You sure she's a wise choice?" I asked, bristling a bit at the
mention of her. Ever since the gargoyle population had gone
up a thousandfold, Emily Hoffert had been Stanis's constant
companion, not just tonight. Having once myself been the one

Stanis used to watch over exclusively, I couldn't help but hate on her a little bit. I didn't have to like myself for realizing that fact, but there it was if I was going to try to remain honest with myself. I wasn't simply going to discount it or sweep it under my mental rug. "It's not like she's much more seasoned at this *grotesque* thing than that troubled monk we found."

"She was the first," Stanis said without any hesitation, "the one who came to me, seeking my counsel out after having been used by the darker forces in my family. And she was truthful at the first about her role in deceiving me. Emily has since given most of her time over to proving herself through her assistance with my efforts to unite all of my *grotesque* kind. So, yes, I trust her with the task. Emily well knows the confusion that comes from inheriting this new life. You need not concern yourself with her affairs."

His words stung, but surely no worse than the short ones I had slung at him earlier in the evening at the Cloisters.

"I wish to be a better ruler than my father was," Stanis said.

"Hard to be a worse one," Caleb said.

The look I shot Caleb shut him down.

"I wish to do it wiser," Stanis continued. "And kinder. I *will* see to those who wish for my aid in this modern era." He looked off across the lush green expanse of my building's rooftop. "Again, I did not wish to intrude on your time together . . . especially in this place I believe you once said you made for me."

Was that an actual dig? I would have been impressed if I hadn't already felt guilty being up here with Caleb.

Caleb raised a hand. "Blame me, big fella," he said. "Lexi's little EPCOT version of Gramercy Park here was the closest thing to actually getting her out for the evening. Lexi's been going too hard. The fatigue of it all is wearing her down."

"Long has it been since I have felt your human fatigue," Stanis said, "but if I am recalling it with any clarity, your human body is not meant to be pushed to such limits."

"And there you have it," I said, settling back down into my chair once more. "I now officially have it coming at me from all sides."

"Do not be angry with us, Alexandra," Stanis said. "Much as I have learned in my short time as a ruler, you cannot take on all challenges at once. Even one such as I cannot do the impossible, and you, Alexandra, are not made of stone. No doubt all who know you care about the state of your well-being. *I* care."

Those last words still had the power to cut to my core and I allowed myself the warmth of their glow for a moment.

Stanis made a sudden grab at my waist, and I stepped back, startled. Was he making some kind of move right here, right *now*, in front of Caleb?

"You have something on you," Stanis said, which relaxed me a bit. Jesus, I was high-strung. Maybe I needed to take a break more than I thought I did.

Stanis plucked his clawed fingers gently against my side and pulled away a long, green tendril of vine that ran all the way down my leg.

Wrapped around me as it was, I was surprised I hadn't noticed it earlier. Once Stanis had it fully pulled off of me, I was doubly surprised to see that the tendril was moving all on its own.

"What the hell is that thing?" I asked with a shudder, losing my appetite.

Stanis gathered a length of it in his fist. He closed his clawed hand over it, but Caleb was over to him in a flash, his hands closing around the gargoyle's wrist.

"No, wait!" he said.

Stanis turned to look at Caleb's hands, his face an unmoving demonic mask. He said nothing, but the look was enough for Caleb to pull his hands away.

"Please," Caleb added. "With a cherry on top and everything."

Stanis looked back and forth between the two of us, but kept his hand open.

"I do not understand," he said. "Would the addition of fruit be a beneficial motivating factor in your request?"

I couldn't even laugh at his misunderstanding of modern language this time. I was too squicked out by the still-writhing vine.

Caleb leaned in close, examining it, his nose inches away. Fearing it might latch onto him or try to snake up his nose into his brain meat, I grabbed his arm to pull him away from it, but he stayed put.

"Well?" I asked.

"This isn't your garden-variety creeping Jenny," Caleb said. "Believe it or not, there are a variety of natural magical plants out there," he added, "but this isn't one of them. The growth on these leaves is all wrong for this area . . ."

I moved a little closer—but not *too* close—to examine on my own, but nothing looked out of proportion to me. "You sure about that?"

"You can't see it," he said, "because you have an untrained eye. But to me it's like being able to tell the difference between a guy who works out and a guy who takes steroids."

"Gotcha," I said. I knew the subtleties of Spellmasonry and how every word and gesture were super important to pulling off what I had learned so far. It made sense that Caleb and his lifelong study of such things would make it obvious to him if there were something unusual about this plant. Other than it clearly being magical.

He stood up and nodded to Stanis, who gathered up the rest of the plant and crushed it in his claw until all life was out of it.

"If that thing tried to snare you, it looks like you drew the attention of some witch, warlock, or druid tonight," Caleb said.

"Crap," I said. "There goes my streak."

Caleb raised an eyebrow. "Of . . . ?"

"I've gone almost a whole week without someone arcane trying to kill me for bringing attention to your community," I said. "Or for infusing this city with an abundance of *grotesques*."

"There's so many reasons to want to kill you," Caleb said with a dark smile. "You need to be more careful, Lexi."

"I *was* being careful," I insisted. "Rory and I didn't see *anyone* at the Cloisters . . . other than the *grotesque* monk we turned over to Stanis."

"You didn't have to see anyone," Caleb said. "If the witches and warlocks are catching wind of the gargoyle sightings the same way you are, then they can set traps out there trying to catch you. Remember working smarter, not harder? Working yourself to the bone in this sleep-deprived state of yours is clouding your judgment."

"Caleb is right," Stanis said, which I knew was never easy for him to admit, even now. "You should rest. I shall see what I can find out from my people."

"*We're* your people, too," I reminded him.

He stood in silence, unmoving for a moment, looking more like the statue that daylight transformed him into.

"Yes," he said, "but it is not the same. The differences between our kinds are great. These newfound men and women of stone are in need of my help. I will look into answers about those who would see to trap you and your . . . friends. Rest well, Alexandra Belarus."

I let go of the dark tone Stanis had used when saying the word *friends*. Even if I had wanted to call him out on it, it was already too late as I watched him spread his wings and take off into the sky.

Caleb and I stood there in the now-cold remains of what had been date night. Knowing that I was being hunted kind of put a damper on the evening.

Caleb leaned down and picked up the broken remains of the vine Stanis had dropped, now nothing more than a ruined piece of greenery.

"Obviously you're not staying obscure enough," Caleb said. "We're going to have to work on that."

I shuddered, unable to shake the image of that creeping vine slowly creeping up my body.

"Fricking witches," I said, and grabbed Caleb's free hand, dragging him back to the secret entrance to my building. I was damned if I was going to let my night job frustrations go without a little recreational downtime that date night was supposed to provide. As a complimentary bonus to that, it would also bring on that satisfied sense of postcoital rest that everyone thought I so desperately needed.

See? I thought to myself. *Already I was working smarter.*

Five

Stanis

The human Marshall Blackmoore had once told me not to "fly angry." Once I had made him explain just what exactly the meaning behind that saying was, I understood the inherent danger in that kind of flight. Tonight, however, I could not help myself. A furious anger had taken root in me upon leaving the Belarus building on Saint Mark's, and it was difficult to focus on the details of exactly what its source truly was.

I dodged between the buildings of the Bowery at a breakneck pace as I flew down to the southernmost tip of the Isle of Manhattan, throwing my sudden aggression into my maneuvers. In the past, focusing my mind on flying had always helped. I needed that tonight to occupy part of my mind, which would free up the rest to try to home in on just what had bothered me so much about my two encounters with Alexandra.

At the Cloisters she had been out of sorts, but I was more than capable of withstanding her occasional foul moods, although they had been increasing as of late. Still, I had not liked the tone she had taken with me, but I forgave it for what it was: the stress of dealing with so many of my kind all around the city—both the good and bad *grotesques.*

So if her mood at the Cloisters was not the sole cause of my frustration, it led me to believe my issue must be over interrupting Alexandra's dinner with the alchemist Caleb Kennedy.

But surely that was not the case, was it? Months ago, perhaps their closeness might have bothered me, but Alexandra had made her choice. I had even encouraged it after Caleb had talked to me about her future. He had been right in his assessment of the situation. Caleb offered her a better life and more constant companionship due to his being human, more than I could ever be again.

I had thought the matter settled in my heart, but as I passed over the neighborhood known as Tribeca, my battle with my newly found emotions told a different story.

No. Caring about such matters was not something I could allow to happen. There were my people to think of, and those of my kind who were still lost out there around this city. There was already more than enough to occupy my mind beyond these foolish thoughts and wasted emotions. I forced the thoughts out and flew the rest of the way home to Sanctuary in silence.

All along the top of Trinity Church, wings of all shapes and sizes fluttered in the moonlight. It was strange to see so many other *grotesques* there as I approached it, more so for the years I had spent perched alone reveling in the glory of its architecture. When they caught sight of me, waves, cheers, and cries of warm welcome filled the air. To see my kind living here in such serenity . . . it did my heart good, improving my mood.

But that grand and glorious structure was not my home, no. I banked away from Trinity Church, heading instead toward my true destination, dwarfed by its shadow. Built by my maker long ago, a small disused church sat quietly across the street from the far more iconic one. I flew for the stained glass window adorning the front of it. Pausing, I hovered there, focusing the next few blasts of my wings toward the window. The force pivoted the stained glass open on two fixed points of its frame, creating a space large enough for a creature of my massive build to enter. I flew inside, the window rocking closed behind me, and I dropped down into the old disused church below.

"Welcome back," Emily said, her yellow marble form coming down the main aisle that led to the front of the church. Most of the standard religious fare of the space had long been removed by the building's previous occupants. The only hint of their presence was evident from the now-abandoned offices along the left side of the worship space and a caged-off section that ran down the right side.

The echo of Emily's footsteps rang out in the stillness of the old church.

"It is a quiet night in here," I said.

"What can I tell you?" she said. "Our brothers and sisters in stone prefer the freedom of the sky."

"How is he?" I asked, nodding toward the caged area. Once, it had held volumes of arcane files and artifacts, but now the repurposed space held only the angelic-looking monk Alexandra had handed over to me earlier.

"He's . . . adjusting," she said.

"Anything violent?"

"He had a fit of grief earlier, taking it out on the cage, but I think that's to be expected."

"Let us hope the cage holds, then," I said. "They were constructed to store books and relics, not preternatural creatures such as our kind."

"Should I let him out, then?" she asked.

I shook my head. "Until he and I have a chance to talk, I think it would be best that he remain there."

Emily looked nervous. "You're sure the *Libra Concordia* won't come back to try to reclaim this space?"

"I am fairly certain," I said, recalling how I had dangled their leader, Desmond Locke, several miles above the building to warn their arcane-curious cult away from the Belarus family. "It would be foolish of them if they tried to take what was once theirs but is now mine." I looked around the space. Office furniture and library tables still filled the main area, all of them empty. "I know this is still not fully our home, but I will endeavor further to make it so. I promise."

My words brought a smile to Emily's face, and seeing it brought one to mine as well. Given the evening I had had so far, it was good to not feel so heavyhearted even if just for a moment, but it passed all too quick. There was work to be done and I glanced over at the cage.

"Do you think our recent acquisition is ready to hear what we have to say?" I asked her.

Emily nodded. "I believe so."

Together we walked over to the holding area. The angelic monk stood there, his fingers threaded through the metal of the cage. His stone-feathered wings twitched, his nerves betraying what looked like an otherwise expressionless face.

"Hello, Jonathan," I said, opening the gated door to the cage. "Welcome to Sanctuary. Come. Walk with me."

Too wary to leave the cage at first, the monk took his time coming out after a long moment of hesitation.

"What is this place?" he asked, his face taking in the whole of the space. "A church?"

"Once, it housed those who sought to understand our kind," I said. "Those who wished to catalog us alongside the other arcane artifacts they kept here. Now this church is as close to a place as we dare call home."

I continued walking, leading Jonathan and Emily to the back of the cathedral.

As we approached what I wanted to show him, I found I did not even need to gesture toward the object in question. The monk's eyes rose to what had once been the altar. All religious iconography had been removed. Instead, what remained of a broken statue hung suspended from the ceiling.

"What is that?" he said, marveling at the figure.

Even I found the statue haunting the way it hung there . . . which was the reason, I suppose, I had put it there in the first place.

"Not what," I corrected. "*Who*. Emily . . . ?"

"He is one of the first," she said as if speaking a litany. "Not as old as Stanis here, mind you, but one of the first like you and I, one of our newborn kind."

The monk turned to me. "Is this meant to be a warning?" he asked with rising horror in his voice. "Do not cross you or this will be our fate?"

I held my hand up, hoping to calm him.

"I am afraid you have the wrong Ruthenia for that," I said with a grim smile, unable to suppress the nervous ruffle of my wings at the thought of my family's dark past. "I am Stanis Ruthenia. My father, Kejetan, would have perhaps made an example out of this shattered creature in the name of fear, to intimidate. I prefer to look on this broken form as a lesson, a cautionary tale, if you will."

"This creature you see before you was once the brother of the woman who gave you over to us tonight," Emily said.

"She made him, too?" the monk asked.

"No," I said. "Devon Belarus was never supposed to be like us. He assumed this form—the living version of it, anyway—through deception. Alexandra had no part in it. However, the way you see Devon Belarus hanging here now. . . That young woman *was* responsible for her brother's final fate."

"What was his crime?" the monk asked, unable to hide the nerves in his voice.

I shook my head. "You speak of crime," I said, "but I wish to be clear with you, Jonathan. I am not the law here. I simply offer guidance as the oldest of my kind that I am aware of. Whether it is a foolish notion or not, I am of a mind that my longevity has perhaps given me some insight into our existence that those like you might find of use."

The monk's eyes stayed on the broken form of Devon Belarus high overhead.

"We know this transition must be difficult for you," Emily said. "As it was for me."

The three of us stood there in silence. I gave the monk time to consider my words, Jonathan's eyes never leaving the static creature above.

"How, then, did this fate befall him?" Jonathan asked after several minutes.

"Through treachery," I said. "He and others like him used trickery to take the form you see. It happened, in fact, the very night that you and others like you were drawn as restless souls into the stonework statues by the kin of my creator."

Emily stepped closer to him, her voice soft now. "Devon

used his new form to exact vengeance on his family, even using me as a tool in his efforts," she said, and I could hear the hint of shame in her words. "He and others like him wished harm upon humanity."

"And that, perhaps, is my point here, Jonathan," I added, "the one thing I will not abide. You see, before this . . . great awakening, I was alone." Emily took my hand in hers, the smooth stone of it calming. "At times I hoped for different, imagining that I occasionally saw others out there, but no. I was a singular creation, and I had but one purpose: to watch over the Belarus family. For centuries I observed humanity. I have come to love these creatures . . . and I will not watch *any* of them come to harm. Every last one of our kind comes from humanity . . . We *are* them, and I will not abide any attack against our forebears."

"Forgive me," the monk asked, his voice quiet, "but in my human life, I knew well of the corruption of man. They are not this paragon you make them out to be."

"You speak true," I said, "but we are gargoyles, *grotesques*. Given the strength of our kind, I believe it is our responsibility to err on the side of protecting humanity first, and then seeking out the corrupt among them second."

I let go of Emily's hand and turned my full attention to the monk.

"You are welcome here, Jonathan," I said. "You may consider Sanctuary your home, and those around you your family."

The angel looked around the space with both reverence and relief on his face. "Thank you," he said. "That is most generous."

"Thank *you*," I said. "My own particular lineage has not always been known for their generosity, so it does my soul good to hear you say such a thing. Before I release you, however, I would ask a boon from you."

Wariness crept into the stone eyes of the monk, but after a second of hesitation, he nodded. "Ask, and if it is in my power to be of aid to you, I will try."

"The many souls that currently inhabit the living stonework of Alexander Belarus are varied," I said. "I cannot fathom why certain souls have lingered on earth long enough to take possession of these forms, but I do know after these many long months that not all of them are as kind as you. For my favor I would ask only that you do in turn what we have done for you. Help another of our kind if you can . . . Bring them to us or inform us of any unquiet souls you come across."

Jonathan nodded. "Very well," he agreed.

"Now, with regard to your own life," I said, "your previous human life, that is . . . it would be in your best interest to stay clear of the Cloisters."

Curiosity filled the angel's face. "Oh, really?" he asked with a hint of disappointment in his words.

I nodded.

"It is best to let go of your past," I said. "Who you were is behind you. Who you *will* be is up to you."

The monk fell silent in contemplation. "You have given me much to think about, Stanis," he said, "but first I would like to thank the three people who gave me over to your care earlier tonight."

"Three?" I repeated. Alexandra and Aurora had been the only ones Emily and I had seen in Fort Tryon Park. Marshall would have been their likely third, but they said he was back at his store.

"There was the woman with the bladed staff, and the one you call Alexandra, and the man at the edge of the forest."

"*What* man at the edge of the forest?"

The angel's face sunk. "He wasn't with them?"

"I do not believe so," I said. "Describe him."

The angelic monk thought for a second. "Everything happened so fast," he said. "I think he had a close-trimmed beard . . . but also wild black hair. Oh, wait! The rings!"

"Rings?" Emily asked.

The angel nodded. "I remember the light of the moon shining off his hands," he said. "They were covered in rings, every finger."

Emily looked to me. "Do you know this person? Is this an associate of your human friends?"

"I am afraid not," I said, "but I will inquire with Alexandra.

She is . . . changed as of late. Perhaps there are people working with her now that I am unfamiliar with." I turned to the monk, gesturing to the stained glass window overhead. "Go, fly. Introduce yourself to the quarry."

The monk cocked his head at me. "Quarry?"

"It is a term my friend Marshall Blackmoore came up with," I said. "A group of crows is called a murder; whales come in a pod . . . He coined the term that a gathering of our kind is known as a quarry."

He smiled at that, and with an awkward leap into the air, the angel headed up and out of the church, fumbling for a moment with the window as he exited. When the window pivoted shut after him, the space was silent once more and I turned my attention to Emily.

"Do you think he will stay? Not every *grotesque* does . . ."

"I think he will be fine," she said, reassuring me. "I almost envy him."

"Why?"

"He knows how he died," she said. "He knows where he is buried. I cannot say the same for myself. It is very unnerving to be in this form, Stanis, without knowing how one got here, not knowing the fate by which my human life was terminated. My death is as much a part of me as my life is, and not knowing . . . It leaves a cold and empty place within me."

I took her hand in mine, squeezing. "Give it time," I said. "You did much good tonight, helping out our newest addition to Sanctuary." I spread my wings and looked out the stained glass window above. "It would seem, however, it is also time for me to help out my human friends."

"How?" she asked.

"I need to find out who this ringed man from the forest is," I said, leaping into flight. "Is he friend or foe? Either way, we can deal with him accordingly."

Six

Alexandra

I wasn't sure I'd ever get used to the strange newness of my family's ancestral home on Gramercy Park, especially up here in Alexander's art studio/library. Even Bricksley seemed confused by it all, his tiny stone golem body waddling back and forth on the tiny legs that supported his single brick of a body.

"I know," I said as I stared down into his big drawn-on eyes. I couldn't help but smile back at the eternal one I had painted on him. "It takes some getting used to, but I tried to at least order the place the way it was before mind-controlled Stanis trashed it. My great-great-grandfather's books on arcane societies go where they always have, in the last row of the stacks. If you would be so kind . . ."

Bricksley picked the small stacks of books from the floor and headed off as I set about sorting out the rest of the tomes still scattered all around the library/art studio that I had spent my life before Saint Mark's hanging out in.

Despite the late hour, I found myself wide-awake thanks to the pit of nerves that filled my stomach and had the added benefit of fighting off sleep.

I worked in silence as I waited, the only sound that of Bricksley's tiny feet scraping along the wooden floor as he went about his business.

"I see Bricksley is hard at work," Stanis said from the doorway leading out to the terrace, nearly causing me to jump out of my skin.

I paused for a second to settle both my stomach and my nerves before turning around. "He's like the Energizer Bunny," I said, watching the animated brick totter across the floor toward the library with another stack of books in his tiny metal arms. "He keeps going and going and going."

"It is a shame he is not built for flight," Stanis said. He collapsed his wings in close and stepped through the doorway, entering the floor.

"I suppose I could work on that," I said, stepping past him as I exited out onto the terrace, leaving Bricksley to his work. "Thank you for meeting me. I know how late it is and I'm sure you want to get back to your people."

"It is no worry," he said, once more stepping out into the night air, his voice short and firm with me. "This would not be the worst place in the world to take my statue form. After all, I did it here for the past hundred years or so."

"Oh, right," I said, feeling a bit foolish. "Of course. That was a simpler time."

"Was it?"

"Before your father came here, before the awakening of all those other *grotesques*. How many people did you talk to in all that previous time?"

"Your great-great-grandfather was the sole person I was in contact with," he said.

"See? Simpler."

"But then you and I would never have conversed," he said with a fanged grin.

I turned away from it, finding it unbearable.

"Don't," I said. "I don't deserve your smile."

When I looked back up again it had vanished from his face.

"What is wrong, Alexandra?" he asked.

"Even before I knew who or what you were, I always

sensed your presence. Watching, protecting . . . I mean, a woman can take care of herself and all but somewhere at the back of my mind, I sensed you. I guess I just miss it, is all . . ."

"I am still here for you, Alexandra," he said.

I bit my tongue.

The person I had been these past few months wanted to scream, *That's not true!* at him. There were all the goings-on at Sanctuary, the hunt for the rogue gargoyles, and of course *Emily.*

But tonight wasn't about me being selfish anymore, and besides, Stanis had made his choice in companionship, hadn't he? He deserved that bit of happiness, the kind only a fellow *grotesque* could give him.

"I appreciate that you're here for me," I said, "and your efforts to help clean up the mess Caleb and I accidentally caused by awakening so many *grotesques.*"

His wings twitched, betraying the nerve I had hit, but I pressed on.

"But it's come to my attention that I could be kinder about it. I bark orders at you, but we are *all* a team in this together. Or we were. I don't know what any of us are anymore."

"Where is this coming from, Alexandra?" he asked. "What is truly bothering you?"

"I don't know," I said. "I value what we have, what we *had*, and I'm afraid I'm losing that—and myself—in all the crazy."

"Do not drive yourself mad," he said. "I have had several hundred years to contend with both the mundane and arcane worlds and I barely know how to process it."

Somehow the optimism with which he was taking my apology made it worse.

"Regardless," I said, holding up a hand for him to stop. "I am sorry if I have been out of sorts with you. I will try to be more mindful."

"I appreciate that," Stanis said after a long moment, "and I will endeavor to do the same."

We stared at each other for a good, long moment in silence . . . until I realized his silence came from the faint rays of the sun that had crept up, rendering him an inert statue.

I turned, once again the fool as I went back into my great-great-grandfather's newly restored library, but I also felt better for having cleared the air with Stanis. However I felt, it *was* a step in the right direction, and one that was better left alone for now.

A dark, smug sense of satisfaction at having him away from his people for a day—and away from Emily, too—rose up, surprising me as much as it shamed me. Lord knows I was far from perfect, but I could contend with only so much emotional growth—or really, baggage—at one time.

Apologies now, slaying the green-eyed monster later. Right now, I needed to sleep, wishing for once I could induce it via the rise of the sun like a *grotesque*. There were other apologies to offer, but if I went for any of them at this time of the morning, I'd have a whole new litany of apologies to make instead.

I scooped up Bricksley from where he had fallen inert from transformation coming out onto the sunlit terrace. I stuffed him in my backpack, grabbed a few of the books I had gathered from inside, and headed back down to Saint Mark's where my bed awaited me.

Seven

Alexandra

I awoke around seven, a rarity given the night schedule I'd been keeping. Considering last night's near-death adventure, I felt remarkably well. I showered, dressed, and even ran errands for several hours before calling Rory and begging her to meet me at Marshall's game store before it could open.

The two of us arrived at the same time outside Roll for Initiative, and when Marshall looked out his store window and saw my arms were full of maybe a dozen or so small boxes and bags, he ran to the door, unlocked it, and let us in.

"This is an odd but welcome surprise," he said, locking the door once we were inside. "You're not really a morning person these days."

"Tell me about it," I said, pushing past Rory. "Not really a fan of that big fireball up in the sky, either, but I thought why not get up early and do something proactive with my day other than hunting gargoyles."

"I'm missing a contemporary class for this," Rory said, laying down her Manhattan Conservatory of Dance bag.

"I know," I said. "Sorry." I walked over to the store's sales counter off to my left and set about unloading everything in my arms.

"What's all this?" Marshall asked.

"Breakfast," I said. "I figured it's been a while since we've all just hung out, so I thought I'd bring everything to you."

Rory picked through a few of the bags, pulling an icing-drizzled muffin from one of them. "And you do mean *everything*," she said.

"Oh!" I said, excited. "That's a cruffin!"

"A *what*-fin?" Marshall asked.

Rory's face transformed to a look of awe and she went from just holding it to cradling it with care in her hands.

"I've heard of them, but I've never seen one," she said. "How long did you have to wait?"

"About two hours," I said. "There was already a line when I got there."

Marshall walked over to Rory, staring at the treat.

"But what *is* it?" he asked.

"It's all the rage," I said. "It's a muffin on the outside, but inside it's got the flaky layer of a croissant. Every food blog in the city has been losing their minds over them, so I figured, why not get the best for my besties? You got lucky. They limit them to two per person, but I promised them a discount here at your store to snag a third."

Marshall looked up. "So generous of you," he said.

Rory held the cruffin up to her mouth, not daring to bite into it yet. "It will be worth it," she said to Marshall. "Trust me."

"And if you don't like it, I hit up a bunch of other places, too." I pointed off to a red and yellow bag at the far end of the counter. "There's an egg sandwich in that one where the 'bread' is made of maple-bacon pancakes."

Marshall turned away from Rory and dove for the other bag. "You had me at bacon," he said, unwrapping one of the sandwiches and tearing into it.

He and Rory fell silent for a few minutes as they devoured their first breakfast treats while I simply enjoyed watching them. When Marshall had polished off his sandwich, he basked in the glow for a moment with a big smile before coming back to earth.

"How's the arm feel today?" he asked.

I flexed it back and forth. "Feels a little tight," I said, "but good. Thanks again for the potion."

"So what's all this *really* about?" Rory asked, licking her fingers clean. "Last night neither of us could talk sense to you and you were practically biting our heads off. Today you're either killing us with kindness or just trying to kill us by way of caloric intake."

A twinge of guilt knotted my stomach. "Consider this a peace offering," I said.

Marshall narrowed his eyes at me with skepticism. "I didn't realize the three of us were at war with each other."

Being honest with myself was one thing, but steeling my resolve to admit my shortcomings to my friends was far more uncomfortable.

Still, I needed to verbalize it out loud to them because just shoving food down their throats wasn't going to be enough. I took in a deep breath, letting out the tension that was starting to build in my shoulders.

"I *know* I've been pushing myself too hard," I said. "And Rory. And you, when we can drag you away from the store. If we keep going like this, we're going to make mistakes, and someone besides me is going to get hurt. I don't know if I can live with that."

"What about the rest of New York?" Marshall said. "Last night you were so concerned with stopping every bit of gargoyle violence before it even had a chance to happen."

"Caleb *might* have pointed out to me that I can't help anyone if we're not careful," I said. "We'll end up too dead to do anyone any good."

"Hey, I'm all for not dying," Marshall said.

"So *we* didn't get through to you, but Caleb did?" Rory asked, crossing her arms.

"Oh, I went down kicking and screaming," I said. "I fought him on it for a bit, but then we made a discovery that changed my mind."

"Which is . . . ?"

Rory grabbed a chocolate-covered doughnut out of one of the boxes and sat herself up on the edge of Marshall's counter.

"Apparently, the arcane community is hunting me down," I said, reaching into my coat pocket and pulling out the now-withered vine Stanis had pulled off my body last night. "Some witch or warlock tried to snare me with some creepy little living plant trap up at the Cloisters. The witches and warlocks of Manhattan seem to be on to us. We've got to be more careful. *I've* got to be more careful."

"Now you're talking sense," Rory said, her mouth covered with chocolate like she was a four-year-old. "It's about time the madness stopped."

"Oh, we're not stopping," I said, correcting her.

"We're not?" she asked, wiping her mouth off with the back of her hand.

"No," I said. "We're just going to be a bit more cautious."

"Speaking of which," Marshall said. He wiped his hands off and popped out from behind the counter, heading off toward the back of the store. "Wait right here."

"There are *cruffins*," I said, finally picking one up for myself. "We're not going anywhere."

While Marshall vanished into the back room of the store, I bit into my treat not really knowing what to expect. An explosion of flaky layers and muffin textures filled my mouth. Each bite's deliciousness added to the last, building to an overwhelmingly sweet but savory explosion. I couldn't consume it fast enough and by the time Marshall came back to us, I had greedily scarfed the whole thing down.

"Oh. My. God," I said. "It was worth waiting in line for."

Marshall stopped. In his hands he held a black velvet bag that was just slightly smaller than your average plastic grocery one.

"Please tell me there are cruffins in that bag," Rory said, as she hopped down off the counter.

I stepped closer, licking my fingers clean. "What is that?"

Marshall held the bag up to his chest as if he were about to clutch it. "After you two staggered in all bloody and wet last night," he said, "I was worried. I guess your recklessness got to me, so I decided to do something about it."

Marshall extended his arms, offering the bag to me, and

I snatched it from his hands with the excitement of a kid at Christmas, startling him.

"Sorry," I said. "Sugar rush."

"What did you buy for us?" Rory asked, clapping her hands together with the same kind of false excitement, which I found adorable.

"I didn't buy anything," he said. "I *made* these . . . for the two of you."

"It's not even Christmas yet," I said.

"I know," he said. "I just wanted to make sure you made it *until* the holidays, what with the way things have been going with you lately."

I gave Marshall a grim smile and pulled the drawstring open. Inside were two small bundles of dark gray cloth. I pulled both of them out, the fabric reminding me of a cotton jersey material that at the same time also felt impossibly coated with something weather-resistant.

I laid the now-empty bag down and shook out the cloth, which upon examination was really more of an infinity scarf that ran in a circular sleeve that was wider along one side of it.

"You made us hoodies?" I asked, throwing the second one over to Rory.

Marshall shook his head. "Just hoods," he said, practically giddy. "Try them on."

I slid the cloth sleeve over my head and wrapped the scarf section around my neck before pulling up the hood.

"It's comfy and all," I said, "but I don't get why you got us matching outfits. You *do* know it's generally bad form to gift a woman clothing, right?"

Marshall pointed over at Rory and I looked at her. She had also put Marshall's gift on, and despite the daylight streaming in through the front of the store, I couldn't see Rory at all within the shadows of the hood.

"Your face is gone!" I said.

"Yours, too," she said, reaching for mine.

"Is it?" I reached for her, my hand vanishing into the darkness within the hood until I ended up grabbing Rory's nose somewhere within the unnatural shadow.

"Neat!" Rory said.

"There's not a lot I can do when we're out on the hunt," Marshall said. "Other than take notes for my monster manual. I don't possess any skill like Spellmasonry and I certainly don't fight like Rory can, but I *can* do some things that can help keep you two safe. There's already enough footage popping up online involving gargoyles and some blurry footage of you two scurrying away from dealing with them. These should at least help keep your identities better hidden."

"You know what this means?" Rory asked, looking really creepy talking while faceless. "We're superheroes now!"

I laughed. "A costume kind of cinches that, doesn't it?" I asked.

Marshall nodded. "Now try to take them off," he said.

A statement like that instilled a little ball of dread in me, but I did as he asked. I ran my fingers up over my forehead to swipe the hood back, but they met with resistance. Closing my hand over the edge of the hood, I gripped it tight and pulled. Only then did the hood come off, and only by using a good deal of strength to do so.

Running my fingers through my hair, I let out a sigh of relief. "You're lucky this didn't take my hair out in clumps," I said.

"This is great," Rory called out, whipping her head back and forth like she was head banging back in our high school days. "It's staying in place."

"Exactly," Marshall said. "The wind won't catch it, and anyone who tries to pull it off of you is going to have a hell of a time doing it. Plus, it'll keep the elements out."

I walked over to Marshall, hugging him. "They're perfect," I said. "Thank you."

"Someone's been working on his alchemy," Rory said. "Caleb taught you well."

Marshall blushed. "This wasn't all me," he said. "I called in a few favors from some of the people I met through Caleb."

Rory shook her head at him. "Careful, there," she said. "I wouldn't trust them as far as I could throw them. Which, come to think of it, is pretty far. Never mind. You get what I mean."

"You include Caleb in that group?" I asked.

Rory scrunched up her face as if she were giving it serious thought. "He gets a pass," she said. "For blowing himself up to aid our escape that time."

"I *am* being careful," Marshall said, sounding like a scolded child.

Rory pulled her hood off, her head finally reappearing. "So . . . now that the band is back together, what's the plan?" She looked at her watch. "I've got to go hurt myself in a make-up dance class in a few." She grabbed up another bag off the counter and pulled out a sticky bun the size of my head.

"How do you keep that body?" I asked. "Seriously."

"I'm carbo-loading," she said, already biting into it. "Do you have any idea the amount of calories I'm burning through in my dance intensive? Almost as many as I do all night when I'm chasing down gargoyles with you."

"You were talking about a plan before . . . ?" Marshall said. "Focus."

"Oh, right," I said. "Like I said, we're not stopping, just being more cautious. We get back to hitting the police scanners. I've got Stanis trying to get a lock on who might be trying to vine me to death. That means we take things slow until I figure out how to deal with whatever arcanists are after me."

Marshall couldn't help but give me a dubious look. "So you're *not* going to keep us out all night?"

I shook my head. "Nope."

"And if the weather sucks . . . ?" Rory asked with a glimmer of hope in her eye.

"We go home," I said. "I promise. We track down one gargoyle a night, and we can call it a night. Starting tonight."

"I'll bring the rope," Marshall said, pulling out a small pad and making a note of it.

I didn't even bother to tease him about his obsession with rope. We *would* need it, and it was nice trying to get everything in order, making it feel normal with just the three of us again.

I craved a little bit of normal right then. Narrowly avoiding the cops at the Cloisters, almost bleeding out, and dodging witches and warlocks would do that to a girl.

Eight

C

Stanis

Flying down Lexington Avenue was a pleasure I had forgotten. With all the assistance I had been giving Alexandra as of late—despite the unfounded anger she had been showing—I had not taken the time to enjoy much of what I loved most about the island of Manhattan.

From Grand Central all the way down to the Twenties, the stone buildings along Lexington Avenue were old world with a strength and beauty that I found I missed. Much of the modern world lacked such elegance, but seeing this craftsmanship of an age gone by—an age I had lived through—filled my heart with a bittersweet twinge I had not expected.

At Twenty-sixth I slowed, spying Alexandra standing alone in front of an ornate French-design-influenced building. While I had thought perhaps Aurora might be with her tonight as usual, as I dropped down in front of the large stone arch of the building's entrance I realized Marshall Blackmoore was with her as well.

"Hey, big fella," Marshall said, coming down the steps with a smile on his face. "Long time, no see." He held one of his hands high in the air as he came over. Once in front of me, he stopped with his arm still raised. "Going to keep me hanging?"

Not understanding what he was saying, I ignored his question and gave him one of my own. "I am surprised to find all three of you here," I said. "How long has it been since *that* has occurred?"

Marshall lowered his arm with disappointment on his face. "At least three months since *I've* seen you," he said.

"Strange," I said. "That does not seem like much time."

"I'm sure," he said. "But for you, after centuries of existence, what's ninety days give or take, right?"

"You speak true, Marshall Blackmoore." My eyes went to Alexandra. "But still there are days with my kind that seem too long to spend away from those I consider myself close to."

Alexandra blushed with a smile and looked away.

"Aww," Aurora said, coming over to me from where she stood at the bottom of the steps leading up to the entrance. "Bring it in. Group hug."

She raised her arms out to her sides, but none of the other humans moved.

"No?" she asked. Her arms dropped back down. "Fine, then. Where's the camaraderie? I thought we were getting the band back together!"

I cocked my head at her. "The band . . . ? Minstrels . . . ?"

"Never mind," Alexandra said, composed this time. She stepped closer. "Thank you for coming so fast."

There was a welcome calmness in the way she spoke tonight. "You seem . . . improved," I said.

Alexandra smiled again, but looked down at her feet, unable to meet my eye. "You mean compared to the Cloisters?" she asked.

I gave her a single nod but said nothing.

"Well, I've gotten a little sleep and it's not raining buckets," she said. "So I'm thinking with a bit more clarity now."

"Let us hope so," I said. Was she being sincere about her attitude being gone, or was it simply the fact that I had chosen to come alone tonight, leaving Emily behind? The complexity of the issue made me think that now was not the time to sort that out. Instead, I looked up at the building in front of us. "What is this place?"

"It's the Sixty-ninth Regiment Armory," Alexandra said.

"An armory," I repeated with understanding in my words. "My father had many of those around the castle grounds. Is this the same sort of place?"

"Not quite," she said. "It used to serve a more military purpose, but over the years, it's been used for all sorts of other functions. Tonight, however, the scanner had a call come in dispatching a car to check out a report about a *grotesque* tearing the place apart from the inside. It was met with laughter by a few others on the line, so I figure we have a little time before anyone takes it seriously and gets over here."

"I looked the armory up on our way over," Marshall said, holding up his phone. "There's some kind of art show scheduled in here this week. We can only hope there's no late-night gala going on. The less people inside, the better."

"I doubt there's anything going on," Aurora said, walking up the stairs to the entrance, taking the handle in her hand, rattling it. "Locked."

I gazed up at the old building rising before me. "There are many other ways in for one of my kind," I said. "Rest assured, we will find this creature." I walked up the steps and stood next to Aurora, examining the heavy wood of the door before pulling back my arm and smashing through it. As I pulled my hand free, the door twisted off its hinges and fell into the building. "This, however, will suffice for a way in."

"Hey!" Alexandra said, offense in her voice. "Historic landmark here!"

"My apologies," I said, looking down the stairs at her, "but do you not wish expediency in this matter?"

"The direct approach," Aurora said with a smile. "I like it."

Alexandra sighed, coming up the steps to join us, Marshall following. "Can we not encourage the wanton destruction of property, please?"

"I do not understand," I said. "The longer we talk outside, the more destruction within from the prey we seek, yes? And there is the chance officers may actually decide to check out the report from the police scanner . . ."

Alexandra opened her mouth but nothing came out. Instead, she stormed past me through the door, Marshall following. "I hate when he's right," she said.

I turned to Aurora and met her eyes. "She makes no sense to me," I said. "I merely pointed out the strategic advantages of the situation and the reason for my actions."

"Don't mind her," Aurora said, stepping through the door. "Stick with me. I tend to break only what I need to when it comes down to a fight."

"Very well," I said, drawing my wings in close to me as I stepped through the empty doorframe. "But I promise nothing. Enclosed spaces and I do not make the best of compatriots."

Once past the doors and the cramped confines of several long, narrow halls, my anxiety passed when we entered a large open space at the center of the building. Artwork ran neatly in orderly rows of tables and hung from wire walls that all left room for me to spread my wings to their fullest without knocking any of it over.

"This is unexpected," I said, surprised at how my voice carried and echoed out over the large expanse of the room. "I should not think such a space could exist within this building."

"Consider it one of the old-world arenas," Alexandra said in a low whisper. "There's a lot of history in a place like this. Indoor track events, basketball games; the first modern art exhibit in the entire United States was held here. Quite the controversy, really. What I *don't* see, however, are any signs of *grotesques*. Present company excluded."

"Perhaps a better perspective will be helpful," I said, and leapt into the air, letting my wings carry me up over the room. The moonlight pouring in through the massive windows overlooking the open space helped as I circled around the room searching among the shadows below.

At the far end, several statues stood in a corralled-off space, and although they seemed solid and still, they begged for my further examination of them. I came down in silence among them, anticipating the slightest hint of fight out of any of them. From above, a few had looked as if they could have been carved by Alexander Belarus, but up close I could see they were not cut in his inimitable style, and I relaxed.

"There is no creature here," I called out, at once confident in my assessment.

"Not only that," Marshall called from somewhere on the other side of the room, "but as far as I can tell there's been zero destruction here."

"Shit," I heard Alexandra hiss out. "Are you thinking what I'm thinking?"

"Yep," Aurora said. The scrape of what must be her pole arm sliding out of the tube on her back rang out like echoing chimes across the open space. "There's no *grotesques* damage, and not a single squad car has shown up with sirens blazing. I'm thinking ambush."

"Marshall, Stanis," Alexandra called out. "Let's get out of here, *n*—"

"Freeze," a man's baritone voice yelled. "NYPD."

"Into the center aisle, all of you," a woman's voice called out with the same authority Alexandra had when casting a spell.

I had long known the letters *NYPD* from the roofs and sides of the red-and-blue-lighted vehicles—we were dealing with members of the city's constabulary. Centuries of observation left me with little hope that the events that were about to transpire would be anything less than violent.

I needed to protect my friends. Leaping into the air, I took flight once more, going high to better assess the situation.

Two people stood at the head of one of the aisles with guns raised. The taller of the two—the male—kept his gun trained on Alexandra and Aurora, while the woman tracked Marshall as he moved to the center of the aisle to join our friends. While I had not recognized their voices, their faces were familiar from the last time I had fled these two at the entrance to the Cloisters.

I swooped down toward them. The redheaded female—Rowland, the man had called her the other night—caught my approach and her head lifted along with her gun.

"Maron!" she called out.

"Sweet Christ," her partner said as he turned his eyes upward. He slid his gun into his jacket and his hands went to a bag he wore over his shoulder. When they emerged, an unidentifiable black mass was between them.

Pulling my wings in, I came down hard, landing in the space between my friends and the two armed officers of the law. The wood floor creaked on impact, but I stood and spread my wings out to both menace the officers and protect my friends from their firearms.

"You shall not harm these humans," I said.

The woman's gun remained on me. "Not who I'm worried about at the moment, pal," she said.

There was fear in her words, and I found it delicious. It meant what I was doing was working.

She called back over her shoulder. "Maron . . . ?"

"On it," he said, and with some hesitance started creeping toward me.

"Hey," Alexandra called out from behind me. "Easy, now. No one has to get hurt here."

"You're the one who unleashed your monster on us," the woman said.

"I do not answer to her," I said. "I am my own monster."

"Comforting," the woman said. "You want to close those wings down, then?"

"I think not," I said, holding my position. "Unless you wish to put your gun away . . . ?"

The woman shook her head.

"I think not," she said. "We've been chasing these three around this city long enough for their involvement in this gargoyle mess, but they always eluded us. Couldn't figure out how they were getting to the scene of the crimes so fast until I guessed they might be responding to our calls on the police scanner. So *we* created a fake scanner call, and they fell for it. Detective Maron and I would like some answers . . . *now*."

"This doesn't have to go down like this," Marshall called out from behind me.

"Yeah," the man said, still closing the distance to me. "It

kinda does." The detective looked over my shoulder. "You, back there! Down on the floor!"

The man lifted the black mass in his hands and flung it toward me. Once free of his fingers, it expanded, opening to reveal a sight I was familiar with from my father's early military campaigns: a net. Amused to see such a flimsy rope-and-cloth item heading my way, I did not even bother to move. It caught on my wings as it draped over me, and I simply flexed my wings, expecting to easily tear free but instead finding resistance.

"Stanis . . . ?" Alexandra's hand fell against my back.

"Steel-reinforced cable core, asshole," the woman said.

I flexed again, but only succeeded in further tangling the netting around me. The cable within did, however, give a little, meaning it might take a little time, but I *would* get free. The question was whether my friends would be safe until then.

"Shit," the woman said, backing away while looking high up in the air behind me. "Reinforcements."

With my legs still free, I managed to spin myself around. Outside, the shadowy figures of *grotesques* were backlit by the building across the way, and seconds later they came crashing through the windows of the armory. Glass flew everywhere as their snarls filled the air, and by the time the sixth or seventh came through, Alexandra was already trying to pull the netting off me.

"Dammit," the male detective said. "We don't need real gargoyles screwing up our fake gargoyle scanner bait!"

"Friends of yours?" Alexandra asked me with hope in her voice.

I shook my head. "I am afraid not," I said. "They may be *grotesques*, but I am not familiar with them."

"I was afraid of that," she said. "Are they attacking us or them?"

"The way they are staring at our group, Alexandra, I think we have our answer," I said. "Forgive me. They must have been following me, hunting me."

"Stanis Ruthenia," a demonic-looking *grotesque* near the front of the pack said. "Our master sends his regards and demands the presence of you and the human known as Alexandra Belarus."

"I'm not going anywhere with you," she said. "Unless your master plans on surrendering to me."

"It wasn't really a request," the *grotesque* said and headed for her. "You will join the Butcher, or you will die. Simple, really."

Alexandra opened her mouth to respond, but the sound of gunfire broke out behind me. Bullets sailed toward the new arrivals, and as I had assumed, none of the shots proved effective.

"It's no use," Detective Rowland called out to her partner. "Stop firing. You're not damaging them and you're more than likely to destroy the property in here."

"How the hell was I supposed to know there was going to be an art show here, Chloe?" Maron asked, his gun still raised. "I would have moved this setup somewhere else."

"Not really the time to talk planning logistics," she said.

"The Butcher?" Alexandra said, snapping with anger at our foes. "Who the hell is the Butcher? Is that your master? I suggest you run back to him before I shatter you and your fellow gargoyle henchmen to rubble."

At Alexandra's arcane command, pieces of stone artwork from around the room began drawing close to her while Aurora swirled her pole arm around in readiness. Marshall appeared to have the best idea of the humans, moving himself out of the aisle and away from the approaching *grotesques*. A wise move. Because as spirited as the two women were, I did not think their odds were good in attempting to hold off so many creatures of my kind at once.

Still trapped underneath the netting, I forced my way past Alexandra and Aurora, putting myself between them and the now-landed *grotesques*. I needed a strategy and quick. If these creatures and I fell to battle within the confines of this building, it dramatically increased the likelihood that the humans might get hurt. There was only one course of action.

I ran toward the oncoming enemies despite my upper body still being trapped in the net. The creatures stopped at my approach, readying themselves for conflict.

Which is *not* what I gave them. Instead, I leapt into the air over them, and while I was unable to fly, I was able to use the net that restrained me to catch some of the gathered *grotesques*. Having caught them off guard, I doubled the speed of my run once I hit the floor again, letting my momentum pull them along. Not all had been tangled in the netting, but I could not worry about the rest just then. I concentrated on my speed instead as I aimed myself for a section underneath the now-broken windows above.

The brick and mortar of the wall was strong, but I was stronger. At my impact the stone gave way, exploding out into the street beyond. Broken brick rained down over cars parked there and tumbled over the single empty police car pulled up on the sidewalk.

It was impossible to keep my footing. My netted *grotesques* and I fell over one another, rolling out into the middle of the street. A car's brakes screeched to life and seconds later I felt the impact of it against our pile of bodies, but it was nowhere near powerful enough to move us. The crunch of metal filled my ears.

Quicker than the rest of my tangle of *grotesques*, I was up on my knees and free of the net. The front half of the impact vehicle was destroyed, crumpled against us, its driver obscured by a large white bag that filled the cabin. Movement against it was proof enough of his or her safety, and as I stood I turned my attention to the hole I had left in the side of the building.

Already Alexandra, Aurora, and Marshall were heading toward me with the remaining *grotesques* and two armed humans following close behind. Behind me, claws tore at the netting as ineffectively as mine had, but several of the *grotesques* were already managing to pull themselves free nonetheless.

Two stood: one looking like a centurion of some kind and another looking more like a snake-faced Egyptian carving. They came at me, and I spread my wings to their fullest, swirling them around to drive my attackers back. The Egyptian one was driven back but the centurion ducked beneath my wings and came in low, grappling me around my waist. Pain erupted along my midsection.

I brought my balled-up fists down hard on its back over and over until its grip weakened and it fell to the ground. While it struggled to stand, I turned to the other, only to find Aurora and Alexandra squaring off with it.

"No," I cried out. "Do not!"

Aurora pulled up her pole arm, still keeping it poised for action, but Alexandra simply stared at me wide-eyed. "What?!"

I grabbed the creature around its neck, and pulled it back from the two of them, looking behind me. The other *grotesques* were now mostly free, and the armed humans were coming up behind my friends.

I met Alexandra's eyes.

"Run," I said.

"And leave you alone in this fight?" she asked. "Never!"

Another of the *grotesques* grabbed for me and I tore a hole through one of its wings as I kicked it away.

"This is a fight I fear not all of us will walk away from," I said. "You and your friends are in more danger here than you can imagine. But I will do my best to remedy this situation. I promise."

Marshall joined the two of them. "How?" he asked, breathless.

"This is a fight you cannot win," I said. I knelt down and grabbed the edge of the now-empty net with my free hand. "Therefore, I will remove what I can of the fight itself."

I snapped my wrist and the net sprung into the air. It settled over the main group of *grotesques*, their wings and claws tangling once more within it. I tightened my grip on the net and spread my wings to their fullest, taking one last look at my companions.

"Now run!" I shouted, and shot off into the night sky with both captive and free *grotesques* following after.

Nine

C

Alexandra

Normally I'm not one to run from a fight, but when a gargoyle like Stanis shouts out that it's time to do so *and* guns are also involved, hoofing it definitely has its appeal.

Stanis was no sooner in the air with a steady stream of gargoyles flying off after him than I turned to my friends.

"Split up!" I shouted. "Rendezvous at the Bat Cave!"

If we went three separate ways, the odds of any of us getting shot by a cop or torn apart by claws went down by a lot. I didn't wait to see who ran off first, and took off on my own. Marshall and Rory knew the drill. Hell, it had been Marshall's idea to set up a rendezvous point. We'd ditch this scene and meet back up at my great-great-grandfather's guildhall, or as Marshall liked to call it, "the Bat Cave."

Running down Lexington Avenue, I headed for the first opportunity to get off the street I could find. I aimed for the open space between two of the buildings coming up on my left.

Please don't be a dead end, please don't be a dead end.

My legs already ached, but turning the corner into the gap between the buildings made my heart soar. Other than a few scattered trash bins, the alley was clear. As long as I could reach the end of it before the cops figured out which one of us they should chase after, they wouldn't get a shot off.

I ran hard.

That was, until the sound of crushing metal rose up behind me accompanied by screams, stopping me in my tracks. I spun in time to catch the empty police car sailing past the open end of the alley. It flew into the deli across the way in a shower of glass and bricks, the front end of the vehicle crumpled like paper.

Fuck.

At least one of the gargoyles hadn't taken the bait. Worse, from the sound of it, they had decided to go for the detectives we had been trying to ditch.

The selfish part of me wanted desperately to flee for my own safety, but I simply couldn't. I ran back up the alley toward the commotion, pressing my legs even harder than before. Those two detectives might have been the asshats from the Cloisters—and clever ones at that—but they were only doing their job. None of that justified leaving them behind to be torn apart by monsters.

I slowed at the end of the alley, moving to the edge to assess the situation before diving headlong into it. Already the street looked much different than it had seconds ago. Parked cars were now flipped over on top of one another, some lodged into the lower floors of nearby buildings, traffic at a standstill behind a street covered in broken bricks, glass, and the twisted metal frames of gargoyle-damaged cars. The source of it all was a more reptilian-looking *grotesque*. Scaly wings like those of a dragon were spread wide, its snarling face sending a chill down my back. The creature towered well over the female officer, the gun in her hand looking like a toy. Across the street, the other officer lay with his leg trapped beneath a pile of rubble where the police car had crashed through the storefront.

"Where is she? Where is the Spellmason?" the gargoyle shouted as I snuck out of the alley, hiding myself behind one of the overturned cars to my immediate right.

Was he asking for me by *name*? More to the point: How did this monstrosity know of me?

While the creature was distracted with the female detective, I chose the easier of rescue tasks at hand and stepped with caution across the littered street to aid her trapped partner. The man stirred at my approach, but remained silent. By the look on his face he was more dazed than anything.

"Is it broken?" I whispered, kneeling down next to him and setting myself to the task of shifting broken bricks off of his trapped leg.

"Hurts like hell," he hissed out, "but no, I don't think so."

"Good," I said, and continued working on the pile until I had his leg free of it.

The man tried to stand, but his leg buckled under his weight. I rushed forward just in time to catch the bulk of his form on my shoulder, struggling not to fall over myself.

"Easy," I said. "I've got you."

"Who's got my partner?" he asked.

"I will have her," I said, "but first things first." Not waiting for a response, I hobbled the man as best I could behind the safety of an overturned car across the street, feeling a sense of relief—until I heard his partner cry out in pain.

From where the two of us were, I couldn't see anything. I laid the man down and moved to look around the car, but before I could, the female officer flew over the vehicle. Crumpling unconscious against the car behind us, she slid down the side of it onto the street.

"Stay here," I said to the man.

As I turned away, he gave a grunt and a pained laugh. "Where do you think I would go?"

He had a point, but I didn't bother to answer, instead stepping out into the center of the street like I was in an Old West showdown.

"Hey!" I shouted, gathering my arcane will around me as I pulled my notebook free and started flipping through it. "Looking for me?"

"Groovy," the monster said, baring its fangs at me. "Just the chick I was looking for."

I almost laughed at the absurdity of what he was saying. *Groovy?* Whoever he had been in his human life, this gargoyle sounded like he must have shuffled off this mortal coil sometime back in the seventies.

The gargoyle wings spread to their full expanse in a move no doubt meant to intimidate, but I had seen enough of them over time to know it was nothing more than the equivalent of peacocking.

I willed my power out all around me and into the fallen bricks strewn everywhere. The power of the cantrips I had memorized might get them in the air, but for what I intended to do I was going to need a little more juice from what was written in my spell book.

I motioned quickly through the arcane gestures, then lashed out with my power. One by one I lifted the loose and broken bricks, sending them sailing at my target. The first smashed into the gargoyle's torso, evaporating into a fine red dust around him.

"Really, now?" he asked with some attitude. "Girl, are you trying to annoy me?"

"Nope," I said, adjusting my aim. "Just disable you."

My next brick sailed off toward its actual intended target, which was the dead center of the open expanse of the creature's left wing. I pressed my power full blast into the next two bricks. The first cracked the dragonlike "webbing" of the wing, allowing the second one's impact to shoot right through it.

The gargoyle laughed, but there was nervousness in it. Its face filled with ferocity as it assessed the damage to its wing. I had hoped to drive it off, but instead it launched itself across the distance between us. The gargoyle tried to take flight with its charge, but damaged as he was, his movement was at best erratic. Rather than crashing to the ground, however, he managed to find his footing, and continued his charge unabated.

I launched the remaining handful of nearby bricks at the gargoyle. The first three flew right past him while I tried to gauge his movement to win a hit, and when the last of them actually *did* strike, it had such little power in it that it bounced off the gargoyle's chest like a bullet off Superman.

Before I could run, the gargoyle lashed out at me, catching my jacket in his clawed hands and lifting me off my feet until I was staring into his dead stone eyes.

"You're coming with me, girl," he said.

"Like hell I am," I shouted out, struggling, but to no avail.

"We will make you our servant."

The struggle went out of me as his words sunk in. "Servant . . . ?" I repeated. "And who's *we*?"

The gargoyle spread his wings, pointing to the large hole I had just punctured there.

"That my master wants you is all you need to know," he said, running a clawed finger around the inside of the puncture wound. "There are none who can fix the damage that our kind experience. For that, we require your services. You were our maker; now you will be our healer."

"I'm not fixing *anything* that happens to gargoyles who act like this," I said, shoving my feet up against the solid stone of his stomach. In a bid for my freedom, I pushed off, hoping my jacket would tear free or maybe his grip would break, but neither happened, leaving my legs swinging back and forth as they dangled there. "I don't know what master you serve or how you know I am your maker, but I'm not uttering spell one to help you."

"We shall see what the master has to say on this," he said, attempting to take to the air with me in tow, even with his damaged wing.

I needed to stop him. Force wasn't going to work now. I could only hope to reason with him to gain my freedom, but before I could say anything else, a voice spoke up from behind the creature.

"Not so fast, asshole," Detective Rowland said, although she sounded full of pain. "The lady has already got a date with me."

The gargoyle opened his mouth to admonish her, but was met by a deafening boom that filled my ears. The stone serpent's head vaporized in front of me, becoming a gray cloud, a few of the large chunks of sharp stone tearing into me.

The twin barrels of a shotgun sat point-blank at what was now the creature's neck stump, the sound of its blast still washing over and through me. The pressure of its sound wave continued to build in my ears and head until all my body wanted was for it to stop.

And it did—darkness closed over me and my eyes fell shut. My thoughts slipped away from me like my sight had, my mind shutting down to embrace the calm quiet of nothingness.

Ten

🌙

Alexandra

My mind swam up to the bare hint of consciousness even if my eyes resisted opening. I hoped there was a special ring of hell for those who created hospital beds, and I hoped its abyssal equivalent was made of jagged glass, steel wool, and pain to match the kind I was currently in.

I'd hated hospitals ever since my childhood stay when I had my tonsils out. Through my current haze of clouded thoughts, my only fond recollection of that time was Rory sneaking Ben & Jerry's in to me until the nurses caught on and kicked her out.

I went to laugh at the dreamlike memory, but something about my body definitely didn't feel right. There were bandages across my face and arms, bringing the events of my evening back to me: gargoyles, cars flying through the air, the shotgun blast . . . After all that, I *had* to be in a hospital bandaged up, didn't I?

As my brain focused in, I assessed my situation to figure out what exactly seemed wrong. For one, the bed beneath me felt less like the painful hospital kind and more like the hard coolness of a steel slab, which, thanks to every police procedural show on TV, reminded me of a morgue freezer drawer.

With a bit of panic awakening in me, I wanted to soothe myself and went to lift my hands, but discovered I could not. Fatigue fully rolled away from me as a dawning realization hit me hard—I was chained in place.

My eyes shot open, my heart pounding in my chest. My "hospital bed" was nothing more than a steel table I was laid out on within a small square room that was not much more than four walls, a single door, and a large mirror off to my left. A blinking red light, that of an active camera, sat high in the corner of the cold, gray space. As I sat up, I discovered that indeed my hands were cuffed and chained to the table beneath me. Between my feet the contents of my backpack were laid out on the steel table, including my notebooks and the inert stone form of my great-great-grandfather's tome.

"Hey!" I shouted out to the camera, met only by the tinny echo of my voice. That went on for a full twenty seconds before finally dying out, the silence that followed it deafening, but thankfully it didn't last long.

A light went on behind the mirror to reveal the officers from the earlier incident in the streets. Now that I wasn't fleeing the detectives, I finally got a good look at the two of them. Both were in the smart-looking suits from earlier, both of their outfits torn here and there as often happens in gargoyle encounters. The male was about a foot taller than the woman, who looked to be about my height. I pegged him at late thirties or early forties from the hints of gray at the temples of his military-length black hair. The woman was more olive in complexion, but the dark red of her long hair was not a color found in nature.

The two of them headed to a door set along the same wall as the one to the room I occupied, both of them limping, but the woman walked with a more pronounced limp than the man I had dug out of the pile of bricks. They exited their room and when they came into mine seconds later, I could hear the woman hiss with her efforts to walk, indicating she was in more pain than her limp alone suggested.

"How are you feeling?" the male detective asked while the other one shut the door.

I looked down at the dozens of Band-Aids covering my arms and chest. Several showed hints of blood soaking through them and they stung, but nothing seemed fatal.

"This has to be the worst hospital ever," I said, adjusting my butt on the cold table to relieve a tingling numbness that had set in.

"This *isn't* a hospital," the man said, moving underneath the camera in the corner.

"I kind of figured that one out for myself," I said.

He reached up and tugged at the cable running to the camera from the wall until the line came free. The indicator light on the camera went dead.

"What gave it away?" the woman asked as she turned from the door. "The lack of get-well cards?"

"The décor," I answered, and pulled at the cuffs connecting me to the table. "And the jewelry."

"Clever girl," the man said, taking a chair at the foot of the table. "I'm Detective Maron. This is Detective Rowland."

"A pleasure," I said.

The female detective went right to my feet at the end of the table and rapped her knuckles on Alexander's stone book and my notebook. "You mind telling me what these are, Miss . . . ?"

"You've gone through my backpack," I said with a smile. "You tell me."

"That's a bit of a problem," Detective Maron said. "You weren't carrying any ID."

I shrugged. "Maybe it got knocked free of me when I was busy *saving you.*"

My words didn't have the effect I had hoped for, and he leaned back in his chair, arms folded over his chest. "Well, was it?"

"Answer this, Detective. Would *you* carry ID on you if both the police and those monstrosities were after you?"

"Speaking of which," the woman said, her voice sharp. "You didn't seem all that shocked or surprised when you saw that winged stone creature."

Her partner nodded. "Most people just flee when they see them," he said. "But not you."

I shrugged, the cuffs and chains jangling. "Maybe I'm just more stupid than your average person."

"This isn't the first time we've seen you, smart-ass," the woman shot out. "You're involved with those things somehow."

"I've seen you before, too," I said to the two of them. "Before tonight, I mean. At the Cloisters. You were the first officers on the scene."

"Correction," the female officer said. She hobbled her way off to my right to lean up against the wall, looking none too pleased. "We were the *only* ones on the scene."

"That is, until the alarms went off," the man added. "Someone or *something* smashed one of the stained glass windows on the side of the tower. Then every officer from the Upper West Side to Inwood suddenly took an interest and came running, only to find us there with nothing but our dicks in our hands."

I shot a skeptical look over to the female officer.

"You don't want to see hers," the male officer whispered, leaning in. "Trust me."

"You want to know why I don't carry ID?" I asked, looking to Detective Rowland. "Why I ran from you? It's simple. I don't take kindly to having guns pointed at me. Of *course* I ran."

The anger in her eyes didn't let up, and I decided it was best to change the subject.

"No offense," I said, and turned my attention back to Detective Maron.

"None taken," she said. "We've got better things to be offended about, like the fact that when we radio a call in, the only response we get is laughter."

"Excuse me?" I said. "Do they not realize what you're dealing with out there?"

Rowland shook her head. "We're the joke of the department," she said. "You think either of us wanted to get stuck with this shit show?"

Maron shook his head. "Mulder and Scully ain't got nothing on us," he said.

"What does she mean by *shit show*?" I asked him.

Detective Maron sighed. "Do you remember when all this started?" he asked.

Of course I remembered, being that I was the cause of much of it. "It was the night the gargoyles awoke," I said.

Maron made a sound like a negative game-show buzzer going off. "Wrong."

I sat up at that. "It wasn't?"

He shook his head. "There've been reports for years of all kinds of weird shit going down in the city," he said. "Crazy stuff."

"Dispatch is used to getting its fair share of bizarre calls," Rowland added from the spot against the wall. "Elvis sightings, river monsters, vampires . . . Dispatch logs the calls, everyone has a good laugh, but nothing ever gets done about it."

"But over the past ten, maybe twenty, years, there's been an increase in all this nonsense," Maron continued. He tapped at his temple. "Can you guess why?"

I thought for a moment. What would increase the paranormal activity in a place like Manhattan? From what Caleb had told me, much of the arcane community had been around for decades—centuries in some cases—so why now?

"There aren't *more* arcane things happening," I said. "It's just that there are whole new ways for it to become faster public knowledge. Cell phones. *Camera* phones."

Maron nodded. "This whole gargoyle mess was just the tipping point for the police department," he said. "It was easy to ignore crackpot phone calls reporting crazy sightings decades ago, but when people started taking blurry night shots of winged creatures in the sky over Manhattan, those calls got flagged and noted down. Then six months ago you have *video footage* of dozens of these stone monsters appearing suddenly, and they can no longer be ignored."

"So they only put you two on it?" I asked. "Seems like putting a Band-Aid on a missing limb, if you ask me."

Rowland laughed, shaking her head at me like I was stupid. "Do you have any idea how the city of Manhattan works?" she asked.

I shook my head. Other than rudimentary zoning laws I'd

dealt with as part of my family's real estate business, I hadn't a clue.

"It *doesn't* work," she continued. "The fact that they've tasked *anyone* to deal with this gargoyle bullshit these last six months is nothing short of a minor miracle."

"Why you two, though?" I asked. "Some kind of Special Forces training in your background?"

Detective Rowland looked away from me. I turned to Maron, and while he met my eyes, his face was crimson in a full-on blush.

"You could call it special training," he said. "Of a sort. I catch a lot of shit for playing World of Warcraft in my downtime."

"And you?" I asked Detective Rowland.

She sighed, but rolled her eyes and looked at me. "I read a lot of paranormal romance," she said. "Apparently in this police department that's enough to render the two of us *experts*."

Marshall had logged countless hours playing World of Warcraft, so I turned back to Maron. "Have I got someone for *you* to meet."

"Your little blue-haired friend, you mean?" Detective Rowland asked.

I blanched at the mention of Rory. Things were so nerdy-chatty for a second there that I had forgotten where I was and the circumstances I was there under. As if being chained to a table wasn't enough of a reminder. I fell silent in the hopes of killing that air of familiarity.

"Yeah, we know about her," she said. "Funny how you two keep showing up wherever the chaos goes down."

"Maybe she and I are just fans of the old Disney cartoon about gargoyles," I said.

Detective Rowland gave me a crooked smile that looked like it might be followed with a punch to my face. "Why don't I believe you?"

I shrugged. "You've got trust issues . . . ?" I offered.

Detective Maron picked up my notebook in his hands, flipping through it. Unlike the protective measure of stone transformation Alexander had put upon his spell book, there was no kind of warding to stop the detective from looking through mine.

"These look like notes for some kind of spell craft," he said. "Would that be a fair assessment?"

The bandages on my face were soaked with sweat, the walls of the room felt like they were closing in, and the cold steel around my wrists burned against my skin as I realized this was probably a freak-out. I had never been arrested for anything in my life, and I certainly didn't talk to random strangers about the arcane legacy of my family.

"Do I get to call a lawyer or anything?" I asked, trying not to hyperventilate.

The woman limped over from the wall to stand beside her partner. "Depends," she said. "Are you going to tell us who you are?"

"Not . . . just yet," I said, trying to get myself together before I seriously lost it. "I can't. I need to think things through. I just need time to figure out what I want to tell you about those creatures, how I want to handle you . . ."

"Handle us?" Detective Maron repeated, amused. "May I remind you that *you're* the one handcuffed to the table here?"

"What are you?" Detective Rowland asked, raising her voice in anger. "Some sort of cultist puppet master controlling these creatures? They're tearing up our city and you're going to pick and choose what you want to tell us? You have no idea the kind of trouble you could be in with us. Right now, you're off the grid here, sunshine. You're a Jane Doe. We can make your life here a world more difficult if you don't cooperate."

My panic subsided the angrier she became with me, a mix of fear and my own anger filling me in response.

"I don't react well to threats," I said, calm.

Detective Rowland leaned against the table, getting so up in my face I could smell her faint perfume. "And I don't take kindly to whatever those things are tearing up my city! Move them to Jersey or Philly. Thanks to their existence, me and my partner have this citywide rampage to contend with." She laid her hand down on top of Alexander's stone spell book.

"Now, you've got answers and I want them, or I'm going to beat you with this chunk of rock here."

"Easy," her partner said, sitting forward in his chair. He grabbed her hand from the top of the book. "Chloe, let's not forget . . . the woman *did* save us from that monster."

Rowland wasn't pleased, but she shut her mouth and stepped back to her spot on the wall, still fuming.

Detective Maron watched her for a long moment until she settled before turning back to me. When he spoke, his voice was soft and calm.

"How about you give us a break, Miss Whoever-You-Are?" he asked. "We brought you here after you passed out. We bandaged you up . . ."

Detective Rowland might have stopped fuming, but not me. I was full of a growing rage and cut off Detective Maron as I held a hand up to him and turned to lock eyes with his partner.

"You'll have to excuse me, Detective Rowland, if I don't seem terrified by your bad-cop routine," I said. "You two don't have the first idea of what the hell is really happening out there. You want my name? Fine. It's Alexandra Belarus, the last and *only* Spellmason. You want a piece of me? Get in line. At the moment I've got witches and warlocks hunting me, and gargoyles trying to tear me apart. Right now New York's Finest seem to be the most reasonable of the bunch. But if you're threatening me? You can get back out on the streets and try dealing with those things yourself."

Detective Rowland, despite her injuries, lunged for me, which was not what I expected. Shocked and more than a little scared, I scrambled as far back on the steel table as I could until the cuffs stopped me.

Maron was up and out of his chair, pulling Detective Rowland back from me. Watching the two injured detectives wrestle with each other might have been comical had my heart not been trying to pound out of my chest.

After a moment of struggle, the fight went out of Rowland and she stumbled back, spinning toward the door.

"Take her down to overnight," she said over her shoulder.

"Wait—you're *keeping* me here?" I asked. "I gave you my name!"

"Giving your name is not giving your cooperation," she said, opening the door. "Enjoy your stay, honey. Maybe you'll prove more cooperative after a night in jail."

Rowland slammed the door behind her, leaving Detective Maron to remove my cuffs from the chains attached to the table. Apparently he, too, had said all he had to say, and escorted me from the room into the hallway of the station house.

Awesome. A night in prison. That was surely something new to check off the arcane bucket list. Strangely, relief washed over me, killing my anger, fear, and panic. Most people would probably dread something like this, but me? Frankly, incarceration seemed like a good way to make sure I got some forced downtime from the world of hunting gargoyles, at least for an evening.

"Lead on," I said to the detective as he led me down the hallway. "And you can skip the wake-up call. I plan on sleeping in."

Eleven

☽

Stanis

"You okay?"

Aurora's voice echoed up and down the squat, rounded tunnel we walked along under the streets of Manhattan. The slosh of the shallow river that rose to our knees was the only other sound as she, Marshall, and Caleb splashed along with me through it.

"In what way?" I asked. "You mean did those *grotesques* from last night harm me? My intent in ensnaring them was not to harm them, but to distract and draw them away so the rest of you had time to escape."

Marshall clapped me on the arm. "Two out of three escapees wasn't bad," he said.

"I'm glad you escaped harm," Aurora said. "We were worried about the odds with there being a whole gang of them."

I gave a grim smile. "The day I cannot outfly a handful of fledgling *grotesques* is a day I do not see in my near future."

"I wasn't really asking about the other night," Aurora said. "I meant just now. You weren't moving at all. You looked . . . I don't know . . . like a statue. "

"My apologies," I said. "I know it makes you humans more

comfortable to feign motions such as respiration. Forgive me. I was distracted, and I also do not care for confined spaces such as this."

Marshall laughed.

"Hey, at least you're made out of carved materials," he said. "So at least your clothing isn't knee-deep in sewage water. I smell like rotting trash and the inside of a tauntaun. I'm going to have a lovely aroma when we get into the police station. *If* we get in."

"Oh, we'll get in," Caleb said from where he searched fifteen feet ahead of us. He turned his eyes up to the top of the tunnel, shining a light onto some numbers along a nearby pipe. "Somewhere between here . . ." He sloshed through the sludge to the next set of numbers, double-checking a map he held in his other hand. "And here."

I moved underneath the spot, examining the top of the tunnel near the pipes. "Very well."

"You sure this is the right spot?" Marshall asked. "We're not going to come up in the basement of a restaurant or shoe store, are we? Although, frankly, I'd prefer either to breaking into a police station."

"Pretty sure," Caleb said. "From what my contacts told me, this would have been the precinct house where they would have taken her into custody. My friends couldn't find a record of her here, or anywhere for that matter, but that doesn't mean she's not being detained."

"It doesn't?" Aurora asked.

Caleb shook his head. "No," he said. "There's some unaccounted space here at this precinct. My people say it's for some of their wild-goose chase files. If what we go through on a daily basis doesn't count as that, I don't know what does."

"It doesn't make sense," Aurora said. "If they took her into custody, why didn't she call her family? Why didn't she call me?"

"Why didn't she call any of us?" Marshall asked.

"Perhaps she was unable to do so," I said.

"That means someone up there is denying Alexandra her rights," Caleb said.

"Why do you say that?" I asked.

"I've been arrested enough times to know what rights she should have," he said. "She's either not being allowed her call or she's not being processed through the system like a regular person would be."

"Then we'd better hurry up and find her," Marshall said.

"Agreed," I said, and reached over my head. Spreading my clawed hands, I pressed them against the stone at the top of the tunnel. There was much resistance, but as I forced more strength into it, bits of it crumbled down onto me, revealing layers of smooth gray beneath them.

Marshall coughed as dust formed all around us. Aurora and Caleb covered their mouths and noses as they waited it out.

When the dust finally settled, Caleb looked up into the hole. "Concrete," he said.

Aurora stepped over and tapped at it with the bladed tip of her pole arm. "This is going to take me a while to chip through," she said.

I shook my head and eased her away before holding up my claws. "It will not be a problem," I said.

I slammed my claws into the concrete, tearing away chunks of it.

"Easy," Caleb called out, looking over his map. "We need to break through, but we're not looking to cause a scene. If my sources and map are right, I *think* I've got an unused part of the station, but we still want to go in as quietly as we can. Got it?"

"Understood," I said. Finesse was not always the way of the *grotesque*, but for the sake of my friends I slowed my pace and worked with caution. After several minutes I had dug my way through the outer layer until I hit another, this one seeming less substantial.

Caleb came back over when he heard the change in the sound of my digging. "That's going to be subfloor and probably tile on top of that," he said.

I looked down at him. "Any suggestions on how I should handle it?"

He clapped me on the shoulder. "Not a one," he said. "You're going to have to break through and that's probably going to make some noise. I say just go for it and let's get up in there."

"Grab and go," Marshall said. "Subtlety be damned."

The subfloor was just beyond my natural reach, but having cleared a large enough space in the concrete for me to pass through—wings closed—I leapt up while locking my arms above my head like a medieval battering ram. The floor above groaned from the first impact, but did not give. I landed with a splash in the tunnel, squatted as low as I could, and forced all my power into my next leap. Arms still locked in place, they tore through the floor above, and to my surprise so did my whole body.

I perhaps did not know my own strength, suddenly finding myself in the dark of a room up above. As quick as I was through the opening, I spread my wings to slow myself before I crashed through the floor above *that*. The cacophony of metal chairs and tables knocking over all around me filled my ears, but I managed to still land myself without a sound next to the hole.

"Everything okay up there?" Aurora called out from below.

"I believe so," I said, staying still in the darkness for a moment, listening.

"Great," she said, passing her pole arm up through the hole to me while keeping hold of one end of it. "Hold that right there."

She turned, grabbed Marshall, and lifted him up to the pole. When his hands wrapped around it, I pulled him up into the room where his feet scrambled to one side of the hole before he was willing to let go.

I lowered the pole back through the hole where Aurora was reaching for Caleb, who brushed her hand away.

"I've got this myself," he said and jumped up, catching the pole. I pulled him up the same as I had Marshall, then did the same for Aurora until the four of us were securely in the room.

"Where are we?" Marshall whispered.

"It looks like my contacts didn't screw me over," Caleb said. "It's a storage room in a disused section of the precinct. If they're keeping Alexandra off the books, this was my best guess as to where they'd keep her."

"Let's hope you're right," Aurora said, going to the one door. She cracked it open, the dull light of the corridor coming into the room. Her head disappeared as she looked out of it for a second. "Come on."

Marshall and Caleb followed after her and I went last, having to constrict my body as best I could to maneuver through the doorway. Once in the hall, I moved after the line of humans as they headed past several dark, empty cells, searching each of them with their tiny handheld sources of light.

At the farthest down the hall, Aurora stopped, her light shining to the back of the cell. I walked up behind the group of them to find Alexandra lying with her back to us on a metal slab that hung off the wall. The rise and fall of her shoulders was slow and steady.

"She is asleep," I said.

"How the hell can she sleep at a time like this?" Marshall asked.

"Let's find out," Aurora said. She grabbed her pole arm near the bladed tip and slid the shaft of it between the bars. It took the full extension of her arm and pressing herself up against the bars to reach Alexandra with it, but she managed to nudge her friend right between the shoulders.

Alexandra shrugged it away, and gave a slow rollover. Shock ran through me when I saw her face and arms. They were covered in bandages.

Alexandra laid her hand on the end of the pole arm and lowered it to the floor, her eyes fluttering open. She followed the length of the shaft until she saw Aurora and the rest of us standing there.

"Hey, guys," she said with words that were heavy with sleep. "Nice of you to make it." Her eyes went from her friends to mine. She sat up. "You're here, too? How'd *you* get a visitor's pass?"

"None of us exactly came in through the front door," Caleb said. "Which explains why we all smell a bit like sewage." He pointed to the bandages all over her body. "You're pretty cut up there. You okay?"

Alexandra gave a slow, sleepy nod. "You should see the other guy," she said. "Oh, wait, you can't. His shiny marble head got blown off by a paranormal romance reader."

Caleb nodded back. "I'm going to pretend that makes some kind of sense," he said and turned to me, slapping his hand on my shoulder. "If you would do your Man of Steel bit on these bars here, we can get the hell out of here."

"Of course," I said.

Aurora pulled her pole arm back out of the cell as Marshall and Caleb stepped away from the area. When Aurora was done, she, too, moved and I came forward, wrapping my hands around the bars of the cell.

"Wait," Alexandra said, standing up.

"As you wish," I said, and dropped my hands from the bars.

"At the risk of sounding rude," Caleb started, "what the hell, Lexi? Time is of the essence here."

"I was half-awake when you asked how I could be sleeping at a time like this," she said, coming over to the bars, sliding her arms through them, and resting them along one of the horizontal crossbars. "After yesterday's fiasco, I think my body and brain just needed a break so it all shut down once the cops brought me in."

"They caught up with you?" Aurora asked.

"Actually, I caught up with them first," she said.

"Excuse me," I said, "but when I drew those *grotesques* away, it was so you and your friends would have time to escape."

"Well, not *all* the creatures went after you," Alexandra said. "One ended up staying behind and it attacked the detectives. Those *grotesques* were there for us . . . for *me*. I just couldn't let anyone die at their hands."

I managed a smile. "Of course," I said. "I did not think to count on your nobility."

Caleb stepped forward. "Yeah, yeah, look, nobility is great and all, but we *really* need to get going, Lex. Our arrival made a little noise and we're not going to be alone for long."

"We don't need to hurry," Alexandra said as calm as could be.

"We don't?" Aurora asked.

Alexandra shook her head. "The detectives brought me in," she said, "but no one's formally charged me with anything."

"That's great," Caleb said. "You're not on record. We can get away clean on this."

Alexandra shook her head. "I'm not running on this one," she said.

Caleb grabbed her hands, shaking her. "Why the hell not?"

"These detectives . . ." she started, then took a moment as she struggled to find the words. "They didn't book me when they brought me in. Why? They just want answers, the same as us. They've been a bit pissed off in the way they're going about it, but after having slept it off for a day here, I get it now. It's all clear. There's an increasing number of *grotesques* coming onto *all* our radars, and the intentions of a wider and wider variety of them are not fully known. I'm sick of running when what we really need is more people on our side."

Aurora handed her pole arm to me. "Let me see if I can find them, then," she said, and headed up the corridor.

Caleb opened his mouth to speak, but words eluded him.

"You wish to protest, Caleb?" I asked.

He pressed his open hand to his chest. "I just don't want to get shot," he said.

"That *is* a compelling point," Marshall added.

"I need answers," Alexandra said. "Like how that one *grotesque*—the one that *didn't* follow Stanis—knew about me."

"Plenty of *grotesques* know about you," Marshall offered.

"Ones that I capture and bring to Stanis, yes," she said. "But this one was different. He knew I was a Spellmason, what my power could do. He implied he was part of a larger group, one that's organizing itself under the guidance of some master who taught them something about me."

"How would your name be getting around?" I asked. "I do not believe the *grotesques* of Sanctuary would share such knowledge of you with outsiders."

A long silence followed, broken only when Marshall let out a long sigh.

"Okay, okay," he said. "I can't stand it. I have a pretty good idea how your name's been getting around."

Alexandra looked at Marshall, but he would not meet her eyes.

"Why do I have a bad feeling about this?" she said.

"Marshall Blackmoore," I said, grabbing the sides of his

face and making him look at Alexandra. "Tell her of what you speak."

"There's been a lot of talk out there in the magical community," he said.

Caleb crossed his arms. "Oh, has there, now? Do tell!"

"The Orders from all five boroughs are planning a meet," he said. "They're freaked-out about how much living stone is in the city now. They want to hold a Convocation."

Alexandra waved me closer and I dragged Marshall over to her cell.

"What the hell are the Orders? What's a Convocation?"

"Each borough is divided up into witching orders," Caleb said. "There's a warden that watches over the covens in each area, and a head witch who runs the Convocation." He turned to Marshall. "But how would *you* know that?"

Marshall looked as if he might be sick at any moment. "I'm a bit more involved with them than any of you know," he said.

"How?" I asked.

"Blame Caleb," Marshall said, pointing to him and starting to babble. "He's the one who got me started down this path. I wouldn't even have started with alchemy if he hadn't got me into it. The surprising thing, though? I'm *good* at it."

"You're *okay* at it," Caleb corrected.

"Fine," Marshall said. "I'm *okay* at it . . . but, not to sound too egomaniacal, on top of that knowledge, I *am* clever. So I started experimenting. Your hoods, for example. Normal material treated with a mixture of potions. Hell, my Dungeon Master's guide gave me plenty of ideas to try out, and a few of the people Caleb *had* introduced me to were curious as well. There's a market for this kind of stuff. The other night when you came in like a drowned rat? Those weren't gamers at Roll for Initiative. Those were witches and wizards coming to check out my latest wares. There's far more money in arcana than gaming, I'm sad to report."

"Marshall!" Alexandra said.

"Hey, I'm the alpha geek. I know better than anybody that with great power comes great responsibility. I'm being careful. I don't sell to just anybody who comes in wearing a pointy hat with moons and stars on it."

"Never mind that," Caleb shouted. "What about the damage you're doing to *my* profit margin?"

Marshall and Alexandra joined in and the group was shouting at one another to the point where I could not follow any line of their arguments. I released my grip on Marshall and let him go completely as he verbally defended himself. Only when Aurora returned with the two humans from the other night did I speak again.

"Enough!" I said, and turned to face the newcomers. The hallway fell silent except for the footsteps of their approach. Aurora's hands were on the back of her head, the two other humans walking with their firearms drawn. I looked down at Marshall with a growl. "What have you told them about Alexandra?"

"Nothing," he said, full of nerves with his hands held up. "I swear! The community is abuzz with talk, but I would never compromise any of you by talking to them about what we do. I've kept my ear open for anything that sounded threatening."

"Is this any way to start a reunion?" Alexandra asked from the cell, as the two new humans joined us. "The tall one is Detective Maron. The other is Detective Rowland. And as you can see they love guns."

When the detectives turned to Alexandra, they noticed me for the first time and both of their firearms swung over to me.

I stepped toward them, my gaze unwavering as I did so. "I think we have learned how ineffective such measures can be," I said. "But if you insist on pointing your weapons, I do prefer them aimed at me rather than threatening my friends with them."

Unsure of what to do, the two detectives slowly lowered their weapons.

"What is this?" Detective Rowland asked with wary eyes darting among us. "A prison break?"

"Depends," Caleb said, pointing at Alexandra. "Is she actually under arrest?"

"She's locked up," the woman said. "What do you think?"

"That isn't an answer," he said. "Is she or is she not under arrest?"

Rowland went silent, refusing to answer.

"Technically?" Detective Maron said. "No."

"So technically," I said, catching on, "we are not breaking out a prisoner."

Maron nodded, unable to take his eyes off of me. "We could book you for trespassing," he said, holstering his firearm, "but honestly, I don't know where we'd hold you."

Detective Rowland pushed her way past everyone to the front of the cell, her firearm raised once again. She tapped it against the bars of the cell and looked back at her partner. "You're not just going to let her walk, are you?"

"I'm not sure," he said. "I didn't imagine such a crowd being around when it came time to make that decision."

"Then let me make the decision for you," Alexandra said.

I watched as Alexandra bowed her head and concentrated her power into the concrete of the floor where the bars of the cage met it. The area crumbled and twisted and slid away in all directions from the base of the bars.

"Alexandra, please," I said. "Refrain from manipulating the building any further. We are well underground and I have already done some damage to this building's foundation."

"Don't worry," she said, stepping closer to the bars. "I'm not looking to collapse the place. I just want to show our new friends what they're dealing with."

I reached for the now-loose bars and pulled them apart with ease.

Alexandra stepped out of the cage to join the rest of us. "I could have left anytime I wanted to, Detectives," she said.

"So why *didn't* you?" Detective Rowland asked.

"After a good night's rest, I'm feeling . . . refreshingly cooperative today. This outpouring of rescuers tonight reminded me of something I've forgotten these past few months—I don't have to bear this burden all alone. You two chasing us down isn't just another problem for me to deal with. It's an opportunity."

"It is?" the woman asked.

"Yes," Alexandra said. "For *you*."

"You want to explain that, Miss Belarus?" the man asked.

"Look," Alexandra said, reaching for Aurora's pole arm. Her friend handed it to her, and Alexandra broke it down into its three component sections, then handed it back to her blue-haired friend. "Your people and my people could have a go at each other right now, but can we agree that's not going to turn out good for either side?"

"I don't know," Detective Rowland said. "We've got a pretty good legal team here. Not as good, I'm sure, as the Belarus family real estate lawyers, probably."

"You've been doing your homework, Detectives," Alexandra said. "But let's try to keep my family out of this, shall we? I'm talking about here and now. You start shooting, Rory here probably would have started swinging her bladed stick thing around—which *is* a thing of beauty to see, mind you. Caleb and Marshall no doubt have some alchemical tricks up their sleeves. And Stanis . . . ?"

All of the humans looked to me and I made sure I stood stone still, giving the grimmest gaze I could muster to the two detectives.

"Well," Alexandra continued. "There's no telling what chaos he'd bring into the fray."

The female detective raised her firearm. "Are you threatening us?" she asked.

"No," I said. "I believe what Alexandra is actually trying to do is be reasonable."

The detective could not help but laugh. "Three people and one gargoyle breaking into our precinct is considered *reasonable*?"

"Actually, Stanis is right," Alexandra said. "I don't think anyone upstairs here has anything written in the law books to cover the world we're all trying our best to deal with now. I've been lamenting how I haven't been able to just spend time practicing actual art lately, but the truth is we're creating something here. We're going to have to make this up as we go along. *All* of us."

Detective Rowland lowered her firearm. "What do you want us to do, then?" she asked.

"I've decided that I—we—will help you with your *grotesque* problem," Alexandra said.

I looked to her, lowering my voice. "We will?" I asked.

She laid a hand on my chest. "We already *are*. I just think it would be better if we found a way to bring in more of the human involvement element. Your kind are public now. It's time we start thinking about how humanity is going to adjust to *grotesques* out in the world . . . or *not* adjust. Our first step is to find a way to better control the rogue population out there, and I think these two might help us with that. I'm tired of fighting the rogue ones alone, especially when being chased by witches, warlocks, and cops alike."

"Witches and warlocks?" Detective Maron asked. "We're talking witches and warlocks as well?"

Aurora held up a hand. "One threat at a time, pal."

"I had something I meant to tell you about them, Alexandra," I said. "Before we were interrupted at the armory. I had wished to impart some knowledge I have learned from Jonathan."

"Who the hell is Jonathan?" the female detective asked.

"A dead monk now trapped in a *grotesque* body," I said, getting dead-eyed stares from the detectives. "It is a long story."

"You can tell them about it another night," Alexandra said. "What did the monk tell you?"

"As you suspected from your vine incident, there was another person in Fort Tryon Park with you, hunting you. A warlock. I believe it was he who had set the plant snare that was meant to trap you."

"Jonathan saw the guy?" Caleb asked.

"He did," I said with a smile that bared my fangs.

"Well, what did he look like?" he asked

"The monk said this man had black hair and a beard," I said. "And he wore many rings."

"Great," Marshall said. "We're on the lookout for some guy with way too much man jewelry. Maybe we should start our search among the Bridge and Tunnel crowd. Head out to Long Island or New Jersey."

"Wait," Caleb said. "Was it wild hair, like kind of an Einstein thing? And fistfuls of rings?"

I nodded.

"You know this man?" Detective Maron asked Caleb.

"That I do," Caleb said. "I've done some work for his family over the years."

Anger filled me. "Once again working for those who would do us harm," I said.

Caleb met my eyes, not looking away.

"Don't start," he said. "All my past mischief predates knowing any of you."

Detective Maron stepped forward, pulling a small notebook from the inside pocket of his jacket. "You have an address on this guy?" he asked.

"No," Caleb said. "Actually, I heard he was dead, but I know some people who might be able to sort that out for me one way or another."

"Let's get on it, then," Aurora said.

"We can grab this guy and hold him," Detective Rowland said.

"Like you did Alexandra?" Marshall asked. "Very effective. I'm sure this place is totally warlock-proof."

"Let us handle it, Detectives," Aurora said.

Caleb shook his head. "I don't think large numbers are what's needed right now," he said.

"Bullshit," Maron said.

"Listen," Caleb said, insistent this time. "I can't risk spooking the whole arcane community by starting a massive . . . well, a perfect term for it, actually, is a witch hunt. What I need to conduct with those people requires subtlety." He looked up at me. "Not brute force."

Detective Rowland was already shaking her head.

"No," she said. "We have to be part of this."

"Absolutely not," Alexandra said. "But it would be kind of you to fetch my things for me. They're going to come in handy."

Detective Rowland tried to argue, but her partner laid his hand on her shoulder. "Let them go," he said. "We've got to start trusting someone sometime in all this."

"I'm not sure releasing our only tie to all this gargoyle madness is our best course of action," she said. "This woman and her friends are the first solid lead we've actually been able to track down. Something tangible, so our brothers and sisters in blue stop snickering at us in the hallways."

"As I mentioned," Alexandra said, "I could have released *myself* anytime I wanted. You know my name. No doubt in your research you've already verified that I am who I say I am. If I prove uncooperative after my release, you have more than enough information to track me down where I live. But don't worry. I'll be in touch."

The woman thought about it for a moment before giving a silent nod.

"I'll get your things," Detective Maron said and headed back up the hallway with Rowland.

"I will see what I can find out about who is organizing this other band of *grotesques*," I said. "I do not like the idea of some sort of dark insurrection rising up out there while me and my people at Sanctuary strive to protect this city."

"Thank you," Alexandra said. She turned from me, and went to Caleb. "Come on. The sooner we find this guy, the sooner maybe I can have one less group of people trying to kill me."

The two of them followed after the detectives, leaving the rest of us alone in the basement.

"Come on," Aurora said. "We'll take the back way out with you."

"Back through the sewage," Marshall said. "Lovely."

I nodded. "If my father the tyrant could see me now," I said. "An emissary of my people, trudging around under the city, going out of my way all for the comfort of humans and the safety of my own . . ."

Aurora slid the pieces of her pole arm into the art tube and strapped it across her back once more. She clapped me on my shoulder.

"You are not your father's son," she said. "He would have caused a scene, tearing his way out of this precinct with as much devastation as possible."

"That is where we differ," I said, heading back to the storage room we had come in through. "I have not half the vain pride he had. I do not have his ambitions."

"Well, what ambitions *do* you have?" Marshall asked.

I stopped at the door leading into the room, casting my eyes back down the hallway just as Alexandra and Caleb vanished around the corner.

"To see those I care for happy," I said. "And for myself? Peace."

Twelve

Alexandra

On one of the quiet winding streets hidden off in the far West Village, the building before Caleb and me was exactly the sort of home I imagined a cosmopolitan wizard might live in. Part low-rise fortress and part spired castle, the odd little town house looked far older than the buildings to either side of it.

"This must be the place," I said. "It looks like a Gothic version of the Weasley house."

"Yes, very understated," Caleb said. "About what I'd expect from a long-lived magical clan like the O'Sheas."

"So do we just knock?" I asked.

"I don't think that's a wise move," Caleb said. "This *is* the warlock that was trying to trap you, after all. Warren's the only guy I know who wears more rings than Liberace, and since he's been sneaking around after you, I think that allows us to give the sneaky approach a chance ourselves."

Climbing the steps, I examined the heavy oak frame that ran around the frosted-glass panel at the center of the door. Runic script wove its way all around the frame.

"I'm going to guess this is bad," I said, tracing one of the symbols, making sure not to actually touch it. "There are different styles of runes, but these aren't overly familiar to me. This one here, though, looks like the symbol for fire that my great-great-grandfather used in his notes." I moved to another section. "And this looks like one for *mal* and health. I don't want to explode in flame."

"Okay, so no front-door approach, then," Caleb said.

"Hold on," I said, considering our options. "We don't need to actually *use* the door." I pointed to the masonry surrounding the entrance to the town house. "The stonework around it is pretty hefty, but I think I can manipulate it."

Caleb wagged a finger at me. "I thought that messing with the lower floors of a building was a no-no."

"Usually, yes," I said. "But this door is set into an archway. Given that specific architectural design feature, a lot of the load-bearing is taken up by the keystone at the top, which then flows down into either side of the arch. That makes it a lot easier for me to concentrate on where to focus my effort and energy to keep the support where it should be, to know what I can and can't shift around. I *should* be able to open up a gap for us along the side of the door where there's no hinge hardware."

Caleb backed down the steps. "You won't mind if I just watch that from afar," he said, not stopping until he was across the sidewalk and out into the center of the quiet street. "No offense."

"Some taken," I said, then shrugged. "But understandable."

I pulled out my notebook, quickly going through some of the power focus sections that I hadn't quite mastered yet. After a few minutes of brushing up, I slid the notebook back into my coat pocket and let out a long slow breath while quietly letting loose one of my family's words of power. My hands worked through the accompanying gestures as my concentration flowed into the stone of the archway.

I searched for any sense of weakness in the craftsmanship. Near the top of the arch I lashed out my power, tugging at the stone there. A block at the top left side of the door pulled out from the door's framing, and as it came free, I added the ones below it to my efforts, attempting to remove them as one column.

The second they were clear, the heavy pressure of the
archway and the building it supported became painfully evident as the invisible sensation of a giant finger suddenly
pressed down on my brain. The force startled me enough that
I staggered back, feeling like my skull might pop open at any
second, barely able to keep control of the wobbling column
of stone at my command.

"You okay?" Caleb called from out in the safety of the
street.

"Get up here," I hissed through clenched teeth. "And get
inside . . . *now*!"

Caleb ran up the stairs, but hesitated before the gap leading
into the building.

"I'll get us in," I assured him. "Then it's up to you to keep
us alive."

Without a word, Caleb slid into the narrow space and disappeared into the building.

Stepping carefully around the stone column in my control,
I pressed myself into the opening and followed after him. The
immediate interior of the town house was dark, but before I
worried about my eyes adjusting to it, I still had work to do.
I reached out my power, pulling the column of stone back into
place behind me, and restored the archway.

As the stones settled once more against one another, I
nearly wept for joy as the crushing pressure in my brain subsided, leaving only a dull headache in its place.

"Remind me to start carrying aspirin," I said, turning
around to look for Caleb.

Caleb held his finger up to his lips, shushing me.

Silently, I waited as my eyes adjusted to the darkness so I
could fully assess the main floor of the town house. From
inside, the rooms of the town house looked far more spacious
than the outside of the building suggested and the furnishings
were a bit more modest and plain than I expected.

"You *sure* this is the place?" I asked in a low whisper. "I
mean, it looks so . . . mundane."

"So it would seem," Caleb said, scanning the hallway.
"What did you think? That there would be a broomstick stand

by the front door or something? A sacrificial altar where the dining room table is?"

"Kinda," I said, then stopped myself. "Actually, I don't know what I thought to expect. I'm pretty sure, however, that the IKEA catalog wasn't it."

Caleb poked his head into a few of the archways off the main hall. "I'm guessing his inner sanctum is probably somewhere on the upper levels," he said, then drank a vial he pulled from his jacket. He tapped his shoes to the floor, but they made no noise whatsoever. He gave me a thumbs-up and headed soundlessly for the stairs.

I followed after, attempting to make as little noise as I could, a little pissed he hadn't offered me at least a swig of what he was having. In a home as silent as this, my every move sounded to me like I was a lumbering giant, but since Caleb didn't turn to shush me again, I kept on trying to do my stealthy best to keep my stair creaking to a minimum.

Once upstairs, the two of us went down its main hall, only to find bedrooms and a plain office devoid of people and any sense of taste. We stopped at the end of the hall where it dead-ended in front of a large wall-spanning mural that consisted of fornicating unicorns.

"Any guesses on the name of *this* masterpiece?" I asked with a shudder, unable to look away from it. "I'm going with *Pornicorn Bacchanal*."

"I forfeit my guess," Caleb said, looking anywhere but at the mural. "I'm trying not to throw up and leave any evidence behind." He looked back down the hall we had just come down. "I thought for sure there'd be something up here."

"Let's give the rooms one more go-over," I said, heading off to the one on the right side of the hall. Checking each carefully, I made sure no secret stairs were hidden in the backs of closets, perhaps leading up to an attic space. When nothing appeared in any of my three rooms, I returned to the main hall, where Caleb had already finished and had against his desire started looking over the bawdy unicorns in the mural.

"Any luck on your side?" I asked.

He gave a weak shake of his head.

"Creepy as this building looks on the outside, maybe you've got the wrong address . . . ?" I suggested, heading back to the stairs down to the main floor. When I realized Caleb wasn't following, I stopped and turned.

"Caleb!" I whisper-shouted. Even with no one home here, I still found myself reluctant to call out in the middle of the evening in a stranger's home.

"I . . . I can't help it," Caleb said, still staring at the mural. "It's like . . . Tolkien porn. It's—"

"Distracting," I finished, walking back to him as an idea hit me. "I know. And the thing is, it's *meant* to be."

I stepped past Caleb to examine the mural closer. About an inch away from its surface, I felt something: a hint of magic radiating from the artwork. Raising my left hand to run over the canvas, I was surprised to find my fingers *missing*.

Startled, I staggered back from the mural, and my hand suddenly reappeared at the end of my arm. I eased it forward once more, and my arm slowly disappeared into the mural itself. Continuing forward with the rest of my body, I stepped toward and *through* the mural as a tingling sensation washed over me and I found myself at the bottom of an ascending staircase.

I turned back around, making out a Caleb-shaped shadow on the other side of the wall. I reached back through the mural, grabbed his arm, and pulled him through.

"Whoa," he said, stumbling into the bottom of the stairwell with me. "You should totally get one of these for your guild-hall."

"I'll stick with my secret-door bookcase, thanks," I said, starting up the stairs. "I like something with a little heft to it."

"Suit yourself," Caleb said. "I just thought it was a cool effect."

I started to respond, but as I hit the top of the stairs, I lost track of my thoughts and let out a low whistle. "Now, this is more of what I imagined," I said.

A large window looked up and out into the night sky, the moon full and bright as it shone down into the large open space up here. The room was neatly arranged into an eclectic mix of furniture and items, which gave it an almost museum quality due to the wide span of history that the collection clearly represented. Trunks upon trunks lined the walls to either side of the space.

Caleb bounded up the last few steps and stopped at my side, taking the room in.

"I've long suspected that the O'Sheas were a bit of a magical hoarding family," Caleb said. "This just clinches it."

"Oh?"

He nodded, stepping into the center of the space, marveling. "I freelanced for them a bunch of times, but they never let me see *this*. They never admitted to owning even a tenth of the stuff represented here." Caleb shook his head. "Warren's a dick."

He chuckled at his own statement, which I found odd until I realized it wasn't Caleb's laughter.

I couldn't pinpoint where the voice was coming from, and by the time I did, it was too late. A lone figure materialized from the shadows at the back of the room. The ominous tone of the laughter had me fishing for the store of small stones I kept in most of my coat pockets these days, hoping I could get off a few shots before the figure could close the distance. I began incanting the spell to drive them with significant stopping force at our attacker, but jumped as the massive trunks on either side of the room exploded open.

Thick coils of heavy chain shot out from the massive holes, and I dropped my spell to dive out of the way of the incoming assault. Despite my attempt at evasion, the chains corrected their course after me all too quickly, wrapping around my ankles and bringing me to the floor.

Caleb went for the inside of his coat, no doubt reaching for one of his alchemical mixes, but the chains attacking him went for his hands, knocking their contents away and sending a fistful of vials sailing off across the room.

I fought to stand despite my bindings, forcing myself up onto my hands and knees, but two more chains wrapped around my hands and dragged me to a hanging position. The last of the chain snaked around my body over and over in a near-solid coil before finally stopping.

Clearly, breaking and entering was something I needed to brush up on, although I couldn't feel too bad about my effort because Caleb—despite his more nefarious past—was just as screwed, mummified in his own set of iron restraints.

"Man, I *really* hope getting caught like this is part of your master plan," I hissed to him through my tight, heavy bonds.

Caleb ignored me, focusing his gaze instead on the man coming toward us.

Wild black hair stuck up in every direction, in stark contrast with the orderly trimmed beard the man wore. Both of the man's hands were covered in a variety of rings, which, given his old jeans and T-shirt, made him look more like an unemployed musician than a sorcerer supreme.

He stopped five feet from me, amusement on his face.

"*You're* not who I was expecting," he said, a bit of wonder in his words.

"Sorry to disappoint," I managed to get out between shallow breaths. "You're not the first witch or warlock to hunt me. You are, however, the lucky one."

"Lucky?" he asked. "How?"

"Not everyone gets me delivered to their doorstep," I said, mustering up as much bravado as I could. "But I'll warn you . . . the others failed in their quests to keep me captured, so the odds aren't looking in your favor."

"Be that as it may," he said, looking me over, "you are a welcome surprise, I must say."

I felt the early stages of panic kicking in, which sucked because if I started hyperventilating, I'd end up passing out from the hundred pounds of chain wrapped around me.

"Easy, Warren," Caleb said, and the man finally looked over to him, recognition filling his face. "Let's not do anything hasty."

"Caleb Kennedy . . . ?" the man said, moving closer in the low light of the room. "This *is* an interesting night, indeed." He jerked his thumb in my direction. "Freelancing for *this* troublemaker, are you?"

"Troublemaker?!" I asked, almost laughing. "Me? How

did you even spot me? I've been wearing my talisman and it's fully charged."

"Your tricks and trinkets might work on the simple-minded," Warren said with a scoff, "but on a warlock in his ancestral home? Not a chance."

"I heard that *you* were dead," Caleb said.

"Excellent," the man said. "That's what I was going for."

The man looked me up and down, curiosity mixed with lasciviousness. "Hello, moppet," he said with the slightest hint of an Irish lilt in his words.

Caleb sighed from within his coil of chain. "Alexandra Belarus," he said. "This is Warren O'Shea. Warren, this is Alexandra."

Warren stepped closer, examining my face like someone who was starving and I was his next meal. "Charmed, I'm sure."

"Why do you want people to think you're dead?" I asked. "In my experience, people who disappear are the ones who most have something to hide, Warren."

"You mean people like you?" he shot back. "Do you know how hard it has been trying to track down the mysterious Spell-mason all the witches and warlocks in my community have been searching for? What do *you* have to hide, I wonder."

"Fair point," I said, knowing how much I wanted to stay off their radar. "But you didn't answer *my* question. Why do you want people to think you're dead?"

Warren sighed and stepped back from me, a bit of the venom going out of him. "I was hoping that by going into hiding, playing dead, I could avoid *being* actually dead," he said.

"You're going to have to explain that."

"Someone wants to kill me," he said. "Better?"

"I want to kill you right now," Caleb said.

Warren looked up and down the chain cocoon that covered Caleb. "I'm not all that concerned about that, funnily enough."

"Who else wants you dead?" I asked.

"For that you'll need to understand something first," he said. "There's a reason witches and warlocks tend to group into covens. There's safety in numbers."

I turned to Caleb. "I thought you once told me that they didn't organize like that."

"I had said there's not a lot of trust out there among witches and warlocks," Caleb said. "And that's true, but when they find those who *are* like-minded, they're willing to form a rudimentary magical grouping like a coven, which answers to their Orders in the boroughs. That's why some groups like the Witch & Bitch ladies don't like using freelancers like me. They've got their little group and simply don't trust outsiders. Now imagine dozens and dozens of groups just like that. That's why they formed the Convocation—to gather and settle the issues that arise from arcane distrust."

"Although," Warren added, "there *was* once a time when *all* the covens of Manhattan joined together."

"When?" I asked.

"In the 1920s," he said. "In fact, my family and I led the charge."

1920s? I thought. "Just how old *are* you, Warren?" I asked.

The man smiled and smoothed down his wild black hair, which immediately popped back up into its disheveled state.

"Let's just say I'm remarkably well preserved," he said. "But vanity aside, yes, there was a time that we all came together for a common cause."

"Robert Patrick Dorman," Caleb said. "The Butcher of the Bowery."

"Correct," he said.

"He sounds unpleasant," I said. "The gargoyles who attacked us at the armory were his henchmen. Just who the hell is this guy?"

"There are a variety of ways to channel magic," Warren said, pointing to me. "Your Spellmasonry, for instance." He moved his finger over to Caleb. "Alchemy. All of these various disciplines are driven by a mix of will and arcane science, but there are also what our kind call wild mages. However they make their magic work, it is nearly unrecognizable to the scientific approach taken by the rest of us practitioners."

"That's not quite right, now, is it, Warren?" Caleb asked. "It's not that you don't understand their magic. It's that you refuse to acknowledge what form some of that magic takes. You don't want to call it what it is."

My face cooled as I felt the color drain from it. "Is that as bad sounding as I think it is?" I asked.

"Actually, it's worse than you're probably thinking."

"Fine," Warren said, forcing out the words now. "*Blood* magic. Out of nowhere people in our community were turning up dead, and that drew attention to us. Witches and warlocks have long suffered at the hands of those who do not practice the arcane arts, but the Butcher's madness and lust for power drove him to more and more public displays of his power, mostly through the carnage that is blood magic. There is a great power in the blood of the living, more so in that of the magically inclined. Once we were able to sort out who was responsible for such a foul practice, it took all of the community's effort to hunt the Butcher and take him down."

"And yet as your community stands today, all of you are fragmented," I said. "I would think that this Robert Patrick Dorman would have proven to be the great uniter of all the tribes forever and always."

Before Warren could answer, Caleb let loose a powerful laugh. "You'd think, wouldn't you?" he said. "But let me see if I understand Warren's people as well as I think I do."

Warren stepped back and lowered himself into one of his chairs, folding his hands over his knees. "By all means," he said. "Give it your best shot."

"After the arcane community took the Butcher of the Bowery down, there was a mad scramble for power," Caleb said. "Everyone was spooked about what had happened and didn't want it to happen again. So everyone circled up in their own little power-hungry groups tighter than ever before, hoping to grab the biggest piece of the magical pie that they could. And others simply disappeared off the grid, fearing their power might be abused. Now you're all a bunch of nomadic arcane tribes operating independently and are far less powerful because of it."

Warren raised his hands and gave a long, slow series of claps. "You understand us better than I would have expected," he said.

"I know my client base," Caleb said. "It's your messed-up thinking and insecurities that keep me in business."

"This is nothing new," I added. "My great-great-grandfather Alexander Belarus understood what madmen in search of arcane power were capable of. He had initially built a guildhall for those he was going to teach, but long before your Butcher, he saw what arcane power did to people in this city. I think that's why he never formed his own guild and chose to hide the ways of the Spellmasons instead." I rattled the chains wrapped around me. "But I'm sure you didn't capture us to give us a complete history of the arcane community of New York City. *You're* the one who's been hunting *me*. Why?"

The warlock waved his hand. The walls of the room all around us shimmered as if I were looking at them underwater. The effect caused my stomach to clench and I fought the urge to throw up until the existent walls faded away completely. What once was a neat and orderly mix of eclectic furnishing was now a broken mess of destruction. Warren spread his arms out to indicate the damage all around him.

"It would appear I have a serious gargoyle problem," he said. "And it is the Butcher, although I could not tell you how or why he's back."

"Can *I* take a guess?" I asked as pieces of this warlock's puzzle started falling into place.

"This is starting to feel like a quiz show," Warren said, pleased to the point of smiling. "Please, proceed."

"I've discovered many of the souls currently in possession of a gargoyle form belong to disturbed spirits, ones that were unwilling to leave this mortal plane for . . . wherever spirits are supposed to go. I don't pretend to know. We can discuss the afterlife another time. Your Butcher sounds like a worthy candidate for Disturbed Spirit of the Century . . . His soul was never going to leave this mortal coil. Now he's got a big, bad, stony form and you're worried he's coming for your family in revenge, for leading the charge against him all those years ago.

"You *do* have a serious gargoyle problem, Mr. O'Shea," I said, repeating him. "I can say that with certainty because *I've* had a gargoyle problem before myself."

"So it would seem," Warren said, walking up to me. "Which is why I've been hunting you. From what I've heard through the grapevine, I have *you* to thank for that."

It pained me to recall the damage a mind-controlled Stanis had done to my great-great-grandfather's library—or that Caleb had been part of its doing—but Warren's home had the same look of furious damage that only a gargoyle could do.

"I know what I've unleashed on this city," I said, the old guilt hurting my heart.

Warren's eyes narrowed at my admission. He raised his right hand, the rings on his fingers glowing bright as he closed his fist. My restraints tightened, making it harder to breathe.

Gasping for breath, I decided to go with reason to get the warlock to relent. "*I* didn't do this to your home," I said. "Or to your family."

"But you *are* the girl with the gargoyles," he said. "In my hunt for you, there hasn't been much video footage, but I still have found bits and pieces of you in the company of a gargoyle."

"My gargoyle didn't do this," I gasped out. It was strange to call Stanis *my* gargoyle, but it was the best way to explain the situation while being crushed by chains.

My bindings tightened even further, Warren's eyes full of anger, burning into mine.

"We didn't have a gargoyle problem until *you* showed up," he growled.

I blushed as a wave of shame hit me. It was true. I could put some of the blame on Caleb for his involvement in the great awakening, but if it wasn't for unleashing the ways of the Spellmasons by reclaiming what I felt was my birthright, things simply wouldn't be the chaotic mess they were now.

With the chains ever tightening, stars began to appear in my vision and I struggled to catch my breath. "I . . . can . . . help," I said, refusing to look away from Warren as I fought to stay conscious.

The warlock studied my face for a moment longer, then turned away, the tension going out of my restraints.

"Let us hope so," he said. "It is, after all, why I was hunting you. I fear for my safety as well as that of my family."

Caleb shrugged off his bonds, the chains clanging to the floor in a circle around him. "You seem to be perfectly capable of defending yourself," he said.

"Yeah," I said. I pulled away my own slack restraints, letting them fall to the floor. "What do you want me to do?"

"You're the Spellmason," he said. "Dealing with rampaging masonry is your bailiwick, not mine. I could harm the Butcher—again—but I am looking for a more . . . permanent solution."

"Oh," I said, and remained silent, hiding the fact that I had zero idea of how to go about so tall an order. If he thought we might be of help and it kept us unchained, I wasn't about to contradict the man.

"You'd think his need for vengeance would have died down a bit over the past century," Caleb said.

"I'm afraid this isn't just garden-variety vengeance," Warren said, sitting back down.

I stepped out from inside the pile of chains around my ankles. "It's not?" I asked.

"No," Warren said. "Vengeance is the obvious choice, although frankly nothing satisfying usually comes from it. Trust me on this. The O'Shea family is a long-lived line in our particular branch of arcane study. Over time we have accumulated more than our fair share of items and devices. Tomes, charms, potions . . . I believe, however, the Butcher came after us because he is on the hunt for one particular item."

"Jesus," Caleb said, "what more does a gargoyle need? They've already got strength, flight, immortality . . ."

"To understand the Butcher's motives, you would have to know Robert Patrick Dorman as well as we knew him," Warren said. "Dorman didn't just feed his blood magic on the power of the arcane community. He seemed to enjoy the hedonistic and carnal nature of his craft against both arcane kind and humanity."

"Gargoyles are created through magic," I said as part of our dilemma became clear. "The fact that they are a supernatural construct means they themselves cannot actually practice the craft of it. The Butcher would need to be human again to regain his arcane power."

Warren nodded. "And while I am sure that today he appreciates just being alive in his new stone form, I am more than certain of his desire to return to the flesh. It is surely what prompted this carnage in my home."

My stomach tightened at the suggestion of such an item that could transform a gargoyle's body out if its stone form.

"Your family has something that will do that?" I asked. "Restore his humanity?"

"It can't be done," Caleb said. "Bringing an alchemical creature back to something human. Not from stone. Alchemists have struggled with debates like this for centuries. You can't bend the material nature of the universe in quite that way."

"Hold on a second," I said, turning to him. "*You* turned from stone to flesh. I saw you. You did it before I knew you, the night Rory and I caught you stealing from the alchemical cabinets in the guildhall."

"Actually, that wasn't *quite* what I was doing," he said. "That was more of a camouflage thing . . . and what I do are tricks compared to the big magic Warren here is implying."

"And Kejetan's boat that we transformed from steel to stone?"

"Allotropy," Caleb reminded me. "An allotrope allows for elementary substances in material matter to exist in other forms, like when sharing the common components in steel and stone. But the difference between the core elements that make us human flesh versus stone . . . I'm sorry; it just can't be done."

"I cannot speak to the alchemy of such matters," Warren said. "But I can tell you that my family was in possession of an item that purported to do such a thing—the Cagliostro Medallion."

"*Was* in possession of?" I repeated. "Then the Butcher already has it. If you want my help in taking care of him, that just made my job a whole lot simpler. It will be far easier to take down a man of flesh than it is one of stone."

"One small problem," Warren said, holding up a finger. "I

don't think the Butcher *does* have it. My family lost track of the Cagliostro Medallion decades ago."

"How the hell does one lose such a thing?" I asked, unable to hide my incredulity. The importance of such a rare arcane item—one that made me immediately think would be of use certainly to Stanis—made it seem impossible that a person might just simply misplace or lose track of it.

"No one can remember," he said. "Some say it was too powerful to be on anyone in the family's radar. I suspect one of us took it upon themselves to secure it away from seeking eyes, but no one recalls it, or is willing to fess up about it, anyway. I have my suspicions, but yet I can confirm nothing."

"So what is it you want from me?"

"I want you to stop this creature that the Butcher has become," he said. "In human form, he was clever, resourceful, and dangerous. In his newfound form, I simply cannot fathom the hell he might unleash on both my family and the rest of this city in his search to regain his humanity. You have some prowess dealing with these creatures that you are in part responsible for creating. I need him stopped."

"Very well," I said. "But where do we start?"

"I think I can send you off with a two-for-one," Warren said with a smile. "If the Butcher is seeking out the medallion, he's going to look where *I'd* look next."

"Which is where?" I asked.

"Our family crypt," Warren said.

"Please tell me you have one in your basement," I said.

Warren cocked his head at me. "Excuse me?"

"My family's ancestral home has one in the lower levels of the building," I said. "I figured you might have the same."

"That's morbid," Warren said with a look of distaste. "You people are creepy."

"Says the guy wearing twenty rings," I fired back.

Warren held his hands up, examining with a look of pride, my barb being lost on him completely.

"Where is this crypt, then?" Caleb asked.

"There is a secret cemetery in this city," he said. "One where most of our kind are buried."

"That's what I was worried about," Caleb said. "I've heard of it."

"But you've never been?" I asked him.

He shrugged. "I'm not really one for planning out my future," he said. "And picking a place to be buried wasn't really top of my list. I always figured I'd end up in some magical potter's field somewhere. I know where this place is, though. Roughly."

I turned my attention back to Warren. "Why send *us* to check your family crypt? Couldn't you do that yourself instead of sending us in there like grave robbers?"

Warren shook his head. "Normally, yes," he said. "In fact, I already tried to do just that, but there's one problem."

"You mean *other* than the Butcher wanting to kill you?" I asked.

He nodded. "I would have gone to the crypt myself," he said, "but it appears to have gone . . . missing."

"Your family's crypt?" Caleb asked.

"Not just it," he said, and looked almost embarrassed by the admission. "The cemetery itself. I can't seem to find my way to it any longer. I searched the path for it, but to no avail."

I sighed. "Of course not," I said. "Why should anything ever go easy for us?"

"Leave it to me," Caleb said. "I'll find the place, don't worry. Now, what was this you mentioned about a twofer . . . ?"

Warren nodded. "If you do indeed find the cemetery, not only will you find my family crypt there, but it is also the final resting place of the Butcher. I am not sure of the way of gargoyles, but if it is like other transformative arcana, he'll want to have secured his mortal remains so none can act upon them. You'll find either them or evidence of their removal. Either way, it is a starting point for tracking him down."

"Fine," I said. "We'll check on this crypt of yours for the medallion, providing Caleb actually finds it for me, and I'll see what I can do about this gargoyle Butcher of yours. But I have two conditions."

Warren leaned back in his chair and folded his arms across his chest. "Name them."

"First," I said. "I'm sick of Manhattan's magical denizens trying to hunt me down. I need that to stop. In fact, I could use their help. It would benefit us all if they could help get the city's gargoyle population under control. "

Warren shook his head. "I have little control over how the various covens of New York conduct themselves," he said.

I leaned over him. "This is a nonnegotiable point," I said. "Put your best foot forward with them. I'll deal with the ones who can't be persuaded by you, but I have a feeling you'll be very convincing."

Warren thought about it for a moment, then nodded. "Agreed. I will speak with the powers that be. There is a Convocation with all the boroughs on the schedule. Perhaps I can arrange something. And?"

"For my second request," I said. "The Cagliostro Medallion. If I find it, it's mine."

Warren shook his head "You cannot ask for such a thing," he said.

I turned away from him, heading back to the stairs leading down into the town house, not even waiting for Caleb to follow.

"I wasn't asking," I said, and walked down the stairs back toward the mural of the fornicating unicorns. "That's the price you pay for getting to live."

Thirteen

○

Alexandra

"I remember when we used to come to Central Park because we were skipping school," Rory said as we wandered down one of its winding, sunlit dirt pathways. "I'm not so much a fan of coming here as grave robbers."

The sun shone down through the trees, creating gorgeous shafts of light all around us. It seemed strange to even be talking grave robbing during daylight hours, but clearly it was still enough to give Rory a look of unease.

"We're *not* robbing graves," I said, loud enough for even Marshall and Caleb to hear from where they walked up ahead of us. "We're ensuring a good relationship with the magical community."

"Yes," Rory said. "By robbing a grave."

"We're doing a favor," I offered. "Or would you prefer this Warren guy and the rest of the witches and warlocks to keep hunting us? At least he wanted a favor. The others of his kind just want us turned into mice or something for unleashing this gargoyle terror on the city."

Marshall turned back to us. "I'm with Rory on this one," he said. "Not too sure how I feel about defiling a crypt."

I stopped for a second and sighed. "We've got permission from the family," I said, "from the O'Sheas. We recover this item for them, we check out the Butcher's burial site, and we're good. We'll do as little defiling as possible."

"I'll hold you to that," Rory said.

"You do that," I replied.

The two of us caught up with Caleb, who was stopped in the middle of the path, consulting a hand-drawn map. I hadn't seen another person on our trails for at least half an hour, and in the middle of New York City, that kind of lonely isolation felt all kinds of creepy.

"I thought you said you knew where this place is," I said.

"I do," Caleb said. "This might sound strange, but I just don't think it wants to be found right now."

I raised an eyebrow at him. "How does *that* work?"

"Let me ask you this," he said, looking up from his map at me. "How many times have you opened a newspaper or turned on the television and heard about a cemetery for paranormals having been discovered in Manhattan?"

"Zero . . . ?" I asked after taking a moment to wonder whether it was a trick question.

"Correct. It's a *secret* cemetery, and not by chance. Whoever chose to put it here meant for it to stay hidden from the hundreds of thousands of tourists who hit New York City."

"So it's like my family's building on Gramercy," I said. "Alexander warded it centuries ago so people wouldn't take notice of it, especially those seeking out the secrets of the Spellmasons."

"Exactly," Caleb said, then looked down at the map. "Thing is, I thought we would have come across it by now."

Marshall shook his head.

"I don't think we're getting anywhere," he said. "I'm pretty sure we've passed that lamppost with that Grateful Dead cover-band poster on it at least six times."

"Dammit," Caleb said. He folded the map shut and slid it into his jacket.

"So let's make a new path," Rory said, pulling the tube off her back to assemble her pole arm.

"I like your thinking," I said. "Have at it."

"Ladies," Marshall added, holding up a finger. "I'm not sure this is such a good idea."

Rory paused with the pole arm over her head. "No?"

"Don't you remember what happened to the orcs in Fangorn?" he said.

Rory and I both shrugged in confusion.

"What the hell is Fangorn?" I asked. "You forget I'm not fluent in geek."

He sighed. "In *Lord of the Rings*. Saruman the White and his orcs destroyed parts of Fangorn Forest to fuel his war efforts. Eventually the living trees there rose up and fought back."

"That's great and all," Rory said. "But this is Central Park, *not* Middle Earth." She swung with a great downward slash into the tall, thick bushes on one side of the path. It sliced through the branches with ease but all around us the rest of the natural growth sprung to sudden life. Vines and brush snaked out onto the pathway from every direction, coming toward our group.

"I told you!" Marshall said, backing away from the flurry of activity as fast as he could.

"What do you know!" Caleb said, digging into the inside of his coat. "The game store owner was right!"

"I hate being right," Marshall said in retreat.

Caleb pulled several vials free from the lining of his coat. He gave a quick study of their labels and then smashed one of them on the ground at his feet. Several of the rapidly approaching vines burst into flame. Some withered or were consumed immediately by flame, but the thicker, older branches kept coming and wrapped around his legs.

"That could have gone better," Caleb said, coughing through the smoke rising up as his pants caught on fire.

Marshall's hands flew into the satchel he wore and he produced several vials of his own. He poured two small silver ones into a larger plastic one, shook it, and opened the end of it in Caleb's direction. Its contents exploded out of the end and onto the vines wrapped around his legs. What looked like wet sand—and far more than the vial could ever have contained—rained down around Caleb's feet and legs, killing the flames.

Being on a dirt path did little to help me as far as my powers were concerned, but I reached my will out to whatever stone I could find nearby. Rocks, pebbles, and chunks of stone flew up out of the woods all around me, and I aimed them at any vine or branch that made a move toward me. Concentrating my will more on the larger pieces I had summoned, I brought them down over and over again, mashing the broken vines and twisted branches into the path, the fight reluctantly going out of them.

My plan was working, but there was just too much violent, enchanted greenery coming for us. For each one I dispensed with, three others seemed to snake out of the wilderness to replace them.

"A little help here," Rory's voice croaked out from off to my left.

I looked over. Since she was the one who had actually dealt the blow, the plant life seemed to have gone for her with a greater vigor than the rest of us. She was *covered* in vines, her arms and legs splayed out in the air about a foot off the pathway.

"Jesus," Marshall said, already running for her. "She looks like Swamp Thing."

I ran to her as well. Vines snaked around her hand that held the pole arm, but I reached for the connection where the bladed section met with the shaft and twisted the pieces apart, freeing the sharp piece of it. I held it like a giant kitchen knife and began cutting away at the vines entangling my best friend. Marshall grabbed the writhing pieces that fell free and poured a thick, black liquid on the severed ends, which caused them to wither away completely.

The whole process was hard going, especially since I couldn't hack or slack Rory's way to freedom. I couldn't risk cutting her that way, but I needed her free of this mass because I could already hear the rustle of more branches coming out of the bushes all around us.

Caleb joined Marshall in handling the ones I was tossing free of Rory, and a minute later I had cut enough away that Rory was able to lower herself and get her feet back on the ground. Immediately, she was back in action, but was coughing up a storm. Her nails tore into a vine wrapped around her throat. It wriggled like it was in pain as her fingers sunk into it, but she was relentless and wild-eyed now behind her glasses.

With a Hulk-like rage, she pulled it free and took in a huge gasping breath.

"Thanks," she said when she had caught her breath. She staggered weakly on her feet, but managed to tap the end of her pole arm on the ground and reach out her hand to me for the bladed section.

I shook my head, keeping the blade poised for the next vine that snaked near me.

"Uh-uh," I said. "We're getting out of here."

"What?" she asked, still wobbling. "You're kidding, right? I just got caught off guard, that's all. It won't happen again, I promise."

"This isn't just about you," I said. "We don't know what we're up against and I'm not about to put all of us at risk in the face of that." I pointed off to the rustling in a nearby clump of bushes. "There's already more on their way. We need a plan. We need more information."

"I know a guy," Caleb said as he danced in great twists and turns to avoid several attempts by the vines to ensnare him.

"Of *course* you do," Rory shot back, lashing out at one of the bushes with what remained of her pole arm, essentially a staff then. The shaft caught in the bushes, and despite Rory's grip on it, it came free and disappeared into the greenery.

"I see your point," she said, staring down into her empty hands. Her knees buckled as the fatigue of the fight caught up with her, but I ran in close and caught her before she could fall.

"I will not be undone by shrubbery," Marshall added, emptying vials of his own as fast as he could, the greenery far too plentiful and overwhelming for him to contend with. "I'll never hear the end of it if this gets out to my gaming crowd."

I slid Rory's arm over my shoulder and dragged her farther

from the center of the commotion back along the path away from the action.

"Let's live to fight another day," I called out.

Another wave of greenery shot out of the tree line at Marshall and Caleb, but the two alchemists were ready this time. They threw down their combined vials a safe distance from their bodies and ran back up the path after us. I didn't wait to see what effect their concoctions had on the living plant life, all too busy making sure our escape up the pathway was clear, but the hissing and popping rising up behind me seemed a good indicator that their attack had been effective.

"This guy of yours better own a Weedwacker," I said, giving Caleb a weak smile.

"Not that I'm aware of," he said, grabbing Rory's other arm to help move her along more quickly, "but I think he'll prove helpful."

"Let's hope so," I said. "At this point I'll settle for a guy with a gas can and a book of matches. Smokey the Bear be damned!"

As the four of us hightailed it back up the path, I shook my head and sighed. First the attempted retreat at the armory, and now this one. I hated that this was becoming a more and more unsettling trend.

Fourteen

Stanis

Waiting was something that a *grotesque* knew how to do, and nowhere did my demonic form look more natural than in the aptly named Hell's Kitchen, where I sat perched for hours atop an apartment building. Years of vigilance watching over the Belarus family had taught me a near-infinite patience, but with the uprising of these hostile *grotesques* causing unrest within my people and with Alexandra, I found waiting for anything or anyone unbearable.

When the familiar red hair of my target came into sight headed for the entrance of the building below, I stood, stretched my wings to their fullest, and stepped off the ledge.

Detective Chloe Rowland was almost to the doors of her building when I landed in front of her, the walkway beneath my feet cracking on the impact. She dodged to her right, a gun appearing as if out of nowhere in her hands. By the time she caught my eye, her face was full of uncertainty, the gun remaining leveled at my chest.

"We need to talk," I said.

"Do we?" she asked, the gun unwavering.

"Yes." I looked down at the weapon. "There is no need for that. Alexandra sent me."

The detective lowered her weapon, then slid it inside the coat she was wearing.

"Sorry," she said. "It's hard to tell your kind apart. You're all carved by Alexander Belarus, so it's not all that surprising."

"We need to talk," I repeated.

The detective looked past me into the building, then back down the sidewalk where there were more people approaching from off in the distance.

"Now? Here?"

"Yes," I said. "And no."

"Make up your mind," she said, but before she could go any further, I reached out, secured her under her arms, and shot straight up into the night sky.

The detective's eyes went wide and white, her mouth falling open. Before any sound could escape it, I came up over the edge of her building, bringing her down on its roof. I released her and she stumbled back from me until she could once again find her words.

"Next time *ask* before you do something like that," she said, smoothing down her coat. "I almost lost my dinner."

I folded my wings in close to my body, knowing just how uneasy they made most humans when they were flourished open.

"Although we met the other night, I do not believe we were formally introduced," I said. "I am Stanis Ruthenia, and I humbly come before you as a representative of our kind."

"You mean to help Detective Maron and I with our gargoyle problem," she said.

I gave a single nod. "That is what Alexandra Belarus asked of me, yes," I said. "I would do anything to see her happy."

"Touching, really," the detective said, then sighed. "But listen up—your kind *are* my problem. So what exactly do you plan to do about that?"

There was anger thick in the woman's words, the kind that set off my own anger in return, but having come here at the request of Alexandra, I forced myself to choose diplomacy instead.

"Let me be clear about a few things, Detective Rowland," I said, meeting her eyes. "I have watched this city clash for decades, when humans went at each other simply for having different shades of skin. And while those problems seem to persist, I also have seen your kind move beyond such grand generalizations. I would ask that in matters *grotesque* and gargoyle, you show the same restraint in lumping all of my kind into the category of being 'your problem.' Am I understood?"

Rowland went to speak, her face cross with reciprocal anger, but she stopped herself. Instead, she pressed the palms of her hands against the sockets of her eyes, rubbing at them.

"I'm sorry if I seem insensitive," she said. "I've just been dealing with chasing down cases of arcane violence—ones where gargoyles *are* involved—for days on end."

"I understand your plight," I said. "Consider me an ambassador of goodwill for my kind. Those whom I or my fellow *grotesques* have been able to speak reason with have been welcome to become part of our peaceful community at a place I refer to as Sanctuary."

"The whole lot of you are holed up somewhere together, eh?" she asked, her curiosity growing.

"Yes," I said with reluctance at her reaction, "but perhaps for the time being I think it is best that I leave that location undisclosed. Until I know I can trust you and your fellow officers of the law."

"Trust *us*?" she asked with a laugh. "We're not the ones tearing up the city."

"Still, you represent the most law-abiding of your kind, yes?"

"Some more so than others, yes," she said. "Many of my brothers and sisters in law enforcement aren't angels, that's for sure, but the people *I* trust are the cream of the crop. I don't know how exactly I'm supposed to prove that to you, other than my word."

"Trust," I said, "is something to be earned, and then only through time. These are early days, Detective. The course we set now will set the course for how the rest of the world perceives *both* our kind . . . the best *and* the worst."

Detective Rowland visibly relaxed before me, and she placed her hands on her hips as she gave a small smile.

"How did you get to be so smart on such matters?" she asked.

"Long life and a penchant for observation," I said, relaxing myself. "I've watched this city of ours grow over the centuries, and I have seen both the good and bad results of the changes that have occurred. In my human life I came from Europe's ruling class, and although a quest for power had maddened some of those who came before me, I have learned much in my quest to broker peace before an all-out war erupts. I wish that I could report it an easy task, but there is much I am still learning to contend with even now. Those who have come to Sanctuary are dealing with their new lives and issues of their own, which makes it hard to motivate them while also handling them with compassion."

"And here I thought you would have a heart of stone," the detective said.

"I remember my time before taking this form," I said. "I had the heart of a man. Even now, there are those among your kind that I care for dearly. And they are a constant reminder that even though I conduct myself as a creature of stone, I, too, was once human."

"How does that work exactly?" she asked, pulling out her phone to type at it.

"All of *grotesque* kind were once human," I said, "and while the animation of our bodies may be an arcane matter, the thoughts and actions of each individual creature come from a spirit within each of them. These spirits were once human."

The detective lowered her phone again. "So . . . what? Let's say I want to become one of you. My spirit just jumps bodies?"

"In theory, yes," I said. "Although from what little I know about the process, it is far more complicated. Alexandra's brother, for instance. Devon Belarus had bargained with my father, Kejetan the Accursed, for an eternal life in stone. His first form was a monstrous one, before many of my father's

followers were finally able to take the forms of Alexander
Belarus's statues. During that process, more than just Kejetan's
men were created, the stonework throughout the city filled by
the souls of restless spirits in search of an empty vessel. That
is where your—and my—greater issue lies."

Rowland was back at her phone again, her fingers flying.
"Detective Maron and I are going to need as much information as you can give me," she said. "If I'm to bring any of this
in front of my superiors, I need more than what sounds like
the next Guillermo del Toro film to present to them."

I did not know who that was, but her point was clear enough.
"Those who have chosen to join Sanctuary seem to share a common theme," I said. "Their spirits seem to have lingered due to
violent or traumatic events that were done to them in their human
lives. Most see this rebirth in stone as a way to either help others
or do their penance for the life they lived."

Detective Rowland looked up from her notes. "And those
who do not join your Sanctuary?" she asked, but it was clear
she already knew.

"You've already seen them in action," I said. "At the armory.
They would see harm come to this city. Perhaps their spirits
linger on this plane because whatever powers that be . . . Well,
neither side wants them, Heaven or Hell. But these creatures are
out there and they are organizing under one *grotesque*."

"Does this creature have a name?" she asked, pausing from
typing. "What does he look like?"

"I have not seen him yet," I said, "but to those who have been
approached or threatened into joining him as I and Alexandra
have been, he is called the Butcher of the Bowery. He was once
known as the arcane warlock Robert Patrick Dorman. You may
recall Alexandra shouting about him at the armory."

Rowland nodded. "I've actually heard of him before that
night," she said.

"You have?" I asked. "I thought you and Detective Maron
were only recently put to the task of dealing with the supernatural."

"Everyone who goes through the regular old police academy
knows of Dorman," she said. "Although the word *warlock* never

came up, that's for sure. His crimes were many, it appears. At first he was thought to be a bit of an eccentric playboy, but that was just the tip of the iceberg. Eventually he was pegged for a series of ritualistic murders that started with women he had been with but branched out much further than that."

"Blood magic," I said. "Alexandra explained it to me. His hedonism only helped fuel the fire that led to the rest of his darkness."

"You need to find this *grotesque*," the detective said. "Maron and I can get some of the department to pay attention to the type of things we're asking them to look for, but not without some kind of real evidence. The best he and I have been able to do is going out during the day to rooftops in search of these creatures and taking a sledgehammer to them when we come across one."

"What?" I asked with a growl, my wings fluttering with a sudden rage.

"Daylight is the only advantage we have!" the detective fired back, defensive. "Don't look at me like that. We've got zero chance in hell of capturing one of them when they can just fly away. But when they're dormant by the light of day . . ."

I stepped closer, unable to stop myself from trying to intimidate her. My wings flared wide behind me. "Tell me, Detective," I growled. "Since minutes ago you said we all looked alike to you, how do you know who exactly you are destroying in your efforts? Some of those may be *my own* people. You need to stop this practice. Immediately."

There was anger in her eyes, which turned to fear the longer I stared at her with my stone-still eyes.

"Absolutely," she said, finally giving a nod. "I can see how maybe that might be read the wrong way by your people."

"Good," I said, settling myself down once more, bringing my wings back in close to me.

"But Alexandra *did* offer your help," she reminded me. "And we *do* need it. We won't find the Butcher on our own."

"I will set my people to the task of flushing him out," I said. "We will find him, and his people will either be made to see reason or be dealt with accordingly."

The fear slowly faded from Detective Rowland's eyes as she slid her phone back into her pocket. I had hated using such obvious theatrics to put that fear in her, but I could not help myself at the thought of one of my kind being destroyed by her ignorant ways.

"Why do I have a feeling that your 'dealing with accordingly' is going to prove to be strikingly similar to what we were doing with our sledgehammers?" she asked.

"Let *me* worry about my people," I said. "You will have my cooperation in your investigation."

"Good," she said with a look of satisfaction. "That's all I was looking for."

"I would, however, ask a favor of your law enforcement in return," I said, letting all the growl go out of my tone.

Detective Rowland eyed me with suspicion. "The New York Police Department isn't really known for doing favors," she said, looking up at me, "but in your case I'll make an exception. Lay it on me."

I raised my hand and gestured toward the roof of the building across the way. A shadow at the top of it came to life, and with a spread of dragonlike wings, Emily flew down from it and landed hard on the roof behind me.

Rowland's face grew wary at the approach of my more snake-featured companion, but made no effort to leave or back away.

Emily stopped when she stood next to me, wings folded close to her in a calm, relaxed pose despite the fact that I knew how nervous she must have been waiting in the wings while I had made sure the meeting with Detective Rowland was safe enough for her to join.

"Hello," she said.

Rowland nodded. "Hello yourself," the detective said, then looked to me. "This is your favor?"

"No," I said. "This is Emily, but yes, I would ask a favor of you on her behalf." I gestured to Emily for her to speak.

"Thank you, Stanis," she said, almost shy now as she turned to address Detective Rowland. "I . . . I . . . I'm sorry. This is difficult for me."

Detective Rowland laughed. "Sorry about that," she said as she composed herself. "I'm used to watching creatures like you destroy my city or throw a bus or cars about. Not used to seeing one so . . . timid."

"Then I suggest you learn the finer points of our differences," I said, a snap of anger filling me.

"All right, all right," Rowland said, holding her hands up. "I get it. What is it you want?"

"I don't recall much of my life before I took this form," Emily said. "I remember Kennedy was my president, and how Manhattan looked much different when I had been human, but beyond that, I am afraid my memory fails me."

"It is that way with many of the other creatures I have taken in at Sanctuary," I said. "Most have decided to leave the past just that—in the past. There are others, however, who have sought out who they were in life or have tried to track down their relatives on their own. Emily, however, has too little a recollection of her past to even begin such a task."

"Is that important to you?" Rowland asked her.

Emily cocked her head at the detective. "What do you mean?"

"I've seen a lot of cases over the years, before I got busted down to the Spook Squad," she said. "And when I see the looks on some of the victims' faces, I can't help but think that they'd be better off if they could just forget what happened to them. Start life anew, move forward without looking back. They could be happy. *You* could be happy, without ever finding out what happened. You sure you want to know your past?"

"My past is a blank," Emily said, "but it *is* part of who I am. Who I was. Now I have this form, and all I can think is that I must be here for a reason. How can I figure that out without knowing who I was?"

"As long as you're sure," the detective said.

Emily nodded.

"Okay, then," the detective said, pulling out her phone once more. "Why don't you tell me what you *do* know?"

"My name is Emily Hoffert," she said. "Although I do not recall who I was, I believe my life was taken from me."

"You were murdered?" Rowland asked as she typed.

"Yes," Emily said, her voice soft now, barely audible. I laid a hand on her shoulder and she reached up to squeeze it.

"Do you know how?" the detective asked.

"That I do not know," she said. "All I know is that when I try to think back to my earliest memory, my stomach clenches and my mind fills with an unexplainable horror."

My heart ached for Emily, but Rowland's face betrayed nothing. She simply kept typing away at her phone until she was done, then looked up.

"Anything else?"

Emily had gone quiet and shook her head.

Detective Rowland turned to me.

"So just to be clear," she said. "I've got metric tons of your kind tearing apart my city and you want me to take the time to investigate a decades-old murder?"

"That is correct," I said. "I would consider it a gesture of good faith between our two people."

"And I would be most thankful," Emily said with a smile that exposed her fangs.

I leapt into the night air, hovering above Detective Rowland. "I will see what I can find concerning the Butcher and his people," I said. "This has been a good meeting."

"It has?" Rowland asked, craning her neck up at me.

I bowed my head to her. "History will look on it well," I said. "A day when our people first came together. And, most important, no one had to die."

"That is a plus," I heard the detective say from far away as I rose higher and higher, Emily already catching up.

The detective wanted answers, and so did I. Hopefully we would both get what we wanted. I banked into a turn south and headed for Sanctuary, eager to get some answers if only to gain Emily some closure on who she had been.

Knowing the past was the first step to moving beyond it—or learning from it—and more than anything I wanted my near-constant companion to be granted some peace.

Fifteen

———— ☾ ————

Alexandra

The press of tourists was thicker in the surprising midday heat of an early October morning when Caleb and I crossed Central Park West at Seventy-second Street. I made it as far as the park's entrance before I doubled over with a yawn so powerful that it stopped me in my tracks. The sea of tourists and locals continued to wash around me as Caleb stopped and turned back, watching with bemusement.

"You okay?" Caleb asked. "Did crossing the street wipe you out?"

"I'm fine," I said, finishing off my yawn with an uncontrolled stretch that ran through my whole body. "Just not used to being awake during daylight hours these days, what with so much happening during my night shifts."

Caleb nodded. "Sleepy is the head that wears the crown," he said, then took my hand in his before leading us into Central Park.

It seemed like such a normal couple's activity—just a day out in the sunshine—that for a moment I allowed myself to forget the troubles of the arcane world that were taking over more and more of my life. For a brief moment all my worries about that or the more mundane but soul-crushing fact I hadn't produced a lick of artwork in months were gone. The two of us simply flowed down the crosstown path until Caleb took the lead and wandered up a side trail to a small open circle nestled inside a ring of trees.

Benches surrounded the outer edges of the space, most of them filled with guitar players, drummers, and what looked like sixties-era flower children. Below our feet the pavement gave way to a mosaic of light and dark green tiles arranged in a radiant sun pattern with the word "Imagine" spelled out at its center.

"You brought me to a drum circle?" I asked, leaning down to scoop up one of the wilting flowers that had been laid on top of the mosaic.

A bearded hippie wearing just an open vest, no shirt, and what looked like forest-colored pajama/yoga pants locked eyes with me, and before I could look away, he was up off his bench heading for me.

"Oh, crap," I said, turning to face Caleb to the exclusion of all else. "Incoming crazy, twelve o'clock."

He looked over my shoulder and chuckled. "I told you I knew a guy," he said, stepping around me.

Caleb opened his arms and the man came in close, giving Caleb a bear hug filled with such strength I feared all the vials lining his jacket would crack and melt him as the potions mixed. Despite my worry, I could not help but notice the genuine warmth radiating from the man giving him the hug.

Caleb broke away from the embrace a few seconds before the stranger and waited until the hippie clapped him hard on the back several times before releasing him. When the moment was over, Caleb turned back to me and extended his arm in my direction.

"This is the guy," he said. "Fletcher, this is Alexandra, a good friend of mine."

"Hello," I said, giving him an unsure smile and a small wave.

Fletcher looked at my hand, shook his head at it, and started for me. "Oh, no, that's not how we do it here," he said. "Bring it on in."

He stretched his arms wide, hands waving me in toward

him, and despite my reservations at hugging a wild-eyed
stranger, I found myself giving in to the warmth of the gesture.
His arms closed around me and the embrace was comforting,
the man himself smelling like an earthier and more pleasant
form of patchouli. His beard itched against my cheek, tickling
me while he tightened his bear hug. While the grip should
have felt intimidating or overly familiar from a stranger, it
simply made me feel safe.

"Hey, pretty mama," he said when he pulled away. He held
me at arm's length by my shoulders. "So very groovy to make
your acquaintance."

Given the raw and powerful vibe coming off of him, I
couldn't help but smile. "Likewise," I said.

Fletcher looked to the wilted flower still in my hand. He
reached out with the index finger of his left hand and touched
it. Leaning forward, he blew a sweet, gentle breath across my
palm. The petals of the wildflower fluttered to life, their
motion tickling the palm of my hand. I looked away from the
flower and stared up at the man.

"*E.T. phone home,*" he said in a mock croak, and laughed
with a childish delight at what he had done. After almost a
full minute of it, he regained control over himself and stroked
his beard before gesturing with his arms out to both sides.

"Welcome to Strawberry Fields," he said.

"Of course," I said as recollection hit me. I hadn't been up
in this part of Central Park in more than a decade, having
almost forgotten about its existence. "This is the memorial to
John Lennon."

Fletcher nodded, his eyes sparking. "Yeah, John was good
people," he said. "Always treated me kindly."

I raised an eyebrow at that. "You?" I asked. "You *knew*
John Lennon?"

He nodded again. "Yoko, too. You know, people give her
a bad rap and all, but she's really a sweet lady."

I shook my head. "But Lennon died, like, *forever* ago, and
you're . . . what? Twenty-seven, twenty-eight . . . ?"

Caleb laid his hand on my shoulder, his eyes telling me to

proceed with caution, but before I could, Fletcher was laughing again.

"Age is just a number, lady," he said, grinning. The smile radiated a preternatural warmth from him, one that confirmed to me that we were dealing with something more than some young stoner hippie. If there was such a thing as Father Nature or whatever you'd call some sort of spirit of the forest, this guy glowed with an aura of it.

The smile slowly faded from his face. "Somehow I don't think you came here to talk about me, am I right?"

"No offense, Fletch," Caleb said. "Listen, I'm sorry I haven't come by lately. I don't want you to think I only show up when I need something."

"But that *is* what you do," the man said, his face going serious with a dark power that danced behind his eyes. I felt the weight of it, and by the way the color was draining out of Caleb's face, so could he. A long silence passed between the two men as I waited and watched, each second becoming more and more uncomfortable.

"It's all good, brother," Fletcher said, with a laugh and a hearty clap on Caleb's shoulder that broke the spell of the tension. "Just keepin' ya honest."

Caleb relaxed while the two of us watched Fletcher scan the entirety of the memorial circle.

"Let's move off to the side here," he said. "We're a bit too much in the middle of everything. I'd hate to harsh the mellow of the mood here."

Fletcher went off to the one side of the circle where there were no benches, only trees. I was relieved, since it moved us farther away from the rowdiest group of guitar players who were busy launching into their six hundredth chorus of "Hey, Jude." With no benches nearby, Fletcher sat himself down cross-legged on the pavement and waited for us to do the same. When we had lowered ourselves, he leaned in, his voice dropping to a clandestine whisper.

"Lay it on me," he said, slapping his hands down on both knees. "I'm all ears."

"We came into Central Park seeking something," Caleb said.

"Hey, man," Fletcher said. "It's all good. You need some herb, no worries. I got the hookup."

I rolled my eyes. "That's *not* why we came," I said.

Fletcher's face fell. He looked almost hurt.

"My bad," he said. "Continue."

"My friend and I were seeking out the special cemetery," Caleb said. "The one for those of a more supernatural persuasion."

"Checking out a plot of your own?" Fletcher asked with a chuckle. "Not planning on dying, are you?"

"He's tried," I said. "Didn't really work out for him."

"Oh?" Fletcher raised one of his bushy eyebrows.

"Long story," Caleb said, dismissing it with a wave of his hand. "Anyway, I thought I was leading us right to it, but I got . . . well, lost."

"Nature can be tricky like that," Fletcher said, erupting into a bout of laughter.

Caleb sighed. "It can also be tricky in that it attacked us. We were covered in vines that were trying to tear me and my friends apart, and green so isn't my color."

A darkness clouded the man's eyes.

"I do not think an attack like that would happen unless nature was provoked," he said.

"Well . . ." Caleb started, but I interrupted.

"That's on me," I said. "We'd been wandering lost for a bit and I thought we might make some progress if we cut a new path. I wouldn't have done it, though, if I had known what might happen."

Fletcher frowned at me from deep within his beard and jerked his thumb at Caleb. "*This* one should have known better," he said.

Caleb shrugged. "What can I say, Fletch? I'm all about finding shortcuts. In fact, if I *didn't* take shortcuts I never would have ended up finding you a few years ago trapped by that wizard who had taken up occupancy in Belvedere Castle."

"Ugh," the man said with a shudder that dispelled his growing menace. "Him and his cat, not to mention all those little blue creatures scurrying around . . . Don't remind me!"

"So can you help us or should we go find ourselves a nice druid?" Caleb asked.

"Druids," Fletcher said with another shudder. "Always disrobing in my woods, calling on my power. Like I have nothing better to do than help them frolic or engorge their phalluses in the name of nature!"

"We just need to check out a few things," I assured him. "I need to make sure a certain family's mausoleum is secure. And . . . there's another, more sensitive matter . . ."

"Are you familiar with the Butcher of the Bowery?" Caleb asked.

Fletcher's face went dark and he nodded. "It was a particularly bad time for those of us who lived through it," he said. "But yes, I recall Robert Patrick Dorman."

"We think he may be back," Caleb said. "In the form of a gargoyle. Judging by a trashed town house we've been to. There are other gargoyles working for his cause every night."

"We need to locate where his body rests in the cemetery, though," I said. "So . . . can you do it? Can you get us to the cemetery? Please . . . ?"

Fletcher examined my face and I did nothing except meet his eyes. After an all-too-long examination of me, Fletcher nodded.

"I will grant you safe passage," he said, "but first, I would ask a boon of you."

I let out a long, slow breath, cringing a bit inside.

"And that would be . . . ?" I asked.

"Lately I've seen a surge of these winged creatures over this city," he said. "Some of them even foolish enough to try to enter my woods, and while either I or the forces of this forest have driven them back, they still have managed to elude me. You want into the cemetery? Fine. I'll grant you this, but in return I first want you to bring me one of these winged creatures."

"In what condition?" I asked. "None of them will want to come willingly. And why don't you just go get one yourself?"

"I wish to examine the nature of these creatures, but it is no matter how one is delivered to me," he said. "As to why I don't capture one for myself . . . I am afraid the park and the woodlands here are my domain. To venture into the rest of this city would prove impossible."

"Fletch, if we could capture the Butcher, we wouldn't need to go to the cemetery," Caleb said.

"I didn't ask for the Butcher," he said, shaking a finger at him.

"No, you did not," I said with a dark smile. "You just want *any* one of these misguided creatures. Fine. I've met enough of them that have wanted to take a swing at me. It's time I return the favor. I'll get you one. Pretty sure I can bring one of them down."

"Really, now?" the hippie asked, looking me up and down. "You sure you're up to that, lady?"

"I know a guy," I said, standing up, brushing my pants off.

"Hey," Caleb said, also rising. "That's my usual line."

"Sorry," I said, heading for the path leading out of Strawberry Fields. "Better ready yourself for that trip to your secret cemetery."

"I like your lady," Fletcher said, laughing and applauding me as I went. "She's got moxie, that one."

"Or a death wish," Caleb said, running to catch up with me.

I didn't bother to correct him. Given the various factions out there either wanting my help or trying to kill me, I couldn't worry about that. All I could worry about was how I was going to find and run down one of my problem gargoyles. Luckily, I *did* know a guy who might prove helpful.

Well, more *grotesque* than guy, really.

Sixteen

C

Stanis

"Could you fly—I don't know—stealthier?"

There was little bite in Alexandra's words, only worry and concern. Cradled in my arms, Alexandra yawned as her eyes searched to either side of us as I flew through the massive canyons of Manhattan's lit-up buildings.

"Excuse me?" I asked, spreading my wings to slow my flight.

"I know it's late," she said, pointing to our right where people moved behind the glass windows of the apartments, "but the Upper East Side is still mostly residential. We just need to be extra cautious and keep ourselves out of view." Then she added, "Pretty please?"

"As you wish," I said and slowed my pace even further as I maneuvered us away from any apartment with its lights on at this time of night.

We circled the area, Alexandra's eyes sliding shut as I flew, only to flutter open with a look of panic again.

"Are you all right?" I asked.

"Just tired," she said. "Three nights of this while researching what I can find written about Dorman, and I'm beat."

When her eyes slid shut again, I smoothed my flight as

best I could, allowing her a momentary reprieve from our worries. I remained aerial, searching the streets below until a crackle of voices rose up from the speaker of Alexandra's phone in her pocket.

She woke with a start, leaned her ear to her chest, then pointed up ahead.

"Dispatch is reporting activity on the next block," she said. "Take us down in the alley between those two buildings, please."

I aimed for the narrow space between the upcoming buildings, drawing in my wings as we approached. Once in, there simply was not room enough to expand my wings and I dropped down into the dark and deserted alley faster than I would have liked. My knees buckled with the impact of my landing.

Alexandra—shaken—took her arms from around my neck as she swung down out of my hold on her and set her feet on the ground. While it took Alexandra a moment to adjust to the darkness of the alley, she kept pressed close to me, which I found I did not mind. She lingered a moment longer before finally stepping away, feeling around as her eyes continued to adjust.

"How's Emily?" she asked from the other side of the alley.

I paused, surprised to find her asking.

"She is well," I said with caution. "I have set into motion the tools that may lead to Emily discovering who she was in life."

"Is that important to her?" Alexandra asked, turning back to me.

"She is unique among my people in that she does not remember *any* part of her past," I said. "Some of those at Sanctuary have shown no concern for who they were, simply embracing what they are now. But as to Emily . . . yes, I think it is quite important to her to understand the person she once was."

Alexandra fell silent, and turned back to examining the contents of the alley, which left me uncomfortable. I decided against reciprocating and asking her about Caleb, and instead took the opportunity to better take in our surroundings.

"I do not see one of my kind here," I said.

Alexandra continued farther away from me as she searched. "Here's a compelling piece of evidence," she said, picking up a crushed trash can that stuck up out of broken slats of wood that I imagined had once housed the can itself. "Judging by the damage, I would say at least *one* of your fellow *grotesques* was here. No doubt they didn't stay long, especially when someone caught sight of them long enough to call in the complaint."

I leapt into the sky, flourishing my wings fully open along the length of the alley, hanging in the air above Alexandra, looking down.

"If the voices on the police scanner were correct a moment ago, it has not been all that long," I said. "And I suspect the trail of the hunt has not yet gone cold."

"Agreed," she said. "You take to the sky. I'll check out the rest of the alley."

"As you wish," I said, and shot straight up into the night sky without another word.

From above the buildings on either side of the alley, I watched Alexandra down the narrow gap toward Eighty-third Street, stepping carefully to avoid the scattered trail of debris from whatever had happened here. I flew along, following the signs of a *grotesque*'s path of destruction. Evidence of its exit from the alley continued out onto the cross street, marked by an off-duty cab half-crushed farther down the block. A pile of broken bricks sat at the corner of the building on the north side of the street and I aimed for it, following the signs of chaos into the gated area between two other residential buildings.

The crunch of stone grinding violently against stone rose up from somewhere in the new alley and I swooped down out of the sky at the far end, stopping myself short when I discovered Alexandra there already.

She jumped back with a tiny yelp.

"My apologies," I said.

"Don't worry," she said, pushing by me, holding a finger up to her lips to silence me. Somewhere nearby the sounds of struggle filled the air. "We need to keep moving."

"There's no one else in this alley—"

Alexandra was already running back past me toward the

end of the alley I had swooped in from. Confused, I spun around to follow her progress, catching sight of her disappearing down a right turn off the main alley I had not noticed.

I followed after her and tore down the even darker interior alley. A struggle echoed out from somewhere far in front of us, but as we approached the dead end of the alley, the sound was already fading.

"Whatever went down *just* happened," Alexandra said. She pointed to the wall to our left, which was in the act of crumbling away from whatever had impacted it.

As I ran to the spot, a few of the bricks rolled to a stop at my clawed feet.

"None of the walls have broken down," she said. "Which means no one escaped this dead end *that* way."

"Then that means . . ."

"Up, up, and away, Stanis," Alexandra said.

I searched directly above us, making sure I had clearance to rise. At the top of the buildings the sky was a flurry of activity, none of it discernible . . . except for the fact that something was falling.

And falling *fast*.

I dashed toward Alexandra. She had not quite registered what I had, a look of fear overtaking her at my rapid approach. She braced herself as my clawed hands grabbed her shoulder, careful not to dig in. Using only the smallest fraction of my power, I shoved her away from where she stood against one of the walls. Even with that small amount of my strength, she shot across the alley as if I had thrown her. Her feet danced on, then tripped over a large trash bag, sending her into a tumble until she came to a rest against the far wall.

Alexandra's head poked up from behind the bag of trash, her eyes furious.

"Stanis, what the—"

Alexandra did not get a chance to finish her sentence. Chunks of stone rained down over me where she had stood a moment ago, a cloud of dust rising up all around.

These were not just chunks of stone, I realized. Hands, arms, and legs stuck up from the jagged pile settling around me.

Through the cloud of dust, I could make out Alexandra's shadowy figure as she stood up and came toward me. "You okay?" she asked, coughing.

I spread my wings wide and flapped them several times to clear away the dust. Alexandra's cough continued until the air around us was clear once more.

"I am unharmed," I said, which took some of the tension out of Alexandra's face and shoulders.

I looked up, unable to make out any sign of activity above.

Alexandra looked up, then back down to the ground as she stepped with caution among the pile of broken limbs, approaching me. When we were face-to-face she grabbed on to my shoulders.

"We need to get up there, now," she said, then added, "Pretty please . . . ?"

"Hold on," I said, and without any hesitation, I shot straight up into the air with all my strength.

Alexandra's arms clenched tight around me and I felt the breath go out of her.

"Are you all right?" I asked.

She nodded, even though all the color had drained from her face.

"It's just the falling sensation in my stomach," she said. "Caused a quick wave of nausea."

"Should I put you back down?"

Alexandra shook her head, locking eyes with me. "No," she said. "There's simply no time for chundering up the great Technicolor Yawn in the fast-paced world of gargoyle tracking."

I did not fully understand what she meant, but I assumed it meant I had just been spared a great indignity. Her eyes were filled with determination, and instead of worrying any further, I concentrated on my flight.

Coming up over the edge of the neighboring rooftops, I searched for movement anywhere. Even with the moonlight being as bright as it was, my eyes caught nothing until I had set Alexandra down on top of the taller of the two buildings.

Only then did I notice the nearly still figure crouched at the edge of the rooftop.

The figure was in the same larger-than-life scale as mine, its features far less bat-winged and demonic than my own. This other creature was a carved angel, complete with full, feathery stone wings, long locks of curled hair, and the smooth skin of its features. It crouched at the edge of the rooftop in contemplation of an object I could not make out in its hands.

Stepping closer, I saw what it was—the head of another statue, its features far more demonic than mine with curved horns rising up from its forehead. The edge of the severed stone head was jagged, bits of stone flaking away from it like burning ash onto its broken body far down below in the alley.

"Hold it right there," Alexandra said.

I flourished open my wings to increase my size in the hopes of looking more menacing. "Do *not* attempt to flee," I said. "You will not find any escape."

The angel contemplated the two of us for a long moment, menace in his eyes as he clutched the demonic head in his hands. I was prepared to protect Alexandra should he throw it, but her face showed no fear. She looked unmovable.

The angel held his ground, neither attacking nor surrendering.

"Easy, there," she said, waving her hand for him to lower the severed head. "Let's take this slow. Why don't you start with who you are and we can get to who that was later?"

The menace went out of the angel as he stepped down off the ledge of the roof.

"Forgive me," he said with a deep bow. "My manners are a bit rusty, what with just having been attacked. Who am I? In my human life I was once known as Nathaniel Crane."

Alexandra smiled, but did not relax, her hand hovering over the pocket she kept her spell book in. "Well, Mr. Crane, I suggest you drop that gargoyle in your hands," she said with more authority than I was used to hearing out of her. "And don't even *think* about trying to fly away. You've got a lot to answer for here, outside of the fact you almost got me killed down below in that alley."

I expected the angel to bolt, to fly off. I did not expect him to stare at us with wry amusement.

"Forgive me once more," he said, "but who made you the adjudicator on such manners?"

The tone was dismissive and I could not help but growl. I stepped forward, but Alexandra pressed her hand against my chest, stopping me.

"Well," she said, "for lack of a better term, I'm your creator. I made you."

The angel seemed unimpressed. "And I should just take your word on that?"

Alexandra shrugged. "That's up to you," she said. "You asked."

"Well, this *is* a rare opportunity," he said. "It is not often one gets to ask their creator questions on the spot."

"Such as?" I asked.

"Oh, let's start with the big one," he said with a wide grin. "Why am I here? I didn't get those answers in my human life, so let's try now."

"I wish I could give you a better answer, but you—all of your kind except Stanis here—were a mistake. One I've come to regret more and more."

"I think, perhaps, you should be the one answering questions here," I said. "Starting with why you are holding the head of one of our kind in your hands."

"This?" he said, holding up the demonic face, frozen in an eternal snarl. "Friend of yours?"

I shook my head. "I have no knowledge of this particular *grotesque*, no," I said. "But I do protect all of my kind . . . or at least attempt to bring them into the fold of my people. What cause did you have for such brutality against one of our own?"

The angel laughed at that. "We may all be carved of stone, and by the looks of it, the same carver, but make no mistake," he said. "We are *not* all of the same kind. This one, for instance."

"Why?" Alexandra asked.

"What grievance had you with him?" I added.

"This one was quite a salesman," the angel said. "He tried to bring me into his fold, too. He wished me to join the cause of one he served."

"It was not my cause," I said.

"Let me guess," Alexandra said. "The Butcher of the Bowery."

The angel looked amused and nodded. "Word of him seems to be getting around, yes."

"And I take it he wouldn't take no for an answer?" Alexandra asked.

"Let's just say it wasn't so much him asking as it was him *telling* me I had to join his cause," he said. "And me? Well, I'm not much of a joiner."

"What did he tell you about his cause?" I asked.

"Our conversation didn't quite get down to that level of detail," he said. "I figured if I was being told to serve someone called the Butcher of the Bowery, it wasn't exactly going to prove to be all rainbows and sunshine."

"So you took his life in stone from him," I said.

"This minion of the Butcher was crafty," he said. "He was the sort to draw things out of you. In his case, he was seeking out . . . I believe *cronies* would be the best term for it."

"And just why did he think you would fit the bill for cronyism?" Alexandra asked.

If stone could blush, I was sure it would have on Crane, given his sheepish look.

"Despite my current appearance," he said, "let's just say that in my previous life I was a bit of a . . . problem child."

"What were you?" I asked.

He pressed a hand to his chest as if deeply offended I even had to ask. "Nothing as gruesome as a murderous butcher, I assure you," he said. "But I had earned a bit of a reputation at what I would call being a purloiner of other people's goods."

Alexandra laughed. "A thief," she said. "Let me guess: stealing form the rich, giving to the poor?"

"I wish I could say I was that noble," he said with a smile, "but no. I was far more self-serving than that, I'm afraid." He flourished his wings to their full and impressive span, showing off the majesty of his angelic form. "It would seem this stone life I've been led to wishes me to atone for those crimes."

"These are interesting times in this city," I said. "I would prefer the violence among my kind to be kept to a minimum."

"Yeah," Alexandra added. "Humanity is already freaked-out about the amount of gargoyle action going on out there."

"We must police ourselves," I said.

"I did not do what I did idly," the angel Nathaniel said.

"Fine," Alexandra said but sounded unsatisfied with his answer. "Then if you have to do something, could you maybe make sure there's not a human standing in the alley below you before crumbling a body to bits?"

The angel thought it over for a moment, as still as a statue in contemplation.

"A fair and reasonable request," he said with a deep bow.

"Good," Alexandra said, relaxing a little. Her face shifted, a look of reluctance overtaking it. She pointed to the head in his hands. "Do you think maybe we could have that?"

"This?" the angel said, twisting the demonic head back and forth in his hand. "I do hope this is not how you spend your nights, collecting souvenirs of the dead."

"No," I said with a shake of my head. "My father was the kind to mount the heads of his enemies on pikes as a warning to others. I prefer diplomacy to violence . . . when possible."

"To each his own," the angel said, and tossed the head in our direction. I reached out and caught it in one hand, the dead stone eyes staring up at me.

"Thank you," Alexandra said, turning to me. "We can gather the rest up from the alley."

"Am I free to go?" the angel asked, making it clear he was not really asking for our permission.

"This is not a police state," I said. "You are free to do as you choose, as long as it does not interfere with the freedom of others. I am sorry to hear that you were put upon by this group that would wish harm upon the people of this city. However, if you hear from any more of the Butcher's recruits, you can find me and my people by flying to the southern tip of Manhattan."

Alexandra nodded. "I'm sure you would be more than welcome at Sanctuary," she added with a hopeful look at me.

"Of course," I said.

The angel gave us a tight-lipped smile. "As I mentioned

before," he said, "I'm not much of a joiner." He spread his wings and leapt into the sky. "I wish you luck in your endeavors. And who knows? Perhaps I will pay your Sanctuary a visit sometime."

I watched in silence as he flew away, the heaviness of the head in my hands growing every moment.

"You okay?" Alexandra asked, resting a cool hand on my shoulder.

"I will be," I said, staring into the lifeless eyes of the demon, then looked to her, only to find Alexandra's eyes locked on it as well.

"What is it?" I asked.

"Look at it," she said. "Stone. So lifeless. This could be you, Stanis. It makes a woman think."

Lost in her own thoughts, it was difficult for me to read her face. "About what?"

"About how short life could be," she said.

"I have had more than my fair share of a lifetime."

She smiled and shook her head. "That's not what I meant," she said, then let out a long, slow breath. "With all we've been through, sometimes I forget it could end at any moment, and I don't want things to go unsaid, especially when they need saying."

"I hope you know you can always speak your mind with me," I said.

"Okay," she said, nerves in her voice. "Here it is. I'm sorry if I've been short with you . . . when talking about Emily. I think it comes from a place of . . . jealousy. I mean, she gets to be with you practically all the time."

"You do not approve of her?" I asked, taken aback by her admission.

Her face twisted with frustration. "No," she said. "It's just . . . Well, why did you never try with me?"

I cocked my head at her. "Try?"

"I miss more than just the protection you provided when you watched over the Belarus family," she said. "It's a dark thought, but since we're being honest, I wonder sometimes if I should have released you from it. I know once you were freed of the bond, you went with your father to protect us, but part of me thought . . ."

She could not finish what she had started to say, but I thought I understood.

"You thought I would choose you once I was freed," I said. She nodded in silence.

"But you have Caleb," I reminded her.

"I know," she said, "and he's great. I just wanted to know why you never tried?"

I gave her question careful consideration as I thought back on it. I had long held a deep affection for Alexandra, but I searched my soul for the answer.

"Strangely enough it was Caleb who convinced me," I said.

It was Alexandra's turn to cock her head at me. "I'm sorry; what?"

"On my father's floating palace barge," I said with a nod. "We had both gone there to contend with Kejetan. It was there he convinced me he would be a better fit for you."

"Frankly, I don't think that's something for him to decide," she said, anger rising in her voice.

"He made a convincing argument," I said. "He is of your kind, can walk in the day with you, live out a mortal life by your side . . ."

"What if you could do all that?" she said, shaking with rage, but her face full of earnestness now. "What if you could be the one at my side?"

"That is not possible," I reminded her.

"But what if it was?" she pressed.

I entertained the idea, as fruitless as it was. Could I imagine myself enjoying a life at Alexandra's side, not as a construct made to serve her but as a companion. Yes, but still, reality kept me from speaking my mind on it.

"I am not sure," I said, my mind turning to thoughts of Sanctuary. "There are my people to think of . . ."

"Unbelievable," Alexandra said with a shake of her head, then looked up into my eyes. "Caleb conned you, Stanis. He took advantage of you to get what he wanted. Me. Stupid, Lex. This is what I get for trusting a reformed freelance criminal."

Had Caleb talked me out of my feelings for Alexandra? I was
not sure. It was something I needed to think about, and judging
by the severed stone head in my hands, there were more pressing
issues to concern ourselves with. I lifted the head up.

"Will this suffice for your needs?" I asked, focusing on
the task at hand. "Will this please this Fletcher of yours?"

"Let's hope so," she said, calming herself, even though I
could sense her brooding underneath it all. "Who knows
what's going to impress an immortal hippie?"

I grabbed her in my free arm, and started our descent to
the body in the alley below. "Is that another idiom of yours
that I fail to understand?"

"Pretty much," she said, "but we can go over that later.
Right now I need to keep from shaking Caleb to death until
his friend Fletcher gets us to the cemetery."

I descended in silence, surprised to find the idea brought
a smile to the corner of my mouth.

Seventeen

C

Alexandra

Having grown up in Manhattan, I was used to the city at night, but the dark twists and turns of deepest Central Park took on such an eerie calm compared to the bustle of the streets that I couldn't hold back a shiver and stopped in my tracks.

Caleb stopped on the dimly lit wooded path. He turned back to me, grabbing my hand and squeezing it in his, which normally would have given me a bit of joy out here in the darkness had I not just heard what Stanis had told me. Still, now was not the time to get into it, especially when there was work to be done.

"You okay?" he asked as we stood alone on the dirty pathway under trees that arched high overhead.

I nodded, suppressing the urge to shiver again. "Get a grip, Lexi," I said out loud, for my benefit more than his.

Caleb laughed. "You've fought stone golems in abandoned subway tunnels," he said, "not to mention that weird water dragon thingie we faced at the *Libra Concordia* before it became Sanctuary. And *this* is what gets to you?"

I slid my hand out of his and wrapped my arms around me.

"I know it's ridiculous, but being isolated out here in Central Park . . . Well, once I started dealing with arcana and *grotesques*, mundane things like muggings in the park or human-on-human violence seem to freak me more, okay?"

"I can do this alone," he said. "I'm sure Fletch can tour-guide me to this burial ground no problem."

"No," I said, adamantly steeling myself. "Warren asked for *my* help. I need to do this. Besides, I can't be letting you have all the secret cemetery fun. Fletcher has had that broken gargoyle to look over for days. It's time your hippie madman lives up to his end of the bargain and takes us to that secret cemetery."

Caleb crossed his arms. "You want to tell me how you came by that stone body, by the way? Let me guess. The Rock helped you."

"Hey," I said, surprised at his sudden jealousy and a little pissed off by it, given how he had talked Stanis out of showing his true emotions toward me. Even though this wasn't the time to get into it, I couldn't help but needle him a little bit to release some of the tension I felt in his presence now. "When you grow wings, I'll let you fly me around the city hunting gargoyles. Fair enough?"

"I can work on that," he said, pulling out a notebook.

"Now?!" I asked, stern this time. "How about we focus on finding Fletcher first and getting to that cemetery?"

A rustling rose up behind me off in the foliage and I spun, my spell book already pulled free from my backpack. I reached to open it, but a hand shot out of the bushes and came down hard on top of mine.

"Did someone say my name?" Fletcher asked, looking even more wild-eyed than when I had last seen him during the day. Hopefully it was just a trick of the moonlight and he hadn't gone feral since then.

"You okay?" I asked.

"Huh?" he said, his eyes fixing on the stone book I held in my hands.

I slowly eased it away from him, but his hand was reluctant to slide off the book. Eventually it came free and I stuffed the book back into my pack.

"You sure you're up to this, Fletch?" I asked. "It was pretty freaky last time we were here, *and* we had greater numbers."

Fletcher nodded. "Absolutely," he said with a jovial laugh. "If I can't find the cemetery in the middle of my own park, who can?"

"So what's the plan?" I asked.

"What I promised you," he said. "I lead you to the cemetery."

"Wait, wait, *wait*," I said, holding up a hand. "We already *tried* that, and you're just going to try and walk us back in there? That didn't work out so well for me and my friends. I'm pretty sure we pissed off your forest."

"That's because you didn't have me with you," he said with a prideful laugh. "Relax, lady."

I tried to, but I couldn't shake my doubt, even if I was dealing with some sort of forest spirit in Fletcher form.

"You're sure you're up for this?" I asked once more.

Fletcher nodded with vigor over and over. "Don't worry," he said. "If I seem out of sorts, it's just that I've been a wee bit distracted examining that broken stone creature you acquired for me."

"Will it work for your purposes?" I asked. "Has it given you any deeper meaning into the magic of Spellmasonry or living stone?"

"Fascinating stuff," he said, nodding over and over to the point he reminded me of a bobblehead. "I've never seen stone quite like it. It's both a natural element and yet . . . not."

I wasn't quite sure what he meant, but before I could ask he patted me on the shoulder.

"I'll get you to your cemetery," he said. "Fear not." He turned to go, then spun back around to us. "Oh, I almost forgot." He reached into the brown hippie satchel he wore slung over one shoulder and pulled out several bundles of leaves wrapped in twine, handing one to each of us. "After studying the stone creature you brought me, I discovered that the spirits within are not wholly bonded with the stone. It would appear that while the stonework of your great-great-grandfather can be a vessel for the spirit, they are always tied back to their original bodies."

I held up my bundle, the smell of it somewhat familiar but not one I could readily place.

"Sage," Caleb said when he saw me sniffing at it.

"So what are we supposed to do?" I asked. "Season him to death? I hope you brought the parsley, rosemary, and thyme to finish the Butcher off."

"You want us to smudge him?" Caleb asked.

Fletcher nodded.

"Smudge?" I asked.

"We light these," Caleb said. "To purify the remains of the Butcher."

"What good will that do?"

"It's the only way to be sure that his body is properly disposed of," Fletcher said. "It's part of why his restless spirit was still able to linger here in the mortal realm. We destroy his body, and his ties to this world are severed. When we find his remains, we burn them. *If* I can find the cemetery, that is."

Without another word, Fletcher spun back around and dashed up the path ahead with a speed and agility I wouldn't have expected from so hippie-ish a figure.

Caleb and I continued down the path in pursuit of him. I glanced over to see whether Caleb was feeling my vibe, but by the passive look on his face he seemed completely oblivious.

"You sure this is a good idea?" I asked. "Trusting this . . . forest spirit or whatever he is."

Caleb thought about it for a good ten seconds, then shrugged. "Pretty sure."

"Only *pretty* sure?" I asked, a sense of dread filling me. "Great."

Caleb stopped while Fletcher scampered off farther ahead.

"Listen," he said, sounding a bit put out by my questions. "I don't know what to tell you, Lexi. I'm working my connections as hard as I can. Fletcher is who I've got for this."

"Tell me we're going to be fine," I said. Nights of dealing with gargoyles, cops, and witches and warlocks who wanted me dead had me craving reassurance.

"Oh," he said. "So you want me to lie?"

"No, but . . ." I stopped myself. Truthfully, I didn't know what was going to make me feel better.

"I can't say that, Alexandra," Caleb said. "I don't know if it's going to be fine. Nothing in life is certain, especially in the matters we deal in. What I can tell you is that Fletch is good people. He's always helped me out . . . He grows a lot of things out here in his woods that are near impossible to get."

"Oh, I can imagine what he grows, all right. The man looks like he's been following the Grateful Dead for decades, despite his youthful appearance. And knowing him, he probably knew Jerry Garcia, too."

"That's *not* what I was talking about him growing," Caleb said, but then he nodded. "Okay, *maybe* that, too, but Fletch has always come through for me and I trust him."

"Even all alone out here in the middle of the night?" I shuddered again, unable to control it.

"Now you're just spooking yourself," Caleb said. "Come on." He started off down the path again, but I wasn't budging just yet. He looked back at me, his eyes full of frustration.

"Hey, Fletch!" he called out at full volume, causing things in the darkness at the sides of the path to scatter off into the trees.

"Yeah, man?" our guide called back after a moment, much farther from us than I imagined he could have gone.

"You're not planning on killing us out here tonight or something along those lines, are you?"

The forest fell silent for a long, drawn-out moment, and for a second I imagined the wild-eyed bearded man sneaking up behind me, but then he called back down the path.

"I don't think so, man."

"Okay, thanks," Caleb called back, still looking at me. "Satisfied?"

"No," I said, although I *did* relax a bit, "but I suppose it will have to do. I just wish there was more stonework around out here so I could better defend us if I had to."

"I don't think that would work on someone like Fletcher," Caleb said.

"No?"

Caleb shook his head. "Whatever Fletcher is, he's more powerful than you or I can imagine. We're in his domain, his grass and leaves and roots . . . I say we tread softly and speak kindly."

"Such a sensible approach," I said. "And coming from you even!"

"I'm not just a pretty face," he said. "And I've learned the advantages of being polite, especially when I'm dealing with someone or some*thing* I don't fully understand."

A moment later we came upon Fletcher once again, this time sitting cross-legged on the ground in the middle of the dirt path.

"Is it break time already?" Caleb asked. "What's up, buddy?"

Fletcher combed his hands though his bushy mane of hair, then ran them down to his beard, pulling at it.

"I don't get it, man," he said. "The path *should* go through here, but the forest is acting all weird and jumpy. I tried being reasonable with it, but no go. It's a dead end."

Caleb stepped past him, examining the end of the trail.

"Come on," he said after a moment. "We can make our *own* path."

He pressed himself in between two clumps of still, leafy branches, forcing his way forward.

Fletcher scrambled to his feet. "Hey, man, I wouldn't do tha—"

Despite there being no wind, the branches rustled all around Caleb, who gave a shocked cry as they parted farther apart and then seemed to swallow him. He grunted from within the mass of leaves, no doubt struggling to free himself, and I panicked because all I could see of him was his legs.

"Help him!" I cried out.

"Whoa, now," Fletcher said, with a mix of surprise, wonder, and curiosity all at once. "Take it easy there, old girl."

In response the bushes and trees rose up higher into the night air as if a giant was waking from its slumber.

"Fletch, what the hell is that?" I called out, backing away from it.

"Hmm," he said, nodding slowly at the creature as the two of us watched Caleb's legs kicking like mad from its "mouth."

"Beats me," he said after a moment. "It's not one of mine, man."

"Well, *do* something!"

Fletcher stood there, continuing to look the monster over, but made no move against it.

"I've got this one," Caleb's muffled voice called out from within its body. "If it's green and leafy, it can burn."

A warm glow sprung to life within the tangle of branches, the hiss and crackle of flame coming to life. The creature twisted around in reaction to it and before I could worry for Caleb's safety—despite having known him to be fireproof from our previous adventures together—the creature spat him free. Caleb flew like a shot through the air until he slammed into the ground, rolling past me as I dodged out of his way. A column of smoke trailed after him, and once he came to rest at the base of one of the trees, his lungs erupted in a fit of coughing.

I ran to Caleb, helping him up as he regained his composure.

"Told you," he wheezed, "I . . . had . . . it."

"Better than what your hippie friend's been able to do."

Caleb started to nod, but stopped and pointed past me back over my shoulder.

I spun around in a quick circle to see the roots of the creature pulling free from the ground all along the path, clouds of dirt erupting into the night air. The tangle of bushes, branches, and trunks rose up to its full height, towering at least twenty feet higher than anything around it. It lumbered forward through the dirt cloud, and although dried bits of old leaves still sparked in flares from within, the cloud damped the fire as the creature shambled down the path toward us.

"Hey, Father Nature," I called out to Fletcher, who simply looked on with fascination at the creature. "You can jump into action at any time, really . . ."

Vines crawled in advance of the creature, snaking down the path toward us, and before Caleb or I could run, they ensnared us. I dropped my bundle of sage, tearing them off me while Caleb fought to pull more and more vials from his jacket in his struggle with the vines. For every one he burned, withered, or slimed away with a concoction, another replaced it.

"Anytime, really," I repeated, some of the vines getting past my defenses and crawling up my body.

"Fletch!" Caleb called out. "Help her!"

This seemed to shake the hippie out of his fugue state of fascination. In a flash he ran from the side of the path until he was standing right in front of me, looking down at the vines that had a grip on me.

"Hey, buddy," Fletcher said, laying his hands on the vine that was quickly constricting across my midsection. "It's all good. We're *friends*."

Despite the soothing tone in his words, the vine continued wrapping itself, snaking up and around my neck.

"Apparently, it didn't get the memo," I said before the tendril slid over my mouth and cut me off.

Fletcher and I both latched onto the vine pulling at it, but it would not budge.

"Don't be like that," he said, using an even more soothing tone than the last. "Come on, now."

The breath in my chest grew shallower and shallower, each exhale allowing the vine to tighten further around me. Stars of light danced before my eyes.

"Stay with me, Lex," Caleb called out from the bushes nearby as his own struggle escalated, his head disappearing completely into it.

I wanted to call out that this certainly wasn't the way I wanted to go down. If Rory were here with that damned pole arm of hers, she's be cutting through our leafy attackers with no problem, but no. I had to go and trust Caleb and his damned hippie friend.

"Shh!" Fletcher said, stroking the vine like it was a pet now. "Don't be like this."

Jesus. If I had to rely on these two, I'd be unconscious or worse in the next twenty seconds or so. Despite vines covering my face I managed to still speak out one of the family's old words of power, reaching out with whatever hold I could get on any kind of stone around me. The sensation came back to me in small dots and jags as I willed what I could latch onto toward my one open hand.

The surface of my hand stung as stone after tiny stone collided with it. The surface of most of them was too smooth or the stones themselves too insubstantial to do anything with. One, however, struck the palm of my hand and a warm trickle of blood opened up on me from its impact.

It had *cut* me. Meaning it had an edge.

I closed my hand around it, making a fist with one end of the stone sticking out of it. I gripped it with such force that the cut across my hand deepened, more blood dripping from it now, but I refused to let go. Instead, I darted my fist up and into the vines, tearing into them with the protruding jag of stone. The alarm of the creature was evidenced by the twitch the rest of the vines gave, but rather than further tightening around me, it lashed away from me.

Fletcher fell back as a whiplike tip of the vine struck him in the face. Startled, his eyes went white and wide, but that did not last long. Even in the moonlight I could see the whites disappear as the blacks of his pupils filled his eyes. A darkness replaced the light, easy nature of the man, an otherworldliness erupting out of him.

"I tried to go easy on you," he shouted, his voice now a fearful roar of wind in my ears, "but you have chosen destruction over living."

Other than his eyes, Fletcher did not look any different. The only change was the distinct sensation of power that radiated off of him like a miniature sun.

The creature towered over Fletcher, focusing its branches and vines on snagging him. With one hand he caught vines one after another, and with a preternatural strength twisted the writhing natural tentacles into a mass of knots. After what seemed like a never-ending stream of them, Fletcher tugged the knotted bunch and pulled the creature down onto the path.

Once grounded, the creature looked more like a beaver dam than anything. Still, it struggled and writhed as it tried to break free of Fletcher's grip, but it was no use. Fletcher advanced on the monster, pulling himself closer as he took up the vines. It reminded me of the world's craziest game of tug-of-war ever imagined. When he had closed within five feet of the giant mass, Fletcher let go, leapt higher into the air than a human could go, and crashed down into the center of the creature's mass, disappearing from sight.

A growl drove into my ears from within the creature. At first I thought it might be some kind of stomach, but then I realized to my surprise that it sounded more like it belonged to Fletcher. It rose to a near-deafening pitch as the bushes and limbs shook. The sharp sound of wood cracking was so intense it felt as if the island of Manhattan itself might be splitting in two.

The vines on Caleb and me went slack, reversing their courses down our bodies and back into the creature's mass. Shifting and twisting, the creature could not hold its shape. The vast trunks that stuck out shrunk one by one into itself, bits of green brush and branches flying off as they came free of it. Glimpses of Fletcher caught my eye through the creature as it diminished in size until it was no more than a pile of dead wood and shredded greenery.

Fletcher strode from the center of the chaos. His hair was wild, his eyes still pitch-black, and his Hulk-like body ripped with muscles that strained for release inside the now-tight T-shirt he wore. The closer he came to us, the more his body seemed to normalize, his hair smoothing as his pupils shrank and his muscles returned to what they were before.

Now that the path was no longer blocked, Caleb held a hand up for me to wait a minute, then took off up the path.

Fletcher leaned forward, winded, and laid both hands on his knees.

"That was . . . impressive," I said, reaching down to re-claim the sage I had dropped earlier.

Fletcher's face was full of distaste. "I wish that this would not come down to that," he said between breaths. "This abomi-nation rising like that, the fear that grew such a creature . . . Something must have spooked these woods to have it act so."

"The path looks clear up ahead," Caleb said, coming back to us.

"Let us proceed, then," Fletcher said, not quite sounding like himself, as if a darkness still held sway over him. "And the wicked that dares turn my own forest against me had better be prepared to answer for its perversion."

The three of us went along the now-open path, Caleb and I having to hurry just to keep up with Fletcher as he scampered ahead. The path twisted and turned several times as we wound our way forward before rising up to the crest of a short hill.

The trees parted as the path opened up onto a grand clearing, one much larger than I imagined. Short, rolling hills were dotted with grave markers—tombstones, statues in mourning, mausoleums—and I was surprised by the sheer number of them. There were hundreds.

"Whoa," I said. "This place is huge. How has no one ever stumbled upon it before? It must take up half of Central Park."

"I doubt this place would show up on Google Maps," Caleb said. "I'm not sure we're really even in the city right now. Look."

Caleb pointed far off in the distance just above the line of trees, and while I could make out hints of the Manhattan skyline, it both was and wasn't there, like a ghost image on a piece of old film that had been double exposed.

"Do I even want to know?" I asked him.

"Freelancing has taught me a few things," he said. "Don't eat *anything* a witch or warlock offers you when you first meet, anyone who says that they can help magically improve your sex life usually means the opposite, and when it comes to the impossibly arcane, it's best to just roll with it and not stress out about logic too much."

"That sounds like good advice," I said, looking away from the existent/nonexistent skyline. "My brain was starting to hurt."

"Come," Fletcher said, pointing to the uppermost peak out in the middle of the cemetery. He started for it, going up and over hill after hill, and the two of us followed.

"The Butcher is kept in a place of honor?" I asked.

Fletcher shook his head. "No," he said. "That is not a place of honor. It is a reminder to all who visit here."

"A reminder of what?"

"To not become a megalomaniac hedonistic warlock," Caleb said. "Am I right?"

Fletcher laughed at that. "You do have a way with words, man," he said, "but yeah. More or less. I think it helps keep those who crave power in check."

"Who keeps *you* in check?" I asked.

Fletcher looked at me, a bit of a stoner smile on his face. "Me? I'm good, man. I'm not looking for power."

"You *are* power," I said.

He burst out laughing. "I am?" he asked, totally oblivious. "Whatever you say, lady."

I looked to Caleb, but he shook his head, indicating it might be best if I stopped asking such ridiculous questions of a creature I didn't know all that well. We walked on in silence, following him for several more minutes.

Fletcher was standing at the top of the hill by the time the two of us joined him there. The hilltop was nothing more than what looked like a pile of rocks.

"Is this a cairn?" Caleb asked.

Fletcher shook his head. "It is not supposed to be, no."

There was no rhyme or reason to the assemblage of stones up there. Only one explanation made sense. Whatever *had* been up here had been destroyed.

"Where's the gravestone?" I asked. "Or the grave, for that matter."

"Well, this is a bit problematic," Caleb said, letting his bundle of sage fall to the ground and kicking over one of the stones.

The letters *ORMA* were carved distinctly into one of the broken pieces at his feet.

"Here be the last resting place of Robert Patrick Dorman," I said. "Guess there's nothing left but to see if the ancient psychotic is still resting here."

I gathered myself closer to the pile of debris as I slid off my backpack and switched my sage for my family's stone spell book. Pressing my palm to it, I whispered the word of opening and the rock transformed to its natural book state of leather and paper. My will snapped to that of the stones scattered before me, and I pulled at them with my will in large groups, forcing them up and away from what remained of the grave site.

When the dust settled after the initial dig, Fletcher plunged his arms into what little dirt was left in the hole. Using the preternatural strength he had exhibited earlier, the forest spirit hefted out the coffin beneath. When the dirt fell away from it, all that was left was the twisted remains of what looked like a metal coffin.

I knocked my knuckles against it as I moved closer to confirm it.

"Iron," Caleb said. "To ward off certain types of supernatural creatures."

"But clearly not gargoyles," I said, running my hand along the clawed-up iron of the lid. I held my phone's flashlight up to the opening. "Empty. That takes care of one of the things we came here to check on. We can confirm that the Butcher's body is indeed missing. That's going to make it harder to track his gargoyle form down."

"No bones about it," Caleb said with a smirk.

I stared daggers at him, so not in the mood for levity right then.

"And correct me if I'm wrong," I said, unable to hide my testiness, "but according to what Fletcher said, won't we need the Butcher's *body* if we're going to stop him?"

Caleb's joviality died on his lips. "We do," he said as the realization sunk in. "No body, no ritual. We can't smudge his bones if we can't find them."

"I'm going to go out on a limb here and take a guess that maybe the Butcher came here and reclaimed his own body so that no one could do what we were about to do," I said. "What do you think, Fletch?"

My question was met with silence.

"Fletch?" I repeated, turning around. The man was nowhere to be seen.

"He's like Batman, I swear," Caleb said, starting down the hill. "Come on. He's got to be around here somewhere."

Having learned a lot from watching *Scooby-Doo*, I decided it was best that the two of us stick together while wandering a cemetery. Working ourselves away from the Butcher's tomb at the center of it, we circled out and around, calling Fletcher's name as we went until we got an answer.

"Over here, man," his voice shouted out from somewhere far off to our left. "I think."

Caleb and I scrambled up over the next hill, and then the next one, in pursuit of it.

"Over where?" I said, hoping to course-correct ourselves as we went.

"What did you say the family's name was again?" Fletch called out from just over the next hill, a little more to our right than I had thought.

"O'Shea," I said.

"Then I found it!"

"That was quick," I said, heading up and over the hill with Caleb behind me.

"It's kind of hard to miss," Fletcher said, and when I saw what he had found, it was most definitely true.

One entire hill among all the rest of them had been removed in its entirety. In its place was a massive domed structure, the designs and carvings all along it of a Gothic yet Celtic nature. It had to be at least the size of the Church at Saint Mark's Place. Over its entrance the word *O'SHEA* was carved in two-feet-tall letters. The entrance itself was an elaborately carved archway that stood at least twenty feet across. Bits of the archway were crumbling, but not from signs of age or wear. Two massive gold-leafed doors lay crumbled mere feet away from it, the hardware that had been holding them in place still attached to pieces of crumbling rock.

"You really need to hire a groundskeeper for this place," I said.

Fletcher shook his head. "No, man, this graveyard wasn't like this the other day."

"All this damage is new?" I asked.

He nodded.

"Let's just hope no one is still inside," I said, starting toward it. "And, against my better judgment, let's check it out. It's quiet, so there should be no surprises, right . . . ?"

Caleb paused at the entrance. "Until someone jumps out of a coffin at us," he said, and turned to look out the archway where Fletcher was still standing. "You coming?"

"No, man," he said. "I like it out here better. Buildings and enclosed spaces give me the creeps. I only promised you I'd take you to the cemetery. I've done that."

"Fine," I said, "but if you hear a bloodcurdling scream out of me, you'd better be prepared to get your ass in here."

"If you hear a bloodcurdling scream out of me, too," Caleb said. "And remember, you've known me longer. You keep that in mind when you think about who to rescue first."

I tugged at Caleb's arm and the two of us headed into the depths of the mausoleum together. "Nice," I said. "Ass."

"Hey, I'm just worried about preserving myself for *you*," he said.

I rolled my eyes and hunkered down to the floor. The dust of ages lay on the stonework everywhere, which made it easy to see that it had recently been disturbed by footprints and claw marks. "There's been more than one gargoyle here."

"You're sure?" Caleb asked, scanning the shadows.

"Positive," I said. "For instance, I know Stanis's tracks by heart. The width of his foot imprint, where the claw marks fall from the way he was carved. All the prints here are varied. There's some claw marks, paw prints, more human-looking ones."

When I stood back up, Caleb's hands were full of vials, his thumb and forefinger on each hand ready to uncap them at a moment's notice.

We continued on, and as my eyes adjusted to the interior darkness, I could see we were alone, if you didn't count the stench of rot and decay that grew the deeper in we went. All around the edges of the space, large stone sarcophagi lay, looking much like the ones from my family crypt in the Belarus building on Gramercy. Unlike the ones in my family's tomb, however, all of these had been opened. Heavy stone lids lay off-kilter on some, others broken in pieces on the floor or lying against the wall of the chamber. Bodies in various states of decay protruded from several of them.

I could no longer contain myself and allowed another shudder. Cemeteries were creepy enough on their own, just the idea that the dead were buried there out of sight, but to actually see the sad mortal remains of these bodies . . . It made the idea of being immortal like a *grotesque* all the more intriguing to me.

"You okay?" he asked.

"Yeah," I said, steeling myself. "You know what we have to do."

"Look for the Cagliostro Medallion," he said, his face full of concern. "If you're freaking, though, my offer still stands . . . I can go it alone."

"No," I said, almost snapping. Caleb might be far more seasoned in this world, but I had no intention of leaving him to do this by himself. "I was the one who made the deal with Warren. It's my responsibility. I won't shirk it, no matter how unpleasant."

Caleb nodded without further comment and the two of us moved from sarcophagus to sarcophagus, searching their contents, respectfully laying the dead back in their last resting places as we went. Although I hadn't caused any of this damage, I still felt like we were grave robbers. A place like this was private, not meant to be looked upon except by the O'Sheas, and this kind of intimacy with the dead made me uneasy at best.

There were rings and jewelry on all the dead—the O'Sheas buried in one kind of ceremonial robe or another—and some of them had been hastily thrown to the floor of the mausoleum by the previous visitors. Caleb went about the business of collecting broken, bony fingers and their rings from all over the floor, for which I was thankful. Still, despite our thorough search, nothing that looked even remotely close to what Warren had described to us as the Cagliostro Medallion was present.

"Well, that appears to be everything," I said when we had been through the entire place.

"No luck, then," Caleb said. "Still, who knows what some of the stuff on these people does . . . Imagine . . ."

"Stop yourself right there," I said, snapping. "Don't even think it."

"Wait, what?" Caleb said, his face going red, noticeable

even in this darkness. "Lexi! I wouldn't . . . How can you even—"

"I saw the glimmer in your eye just now when you were talking!"

"Hey," he said, sounding genuinely offended. "I *may* be an opportunist, but I'm *not* a ghoul."

"You sure about that?" I asked, unable to hide the venom in my question.

"Excuse me?!" he fired back, offense filling his face, which only fueled my agitation with him.

Exhaustion and frustration with a lack of results tonight had let the words just slip out, and once the dam was broken, there was no stopping it.

"Were you simply being an opportunist when you manipulated Stanis?"

"What are you talking about, Alexandra?" he asked. Already I could see the wheels turning behind his eyes as he fought to no doubt figure out which particular thing I might be calling him out on.

"When you ran your biggest con against him," I said. "To win me, like I'm a prize to be had. Telling him he should back off, that there was no future with me for a man of stone, that I should stick to my own kind if I wanted to be happy."

I expected him to be ashamed or at least surprised, but instead his brow furrowed and he glared at me.

"And I stand by what I said," he shouted just as angrily right back in my face. "What kind of life would you have had with him? Tell me. Skulking around at night, scratching your face up on his stone skin trying to make out with him? And long after you and I are gone, he'll still be here unchanged. In the long expanse of his time, you would be a blip on his radar. Nothing more. I did it for *you*."

"No," I corrected. "You did it for you. Just like you've always done. Conning your way through your entire life."

"He can't make you happy," he said. "I can."

"Well, I'll never know now, will I?" I spat out. "You made sure of that."

Caleb looked confused. "How?"

"You always pride yourself on your ability as an arcane freelancer," I said, "talking your way into this deal or that deal to make the highest dollar. You're such a natural at making a case for something that benefits you that Stanis fell for what you told him. Maybe being just a blip on the radar of his long life would have been enough. Your con was so convincing he's committed himself to his cause, to his people. Thanks to you, I never stood a chance of being on his radar. You manipulated the whole situation." My anger flew from my lips with every word, and my breath caught in my throat as the truth of what was really bothering me hit me. "You manipulated *me*."

"Lexi," he started. "Come on . . ."

I held up a hand to silence him. "Can we just get out of here?"

Caleb knew better than to speak. He nodded and without another word led the way back out of the mausoleum with a heavy, angry gait. Once outside, the graveyard felt almost homey in comparison to the super creepy interior and emotional whirlwind I had stirred up in the O'Shea family plot.

Fletcher, however, was nowhere to be seen, and the two of us stood in awkward silence for a long moment.

"I guess we're supposed to show ourselves out," Caleb said finally, but there was still bitterness in his words. "Presuming another tree monster doesn't get all hungry up on us."

Free of the mausoleum, I snapped. I craned my head up to the sky and gave a feral-sounding cry.

"Why can't this for once just be *easy*?" I shouted to the heavens. "This gargoyle situation, my situation with you."

Caleb shrugged. "What part of alchemy, arcana, witches, and warlocks made you think any part of this life would be a cakewalk?"

"A girl can dream," I said. "Or in this case, a girl can nightmare." I looked at him until he met my eyes, and I did not turn away. As the weight of everything hit me at once, I couldn't help but laugh as I fought back tears. "We're good and tangled in all of this now, aren't we? We live through this whole thing, I'm seriously going to reevaluate if we're even friends then."

I turned to walk away.

"Lexi—" he said, stopping me, but when he couldn't follow it with anything, I simply walked off.

Caleb wasn't dumb. He knew there was nothing he could say or do right now that I could trust.

I picked my way past the crumpled doors of the mausoleum that lay nearby and headed off in what I thought—what I *hoped*—was the right direction out of the cemetery.

"For the sake of everyone's involvement and well-being, let's just keep this business right now," I called back to him, calming myself in an attempt to regain some semblance of composure. "Let's hope Warren has secured us our meeting with the Convocation. Outside of getting them off my back, maybe they can help with our gargoyle problem and recovering the medallion." I stopped and turned back to him. "And make no mistake about it: You're going to help me get it and then you're going to give it to Stanis. I don't think that's asking too much, do you? It's the least you can do."

Caleb remained silent as I walked off, but he had been right earlier.

I should have known involving myself in the affairs of witches and warlocks—and *especially* freelancing alchemists— was something that would not prove easy.

Eighteen

Stanis

I knew the concrete canyons of Hell's Kitchen as well as any of my Manhattan neighborhoods. Nonetheless when Emily called out, "Heads-up," I looked up only to catch Detective Rowland's building coming up fast in front of me. I spread my wings to the extent of their span to slow myself, but I had simply picked up too much speed in my distracted state. I arched my back as far as I could, twisting my body as I banked upward just enough that I felt the bricks of the building's side scrape against my chest.

My momentum slowed the higher I rose until I set myself into a hover once I had cleared the building. Moments later Emily joined me, the effort of her wings bringing her into a hover of her own that had become much improved as of late.

"Forgive me," I said. "I did not realize we were already here."

"You're distracted," she said, with understanding kindness in her words. "It's understandable."

"Is it?"

She nodded. "Of course," she said. "You have everyone at Sanctuary to think about, not just me. Your mind must not get a second of rest or much of a thought all your own."

She was right, of course. There were all those things in my mind, as well as thoughts about finding the Butcher, keeping my people safe . . . and of course, Alexandra.

There was less and less time to help out my maker's kin track down the warlock Warren O'Shea's leads, but Alexandra was not something I felt comfortable discussing with Emily. My gargoyle companion had enough worries of her own to contend with without having to contend with my feelings for the last of the Spellmasons.

I reached out to Emily, taking her clawed hands in mine.

"Hopefully tonight shall give you the answers you seek," I said.

"I hope so," she said, her expression worried. Despite her serpentine features being hard to read, I had still been able to learn all the subtleties of her face over the past few months and it pained me to see her unhappy.

"You know who you are, why you are here," she continued. "I do not."

I gave a dark smile to her. "Patience," I said, "Do not forget . . . I spent several centuries *not* knowing, not even considering what or who I had been. My having ever been a part of humanity did not seem possible."

"You're right," she said with a smile of her own. "I know it. But knowing something and suppressing the emotions about it are two different things."

"Come," I said, holding my wings open in place.

The two of us descended down along the side of the building below, our wings spread wide to slow our fall until the windows of Detective Chloe Rowland's apartment were in front of us. I latched onto the brick of the building with my claws, and moved along the row of glass panes until I spotted the detective.

Her long red hair was down, and the clothes she wore were far more casual this time. Rowland sat on her couch in an oversized T-shirt and what Aurora called *sweatpants*. The detective's striped sock feet sat upon a low table that was covered with paperback books. A book with two humans in an embrace lay on her chest, her face awash in the glow of her television set, her eyes half-shut.

I tapped on the glass of the window but despite my quiet, gentle approach, the human jumped from the couch, knocking over the stack of books, and had her gun out of the waistband of her clothes faster than I would have imagined. When she saw it was Emily and me, the gun remained out but she lowered it as she approached the window, sliding it open.

"Can't you people call first?" she asked. "I don't want to explain gunshots to my neighbors when I accidentally fire on you."

"Forgive me," I said, "but I do not think phones are meant to be used by our kind."

"At least not the modern ones," Emily said with a smile. "I might be able to master a rotary with these claws of mine, but I don't think the phone company is really ready to deal with our kind just yet."

Rowland looked at the sides of her window, then back to us. "I'd invite you in," she said, "but I don't think either of you'd fit. And I'm certainly not crawling out my window, not after last time's little flight."

"Your roof, then, at your earliest convenience," I said, and pushed away from the building. My wings caught the air and with two great flaps of them, I came up and over the side of the structure, landing on the roof.

Emily landed seconds later with a poetry and gentle grace in her motion. Composed as she was, her wings betrayed her nerves and fluttered even as she brought them in close to her body.

Detective Rowland arrived a minute or two later, having changed into jeans, boots, and a leather coat over the T-shirt she had been wearing earlier. In one hand she held a yellow folder and with her other she pulled the jacket close around her as she walked over to us.

"If this is going to become a regular thing," she said, "I should probably install a gargoyle symbol up here. Shine a beacon into the night sky when I want to summon you and all that."

I contemplated what the detective meant for a moment before answering. "I do not think such measures will be necessary," I said. "And as a reminder I prefer the term *grotesque* over *gargoyle*."

"Right," she said. "Sorry."

"Forgive my impatience," Emily said, stepping past me and right up to the detective, "but have you found anything concerning my death?"

Detective Rowland gave a grim smile. "I'm not sure I'm ever going to get used to hearing questions phrased like that," she said, "but I guess that comes with my new job description, huh?" She held up the folder in her hands and opened it. "Emily Hoffert. You died—your human form, that is—August twenty-eighth, 1963. It was reported in the media that you were slain as part of a series of killings called the Career Girl murders."

"Career Girl?" I asked.

"It was 1963," Rowland said with a bit of bitterness in her voice now. "The idea of women in the workforce was still a novel concept. In cities like New York, however, women were flocking in droves to seek out their big opportunities."

"Some opportunity," I said. "Become a Career Girl and come to this grand city only to have your life taken from you."

"What career did I pursue?" Emily asked.

"You were a schoolteacher," Rowland said. "That's got to be a good thing, right?"

Emily managed a smile despite the grim subject matter. "I like that," she said.

"It would explain why you have been so natural at helping to educate our ever-growing population at Sanctuary," I said.

"And . . . I was murdered along with several other of these 'Career Girls'?" Emily asked, her wings fluttering once more with nerves.

Rowland shook her head. "That's the odd part," the detective said. "Yes, you were reported as part of the murders, along with a roommate, but the circumstances of your death were a bit more complicated than what was reported in the papers."

"How so?" Emily asked.

Detective Rowland stopped and lowered the folder. "You sure you want to hear this?" she asked Emily.

"Is it that bad?" I asked.

"It's not good," the detective said without taking her eyes off my companion. Emily nodded, and her clawed hand reached out to mine. I took it.

The detective let out a long sigh, then went back to the folder. "It seems your body was used for some sort of dark ritual. I've been over the coroner's reports and the lead investigators' notes on it. They wrote it off as some sort of Satanic ritual. Is that the sort of thing your Alexandra and her friends are into?"

I shook my head as I tried to control my temper. "Your ignorance on such matters will be your undoing," I said. "You understand little of what the arcane in our world is."

"Well, there's not really a lot for me to go on, now, is there?" she said with a bit of bite in her words, shaking the folder at me. "In our department it's practically hippie-liberal-progressive that we've got Detective Maron and I even dealing with these new paranormal cases, and you see how ridiculed we get. This was *1963*. Jesus, America, Apple pie. Hell, Kennedy wouldn't even be shot for another three months. 'Satanic ritual' was the best diagnosis of the time they were going to give. The only thing that's progressed since then is cynicism, but until your people start teaching me the ways of your magical little world, the idea that dark powers do dark shit like the stuff in this folder seems entirely reasonable to me."

I let go of Emily's hand and stepped over to the detective. "May I see the photographs?"

There was no anger or demand in my voice, only a natural curiosity. The detective was right. I had lived too long, and understood little myself about the changes in the human world. From a Europe where people were occasionally burned at the stake to this modern one, there was too much for me to process, let alone for me to lay blame.

Some of the fire died down in Detective Rowland. Instead, there was reluctance on the human's face. "You sure *you* want to look at all this?" she asked. "It's gruesome."

I nodded. "Long have I seen the things that have happened in this city," I said. "The night has always been a time and place for dark deeds to transpire. And do not forget: I also come from a long line of misguided men whose abuse of power drove them to do horrible things."

The detective reached into the folder and held out large sheets of photographs to me. "Then by all means, suit yourself."

"Thank you," I said, taking the thin, fragile sheets from her. I moved across the roof away from both her and Emily, and my fellow gargoyle made no move to join me. I am not sure that I would have been able to take photographic images of my mortal death well, either. My own memories were bad enough.

Although I knew the photographs to be of a human, there was little I could see in them that would have convinced me. A mangled twist of crimson brown was splayed out all across a large living area. While the sight itself had a chaotic horror to it, it was also clear that there was an order to how things had been arranged. The floor and walls of the living space bore arcane symbols written in what I assumed was Emily's blood.

I do not know how long I looked through the photographs, but when Emily moved toward me, I gathered them together and shook my head at her.

"You do not wish to see such things," I said, and brought the photographs back over to Detective Rowland.

Emily crossed over to the detective and held her hand out. "I'll determine what I should and shouldn't see," she said.

If Detective Rowland had any thoughts on that, she kept them to herself as the two of us watched Emily in silence. By the way her wings worked subconsciously behind her, my fellow *grotesque* was not taking the images well.

When she was done looking through them, she carefully arranged them back together as neatly as she had been handed them and gave the photographs back to Detective Rowland.

"Thank you," Emily said quietly. "Perhaps Stanis was right."

"Yeah, well, he strikes me as an observant guy," Rowland said.

"I believe you should share those with Alexandra, Marshall, and Aurora," I said. "Some of the symbols remind me of those used in my creation, but I have no true mastery of such arcane things."

"Got it," she said, pulling out her phone to make a note of it. "Now perhaps you have something for me . . . ?"

"We have not come across the Butcher ourselves, Emily and I, but my people have been keeping an eye out for him."

"Great," the detective said with a heavy sigh. "*This* is what you got me out of my pj's for?"

"I did, however, meet someone the other night who *has* met at least one of the Butcher's men. He had turned the Butcher down, and then, to my surprise he turned down becoming a part of my Sanctuary."

"And he might be able to tell me more about his encounter with the Butcher," she said. "Where can I find him?"

"I do not know," I said. "But fear not. This Nathaniel Crane is not one to hide away. You will find him, if he does not find you first."

Detective Rowland tapped away again. "Nathaniel . . . Crane," she said. "We'll see who finds who first. What am I looking for out there? Something demonic like you, or maybe something more serpentine like Emily here?"

"We do not all look alike, Detective," I said, scolding her.

"I know *that*," she said. "Just help me out here, okay? Maron and I are dealing with chasing the impossible. We need as much help as we can get."

"Very well," I said. "First, you will need to find an angel."

Nineteen

—— C ——

Alexandra

I'd been to Madison Square Garden for countless concerts over the years, but I had never shown up there at midnight. The usually busy arena was practically dark except for the barest minimum of work lights from within. Still and silent as it was, all Rory, Marshall, and I could do was stare up at the enormous space. The only one of us who was oblivious to its urban majesty was Caleb, who was too busy to notice as he scarfed down a pretzel he may or may not have just stolen off a street vendor. The short leash I had put him on earlier had me trying to keep things all business with him, which only made him overcompensate in the opposite direction and act out.

"You sure about this?" I asked him.

"Pretty sure," Caleb said, wiping a spot of mustard from the corner of his mouth. "Unless Warren was screwing with me."

"How likely is that?" Marshall asked.

Caleb shrugged. "I'm not sure. You never can tell with these arcane types."

"That's reassuring," I said. A day ago I found his antics

charming. Now? Not so much. "And now we're supposed to go before a whole bunch of them?"

"Relax," he said. "You'll be fine."

Rory shook her head. "I don't suppose I should break out the *glaive guisarme* . . . ?"

"Let's try the friendly approach first," I said, "and if that doesn't work, I promise *then* you can get all stabby."

Rory smiled. Despite the implication of things going wrong, my promise seemed to make her twistedly happy.

On the other side of her, Marshall dug through his pockets like he had lost his keys. "Do you think it would be gauche to hand out business cards?" Marshall asked, more to Caleb than any of the rest of us.

"Depends," Caleb said. "Do you really want to start handing out physical evidence with your name on it? Don't we already have enough cops in our lives without you leaving a paper trail?"

Marshall went red-faced and stopped his search, going silent while we waited. It wasn't long before the scruffy, familiar face of Warren O'Shea appeared at the main entry doors that were set back from the bustle of Seventh Avenue. His hair was a wild mass of black tangles, and the rings on both his hands holding the doors glowed with a constant shift of colors. His long formal coat blew in the wind as he held open the door for us, waiting as we crossed the vast expanse of the open sidewalk.

"The Convocation will see you now," he said. "Hopefully you will prove yourself a bit more impressive than when you broke into my home."

"No promises," Caleb said, pushing past him with a bit of bite to his words.

"Fine," Warren said, closing the door after we were all in. "Take your chances with every witch and warlock in the five boroughs. Smart move." There was a bit of disapproval in his voice, but when he noticed me noticing it, he switched on a dime and offered me a cheerful smile. "But I *did* promise to bring you before the Convocation . . ."

He turned before I could speak again and led our group

along one of the lower circular corridors around the lower floor of the arena. Rory ran ahead to catch up with him, matching his pace.

"Umm, how many witches and warlocks are we talking here that they needed to hold this thing at Madison Square Garden?" she asked.

Warren made a sudden right toward the center of the building, entering one of the corridors that led to a set of double doors that obviously led into the arena itself. He spun back around to us, his arms spread out wide across the doors, blocking our path.

"You don't understand," he said. "This isn't about being able to house massive amounts of people. It's all about location, location, location. Our kind have . . . trust issues. Therefore, our meetings—when we can agree to all get together, that is—are like a moveable feast. They are rarely in the same place twice, although truth be told, I am rather fond of this venue for it."

"Why?" I asked.

Warren gave me a smile from one corner of his mouth. "You'll see," he said, and turned with a flourish, arms still out to his sides. The warlock flicked his wrists and the doors shot open without him touching them.

Warren stepped through them as they clattered against the walls, and the rest of us scrambled through after him, a nervous excitement running through us. I was ten again, coming here with my family to catch the circus.

In the dim light beyond the doors, stadium seating rose up on either side of the corridor, the click of our heels echoing as we went. Moving forward, the confined space opened up to the Garden itself, and as we came to a stop at the edge of the stadium floor, the silence within the space was deafening.

"It's empty," I said.

"What the hell?" Rory asked, one of her hands coming to rest on the art tube she was wearing.

I didn't blame her for reaching for her weapon. "Is this some kind of trick?" I asked. "You get me on the hunt, I take your case, then you lure us here out in the open . . . for what exactly?"

Warren sighed, shaking his head as if disappointed. "It is amazing you have survived this long," he said. "If you didn't have your gargoyles watching over you, I shudder to think what might become of you."

"Hey, we don't need protection," I countered, but secretly I wished we *had* brought Stanis along. At the time, it just hadn't seemed like the best way to show up when you were trying to make nice with an entire magical community. Flustered, I started for Warren, wanting to get right up in his face, but Marshall grabbed me by the arm, stopping me.

"Hold up," he said. "This is it, isn't it?"

Warren didn't shake his head yes or no, but raised an eyebrow. "This is *what*?"

"This is like part of the audition," he said, looking all around at the empty space, walking in a complete circle until he faced us again. "This is a test."

"Is it?" I asked Warren.

The warlock simply shrugged at me, which only made me want to punch him in the throat.

"He's right," Caleb said, starting to search the space as he walked out onto the empty basketball court. "All is not as it seems."

Marshall joined him, his eyes squinting as he tried to focus his attention off to the far end of the court. "We are not alone," he said.

"We're not?" Rory asked, assembling her pole arm as she crossed the court to join them.

I followed, not wanting to be left alone in the giant space.

Marshall shook his head, narrowing his eyes to the point that they looked shut. "I'm not sure who or what else *is* out there, but if I concentrate, I can feel some sort of resistance in the air. Whatever it is does not wish to be seen."

I looked to Warren. "Well?"

Warren drew his fingers across his lips, twisted the tips of his fingers against them in a locking motion, then motioned as if he were throwing away a key. To my surprise a little key that glowed an eldritch green flew away from him, fizzling out and disappearing before it could hit the floor.

Marshall turned back to us, his eyes lighting up and a smile that threatened to split his head in two lit his face.

"I have it!" he said, practically giggling.

"Have *what*?" Rory asked with frustration.

"Everything that you're seeing right now?" he said. "All of it is an illusion."

"It is?" I said, looking around. I knew the Garden and it looked pretty damn real to me. I turned to Caleb. "Is it?"

He looked like he was trying to find the right words, but in the end scrunched up his face at me. "I'm not really at liberty to say," he said.

"Jesus," I said, pushing him toward Warren. "Go stand with him if you're not allowed to participate."

Marshall was looking all around the empty space, his eyes darting about.

"Marshall!" I called out, catching his attention. "You look insane. Like cheese-slipped-off-your-cracker insane."

He ran over to Rory and me, grabbing us by our shoulders and spinning us to face the far end of the arena. Lowering his voice, he spoke.

"Growing up, the bane of my gaming existence in Dungeons and Dragons were Illusionists," he said. "Much like when non-gamers go see a magician like David Copperfield, illusions rely mostly on the audience choosing to believe in it. So every time I came across something impossible in the game, my knee-jerk reaction was to roll to disbelieve what I thought might be an illusion."

"Roll?" Rory asked.

"A saving throw," he added, like we were being stupid.

I started to ask what the hell a saving throw was and what it had to do with this, but Marshall cut me off.

"Look, that's not really the important part," he said. "I just need you to trust me."

Rory shot me a look of doubt and I couldn't help but return it.

Marshall looked hurt for a second, but whatever had him

giddy was too overpowering for him and he went back to his manic look. "Nice," he said, dismissing us. He dug his fingers into our shoulders, pulling us close and lowering his voice.

"I'm not kidding about needing to trust me," he continued.

"Okay," I said, a bit confused. "Consider yourself trusted."

He looked to Rory.

"After everything we've fought together?" she said. "Done! Trusted!"

"Now, I need you to disbelieve what you see," he said.

"And how does one go about that, exactly?" I asked.

"I'm not entirely sure," he said without losing a beat of enthusiasm. He thought a moment. "Years of gaming must have helped shape that particular mental muscle in me. Let's see . . . I guess you just have to trust me over your senses. Normally you believe what you see, right? I'm asking you to believe what *I* see."

He motioned out across the floor of the empty arena. "For instance, I need you to imagine that this entire space looks like an impromptu Renaissance festival. There's people scattered about, people like you and me . . . although there's a lot of eccentric-looking folk here, too. There are aisles and little shops, and overhead . . . just imagine a pyrotechnic Quidditch match going on."

Rory sighed. *"Marshall . . ."*

"Just trust me."

Although I felt as ridiculous as Rory clearly did, I doubted my own senses and decided to buy into exactly what Marshall was telling me. I couldn't see any of what he was saying, but I believed it was there.

Something in my mind shifted, feeling like a sharp and sudden dizziness. Much like the changing appearance of Warren's home from composed to destroyed by a gargoyle, the empty arena all around me began to shimmer, the motion disorienting to the point where I had to fight not to throw up. I didn't think puking was going to win me any points with whoever was watching. Then everyone else seemed to see it as well, keeping it together, but Rory stumbled and fell to her knees as she tried to take it in.

The empty arena filled with pockets of people everywhere, although it was far from full. They gradually appeared along with sections of tables, stalls, thrones, and chairs throughout the space. Great cauldrons of fire held flames that rose high into the arena, the lighting giving the space an almost primitive cavelike quality. High above, witches and warlocks flew to and fro with the aid of traditional brooms, cloth wings, or by some means I could not quite see. Colors erupted like fireworks as several blasts of energy shot across the open air or at each other, the impacts bursting with explosive lights before fading away with a distinct sizzling sound.

"Holy cats," Rory exclaimed as she stood back up.

Marshall craned his neck straight up as he tried to take it all in. "This is *exactly* what I had imagined something like this would look like."

Rory steadied herself by using her weapon to lean on, marveling at the spectacle all around us. "Whoa," was all she managed to get out.

"Looks like we found Platform Nine and Three-Quarters," I said.

Warren had already taken off again, now weaving through the stalls, tables, and people on the floor of the arena. Caleb kept up his pace, ignoring just about everything going on around him. I guess having been part of this world for so long had left him unimpressed.

Rory and I were still busy pushing through the noisy crowd when Warren and Caleb stopped far ahead before an ornate heavy table carved with runic symbols. A single wooden throne sat behind it, several feet higher than the table itself, occupied by a blond woman who looked maybe ten years older than me. At the table before her several men and women worked at a frantic pace on its clutter of maps, stacks of books, and loose paper everywhere.

"I told you they pose no threat," Warren said to the woman.

"We will determine that," the woman's voice boomed out in the space. "Bring them closer."

Warren beckoned us to him, and the crowd parted as we went. He moved around to the other side of the table, leaving

Caleb behind to line up with the rest of us before the woman. I felt like we were being summoned before the principal.

The woman's hands rested on the arms of her throne, her nails stereotypical with a witchy black gloss coat, giving her a real Goth-past-her-prime look. I had expected someone looking like Maleficent, but this woman's features were gorgeous—her face soft and full, all of it surrounded by a cascade of wavy blond hair that was equal parts *Some Like It Hot* and *Baywatch*. Her face betrayed nothing as she looked us over, running down the line of us. They passed over me and I met hers despite my nerves screaming for me to look away. When she finished examining all of us, her eyes came back to rest on me.

"Are you the one who demanded parlay?" she asked.

Parlay?

Given how relatively young she looked, the word came off ancient on her lips.

"That's correct," I said, then gave a nervous laugh.

One of her perfectly plucked eyebrows went up. "You find your presence before me amusing somehow?"

I covered my mouth and turned away for a second only to find Rory staring daggers at me.

"Forgive me," I said, doing my best to compose myself and suppress my nerves. "I'm just not sure how to address you . . ."

The woman looked to Warren, and the warlock turned away from her gaze.

"Tsk, tsk, O'Shea," she said. "Formalities, formalities . . . What would happen if our kind gave up on the finer points of civilization, hmm? We'd still be trying to sling plague spells at each other from our respective caves. Manners, Mr. O'Shea."

Warren nodded, and though I could see a fire burning in his eyes, when he spoke there was no vitriol in it. "Yes, of course," he said. "My apologies."

She turned back to us. "I believe introductions are in order," she said, eyes moving to Caleb. "Hello again, Mr. Kennedy."

"Hey, Laurien," he said. "How are those special creams working out for you?"

"I've felt younger," she said, sounding completely and utterly unimpressed.

"Haven't we all?" Warren muttered off to the side.

She held her smooth-skinned hands up, flexing them. For a split second they appeared wrinkled, then went back to their state of perfection.

"I can fix that," Caleb said. There was no hint of worry or concern in his voice, charm oozing out of every word and finished off with that crooked winning smile of his.

"For what I paid, I should hope so," she said, and moved down the line to Marshall.

"A pleasure to see you again, Mr. Blackmoore."

Rory and I both shot Marshall surprised looks.

"What?" he asked. "Laurien is a steady customer. How was I supposed to know she was the Wonderful Witchess of Oz?"

"Isn't 'know your customer,' like, job one of owning a business?" I asked.

Warren cleared his throat, and I stopped bickering long enough for Rory to step forward.

She tapped her pole arm on the floor and gave a low, deep curtsy with all of her dancer's grace. "I'm Aurora Torres," she said. "Your Majesty."

"'Your Majesty,'" the woman repeated. She looked to her group of people working at the table. "I like that. You could all take a lesson from her."

Either they were too busy to respond or they didn't want to. By the eye rolls I saw, I was banking on the latter.

"I'm Alexandra Belarus," I said, adding, "Your Majesty."

The woman smiled. "Belarus," she said. "Interesting . . ."

"Is it?" I asked.

"It is," she said, giving a single nod. "I am Laurien du Lac. And you need not call me 'Your Majesty.' Laurien will suffice."

I relaxed at that, but only for a second.

"Why do you find my family name so interesting, Laurien?"

"Oh, we are quite aware of the activities of your kind," she said.

"*Our* kind?" I asked, not sure whether I should be offended. Rory, on the other hand, had already decided.

"What the hell is *that* supposed to mean?" Rory asked, stepping forward with enough anger on her face that I had to grab her arm.

The assembled people at the table had stopped working now, their eyes all on the exchange that they just happened to be in the middle of.

"I've got this, Ror," I told her and turned back to the head of the council. "Forgive my friend, but that came out sort of accusatory."

"*J'accuse,*" Laurien said, holding a hand up as if making a solemn swear.

The smug look on her face and the whole holier-than-thou tone grated on my last nerve. Rory hissed in pain and I looked over to find that my nails digging into her arm were the cause of it.

"Would you care to elucidate?" I asked. "Or would you prefer I unleash my friend on you?"

"Long have we known of the Spellmasons," she said. "And long have we been relieved to see them absent these past few centuries."

"Hey, this is my family you're talking about!"

"Understood," she said, her voice becoming more hesitant and diplomatic, "but be that as it may, my people were happy to hear of Alexander Belarus's disappearance."

"You know of my great-great-grandfather?" I asked. "Then why would you say that?"

"You seem to be under the impression that he should be held in some kind of high esteem . . . ?" she said. I nodded. "Let's just say that introducing an old-world creature such as the gargoyle into this country was not considered by most of the existent magical community to be the most welcome of choices."

"My great-great-grandfather was a great man," I said, hearing how defensive my voice was.

"I know our history," Laurien said with a triumphant smile. "Do you know *yours*, Miss Belarus?"

"I . . . I thought I did."

"And now you come before me with little understanding of your family's past or the chaos you have unleashed upon our city."

"We came here because we wanted your people to stop hunting us down," Rory added. "We came here in peace!"

"I suppose that's a weapon of peace, is it?" Laurien said, pointing to the pole arm in Rory's hand.

"The important thing is that we came," I said, talking over the two of them. "*I* set this up. *I* wanted to lay things out on the table."

"It's taken you some time to come around to it," she countered.

"Hell, six months ago, I didn't even know there *was* a magical community," I said. "It wasn't until I met Caleb that I even heard about all of you. And again, I did make the effort to come before you."

"But only after unleashing hordes of gargoyles all over our city," Laurien said pointedly.

"I'll own that," I said. "I'm not making excuses, but it *was* an accident—"

Caleb stepped between us. "Ladies, ladies . . . this is no time to play the blame game about who may or may not have been responsible for the Great Gargoyle Fiasco of last year."

Rory *hmph*ed, drawing a look from Caleb, but she said nothing.

She might be pissed about Caleb's part in all of it or that he was quickly trying to cover his own ass, but she was also smart enough to realize that here and now was not the place to bring it up.

"That's not the only reason I'm here," I said. "This is about the Cagliostro Medallion and one particular gargoyle who wants it. You may have heard of him in his previous human life as the Butcher of the Bowery."

"An enemy of the Convocation," Warren added, giving no indicator of his involvement in all this, which I found strange.

Laurien raised an eyebrow at that. "This is a serious threat of which you speak," she said. "Why should I trust the word of a Belarus?"

"I came here to help as best I can!" I said with exasperation starting to take over. "What is your problem with my family anyway?"

"It seems you know less of your history than you think you do," Laurien said with a little smugness to her words. "Your family's disappearance from our circles is looked upon as a great day. The cowardly disappearance of the last Spellmason was a boon."

"Alexander Belarus wasn't a coward," I said with rising anger growing in me. "He *chose* to disappear. He went off the grid because he worried what people would do if they got ahold of his secrets. He knew the chaos that would ensue if madmen were to learn the arcana of the Spellmasons."

Laurien sat in quiet contemplation on her throne for a few moments, then stood, walking around the table to me. She took my hands in hers, which I found remarkably cold. I couldn't suppress a shiver. Laurien smiled.

"Walk with me," she said, and led me off in silence into the impromptu marketplace.

"You speak of Alexander Belarus with pride," she said when we were halfway down one of the aisles, "as if he were noble."

"He was."

Laurien laughed. "That is not the man our history remembers."

"No?"

"You call him hero, no doubt, given your name," she said. "We call him killer."

I stopped in the aisle as if slapped. "Excuse me?"

"He came before this Convocation wishing to form a guild," she said. "He seemed lonely more than anything, hoping he could find connection among our arcane kind, but he did not fit well. He was closed off, a reluctant teacher, wanting to reap the benefits of being one of us, but keeping much of his work secret."

"It doesn't surprise me," I said. "Alexander had come to this country in fear of his life. Even when he found likeminded practitioners of the arcane arts, no doubt that fear crippled him from sharing. Even my own education on Spell-masonry has been hard-won, like assembling a giant puzzle. I take it his reluctance to share made him unwelcome among your people?"

"Worse," Laurien said. "One day one of his students went missing, and while none of our people could find damning proof, Alexander's disappearance—and that of the Spellmason secrets—seemed a rather telling jury."

"I don't come from a long line of murderers," I said. "I can promise you that."

"We shall see," Laurien said.

"My great-great-grandfather went off the radar to protect people, to keep others from abusing his power. If one of your people crossed him, I'm sure he took care of it, but I don't think he would have murdered them."

I didn't mention the large stone golem that *might* have done a bit of that handiwork on his behalf. The last thing I needed was for Laurien and her people to have confirmation of my family's hand in direct gargoyle violence.

Laurien's face shifted to a softer look as she considered my words, lightening the mood even though she looked far from convinced by them.

"You know, I can understand his wanting to disappear," she said. "As you say, I am sure there were those who wished to take advantage of his knowledge, of his power. There are times when I wish I could disappear as well."

"You're a witch," I said. "I'm sure you can disappear if you want."

"Yes, but not the way Alexander did."

"You talk like you were there," I said. "How old *are* you?"

She smiled, and looked down at me. "Surely you know it's impolite to ask a woman her age."

"Fine," I said. "Let me rephrase. Is it possible you knew my great-great-grandfather?"

Laurien shook her head. "There are ways for humans to extend their lives, especially among our kind," she said, "but none that I know of that will last for centuries upon centuries. Would that there were!"

We continued along through the stalls, the witch examining table after table of laid-out items. While she perused the goods there, I watched the stalls' owners. Face after face at booth after booth was filled with an eager hope in their eyes. These people wanted her approval; they *craved* it. She tapped her dark nails at several items as we went, and the owners would pull them from the tables and pile them away from the rest of their wares.

I had a million questions, but I decided to take things easy with her as I sized the woman up. After several minutes of shopping silence, she took me to the far end of the arena away from everyone.

"Tell me, Alexandra Belarus, what is your intention in my city?"

"Not to sound competitive," I countered, "but I sort of think of it as my city, too."

"That does come off as competitive," she said. "Do you think to take this city over with these gargoyles you have unleashed, then?"

"What?" I asked, a little shaken. "*No.* I simply meant I grew up here. Born and raised. I love New York. I'm not looking to take it over."

Laurien studied my face, no doubt looking for a hint that I was lying or was being insincere, but I had nothing to hide.

"Good," she said. "Personally, I always wanted power, but now that I have it . . . Well, I spend much of my days settling petty squabbles."

I looked up at the explosions and flares of light that the flying witches and warlocks were hurdling at one another.

"Is that what's going on up there?" I asked.

She nodded. "There are many issues that need resolution when it comes to the arcane community of the greater New York area. Decision by Right of Conflict is one of the ways our people can seek resolution."

"What could there possibly be to fight about?" I asked.

"Territory disputes," she said. "Access to certain arcane supplies that can only be found naturally in certain parts of the city. Every borough rules itself, but our meetings help to keep the peace among them." She gestured across the arena floor back toward the throne. "That paperwork I have my people working on? That's what covers a lot of the more mundane conflicts going on . . . rituals, permits, fishing rights, reagent material harvesting, treaty agreements between the various factions that simply don't play well with others. It's for reasons like this that I decided to take you aside for the moment, so that you might better understand . . ."

"I think I do," I said. "The lives of witches and warlocks are complex."

"And I want you to understand your part in it," she said. "I would give you a chance to hear it first away from the crowd. Tell me, why do the Spellmasons return to us now? And why this grand gesture of summoning all these gargoyles to life?"

Laurien's eyes examined my face as I tried to figure out how to respond. It was clear there was a perceived threat in what I had unleashed upon this city.

"A year ago, I had no idea what a Spellmason even was," I said. "All I knew was that I was named after my great-great-grandfather and that I had a passion for the art and architecture he had created."

Laurien raised one of her perfectly plucked eyebrows again. "You have only been at this arcane work a *year*?"

I nodded.

"My girl, I would not let that get around. The power you wield in such a short time will bring out the jealousy in some, and wrath in others."

"Thanks for the heads-up," I said. "We didn't come here to brag or anything. I'm still trying to figure out much of what Spellmasonry even is."

"Why unleash the gargoyles?" she asked. "What purpose does it serve, other than to put the rest of us on guard, not to mention you've outed the arcane world to others."

I took a deep breath. "My friends touched upon it," I said, "but the truth is that the creation of so many creatures, so many *grotesques*, was . . . an accident."

"An accident?" she asked, her eyes narrowing.

I had to tread carefully if I didn't want to ruin Caleb's

reputation around her, since he had been party to the whole
fiasco. "There was an enemy from long ago who had come
to this country, seeking the secrets of the Spellmasons. We
were trying to remedy the situation to keep him at bay, but . . .
things got out of hand."

"I should say so," Laurien said. "I have long thought the
secrets of Alexander Belarus died with him."

"I stand before you as living proof they didn't," I said.

Laurien looked me up and down once more, which made
me feel like I was under some kind of microscope inspection.
I felt naked in her gaze.

"So you do," she said, with a tight-lipped smile. "So you
do. Come."

We walked in silence back through the crowd on the arena
floor, the air above us filled with chaos, explosions, and shouts
as conflicts raged on and resolved themselves. The closer we
got to her throne, the more I noticed a shift in her. Her body
became more poised and she walked with an air of authority
that she had discarded when we were out among the stalls. Her
carriage was almost royal, and when she rounded the table, she
took her throne with all the grace of a queen once more, the
noise of the crowd all around us dying down.

Marshall, Rory, and Caleb were all staring at me with
intensity as I moved to rejoin them, their eyes searching my
face for some sort of indication of what had just gone down.
The thing was, I wasn't sure what *had* just gone down. The
best I could muster for my friends was a halfhearted smile,
which seemed to annoy them more than help.

"So," Laurien said, her voice quiet yet booming out as if
being broadcast to the entirety of Madison Square Garden.
"What is it you wish from us, Alexandra Belarus?"

Walking among the people talking had been easy. Answering in front of them with all eyes falling on us had my heart
in my throat. I controlled my breathing before answering. If
I could just keep from hyperventilating, I wouldn't have a
panic attack. I collected my thoughts, and when the pulse in
my throat lessened, I spoke.

"I'd like your people to ease up on us," I said. "I'm trying to deal with the gargoyle situation I've created, and it would go a little easier if I didn't have to worry about witches and warlocks gunning for us at the same time. I've spent six months dodging them. It needs to stop."

Laurien looked out across the gathered crowd. "I am sure none of our community wish to interfere with your efforts," she said, meeting the eyes of those hers landed on. "This council and I would not take kindly to hear of anyone barring their progress."

"And actually," I added. "We could use a little help."

Laurien shook her head. "I am afraid not," she said.

"What?" Rory asked.

"Laurien," Caleb said. "Come on. Be serious."

"I *am* being serious, Mr. Kennedy. We cannot offer you help . . . yet."

"Why not?" I asked.

"Try to understand my position," she said. "The great-great-granddaughter of a known menace to our community unleashes an even worse problem and now wants our help in cleaning up the mess?"

"We're here because Warren asked us to help him clean up *his* mess," I said. "The one where the Butcher has already torn apart his home in gargoyle form looking for the Cagliostro Medallion."

Laurien looked surprised. She turned to Warren, who had locked eyes with me the second I mentioned his name.

"Is this true?" she asked.

Warren ran his hands through his wild hair, the rings catching in it. He walked over to stand with us on our side of the table as he freed them.

"It's true that there has been an attack on my home, yes," he said. "And it would appear that it is the work of a gargoyle if the claw marks and destruction are any indicator. That's why I hired Miss Belarus here. Isn't that right?"

I could have told Laurien that the source of Warren's trouble wasn't as "undetermined" as he was letting on, but given the grip he had on me, I decided that could wait until later if I had to bring it up at all.

"He did," I said.

"And she charges a *lot*," Caleb added, joining in on whatever web of lies we were suddenly spinning on our side of the table.

"How do I get you to help us?" I asked.

"Think of this like getting into Juilliard," she said. "You have to audition."

"This is going to be harder than me getting into the Manhattan Dance Conservatory," Rory whispered.

"Why do I have to audition?" I asked, stepping forward. "It's *obvious* what I can do. There are several hundred gargoyles out there right now that prove my abilities."

"Just because you can sing in your living room doesn't make you *American Idol* material," Laurien said. "You don't get to be part of our community unless *I* say you are part of our community."

"And what if I'm not really a joiner?" I asked, recalling Nathaniel Crane's words.

"Then you fail to receive all the benefits of practicing magic in the New York area," she said. "No protection and no aid."

Marshall held a hand up. "How exactly does she have to audition?"

"That's the beauty of it," Laurien said. "She already is."

"I am?"

"I think the aid you are providing Mr. O'Shea should prove sufficient," she said. "I'll consider the resolution of his problem a step in the right direction with the community. Then we can discuss how best we can aid you."

It wasn't the ideal solution. I figured having Warren bring us before them might prove enough, but it seemed like the best offer I was going to get.

"Fine," I said, "but understand this. Anything that befalls the people of Manhattan in that time is on you." I turned and addressed the entire assembly. "All of you. As it already is with me."

I didn't wait for a response and headed away from Laurien on her throne to one of the exits off the arena floor.

Rory, Marshall, and Caleb caught up with me halfway around the circular corridor heading back to the entrance on

Seventh Avenue, but it was the voice of Warren calling out from behind them that caused me to stop.

"Alexandra, wait!"

Warren ran around my friends and slowed when he finally caught up with me.

"Get away from me, Warren."

"Easy, now," he said. The rings on both his hands glowed, and he pressed them together, a vine of colorful flowers twisting up out of his hands.

"Really?" I asked, pulling the flowers from his hands and tossing them on the floor. "That's the best you've got? The cheap tricks of a stage magician?"

Caleb grabbed him by the shoulder and spun him around. Warren's hands flew apart and the flowers fizzled out of existence.

"What the hell was that?" he said.

"You want to tell us why you clammed up in front of your people about the Butcher of the Bowery returning?" I asked.

Warren looked down at the ground. "Right now was not the time to get into those particular details," he said. "And this is a family matter for now."

"I could probably resolve your family matter a lot quicker if we had, say, those hundreds of people in there helping out!" I shouted at him.

"You want to put us in jeopardy?" Caleb asked, grabbing Warren by the lapels of his coat. "Put us more at risk than we have to be? Don't put us in front of Laurien like that and then dodge the questions."

Warren didn't struggle even though Caleb's anger was growing by the second. I would have felt bad for the warlock if it weren't for the fact that my anger was also on the rise.

Smoke fumed out of Warren's jacket. Large, dark puffs rose and covered his head and hands as if his body were on fire from within it. Caleb began to cough, turning his head away from it, but his hands remained clutching the warlock.

Or at least his jacket. As the smoke wafted up to the ceiling and cleared the hallway, Caleb had the warlock's coat, but not the warlock. Warren was gone.

Rory was already poised for combat with her pole arm stretched out in front of her. Marshall was already strategizing and had pressed himself back-to-back with her as he assessed the room, his eyes darting over to a strip of darkened food counters along the inner wall.

Warren sat cross-legged on the countertop, his hands pressed down to either side of him. He shook his head at us.

"Let me ask a question," he said, looking the group of us over. "And I'm going to keep it real simple. Sherlock Holmes deduction simple. Which is more likely: that you, first-time visitor to our Convocation, have assessed our gathering perfectly, or that perhaps an esteemed member of said group—say, a warlock with decades of participation in these gatherings—might have been finessing this first contact situation?"

The fight went out of me as I stood there. "I . . . I just thought—"

"You *didn't* think," he said. "None of you. I've seen many a thing go wrong over the years at a Convocation. Most of those covens would gladly tear each other apart."

"Why would they do that?" Marshall said. "They have a common interest."

"Much of it is fear. Not all who wield such power do so with the same level of responsibility. There is little trust among most of them. It is an uneasy peace that we have fought to maintain for well over a century, but it *is* a peace."

"You didn't think mentioning that the Butcher is back was important?" I asked.

"It *is*," he said, hopping down off the counter. He started walking back over to us. "However, tonight was not *about* that. Tonight was about granting you an audience and an introduction to the community. The Belarus name is not a beloved one among my kind, and you saw the chaos that these meetings are. Things like where and when to reveal things to the Convocation's council take time, Alexandra. I need time to talk to the right people there . . . people I can trust."

My face went hot with red, his words humbling me. I *didn't* know what we were getting into. I hadn't really known that for over a year, making it all up as I went along.

"I'm sorry," I said. "I get it now. I don't know what I expected going in there. Given the hatred that there seems to be for my family name, I'm glad we had you to vouch for us."

Rory lowered her pole arm and came up to me. "What exactly did that woman tell you when you were out in the crowd, Alexandra?"

"Yeah," Caleb said. "You probably had more time with her tonight than I've had in counsel with her during the last decade!"

"She said much," I said. "I'm still trying to process it all."

"Why do they hate Alexander so much?" Marshall asked. "What did your great-great-grandfather do to piss off their entire community?"

"He may not be the man I've always thought him to be," I said, hating that I even had new and nagging questions forming in my mind. "If I'm to give due diligence to what she told me, my great-great-grandfather might have been a bit more murderous than we thought."

"What?" Rory asked, practically laughing. "That's *insane*."

"Is it?" Warren asked.

I stared at him, wanting to deck him as my knee-jerk reaction, but upon examining his face I realized there was no malice or snide to what he was asking, only genuine concern. Having nowhere to channel my anger only angered me further, and I turned from him and started walking off toward the doors leading out onto Seventh Avenue.

"You do what you need to, Warren, and leave the hunt for the Butcher to me," I said. "But the sooner you get those people on our side, the better protected you're going to be."

Once again Caleb, Rory, and Marshall struggled to catch up with me, only doing so once I was out the doors and back on the streets in the cool autumn air.

"Lexi!" Caleb called out, taking my hand. "You okay?"

I nodded. "As okay as I ever am with this business," I said. "By the way, nice crowd you hang with."

"Easy," he said as if I had slapped him, letting my hand go. "I never said I hung with them. They're just business. It's all professional and customer service with them. Freelancers learn not to start making friends in those circles. That way you're not playing favorites. A job is a job."

"How ethical," Rory said.

"I kind of get it," Marshall said.

"Of course you do," Rory fired back. "You were there sizing up the crowd and practically handing out flyers to your store."

Marshall said nothing as I turned down Seventh Avenue.

"So what now?" Rory asked, catching up to me.

"Go home," I said. "It's late."

"Given the irate pace you're walking at, why do I think you're not just going to jump into bed and catch some zzz's?"

Sometimes I hated that she knew me so well, but I had things I needed answered right now and I didn't necessarily feel like getting into it with everyone just yet. Things had taken a personal turn in there.

"You guys get some sleep," I said, already plotting my course through the city back to my home on Saint Mark's Place. "I've got questions I need to find answers to, for myself."

Twenty

●

Alexandra

Much like the road to Hell, my walk home alone was paved with good intentions. I'd hit the guildhall and start searching through the books of Alexander Belarus, hoping to unwind truth from fiction in what Laurien had told me. My kin was *not* a murderer, not that the witches and warlocks were going to take my word on it unless I had proof to the contrary. I needed to know the truth about my great-great-grandfather's activities, if only to help get the Convocation on my side, and that would hopefully be found hidden in his secret notes throughout the books I'd accumulated back at my place. I made it all the way down to the basement of my building and into the hidden guildhall, but after only thirty minutes of preliminary research my body shut down.

I awoke later to Rory nudging me. When I lifted my head heavy with sleep from the stone table at the center of the subterranean chamber, my notebook came with it, plastered to the side of my face.

"What time is it?" I said, snapping up to a sitting position.

"It's like nine," she said.

"Okay, good," I said, stretching. "We can get breakfast, then hit the books."

"Breakfast?" Rory asked. "It's nine, Alexandra. *At night.*"

"Shit," I said, panicking. "You're kidding, right?"

Rory rubbed my back. "You needed the rest after last night," she said. "All of us did."

I set about rearranging the table I had messed up in my sleep, moving my spread-out notepapers to one section and organizing them into the order they had started in. "What time did you get up?"

"Me?" she said, laying down her dancer's bag on the stone floor. "I was up and at 'em about seven thirty this morning, but I only had dance rehearsals, not all this obsessive compulsive bullshit to contend with."

"Don't start," I said, going over a sheet of book reference numbers I had jotted down before falling into my coma last night. "But if I beg you to run upstairs and get me something to eat, I'll be your best friend forever."

"You're already my best friend forever," she said, turning and walking toward the exit of the guildhall. "Since elementary school."

"Well, you wouldn't want to jeopardize it all starting now . . ."

"Yeah, yeah, yeah," Rory said, heading out the secret door.

Since she seemed like she was actually going to do it, I decided not to press my luck and went back to sorting out all the reference book numbers I had notated. I was so deep into the detective work that I didn't snap out of it until Rory dropped one of my breakfast-in-bed trays in front of me, a pizza box from Lanza's sitting on top of it.

"You went out to Second Avenue?" I asked, opening the box. Black olives and artichoke hearts beckoned from within the cheesy, saucy goodness that met my eyes.

"It just seemed easier than sorting out your kitchen," she said, grabbing a slice before pulling herself up on the one clean spot at the far end of the massive table.

"Fair enough," I said, digging into a slice while looking over my notes.

By the time I pulled my face out of my notebook, I was surprised to see more than half the pizza was gone, four discarded crusts on my plate alone.

"Whatever happened to you not working so obsessively?" Rory asked.

"This *is* my non-obsessive pace," I said with a smile. I pointed at my face. "But I'm in a good mood, despite having lost a day of research."

Rory gave me a funny but suspicious look. "You *are* smiling; I'll grant you that," she said, "but this doesn't seem like the kind of letting up you promised me and Marshall, Lexi."

"It *is*," I insisted. "First of all, you're here *by choice*, right?"

She nodded. "You didn't nag me into participation today, so yes."

"Getting the band back together doesn't mean less work," I said. "It just means I have more support when I need to get things done. And besides, my promise to relax more was made *before* last night's Witchapalooza."

Rory gave me a thumbs-up. "More work, less bitching," she said. "Got it. What exactly are you looking for?"

"I'm not entirely sure," I said as I headed off to the ever-growing wall of books that had overtaken one entire side of the guildhall. My current top-shelf titles had little room left for them. I whispered out to the stone, willing a piece of it to protrude farther out of the wall so I could force my latest addition into place. "In the same way Alexander had discreetly recorded the secrets of the Spellmasons in dozens of cross-referenced books to ensure their safety, his historical notes on his lifetime are also stretched out over the same number of volumes. If what Laurien told me about Alexander is true, I *need* to find out the truth about my great-great-grandfather. He built this guildhall, I assume with the intent of using it, but there's no record of an actual guild forming, as far as I can tell. He simply closed up shop and set about building the grand old architecture of this city instead. If I can figure out why, then maybe that's one more way to get the Convocation on our side, by changing their minds."

As I placed the book upon the newly formed shelf,

something scraped across my shin. I startled, looking down to find my trusty golem Bricksley there, his tiny arms cradling a different book.

"Thank you, Bricksley," I said, taking the book from him, slotting it into its space upon the wall.

"All hands on deck, I see," Rory said, picking him up. "Even the tiny ones."

"I could use a little help from someone a bit more advanced than Bricksley, though," I said, offering Rory a stack of books I had noted as I pulled them from various spots on the wall.

Rory did not look stoked as she took the pile from me with some reluctance and picked up my brick golem, but nevertheless she settled in at the end of the table.

"What am I looking for exactly?" she asked, setting Bricksley down on the table next to her. He set about straightening things in that OCD, paranormal-automaton way of his.

I set down a pile of books I had pulled for myself as a starting point. "I think we can kill several birds here with one stone," I said. "We're looking for anything you see that references my great-great-grandfather either talking about the guild he wanted to form . . . or maybe an apprentice he took in."

"Got it," she said, and flipped open one of the ancient tomes in front of her.

"And while we're at it, keep an eye out for anything that mentions Robert Patrick Dorman."

"The one who has a rage on for Warren," she said. "The one who destroyed the family tomb."

I nodded. "Look for mentions of Warren, too, while you're at it."

Rory looked up from her book at me. "I'm surprised you're so focused on this warlock's case," she said.

"Why?"

Rory shrugged. "Your dance card was already pretty full," she said. "But I get it. He's a bit eccentric looking, but Warren's not too hard on the eyes . . . in a magical-hipster sort of way."

"What?" I asked, somewhat astonished. "No. He's strictly business for me. And don't let him hear you call him a magical hipster. I'm not sure what he can or can't turn you into if he hears that, but trust me, it won't be good."

"You *sure* he's not dating material?" she asked, more as a gentle dig than anything by her tone.

"Like I need another man in my life," I said.

"But he *is* in your life," she reminded me. "Why go out of your way to do anything for this new guy when you've already got more than you can handle going on?"

"Because he's a finite set of problems that intersects with my interests," I snapped. "Okay? Most of the gargoyle violence in this city is random. They hadn't been organized until the Butcher started forming his band of cultish cronies. Warren O'Shea is an actual target of the Butcher. *That's* something I can focus on."

"Easy," she said. "I was just kidding about him being more than a business thing. Don't be so touchy."

"Sorry," I said, calming myself.

"Why does the Butcher even want him anyway?" Rory asked.

While Caleb and I had been the ones who dealt with Warren initially, I realized there was much I hadn't told Rory. And, it dawned on me, I realized why.

"To settle a score with the family who helped take him down the first time," I said. "But . . . there's another reason that's really driving me on this."

Rory hopped up on the edge of the table. "Okay . . . Spill it, Lexi. I know that look. You're hesitating."

"While the Butcher may want Warren dead, he also has this thing called the Cagliostro Medallion now. When Caleb and I went to the cemetery, we weren't just looking for the Butcher's remains. I wanted to check the O'Sheas' family plot. It had been destroyed. The Butcher tore the whole mausoleum apart, in search of the medallion, and it's most likely in his possession now."

"Why do you care so much about that damned piece of jewelry?" she asked.

"It does something that I want."

Rory hopped down off the table and came right up to me. "What, Lexi?"

"It has the power to turn stone into flesh," I said. My face rushed red as I awaited her judgment, but all my friend did was stare at me with surprise in her eyes.

"Oh," she said. "I see."

"Do you?" I asked with sincerity.

"That's . . . that's a game changer, Alexandra, now, isn't it?" she asked. "Have you told Stanis?"

"Not yet," I said.

"Why not?" she asked. "If he knew, maybe it would help motivate him, help get his people working double time looking for this Butcher."

"I don't know why I haven't told him," I said. "What if it's something he doesn't want?"

Rory shook her head, almost laughing. "Why wouldn't he want it?"

"He's got Emily," I said.

"Emily?" she repeated. "Are you kidding? Look, I liked the lady gargoyle well enough the few times we've met, but she's charity work. She's Stanis's pet project, a broken person locked in stone form. Don't mistake that for anything more than it is."

"And what about Caleb and m—" I started, but Rory cut me off with a raise of her hand.

"As your oldest friend, I'm going to support you no matter what, but let me just say this one thing," Rory said. "And I say it with love: Caleb is no Stanis."

"I know," I said with a laugh. "Believe me, I know."

That stopped my best friend short. "I'm surprised to hear you say that," she said.

"So am I," I said. "But after what I found out last night . . ."

"What?" Rory asked.

"I'm done with Caleb," I said. "He manipulated Stanis into keeping his distance. I don't know if I can forgive him for that."

"Yeah, that sounds like the Caleb we met," Rory said. "Sorry, Lex."

"I'm the fool," I said. "I thought he had more than proved his worth. He always proved helpful and atoned for the mistakes he's made. Sure, he used to run with a bit more dangerous crowd, if those witches and warlocks we saw were any indication, but I guess some people are incapable of real change. We *were* good for each other."

Rory grabbed my shoulders and locked eyes with me. "Who are you trying to convince here, Alexandra? Me or you?"

I fell silent. When the girl was right, the girl was right. For as long-lived as our friendship was, it was one that rarely got into a cycle of guy talk. Oddballs that we were, our dating lives had both been less than interesting and our conversations always gravitated to more fascinating subject matter like books, music, and, as of late, the arcane world.

A talk like this seemed long overdue, and I couldn't argue about which of us I was trying to convince more.

I realized Rory was still waiting for a response in the growing silence that was passing. Instead, I stepped past her, scooping up Bricksley and the book he was carrying.

"We should get back to work," I said.

"Oh, no, no," Rory said, grabbing my arm and spinning me around so hard I almost clocked her with our little brick friend. "You've had enough braining for one day."

"I have?"

Rory nodded, handing me my backpack. "Yes," she said. "You have. I'm getting us out of here."

"But there's so much more I need to look up, trails I need to follow through these books and the ones up at my parents' building on Gramercy."

"That can all wait until later," she said, dragging me toward the door that led out of the guildhall. "All work and no play makes Lexi a dull girl, remember?"

"Okay, fine, fine," I said, finally giving in and walking without being dragged along. "But where are we going?"

Rory pushed me through the door hidden behind the bookcase leading out into the basement library of my building. She pirouetted as she passed through the arch of the doorway.

"It's just a jump to the left," she said, and ran for the stairs leading up to the door that opened up onto Saint Mark's.

I slid Bricksley into my backpack, giving him a little smile. "Dammit, Janet," I said, then shoved him down in the bag before throwing it onto my shoulders and running after Rory.

Sometimes your friends were the only ones that could remind you to be sane, especially when your own brain was so far down an obsessive rabbit hole that you thought about changing your name to Alice.

Twenty-one

Alexandra

I had forgotten there was actually such a thing as a good kind of exhaustion, but there we were—Rory and I—covered in post–*Rocky Horror Picture Show* rice, newspaper, confetti, and bits of toilet paper. I might pay for it all come morning, but getting my cult music theater on was still an easier task than reading my arcane brains out or running all over Manhattan playing superhero. I hated to admit it, but Rory had been right to pull me away from my day-to-day insanity.

Tired as we were, I chose for us to walk across the Village like we were all of sixteen again, when the worst that would have happened was a stern talking-to from my parents. The stretch of Fourteenth Street between Fifth and Sixth was relatively quiet at three a.m., and I couldn't help but yawn over and over as we moved crosstown.

"Not to alarm you," I said, my voice cracked and shot from singing along with the show tonight, "but I may start snoring as I walk."

Rory laughed. "That tired?" she asked. "You're the night owl."

"Relaxing is *exhausting*," I said, leaning my head on Rory's shoulder. "Seriously. It's like my brain doesn't know what to do with itself when it's not soaking up arcana. I miss the simple life of just wanting to be an artist, but truth be told? I'm not sure I'd know what to do with only that on my plate."

"You *are* an artist still," Rory insisted. "Just in a different medium than you expected."

"I suppose," I said. "I just wish my creations didn't tear up the city so much. The sooner I figure out the truth about my great-great-grandfather, the sooner I can get the Convocation on board with our greater efforts with Stanis to bring this gargoyle population under control."

"And if you happen to score the Cagliostro Medallion along the way, well, that's just a bonus."

"Please," I said, rubbing my forehead. "Stop. It's hurting my brain just thinking about it right now."

We walked east in silent exhaustion down the rest of the block, but as we turned the corner onto Broadway, the sight there woke both of us in an instant.

For three a.m. I expected Union Square Park to be at best filled with a few late-night stoners and students drunk off their asses. I certainly wasn't prepared to find it filled to over-flowing with people everywhere.

"What the sweet crap is all this?" Rory asked. "Some kind of late-night NYU rally?"

"I don't know," I said, grabbing the magical loop of cloth around my neck that Marshall had given me, "but hoodies up, okay? We don't need this many eyes on us."

I pulled mine into place, which I was surprised to find so relaxing. There was a comfort in anonymity, and thanks to Marshall, Rory and I could walk among the crowd without drawing any undue attention to ourselves.

"There," Rory said, pointing off to our right far ahead.

At the north end of the park the crowd was even thicker where the pathways and benches gave way to a large paved section. I knew it well, having explored the spray-painted labyrinth mazes that now were underneath the mad crush of people.

But not just people. Towering shapes several feet higher than the tallest person in the crowd moved among them.

"Gargoyles," I said. "Look at them all."

"There have to be at least a dozen," Rory said.

The *grotesques* moved like slow ships among the sea of humanity, a sight that was hard to absorb given the general state of relationships between our two species.

"What are they doing?" I asked, and without waiting for an answer, I started pushing my way north toward the far end of the park. Though the going was slow against the tide of people, moving closer made it easier to make out the details of the individual gargoyles involved here.

When I saw a familiar angel among them, I relaxed and smiled. I leaned over to Rory, lowering my voice. "That's the one Stanis and I met," I said. "Nathaniel." The angel meandered through the crowd, taking his time as he strode along in silence. "It looks like someone decided he *is* a joiner, after all."

"Yeah," Rory added. "A real gargoyle of the people."

The other gargoyles came to rest, simply standing silent and still among the crowd. If I didn't recognize my great-great-grandfather's artistry in their carving, I would have thought them just statues.

Nathaniel alone moved through the crowd then. People pressed closer and closer, their arms and hands stretched out just to touch him as he passed. Stanis's father would have torn them apart, but Nathaniel's face was awash with patience, not shying away from their touch.

I turned to Rory for her reaction, but she gave a simple shrug.

"I guess it's a unique approach," she said. "You wouldn't find Stanis doing this."

"True," I said, "but he spent centuries avoiding contact with humans because of the rules my great-great-grandfather bonded him with. I do think, however, that the gargoyle Stanis is now would have eventually gotten around to something like this."

"I don't know about that," Rory said.

"He's just cautious. I would be, too, if I had the maniacal mad-lord father he had. He's one to choose to err on the side of caution first."

"This doesn't seem all that cautious, either," Rory said.

"I'm not sure causing a mob at three a.m. is such a smart idea on the part of Nathaniel and his friends."

"Me, either," I said, "but the crowd seems to be enjoying it. I think Stanis would be jealous."

Rory cocked her head at me. "How so?"

"Just of the acceptance."

"I'm not sure this is acceptance, Lexi. Look at everyone's faces."

I examined the bunched-up areas of the crowd that pressed in closest to the gargoyles. There was awe in the eyes of those people, the kind usually reserved for the faces of celebrity stalkers on *TMZ*.

"It's like a cult," I said.

"Yeah," Rory said. "It begs the question, doesn't it? Why are these gargoyles doing this? Why is this crowd so enthralled? I don't get it."

"I do," I said. "In a city as big as ours, everyone is looking for something, some kind of meaning, right? To these people . . . Well, who knows what they make of these *grotesques*? It's the closest thing to superheroes they've got, right? Imagine what Marshall would be like if he ever met Spider-Man."

"I don't have to imagine," she said. "He was pretty unbearable the time he met Stan Lee."

Two people shoved past me in the crowd as they headed toward the gathering of gargoyles, nearly knocking me over. I was about to yell at them, until I realized I recognized their faces.

Detective Rowland hobbled through the parting crowd like a train pushing its cattle catcher. Even with the limp, she was still outpacing her partner as he followed after her.

"Hey!" I called out to them, but with the dull murmur of the crowd all around us, it was hopeless.

"Detective Rowland!" I called out, louder this time. "Maron!"

The two of them were wary-eyed and looked about ready to jump out of their skin, but hearing the formality of their names gave them something to latch onto in all the chaos. When Maron caught sight of Rory and me, his face relaxed, but Rowland wore her now-familiar scowl.

"Is this your doing?" she shouted across the crowd, whose entire focus was on all the gargoyles off in the distance.

"Nice to see you, too, Detective Rowland," Rory shot back.

I laid a hand on her arm to shut her up.

"This isn't something of my doing, Detective Rowland," I said. "We just stopped to see what all the commotion was about."

Maron's eyes searched out over the crowd. His finger went from gargoyle to gargoyle as he counted them and scribbled in a notebook cradled in his hand. "Any of these creatures yours?"

I shook my head. "I don't think so," I said. "Although I have met one of the angelic ones." I pointed to where Nathaniel was moving among the crowd, wings spread wide as he took his time so everyone had a chance to reach out and touch him. "He's one of the good guys."

"So what is this?" Maron asked. "A simple meet-and-greet?"

I couldn't help but shrug. "Your guess is as good as ours," I said.

"We have no idea," Rory said.

Detectives Maron and Rowland moved closer, all four of us trying to absorb the entire scene. Far away, Nathaniel's lips moved, but between the excitement of the crowd and our distance from him, none of our group could make out what he was saying.

"Screw this," Rowland said, pushing forward through the crowd once again. "We need to know what he's saying."

Maron fell in behind her, and Rory and I did the same, passing through the crowd in their authoritative wake. Even in plain clothes, the two detectives still carried themselves as cops, and as they went, people seemed to sense their authority and got out of the way.

When they closed to about twenty feet away from Nathaniel, they stopped. Rory and I followed suit, and were pleased to find we were finally able to hear Nathaniel's voice.

"That's right," he said to the people he passed among. "Get a feel for your future. The Life Eternal is humanity's next great evolution."

"The Life Eternal?" Rory repeated in a whisper to me. "Please don't tell me this is the new Scientology."

"Let's hope not," I said. "Although as far as religions go, I'd say actual physical proof of gargoyles beats out theoretical space aliens on the believability scale . . ."

The gargoyle Nathaniel continued examining the crowd as he went. When his eyes came in my direction, I couldn't help but slip behind someone taller in the crowd. Even though the gargoyle couldn't see my features within the artificial darkness of the hood, I feared even the hoodies might give us away. I didn't want to draw any notice if I didn't have to, at least not until we had heard what he had to say.

"There are those of my kind who would keep themselves secret from you," he said. "Doesn't that make you wonder what they have to hide? *I* come before you with others of my kind, an angelic messenger sent to give you guidance in these chaotic times. The skies are full of winged beasts, filling you full of terror, no doubt, but I am here to tell you there is nothing to fear. We welcome you among us; we have nothing to hide."

A smatter of applause broke out among those closest to him, and grew as it worked its way out into the crowd. Cries of "Hallelujah" and praising of various gods broke out here and there across the park.

I sighed and shook my head. "I fear Nathaniel Crane has traded up his human life for a more evangelical stone one," I said.

The detectives nodded in agreement, but their eyes remained fixed on Nathaniel as he basked in the crowd's adoration.

"We do not shy away," the angel said. "We do not fly above you, judging, hiding . . . and why should we? We are the Life Eternal. And those who wish to join us will well have a chance at our kind of life."

The hair on the back of my neck stood up as I started to tense in anger. I had watched my father give the greater part of his life over to religious zealotry, and listening to this crock of shit out of this gargoyle was more than I could take. I pushed forward through the crowd past all my friends, unable to control myself.

"Oh, really?" I shouted, losing control of my astonished anger. "And how exactly do you plan on going about that, Nathaniel?"

The angel stopped midstride in the crowd and gave a slow turn until he caught sight of me moving toward him. Even though he couldn't make out my face within the sheer darkness of the hood, there was recognition in his look. "Well, well . . . ladies and gentlemen, this is *indeed* a rare treat. May I introduce . . . *my* creator."

This time it was wild applause that erupted throughout the crowd, the enthusiasm a strange counterpoint to my anger. These *followers*, these *easily swayed*, these *sheep* . . . Their ignorant clapping bliss only enraged me further.

"Oh, no, no . . . I'm not responsible for that guy," I shouted to the people all around me. "Nathaniel, tell them!"

The crowd parted as the massive form of the angel closed with me, even the detectives backing away to leave only Rory to come forward to stand at my side. Nathaniel stopped in front of me, leaned close, lowering his voice.

"Like it or not, you *did* create me, Miss Belarus." His words were calm and calculated, and I hated the truth in them.

"What exactly are you promising these people, Mr. Crane?"

"I only offer these people the same chance that was given to me," he said. "The Life Eternal."

"My creation of you wasn't some grand plan," I said. "I hate to break it to you, but you were at best a mistake."

Nathaniel grinned. "What you call a mistake, I call divine intervention," he said.

"You can't expect these people to take you seriously," I said.

"Look at them," he said, raising his hands straight out over the crowd. "We walk like gods among them, each and every person wishing they could become like us. And through their servitude, they will get that chance. They, too, can take the stone form and live forever."

The crowd erupted into wild applause once more.

Rory scoffed. "If you think Alexandra's going to start churning out *more* gargoyles like she's some kind of factory, you are very sadly mistaken, pal."

"How quaint," he said, looking at her. "You think we need your little friend for that?"

There was so much confidence, so much *hubris* in his voice, I wanted to drop the nearest building on him.

"Don't you?" I asked.

Nathaniel shook his head, and turned his back to us, his wings almost knocking over the detectives at the side of the open circle. The gargoyle's people crowded in around him like remoras to a shark as he walked away from us. Several of the other gargoyles moved through the crowd to assemble behind him. At about twenty feet away, he turned back to us.

"Think of yourself as a chef," he said. "There isn't one be-all and end-all way to properly prepare a meal, is there? There are many variants of recipes for each dish. So it is with the taking of the stone. If you won't serve us, rest assured, we *will* find a way of our own."

"Good luck with *that*," I said. With the secrets of the Spell-masons known only to me, I knew the guy was screwed. Now if only these people knew it . . .

"Of course," he said, his words having a dark whimsicality to them, "we *could* always make you." Nathaniel switched his focus to address the sea of humanity. "People of New York City . . . if you so desire the Life Eternal, your first act will be to secure these two women."

Rory reached for the art tube across her back, but I stayed her hand.

"Don't give anyone ideas," I whispered to her. "You pull that *glaive guisarme* out here, our detective friends will probably go for their guns. We don't want anything escalating too quickly."

I checked the detectives, praying they didn't do anything rash. When I caught their eyes, the crowd behind them was already getting restless as they sized us up. Thankfully, the two detectives *didn't* go for their guns, instead choosing to run over to us while the mob was still contemplating how invested they were in doing Nathaniel's bidding to earn the Life Eternal.

As an initial answer, a trash can crash-landed next to us with a clattering of cans, crumpled papers, and breaking glass. And not to my surprise, it had been someone in the crowd and *not* one of the gargoyles. In fact, the gargoyles had taken a position of observation farther away as if waiting to see which of their gathered humans might take us down.

Sadly, the trash can wasn't the only thing thrown at us. As mob mentality took the crowd over, anything and everything they had in their hands or that they found came flying in our direction. Bottles, cans, books, and bits of stone from the park itself rained down over us.

A full plastic cup of soda struck Detective Maron in the chest, the lid and straw popping free as its contents spilled out, soaking him. Both detectives reached inside their coats, but I reached out and grabbed both their wrists.

"Unless you've got bullets enough to take down this entire crowd, I suggest you keep your guns out of sight."

The two of them hesitated, but their hands remained inside their coats, still poised to draw.

"With a growing crowd like this?" Rowland asked. "Don't worry. Other cops will be arriving here in no time."

The mob was closing in on us quick, the faces of our fellow New Yorkers filled with a hatred for us then. We were to them, after all, in defiance of an angel.

"No offense but NYPD's response time will be too damned late," I said, dragging the two detectives by their wrists. "Follow me."

Rory didn't need any prompting and was already backing away from the oncoming press of people.

Pushing my power out around me like a plow, I started west crosstown, hoping to clear a path toward Eighteenth Street. Our magic hoods would keep our identities concealed, but a display of power was what we needed if we were going to escape the hundreds and hundreds of people bearing down on us. The pavement below my feet resisted my power, but I was far too in need of an escape, not to mention feeling

damned well determined. As we walked, the painted laby-
rinths below tore apart as chunks of pavement cracked and
rose up on either side of us, driving the crowd back. My intent
wasn't to hurt anyone, merely keep them from getting at us.
Exacting control of my power proved impossible. Finessing
it as the entire population of the park moved in on us was far
too distracting to keep plowing a steady path.

Several cries arose from the mob as large chunks of the
pavement slipped free from my manipulation and rolled off
into the people all around us, all of it moving at a velocity
meant to scare, not harm.

"Sorry," I cried out to no one in particular.

"Sorry?!" Rory said, her back pressed to mine as she used
her now-assembled pole arm to swat at anyone who dared
cross into the wake of our escape path. "Lexi, they'd tear us
apart if they could!"

"I know," I said. "Doesn't mean we need to stoop to their
level, though."

I shut up and redoubled my efforts to plow through the
crowd, and as we approached Eighteenth Street just off Broadway, my continued attempts at finesse finally paid off. The stone
of the broken pavement pressed out of my way and drove the
crowd back, forming a short wall that proved difficult to climb
for the few insistent pursuers who tried to scale it. Still, several
people managed to come over it and run after us.

"We're not going to make it," Detective Rowland shouted
from behind me, and I turned to see her pulling her gun out.

Immediately the crowd roared, a mix of fear and anger
that added a new and nervous energy to an already nerve-
racked situation.

"We *are* going to make it," I shouted back to her, not even
able to start arguing about her foolishly pulling her gun.

"We're *not*," Rory said, which surprised me. I had expected
to hear something disparaging from the detectives, but not
my best friend.

"I hate to say it," she continued, "but there's simply too
many of them. They're going to swarm us."

"Not if I can help it," I said and sprinted forward, the

pavement of the road spilling before me like I was Moses parting the Red Sea.

We crossed over Broadway and started onto Eighteenth Street heading for Fifth Avenue, leaving the open space of the park behind, but not the mob of people. They streamed behind us into the canyon of buildings rising up on either side of us, the roar of the crowd becoming deafening.

"Keep running," I shouted to the only three people not intent on killing me, and stopped. Rory and the detectives passed by me as I spun around to face the crowd.

"Lexi, what are you doing?" Rory asked, stopping right behind me.

"Just a little construction," I said, raising my hands high above my head as they went through a series of somatic rituals as fast as I could switch their positions. I forced all of my will forward in me, the rush hitting me like a brain freeze after an ICEE, and whispering my family's ancient words of power, I brought my hands down onto the pavement.

There were only two outcomes possible: either my hands would break as they slammed against the pavement of the road with all my might, or the entirety of the road would give way to my power. I had to count on my will in this. I could not hesitate in what I was about to do, although every bit of my rational mind told me to kiss my hands good-bye.

I fell to my knees as I brought my hands down, and just as I felt the scrape of pavement against the skin of my knuckles, the road buckled and my hands sank into it. I might as well have been thrusting my hands into a sink full of water given how effortless it felt, but I didn't take the time to pat myself on the back just yet. That was the easy part.

My will ran down my arms like an electrical charge. From sidewalk to sidewalk I bent and buckled the entirety of Eighteenth Street. I imagined snapping it the way you'd shake out a rug, and the road rose up in response like a grand wave. Cars flew, rolled, and crumpled as the street bent and twisted like a Dalí painting. The front line of the mob stopped short as the pavement wave rose up, the next few rows of still-charging people slamming into their front line.

My last sight of the crowd as the pavement wall rose higher and higher was of them scrambling over one another as they tried to retreat. With every inch I raised the wall, the pressure in my head grew and grew, but I was determined. *Higher,* I thought. *Higher.* We needed something that the crowd would think twice about even attempting to scale.

As the road rose up to about the third floor of the buildings on either side of us, a cloud of dust filled the street and something in the pressure within my head gave way. Dizziness overtook me and I slumped forward, my arms pulling free from the pavement, my face hitting the solidity of the street.

"Lexi!" Rory cried out, and was down next to me on the ground in seconds.

With care she eased her hands under me and rolled me over, sitting me up. My head spun but before I could bonk myself real good again, Rory had her arm underneath both of mine and lifted me to my knees.

"You okay?" she asked.

"I think so," I said. "I feel a bit disoriented and shaky, a bit scraped up, but I think I'm fine."

Detective Maron joined Rory and the two of them lifted me up, holding on to me for a moment until I could support my own weight once more.

"I'm fine," I said, brushing them both away. "Really. I just feel like I have the worse migraine ever."

"Gee, good thing that didn't escalate," Rory said.

I went to speak but a warm sensation running down my face prevented me.

"You've got a nosebleed," Rory said.

Detective Maron reached into his inner pocket and produced a handkerchief. "Here."

I took it from him and held it to my nose. When I pulled it away, the entire cloth was bright crimson. My knees buckled at the sight of so much of my own blood. I pressed the cloth back to my nose.

"I think I've got some studying up to do," I said.

The detectives both stared up at the massive wall that separated us from the mob.

"This seems more than sufficient," Detective Rowland said, managing for once to crack a smile.

Maron whistled. "No shit."

As the bleeding stopped and the dust all around us began to settle, I dropped the handkerchief and hurriedly pulled off my backpack. I opened it and pulled Bricksley free from it, both detectives giving me a wary look.

"What the hell is that?" Rowland asked.

"It's my stone golem extraordinaire," I said. "Bricksley."

"Bricksley?" Maron repeated.

I nodded.

Rowland sighed. "I don't even want to know."

Maron took off his dust-covered coat and shook it out. "So that Nathaniel is one of the *good guys* . . . ?" he asked.

Detective Rowland broke into a coughing fit over where the dust was still kicking around against the pavement wall, and I joined her, searching along the massive stretch of it.

"If he's one of the good guys, I'd hate to see the bad ones," she said.

"He's *not* a good guy, apparently," I said.

"Really?" Rory asked as she fought to catch her breath. "How could you tell? Was it the ordering those people to attack us?"

"Did you check out any of the gargoyles who were with him?" I asked.

Rory shook her head. "Sorry," she said. "I was too busy thinking about our chances of dying."

"I did," Detective Rowland said, which didn't surprise me. I would have expected an officer to be taking in all the details they could, especially in a crisis situation.

"And?" I asked her.

"I recognized a few of them, actually," she said. "They were part of the gargoyle crew that showed up the night Detective Maron and I tried to apprehend you and your friends at the armory."

"Exactly," I said. "And what did the serpent-headed one say . . . you know, before you blew his head to dust with a shotgun? He said that they served a new master."

"Hold on," Rory said. "You think this Nathaniel Crane is the guy they're serving? I thought you and Stanis had him pegged as a petty thief when he had been human. Hardly sounds like leadership material, you know?"

"That's the thing," I said. "I don't think that angel *is* Nathaniel Crane. I think that's what he told me on the night Stanis and I found him because we caught him by surprise and he was outnumbered. Maybe that gargoyle he destroyed right before we got there was Nathaniel Crane and he just used the name when we interrogated him. But that display by 'Nathaniel' in the park just now? That's the kind of gargoyle angel who is leadership material. The way he carried himself, the pomposity. He's not just a crony in servitude like the rest of them to the Butcher of the Bowery. I think the gargoyle who called himself Nathaniel Crane is really Robert Patrick Dorman. That angel *is* the Butcher."

Rory sighed as she began dismantling her pole arm. "Looks like he's traded up butchery for playing a minor deity to the masses."

"We're going to need more than just your hunch to go on," Detective Rowland said. "Procedures and all."

"I know," I said, holding up Bricksley, his tiny arms and legs flailing, his permanently drawn-on smile always bringing me a bit of cheer no matter how grim the occasion might be. "That's why I've got my little friend here."

I pressed him up against the hole at the side of the pavement wall so he could see into the park beyond.

"Bricksley," I said. "You see that large angelic creature there? The one at the front of the crowd?" His tiny left hand on the end of his metallic arm gave a thumbs-up. "I want you to follow him. See where he goes, what he's up to. Don't get caught . . . by him or other humans, okay?"

Another thumbs-up.

"Great," I said. "Then I want you to come home, to our guildhall on Saint Mark's. Be careful, Bricks."

Stupid as the cops might think it was, I hugged the rough texture of the brick golem and slid him through the hole in the wall. The crowd beyond was already turning from it, much of the fight having gone out of them, which was fine by me. By the time the cops would actually arrive, hopefully there'd be less of a riot quality for them to deal with.

Bricksley—well below eye level—skittered away across the park, vanishing from my sight into the whole of the crowd when he was about fifty feet away.

"Gargoyles going this public, interacting with the crowd and stirring them up into a bloodthirsty mob," I said with a shudder as I stood up and shouldered my backpack once more. I started down Eighteenth Street. "I need to talk to Stanis."

"Hey!" Detective Rowland called out from behind me. "What about all this property damage?"

The sounds of car alarms and broken store windows rose up into the night air.

I turned and gave the two detectives my sweetest smile. "You heard what Rory said. The Butcher thinks he's a minor deity now. Have the city write this off as an act of God for the insurance."

I didn't wait for a response. A few hours of relaxation with Brad, Janet, and Frankenfurter had done me good, but now? I was back on the clock and there was a gargoyle I needed to see before the sun came up in a few hours.

Twenty-two

◖

Stanis

The opportunity to simply wander the paths of Gramercy Park had been rare over the past few centuries, but thanks to Alexandra, I had my own version of the park at my disposal. I tried to forget the date-night intrusion my last visit had caused her and Caleb, but tonight the park was all mine as I awaited my maker's kin.

Nearby the tiny brook babbled, the wind rustled through the trees, and the only thing to disturb their calming sounds came around forty minutes into my wait as the sound of stone scraping against stone caused me to turn. Alexandra stood in the frame of the door hidden in one of the pillars.

"Glad to see you're getting some use out of the park," she said as she shut the secret door behind her.

"It does me good to come here and think sometimes," I said. "To get away from Sanctuary, my fellow *grotesques* . . . everything. I find the tranquility and stillness up here of some comfort."

"Things good with Emily?"

Her question surprised me. It was rare that Alexandra asked about my near-constant companion. "Yes," I said.

"Where is she?" she asked, propping herself up on the short wall along the edge of the pathway I stood upon.

I smiled. "As I said, it does me good to get away from *everything* at times." I studied Alexandra with a bit more care. Her eyes were heavy, her hair more tangled than usual. A single flap of my wings would drive her right over the wall into the man-made stream behind it. "You look exhausted."

She rubbed the heels of her palms in her eyes and pulled her hair back into a bun. "Long night so far," she said. "And it's not over yet. Have your people had any luck tracking down the Butcher?"

"It has become a bigger project than I had imagined," I said with frustration.

"How come?" she asked.

"These *grotesques* at Sanctuary are not like my father's army," I said. "His men were old-world militia, men raised to fight and follow. These creatures that I have gathered . . . They were lost souls, all of them damaged somehow from their humanity. They come from all walks of life. The transition is not a smooth one for all. Still, there are some who show promise. That monk you brought me from the Cloisters, Jonathan. He considers himself still in the service of the Lord and has been most helpful in trying to help my people cope with their transformations and new life."

"That's great," I said. "But any ETA on getting them on board?"

"Every night we are expanding our search parties, but so far there has been no luck."

"Well, *I've* had a productive night," she said.

"Have you?" I asked.

"I've found mention of an apprentice who briefly studied with my great-great-grandfather," she said.

"Really?" I asked.

Alexandra gave a weary nod. "The mention disappears quickly from my grandfather's notes," she said.

"Interesting," I said. "I do not recall my maker taking an apprentice."

"More importantly," Alexandra continued, "after a little 'Time Warp' action with Rory, we met the Butcher."

I was not sure what "a little 'Time Warp' action" was, but all questions about it died as I took in the last part of her sentence. "You met the Butcher," I repeated.

"Yup," she said, "and guess what? So did you."

"I think not," I said. "I would remember such an occurrence."

"Remember the *grotesque* we met on the roof the other night?" she asked. "The one who was acting all calm and gentlemanly, carrying that other *grotesque*'s head around?"

"Nathaniel Crane," I said. "Yes. He had just done away with one of the Butcher's men."

Alexandra shook her head at me. "Not quite," she said. "I'm pretty sure Nathaniel Crane *is* the Butcher."

"I thought we were looking for a Robert Patrick Dorman," I said.

"He was *lying* to us," she said, her voice darkening with anger.

"So that angel statue is host to one of the most reprehensible warlocks ever known?"

"And we *had him*," she said, her exhaustion mixing with her anger now. "We even caught him red-handed having destroyed another gargoyle. How did we miss that?"

"Simple," I said. "We were looking for someone more . . . openly sinister. Take my father, for example. His madness for power made him obsessive. That obsession led to irrational behavior, which is not something easily hid."

"I still should have known," she said, apparently adamant on the point.

"Do not beat yourself up too much about this, Alexandra," I said. "Mad men of power do not rise by luck alone. They are clever. They possess charm; they are charismatic. How else do you think they rise if not by the use of these skills of enticement?"

"No," she said. "If I hadn't been running myself ragged, I would have caught it."

"*I* did not catch it," I reminded her. "And I do not get this 'ragged' of which you speak."

Frustration filled her face, her eyes on the verge of tears. She wiped at them with the sleeve of her coat and took a deep breath.

"I'm really trying here, Stanis," she exploded, her words coming fast. "I really am. I've been head-deep in books today, then running around town. There's just too much going on. It's overwhelming." There was anger and despair in her words, in the way she spoke. Then she looked up at me with a pained laugh as she fought to pull herself together. "But I don't suppose you'd know anything about that, huh?"

I cocked my head. "What do you mean?"

"You never need to rest," she said. "You're like that Energizer Bunny. You keep going and going and going. Most of my problems exhaust me, but you? You don't exhaust. You *can't* exhaust."

"You mistake a need for sleep for exhaustion," I said. "My mind often fills with exhaustion, and I wish that I could sleep."

"But you sleep during the daylight hours," she said.

"I would not call that sleep," I said.

"No? What would you call it?"

"Oblivion," I said.

"What's the difference?"

"Even though centuries have passed, I can still remember sleep," I said, smiling with the recall. "There is little left that I recall from my human life save for sleep. To sleep was to dream."

"And now?"

"With the rising of the sun, it is true my form changes, but there is no sleep in it. It is truly oblivion. My mind ceases to exist. There is not the chance to dream. It is this I miss most of all."

Alexandra adjusted herself on the stone wall of the path, looking down at her feet. "What if . . . what if there was a way you *could* dream again?"

"I do not understand," I said.

"Before we met with the witches and warlock community of Manhattan, we had met with Warren O'Shea."

"This I know," I said.

"You don't know all of it," Alexandra said. "We have a mutual agreement of sorts going on."

"One should never enter lightly into a pact with people of an arcane nature," I said as if addressing a child. Given her inexperience in the ways of the magical world, perhaps she was one.

"I know, I know," she said. "But Caleb was there for it."

"That does not give me any additional comfort," I replied, saying it as evenly as I could, hiding my ire.

"Nor me, either," she added.

I cocked my head. "What do you mean?" I asked.

"I confronted Caleb about what you told me," she said, looking up at me with soulful eyes. "We're working through this arcane crazy, but as far as the two of us . . . we are over."

I did not know what to say to that, and after several moments of silence, I went back to the real conversation at hand.

"You spoke of a mutual agreement you have with Warren O'Shea . . . ?"

"You and I are already trying to deal with the *grotesque* situation here in Manhattan," she said. "Warren's problem just happens to intersect with our goals. He wants this Butcher dealt with and so do we."

"And for saving this warlock from destruction, what do we get in return?"

"He's taken me before the Convocation," she said. "The witches' council."

"Alexandra," I said with disapproval in my voice. "You went before them without me? Did you think for a second you did not need protection among their kind?"

"I *had* protection," I said. "Warren had invoked his right of parlay with the head of their council, Laurien. And I brought my own backup. Caleb, Rory, Marshall . . . Besides, you weren't even around."

"I had business of my own," I said, thinking back to my conversation with Emily and Detective Rowland on her rooftop. "You should be hearing from Detectives Rowland and Maron about that."

Alexandra's face filled with confusion. "What have they got to do with you?" she asked.

"I went to assist them, like you asked," I said. "And I may have asked a favor of them in return. Something I had them looking into looked like it might be blood magic, but I could not be sure. I asked them to show it to you."

"You should have brought me along," she said, her voice short and curt.

"These days it is difficult to find you."

"Try harder, then," she insisted.

"Forgive me," I said, not appreciating her tone, "but the world does not revolve solely around your schedule, Alexandra. I have my people to think about, Sanctuary . . ."

"And Emily," she said. "Don't forget Emily."

"I am sorry," I said. "Is that what this is about? Have I offended you somehow?"

Alexandra jumped down off the wall, pacing with her arms folded across her chest. She shook her head. "No, I . . ."

I grabbed her by her shoulders, stopping her and forcing her to look up at me. "Easy," I said. "Take your time."

"That wasn't the only bargain I made with Warren O'Shea," she said. "There's an arcane artifact. The Cagliostro Medallion. It belonged to his family for generations. If I can reclaim it from the Butcher, he promised it would be mine."

"What does this medallion do?" I said, letting go of her shoulders.

"Cagliostro was a well-known alchemist," she said. "It's said the medallion can turn stone to flesh. I bargained with O'Shea for it, because I . . . I thought you might want to wear it. I thought . . ." With growing frustration she turned from me and walked farther down the path before turning back around. "I don't know what I thought, okay?"

Her words hit me harder than anything that had managed to take a swing at me over the last century. "An item like that is a fairy tale, Alexandra," I said. "No such thing exists."

"Warren assured me that it *does*," she said. "And I believe him."

Alexandra composed herself and came back over to me, wrapping her arms around me.

"Alexandra . . ."

"Think of it," she said, not letting go as she laid her head against my chest. "Really think of it. I never gave it much thought before. I've always pushed away the idea because I was with Caleb and it seemed impossible, but after we talked about how Caleb dissuaded you from pursuing me, I had it out with him. I can't deny it any longer. There's always been a connection between you and me, Stanis. I just used the fact that you were what you are and I was what I was as a reason to not go there . . . but now, when there's even the slightest possibility that you could be human again . . ."

I found comfort in her words, and returned her embrace, always careful to control my strength. Feeling Alexandra this close reminded me of the early days of our meeting, of the bond and connection that had existed back then. While some of it had been due to the connection to her that her great-great-grandfather had set upon me centuries ago to watch over the family, it had always been more than that, had it not?

Still . . . I took my arms from around her and gently pushed myself away from her.

"What of my people?" I asked.

"What of them?" she asked.

"I cannot abandon those at Sanctuary," I said. "Although they may be people of stone, they are *still* my people. I have sworn to protect them . . . to lead them, to keep them from harm, to offer them sanctuary. Who am I if I am not a creature of my word? My people need me."

"No," she said, her voice shaking now. "Say what you really mean. Emily needs you. And you need her."

"I . . ." I stopped myself. "I do not know if that is true."

"It's true," she said. "You just don't want to say it in front of me."

I could not admit it, but Alexandra was right.

"Perhaps we should allow this magical community of yours to decide the fate of this medallion," I said in an effort to maneuver the conversation to a different topic.

Alexandra laughed.

"I can't even get their commitment to help with our gargoyle problem because they're so tied up resolving their own infighting," she said. "You think they're going to be able to decide which one of their factions gets so precious an item? No. *I* bargained for it with the man who has a rightful claim to it. It's mine to do what I want with. If I can find the damn thing."

I nodded. "As you wish," I said.

To my surprise, she threw her arms around my neck and jumped up so I had to catch her, cradling the last of the Spellmasons in my arms. The closeness was not an unwelcome sensation, I realized.

"What are you doing, Alexandra?" I said, wary.

"There is a great freedom in speaking about how I truly feel," she said. "Even if you can't reciprocate. So let's get back to work, shall we?"

"Very well," I said, her sudden easiness with me almost contagious, relaxing me. "So what next?"

"I'm thinking a fresh set of eyes—*yours*—might prove useful in rechecking the last known whereabouts of the medallion," she said. "How do you feel about a trip up to Central Park?"

I leapt into the air and shot off into the night sky, heading north.

"It would seem you have already answered that question for me," I said, allowing myself to enjoy the collaborative effort for once. It reminded me of the old days, which was not the worst thing in the world.

Twenty-three

Alexandra

I can sleep when I'm dead. I can sleep when I'm dead.

The words repeated over and over in my head like my own personal mantra as Stanis and I flew across the night sky.

Although I had caught up on sleep the night before, since then it had been nonstop research, a break for the most cardio-driven cult classic movie ever made, and an evening almost exploding my brain while summoning a pavement wall to escape a mob engineered by gargoyles. Why not add an emotional breakdown with the creature whose arms I flew in as we headed up to Central Park at three a.m.?

The only thing keeping me awake right now was the cool night air in my face and an adrenaline rush as we darted across the night sky.

"Who are you taking us to?" Stanis asked.

"His name's Fletcher," I said. "He's . . . I don't know what he is, really, but he *did* get me into the secret cemetery last time. He's . . . special."

I guided Stanis up Central Park West until we hit the Seventies and I had him bring us down just beyond the tree line along the wall. Stanis stood still, taking in the area as I jumped down out of his arms.

"Don't worry," I said. "The park is empty. I think it technically closes at one, but few stragglers are out and about now."

The big guy seemed to relax a little, folding his wings in close to him.

"Come on," I said, heading for the path.

Stanis looked down at the sign with its arrow. "Strawberry Fields," he read.

I stopped and turned to him. "Have you not been before?"

"I do not believe so," he said.

"It's a monument to John Lennon."

Stanis's face didn't move.

"Of the Beatles . . . ?" I added. "Come on now!"

Stanis's face lit up. "Ah, yes," he said. "I know of this particular group."

"I should hope so," I said, starting up the path. "They're only one of the biggest rock-and-roll bands of all time."

"Yes," he said. "I have seen them perform."

I stopped and spun around on the cobblestones. "I'm sorry; what?"

"Out in Queens County, there once stood a public arena. Some nights I heard music coming from there and I would go see what was going on. Perhaps a handful of decades ago I heard so grand a commotion I could not pass up a visit. It was there I saw the ones you call the Beatles."

"Unbelievable," I said. "You saw the Beatles at Shea."

"You know of this performance, then?" he asked.

"*Everyone* knows about it," I said, laughing. "It's a huge part of America's music history." I turned and headed back up the path. "You're going to love this, I think. Come on."

"As you wish," Stanis said.

I *hoped* Fletcher was here. I mean, as a spirit of the forest, or whatever he was, that appeared bound to the park itself, where the hell else would he be? If I couldn't find him, maybe I could use the mosaic with "Imagine" across it as some sort of summoning circle. It seemed to make decent sense to check there first. After all, this was where Caleb had brought me to first meet the guy.

"Fletcher . . . ?" I said as the clearing opened up in front of me onto Strawberry Fields.

Fletcher was there at the center of the circle. In fact, he was all around the circle. There were pieces of him everywhere.

Immediately Stanis's wings were up and out as he dashed forward into the open area. I stayed in place, examining the situation before daring to move farther into it.

The space was devoid of any other people or creatures save for the fallen form of Fletcher. Once I felt confident there was no one lurking, I moved forward with great hesitation. The figure was so lifeless, his body broken, torn apart.

"Is this . . . *Was* this your friend?" Stanis asked.

I nodded, still unable to speak with the sudden shock of finding him like this.

Stanis walked around the edge of the mosaic, looking at the murder scene from every angle.

"There's so much blood," I said when I could finally find my voice once more.

"There is a pattern to this," Stanis said from the other side of the circle.

"What?" I said, forcing myself to look back down at Fletcher.

Fletcher's body was laid out like da Vinci's *Vitruvian Man* and circled by his own blood. His form was barely recognizable with so much damage to it, what was left barely torn bits of flesh.

"Whoever did this must have great power at their disposal," I said, trying to take in the terrifying scene. "I'm not sure what Fletcher was exactly, but he wasn't just human. He was long-lived and there was a force of nature to him. If something took him down like this, we've got serious trouble."

Stanis kneeled down along the edge of the circle, examining the body. "This was done by a gargoyle," he said. "Or several."

"You sure?"

"I know the claw marks of my own kind," he said, "having inflicted some of my own over the years."

"I need to call Caleb," I said, my hands shaking as I pulled out my phone. "He needs to know what's been done to his friend."

By the time Caleb arrived, I had taken the time to write most of the symbols drawn in Fletcher's blood down in my notebook. The gruesome nature of the task had me trying to pretend it was some macabre art project, if only to keep me from throwing up.

Stanis had gone silent while waiting, looking more like a statue in the park than anything. Caleb hugged me and I let him. When his eyes met mine, I couldn't help but tremble a little as the stress of the evening caught up with me.

"Jesus," Caleb said as he walked around the circle. "This is ritualistic in an arcane way, all right."

"That would be my guess," I said, "but this is so far out of my league I wanted you here to check it out. And I thought you should be the first to know."

"Thank you for that," he said, and got down close to the ground to examine the scene better. "Whoever did this didn't just want him dead. They wanted his power for their ritual."

"To what purpose?" I asked.

"I'm not entirely sure," he said, "although a few of the symbols look familiar. This is some strong blood magic."

"Warren said that the Butcher was into that, right?"

Caleb nodded.

"And these marks," I said, pointing out the different claw marks on what remained of Fletcher's body. "Stanis said they were made by a gargoyle."

Caleb hunkered down over a particularly bloody part of the circle, hovering his hands over the area. "From the feel of it, the spell isn't that old."

"From the feel of it?" I asked.

Caleb waved me over. I got down on my knees next to him,

and he took my hands. "Hold your hands over these two marks," he said, easing my hands forward into the circle.

Below my hands were two distinct claw patterns, as if someone like Stanis had pressed them into the blood itself. At about six inches over them, the dull crackle of power rose up from the prints.

"Feel that?" he said, letting go of my wrists.

I nodded.

"That's blood magic," he said, standing. "That's the power of life, twisted to arcane use."

I looked up at him. "If you had to guess, what do you make of it?" I asked.

"As I said, some of the symbols are familiar," he said, "and that major one at the top of the circle is the one for 'seek.' It's some form of detection spell."

"Maybe he *doesn't* have the Cagliostro Medallion yet," I said.

"But I thought you said he got it when he desecrated the tomb of the O'Sheas?"

"What if someone beat him to the punch?" I asked. "What if someone took possession of the medallion before he could get his claws on it?"

Caleb considered it as he looked down at the remains of his friend. "Either way, Fletcher died to power this spell of the Butcher."

"And it's my fault," I said. "For not having acted against the Butcher when Stanis and I had a chance to. I won't make that mistake again."

"And how do you plan to go about doing that?" Caleb asked.

"Like *this*," I said, and before I could overthink it, I slammed my hands down on the two claw prints. The dull tingle of arcane energy crackled to life like lightning running up my arms, shotgunning to right behind my eyes, and my neck snapped back. Although I knew I was looking straight up into the night sky over Manhattan, that was not what I saw.

My brain felt like it was being pulled in all directions at the same time and my mind's eye filled with visions of the streets of Manhattan. I wasn't anyone or anything that I could identify, but my vision was moving at a breakneck speed. I passed through cars, trucks, buildings. It was all I could do to try to keep my bearings, but it wouldn't have mattered. A familiar sight where I had been hours earlier filled my vision—Madison Square Garden.

My jaw clenched tight, the muscles in my neck clenching harder the longer I was in the vision. I phased straight through the glass doors we had entered through earlier, only this time passing through the walls and seating beyond. The arena was in a greater display of raw power than before. Explosions, sprays of color, and lightning filled the entire arena, much of the earlier fighting seeming to have escalated to larger conflicts.

The vision became frantic, darting around the room from conflict to conflict, searching. The volume of arcane activity only confused me, the motion too much for my head, and just as quick as it had come upon me, the image of Madison Square Garden slipped back down a tunnel of darkness like the end shot of a movie.

My head spun as I returned to the real world, and I was falling. I would have ended up facedown in the circle of blood if Stanis had not swooped low across it to catch me. He arched his back and brought me to stand, letting go as he opened his wings and dropped back to the ground in front of me.

"Are you okay?" Stanis asked.

Caleb was by my side a second later, throwing an arm around my shoulder, steadying me on my still-shaking legs.

"I think so," I said. "Although I feel like my head might split open or I might throw up. Or both."

"Good," Caleb said, and there was an anger to it.

"Excuse me?" I asked.

"You're lucky that's all that happened," he said. "What were you thinking, jamming your hands down on those claw prints?"

"I'm fine," I said.

"Yeah," he said, not letting up. "*This* time. Tell me, Lexi, what do you know about blood magic?"

"What did you want me to do?" I said, getting testy myself. "I took a chance. You said yourself the magic wasn't that old. I wanted to try it before it faded any further."

"You don't know what you're dealing with!" he shouted. "You don't know what power you're channeling or what the consequences of that will be. For Christ's sake, Lexi, look at your hands."

I looked at my own hands, dizziness overcoming me when I saw they were coated with blood. Fletcher's blood.

Hot tears poured uncontrollably down my face. I couldn't stop looking at my hands. They looked positively black and shimmering out here in the dark.

Caleb kept his arm around me and reached into his coat with his free hand. He pulled out one of the more fragile vials he kept rolled in cloth, undid the wrapping, and slid the vial back into his coat. Using the rag, he wiped at both my hands until the blood was gone.

By the time he was done, I had pulled myself together, or at least as together as I was bound to get this time of night.

"What did you see?" Stanis asked when he saw I had calmed down.

"I was back at Madison Square Garden," I said. "That spell was actively trying to seek something or *someone* out. Whatever it was, it was there at the Convocation, but there was too much magical interference for it to zero in on what it was looking for." I turned and looked down at the circle once more, my heart aching for the person who had once been Fletcher. "I'm not sorry I risked doing that. I'll research the symbols in the morning."

I picked up my notebook and slid it into my backpack.

"I have seen this before," Stanis said. "This sort of circle."

Caleb and I both looked up at him.

"You have?" I asked. "Where?"

"These markings are similar to the ones used in Emily's murder."

"Is that what you've been investigating with Detectives Rowland and Maron?" I asked.

Stanis nodded.

"Great," I said. "Then I can call them in on this."

"You sure you want to do that?" Caleb asked. "You bring in the police and who knows what they're going to make of this. Fletcher wasn't even *human* as far as I can tell. They bring in the coroner on this, we may be opening up a whole brand-new can of worms, anatomically speaking. They'll cart Fletcher off to Area Fifty-one, and next we'll be seeing photos of him on conspiracy theory websites alongside alien autopsies."

"Loath though I am to admit it," Stanis said, "Caleb does have a point."

"Like it or not," I said, "the world *is* changing. We all already bear the heavy burden of responsibility for that. Maron and Rowland are just the tip of the iceberg as far as the regular world absorbing what they've being exposed to more and more every day. I think it's time we got the rest of the force off their back treating them as a laughingstock and gave them something like this to deal with. It may be a para-normal murder scene, but it's *still* a murder scene. I'm calling it in to them."

Neither of them spoke as I pulled out my phone and dialed Detective Maron. I only hoped I was making the right deci-sion in doing so. If bringing the police in on this created more problems than it solved, I wasn't sure there was room enough left in my guilty heart to add anything more on top of poor Fletcher's murder.

Twenty-four

Stanis

I awoke in Alexandra's replica of Gramercy Park as the last rays of sunlight disappeared behind the horizon, my body aching as always from the painful transformation back into living stone. Having stayed in Strawberry Fields with Alexandra, Caleb, and Detectives Rowland and Maron most of the night had left me with little desire to rush back to Sanctuary. I had returned here after last night's madness, craving once again the solace and comfort of the space Alexandra had created for me.

The interior of her building on Saint Mark's was silent as I made my way down through it, my wings drawn close to prevent any damage to Alexandra's belongings. It was not until I entered the library on the bottom floor that I heard the quiet sounds of activity.

The hidden door to the guildhall was ajar, and, moving the stone with ease, I entered the room behind it. Within the chamber, Alexandra, Aurora, and Marshall were all gathered around a stone table, each of them involved in their own piles of work, no words being exchanged. I watched them for several moments, letting their somber mood settle over me.

"Have I come at an inopportune time?" I asked.

The humans looked up from what they were doing.

"It's *all* an inopportune time," Alexandra said and went back to the book in front of her.

I looked from her to our blue-haired friend. "Is this how you have spent your daylight hours?"

"This is what she does," Aurora said with a shrug. "She throws herself into her work. Forgets to eat, forgets to shower . . . That's why Marshall and I hang around. Someone's got to mind the care and feeding of the Alexandra."

"Alexandra," I said, stern, but all I garnered from her was a quick glance in my direction.

"Shouldn't you be giving a speech at Sanctuary or something?" she asked. "Rallying your troops?"

"Many of those who have come to Sanctuary came there for refuge," I said. "It is at best a difficult task to convince them to put their newly reclaimed lives on the line to seek out this nefarious Butcher and his men. I have those such as Emily and Jonathan who are working among my people, but it will take some time."

Aurora looked up from the book in front of her and brushed her bangs off her glasses. "The sooner you get them on board, the sooner you might find that Cagliostro Medallion, and could, you know . . ." She nodded her head toward Alexandra.

I looked over to her, but the Spellmason was so intent on writing something down it was clear she had heard nothing Aurora had just said. "So you know about the medallion, of Alexandra's intentions with it."

"I do," Aurora said with a smile. "Don't you think it would be cool to be able to hit the town with us without it being all combat or shrieks of horror?"

This was not a conversation I wished to have among our mutual friends, realizing we were actually down a member.

"Where is the alchemist?" I asked.

"Fletcher's death is not going to go over well with the witching and warlocking community," Alexandra said. "Caleb felt the news would go over easier if he told them. And . . ."

Alexandra looked away as she crossed her arms across her body.

"And what?" I asked.

There were tears in her eyes when she looked back to me. "I *made* him go talk to them," she said, "but not because their community lost a powerful ally. I made him go because I thought this would be the best way to try and get them on our side. I'm using Fletcher's death as a bloody *opportunity*."

Her last word came out with such disgust in it, I wanted nothing more than to offer her comfort.

"You did what needed to be done," I said.

"That's what I've been telling her," Aurora said, "but she won't hear it coming from me."

"What would you have me do?" Alexandra said, slamming her book down. "Someone else died because of what *I* set into action. And not just someone . . . a spirit of some kind that was trying to help us."

"Lexi, calm down," Aurora said, turning to Marshall. "Tell her to be reasonable, Marsh."

"I'd like to," he said, "but I can't."

"Excuse me?" Aurora asked him as she walked over to him.

Marshall laid down the materials in his hands and leaned across the table to look at Alexandra. "How can I tell her to be reasonable when none of what is happening to us *is* reasonable?" he asked. "I'm not going to invalidate how miserable she feels about it when I can't think of a better way to process it. If she wants to get down and be obsessive in her research, then let her. There's no playbook for any of this."

Marshall's words silenced all of them and actually brought a smile to Alexandra's face, which I found myself thrilled to see.

"Thank you, Marshall," she said.

"For the record, though," he said, going back to his work, "I don't think any of us blame you for what happened to Fletcher."

Alexandra nodded with pursed lips, and without arguing went back to her notes and books. I stepped around the table to her and rested my hand on her shoulder. "These are unusual times," I said. "Therefore to *not* react with frustration would be unusual."

Alexandra leaned her head against my chest, and for a brief moment I allowed myself to wonder what it would feel like if we found the medallion and it could be my skin against hers. There was also frustration in the thought for me, but I did not wish to add to Alexandra's burdens.

"What is it you hope to find in these books?" I asked, stepping back from her.

Alexandra composed herself and went to one of her open notebooks.

"Laurien had said that the Convocation had turned my great-great-grandfather away after one of his first students with them went missing," she said. "I won't believe he had anything to do with that, but Laurien was insistent he was up to no good. She practically laughed when I tried to defend his nobility."

"How would she know?" Marshall asked.

"They have their history," Alexandra said, holding up the current book in her hands, "and we have ours."

Marshall shrugged and went back to working on whatever the project was in front of him, tinkering with the bits and pieces of metal as he consulted a notebook of his own. I stepped around the table to him.

"And how does this relate to your search?" I asked, gesturing to his handiwork.

Marshall held up a gleaming cylindrical pipe that was slightly longer than the length of his hand to his elbow. He swung it through the air like he was casting a spell.

"This doesn't relate to her search," he said. "But I think it may prove of some help . . . at least to Rory."

"What is it?"

"Just something I've been experimenting with," he said, gesturing to the empty fixture at one end of the shaft. "I'm making a set of Horseman's picks. There's going to be a hammerhead on one side and a sharp point on the other."

"It is like a maul," I said, nodding with some understanding. "My father's men used them in defense of his lands back in Europe."

"Like a maul, yes," Marshall said. "Only smaller. Rory should be able to use two at once."

"If you can get them light enough," she said, joining us. "Marshall made me try wielding a couple of miniature sledge-hammers at Home Depot. I thought I was going to pull my arms out of my shoulder sockets."

"I'll work out the enchantments when they're done," he said, a bit short with her. "I wish you had half the faith in me that my store clients do."

Aurora mussed his hair. He tried to duck away, but she was quicker. "That's because they don't live with you, roomie," she said. "Hard to expect attention to detail from the guy who can't seem to put the toilet seat back down."

Marshall had nothing to say to that, letting Aurora muss his hair until Alexandra cleared her throat loudly behind them. They turned to her.

"We're never going to find out if my great-great-grandfather was an apprentice-murdering madman if you two keep screwing around," she said.

Aurora looked as if she could have argued with her friend, but instead silently went back to the pile of books she had been working on before.

I turned to Alexandra. "You mentioned this apprentice to me the other night," I said. "If Alexander had an apprentice, do you not think I would know about it?"

"No offense," Marshall said, going back to his notes and bits of metal, "but you've never been the most reliable one as far as memory is concerned."

"That was *before*, Marshall Blackmoore," I said, doing my best to hide a bit of exasperation. "My past was locked away from me until Alexandra recovered it for me. And she gave *all* of it back to me."

Marshall put down the shaft of metal in his hands and looked up at me with complete sincerity in his eyes. "Riddle me this, Stanis," he said. "If you don't *know* something, how can you *tell* that you don't know that something?"

I thought for a moment, my wings fluttering with agitation when I realized I was having trouble following his question. "What do you mean by that?" I finally asked.

"Let's say several centuries ago you *did* know about an apprentice," he said, "*but* Alexander blocked it from you. If that information suddenly isn't in your brain anymore, how can you be certain that it was being blocked, or was it simply something you just never knew anything of in the first place?"

"Stop it," Aurora said. "You're giving me a headache."

"Does it matter?" I asked him. "Either way, I do not recall or think Alexander took an apprentice."

Alexandra walked over to me, holding open one of her notebooks. "But according to some of his writing, he did," she said. "Scattered in all his books, there's a record—a very *short* record, mind you—of his taking an apprentice, but there isn't all that much to go on. He's spread the notes in that secret code of his over several books, but the trail goes dead pretty quickly."

Aurora shut the book she was reading, rubbed her eyes, and sat herself up on the edge of the table. She looked up at the ceiling. "Why build all this, then, if you're not going to train people?" she asked.

"I did not even know of this guildhall until Alexandra's brother's death," I said. "When the original building collapsed, we dug, discovering this place and thinking Devon dead."

"Could you at least get back to helping, please?" Alexandra asked. "These books aren't going to read themselves."

"I'm sorry," Aurora said, not moving, "but when I read words like *capitulary* and *catechumen*, my brain starts to hurt."

Alexandra looked up from her book. "That's what you were reading? It actually said *catechumen*?"

Aurora nodded. "Why?"

Alexandra moved down the table and snatched up the book.

"In the ecclesiastical sense, it's a person being instructed in the rudiments of Christianity," she said, flipping through the pages. "But another, more laymen term for it is *neophyte*, which is anyone being taught the elementary facts or principles of any subject. Like Spellmasonry."

Like a creature possessed, Alexandra tore through her notes and went through the book before her, and several minutes passed in silence before she slammed her main notebook shut.

"Well?" Aurora asked.

"The book talks about a hidden catechumen, a lost apprentice," she said. "Marked by the Belarus family seal among the sconces of the wall here."

Alexandra stepped away from the table and went to the edge of the circular room. She looked up at the protruding stones, but there was nothing carved on them.

Marshall and Aurora ran to others, but they, too, were blank.

I circled around the room looking closely at all the sconces that jutted out of the wall, stopping at a section thirty feet away from Alexandra.

"Only these two are marked," I said, indicating the ones in front of me. There was no mistaking the stylized *B* set over the batlike wings carved there.

Marshall came over to me, pulling out a small flashlight from his pocket. He shone it across the stone that stuck out from the wall, moving from one to the next.

"He's right," he said. "All the rest were definitely blank."

Alexandra readied herself with a spell, falling into a stance and moving through the motions of it, but unlike the rest of the guildhall, this section of stone would not react to her command.

"There's resistance," she said, lowering her arms. "Like it's locked."

"So what do we do?" Aurora asked.

The humans fell silent for several moments as they contemplated their next move, but knowing the puzzle-building nature of Alexander so well over the centuries, I had a thought.

"Your great-great-grandfather marked the location on the sconces along this section of the wall," I said, looking to Alexandra. "I believe you should light them."

Alexandra's eyes sparkled with delight. She turned to Marshall. "Can you make some kind of arcane fire?" she asked.

"Can I!" Marshall said with excitement. "Wait . . . Can I?"

He went to his coat lying on the table, pulled out a notebook of his own, and began looking through it.

"I think I can," he continued, and ran to the glassed-in shelves and started pulling down different alchemical mixes.

Aurora hopped down off the table and moved closer to the door. "I'll be over here," she said. "In the non-exploding section . . ."

I doubted any mistake Marshall might make would harm my form and stayed where I was.

Marshall ignored Aurora and continued working, changing the contents of several vials, flasks, and tubes over and over until he decided on two and held them up. He walked to the area between the two sconces and looked up at them before looking over to me.

"A little help here . . . ?"

I walked over and lifted the man with ease, using care not to exert too much strength for fear of crushing him. He poured half of the two vials together in one sconce and then the other, blue flames flashing to immediate life within them.

"Try now," Marshall called out to Alexandra.

I set him back down as Alexandra took up her pose once more, foreign words springing from her lips. The section of wall between the two fires began to shift. Stones moved around one another, sinking into the wall, disappearing and reappearing in stacks just inside the room itself, revealing a dark opening behind it.

The grind of stone against stone continued in the wall as the space continued to shift, carrying something forward out of the darkness.

"What the hell . . . ?" Marshall asked, shining his flashlight into the space.

A long wrap of off-white cloth moved to the edge of the hole in the wall until it passed through and upended onto the floor of the guildhall.

The bundle shifted, unraveling. The taut skin-over-bones of a human hand and forearm tumbled free of it, the metal rings on it clacking against the stone floor—the kind a witch or warlock might wear.

Alexandra dropped her spell and ran forward as the stones ground to a halt. Kneeling next to the bundle, she grabbed the edge of the cloth and pulled it away using just the tips of two fingers.

"Congratulations," Marshall said, although his voice was quiet and did not hold the tone usually associated with the word, "the Belarus family has an actual skeleton in their closet."

Aurora joined us by the body. "But *whose*?"

"Apparently, my bloodline is more murder-y than I thought," Alexandra said, standing up, the color gone out of her face as she turned away. "My great-great-grandfather *did* murder his apprentice."

Twenty-five

Alexandra

I awoke to a low, steady thud against the door to my building, only to find Bricksley slamming himself over and over against it out on Saint Mark's. I was relieved to see that my little golem looked unharmed from the mission I had set him to the other night. How long he had been throwing himself at the door, I had no idea, but the scattered chips of wood from the door itself indicated it couldn't have been all that long.

Curious what his findings would be, I risked waking everyone as I phoned around to my crew and gathered them in my living room in just under an hour as I filled and checked over my backpack in prep for wherever Bricksley's expedition would lead us.

"You look like Luke Skywalker with Yoda when they're training on Dagobah," Marshall said from his place on my couch. "You know, from *The Empire Strikes Back*."

"I know what it's from," I said as I adjusted the zipper so that Bricksley was securely fastened in but also protruding from my backpack. "I'm not a total cultural illiterate."

"We ready?" Rory said, dropping her dancer's bag in my living room. Her hood hung around her neck like an infinity scarf, her art tube poking up over her shoulder.

"If you're packing Mr. Hack and Slash in that thing, sure."

The four of us headed out of my building onto Saint Mark's Place.

"Just keep it out of sight for now," Caleb said. "This is strictly recon. We don't want to draw any attention. We simply check out whatever Bricksley discovered; then, once we have evidence, we bring it before Warren, Laurien . . . the whole Convocation if we have to."

"Lead on, Bricksley," I said. My golem's tiny clay hand came up and pointed uptown, so we headed over to Second Avenue and then began walking uptown.

Rory fell in step next to me as we went.

"You sure this is going to work?" she asked. "I mean, I love Bricksley probably more than is healthy, but he's not the most complex golem out there."

"I was explicit in instructing him," I reassured her. "Follow the Butcher, and come back to us when you know where he is. He might not be the sharpest brick in the pile, but I trusted him with the task. It's bad enough I felt guilty sending him out all on his own, alone."

We walked along in silence for a few more moments until I felt a tear at the corner of my eye and wiped it away, drawing Rory's attention. "When they lock me away," I said, "make sure you tell them how emotionally wrapped up with a living brick I was, okay?"

"Tell them yourself," she said. "Chances are we'll be cell mates."

"That is some comfort."

We continued up Second Avenue until Bricksley indicated we should head west on Fourteenth Street, and our journey turned crosstown. Just past Irving Place, the little golem guided us to the intersection where Park Avenue South split into Broadway and Fourth Avenue.

"Union Square," I said, and although Bricksley was prompting us to enter, I hesitated.

"The park is *packed*," Marshall said, "and from the looks of it with an extra heaping spoonful of crazy."

Much of Union Square had become a shantytown since the other night. The green grass of it was set up with make-shift tents, lean-tos, and people just sleeping out under the night sky. With some reluctance we crossed the street and headed into the park. Up close there was a creepy, cultish vibe to everyone there. Some wore shirts with the words "Show Me the Eternal LIFE!" on them while others had signs lying against their makeshift homes with hand-drawn gargoyles on them, their messages swearing allegiance.

Rory drew in close, whispering, "May I remind you that some of these people were probably part of the mob that wanted to kill us the other night."

"I'm trying not to think about it," I said, concentrating instead on where Bricksley was indicating we should go. "Marshall, Caleb, walk in front of us."

The two men moved into place, Marshall leaning back over his shoulder.

"And we're doing this why?"

"None of this crowd will know either you or Caleb," I said. "Rory and I, on the other hand, might get torn limb from limb."

His face went pale, and with no further questions he turned forward and kept moving as I steered the four of us through the crowd.

"I would have thought the mob would have dispersed by now," Rory said.

"Me, too," I agreed.

"Are you kidding?" Caleb asked. "Remember Occupy Wall Street? It doesn't take much in this city to get people to drop what they're doing and jump on a bandwagon." Standing taller than the rest of us, his eyes scanned the crowd. "Although there is an abnormal amount of police on duty here."

"At least Maron and Rowland got them to take some of this seriously," I said. "Although, I bet they had to sell them on the simple premise of crowd control. I'm not sure how they would have fared if they said they needed more patrolmen to take on any gargoyles that might show."

As we approached Union Square West around Seventeenth Street, I could see the efforts of my handiwork from the other night. Much of the pavement wall still blocked off Eighteenth Street going west, although even now construction crews were working on its removal.

Its sheer enormity had me hiding in the back of my hood, as if it somehow absolved me of the chaos and destruction I was responsible for. Luckily, the gargoyles were nowhere to be seen and no one seemed to be paying any attention to us.

Bricksley motioned us down into the subway station at the north end of the square, and the four of us hurried down the stairs, glad to be away from the vibe of the crowd above.

"Bricksley has a MetroCard?" Marshall asked as we approached the turnstiles into the station.

"The implications!" Rory said.

"Shush," I said, and followed the pointing of my little brick golem through the station to the end of one of the platforms.

"Guys," Marshall said. "You know where we are, right?"

"Give me a minute," I said. "It will come to me."

Caleb looked around the mostly empty platform. "You mean we're *not* in a subway station waiting on the N to arrive?" he asked.

"You weren't around," Marshall said with enough bite to it that it shut Caleb down.

I looked to Bricksley. His tiny clay hand was pointing into the tunnel and up the tracks that led to the distant glow of lights at the Eighteenth Street station one stop up.

"I don't believe this," I said as it hit me. Checking the tunnel first and then the platform to make sure no one was paying attention, I jumped down onto the tracks. Rory nimbly leapt down as well, while Marshall sat down on the platform and lowered himself with care onto the tracks.

Caleb made no move to follow and just stared down at us. "You're kidding me, right?"

"Hurry up," I said, not waiting as I started down the tracks. "You'll want to see this place."

"See that rail over there?" Marshall asked him. "The one

I'm trying to stand as far away from as I can? *Don't* touch that one, got it? Otherwise, you should be fine."

"Comforting," Caleb said, jumping down to join us. "And what if a train comes?"

"You're the indestructible one," I called back. "I don't see what you're worried about."

Caleb ran past Rory and Marshall to catch up to me. "Just because I'm indestructible doesn't mean it wouldn't *hurt*."

"You'll be fine," I said. "Trust me."

The last time I had come this way more than a year ago, the path had been a difficult one, but now the boards and blockage that had once blocked off access to the older, unused sections of the old subway system had been removed. In fact, once we had ducked off the tracks between Fourteenth and Eighteenth, it was clear that all the passages had been expanded for something bigger than me.

"Large enough for a gargoyle to fly down, let alone walk through," I said out loud.

"Where are we going?" Caleb asked.

"Some of the old stations fell out of service over the years," I said as I continued down the unused tracks. "One of them was built by my great-great-grandfather. We had to come down here last year to recover something he had hidden away."

"And let's just say it didn't go flawlessly," Marshall said. "Not that I had a chance to plan for it, mind you."

"Oh, I'm sure this is going to go so much better," Caleb added, but I shushed him.

"There's noise up ahead," I said, and stopped in my tracks, as did the rest of my friends.

When I was certain the commotion I heard wasn't moving toward us, I switched to the set of tracks off to our left, using the darkness there to hide us from growing light up ahead.

As the familiar sight of my great-great-grandfather's grand old subway station came into sight, Caleb grabbed my arm.

"Remind me this is just reconnaissance," he said.

"Oh, yes," I said as I examined the station. The ceiling vaulted high over the main platform. The ornate carvings made by my great-great-grandfather covered the walls on either side of the tracks—stone Grecian soldiers towering three or four times our height, the grand scale of the place hauntingly awesome yet terrifying now that the platform was covered with gargoyles instead of just dust and broken statues as it had been on our last visit. I took a deep breath and let it out. "Just reconnaissance."

"I think I've reconned enough," Marshall whispered, and tugged at my sleeve. "We can go now."

I didn't move. "No wonder Stanis and his people were having a hard time finding them," I whispered back. "They've been flying the friendly skies while the Butcher and his people have moved where you'd least expect to find airborne creatures: underground."

There was much commotion among the gargoyles all along the platform, but it was what was happening at the far end that drew my attention.

The Butcher and his men had fashioned a long, low surface out of several of the fallen pillars. Crane himself sat on a raised platform that stood in front of the carving of the Greek Titans that overlooked all of the station. As we moved closer in the shadows off to the side of it all, the sounds of the chatter changed to that of whimpering. Upon the fallen pillars, a heavy-set man with long black hair was chained in place, the center of the platform itself caked in blood. Next to him a small blond woman was secured in the same manner.

The Butcher stood up and spread his angelic wings, and much of the platform settled down.

"Daniel Hoffman and Tara Novello," he said, looking down at the two figures, "those who seek Eternal Life among my kind must be prepared to give up their flesh. Are you prepared to do so?"

The man's head nodded up and down repetitively "I am ready," he said. "I no longer wish to be a part of this world."

"I am ready," the woman said, proving the less worked up of the two, her voice calm and even.

"Not all who come before us have been deemed worthy of the Stone," the Butcher said. "Not all are worthy. One will serve as a sacrifice to fuel the Taking of the Stone for the other. Tonight we let the fickle hand of fate decide who lives eternally and who dies, as is our custom."

A ripple of approval went through the crowd.

"This is, like, the worst lottery ever," Caleb whispered in my ear.

"On one clawed hand," the Butcher continued, moving to stand over the large man, "we have a man after my own heart. One does not come to such sloth easily, no. Our large friend Daniel here no doubt had to work hard to achieve this girth, and for his commitment to that, he must be given praise. The pleasures of the body—food among the highest of them—are something I miss greatly, hedonist that I was." He turned and moved to stand over the woman. "And here we have darling Tara. A nubile young thing. Once I reclaim my human form, oh, what fun we could have had together. Flesh is a weakness, but oh, what a weakness!" He ran his clawed hand down her side. "Alas, since tonight I have yet to reclaim my own flesh, I leave the choice to our assembly."

The crowd roared to life as they voted their approval for each one, shouting the name of who they thought should either die or become one of them. Through the noise of it all I honestly couldn't tell who was winning.

The Butcher studied the crowd before holding up a hand for silence. He walked over to the man, and looked down at him. "You, Daniel, have been found *unworthy*."

"Wait . . ." the man started, but the Butcher simply talked over him, dismissive.

"My dear man, I cannot simply have every last one of your dreadful kind coming before me expecting to receive the Life Eternal."

"Then let me go!" the man cried out.

"But we still need you," the Butcher said. "Your blood will fuel Tara's binding to the Stone."

The man began to struggle against his chains, his voice slipping into a keening cry that echoed throughout the platform.

I stood up from my crouch, and slipped between the support struts leading over to the track next to the platform.

Caleb grabbed my arm. "Whoa, whoa, whoa," he whispered. "I thought this was recon."

"It was," I said, pulling free, "until they were about to kill someone."

Rory's art tube was already off her back as she pieced together the pole arm within it. I slid my backpack off my shoulders and went for my great-great-grandfather's spell book instead of the one I had been creating for myself.

"Lexi," Marshall said. "Let's think this through."

I shook my head. "You can stay here and think. I've got someone I need to help. Or would you rather watch him die?"

Marshall sighed. "Of course I want to help," he said. "But we are seriously outnumbered here."

"No, we're not," I said. Without another word, I turned and snuck out across the track and lifted myself up onto the platform where the gargoyles were assembled.

I looked back at my friends down on the track. Caleb and Rory were already in motion, but Marshall was just staring at me. "How are we not outnumbered?" he whispered in a panic.

The gargoyles closest to me stirred, some looking over at us the way a human might look at a fly buzzing around them.

"Come on," Rory said as she jumped up onto the platform, her boots echoing as they hit. "Can't let Alexandra have all the glory or insanity, can we?"

"Fine," Marshall said, finally moving, "but if she gets us killed, I'm *not* forgiving her."

"Me, either," Caleb said, unbuttoning his coat, already going through the vials lining it.

"Fair enough," I said, starting my way through the crowd. "I, for one, am going to try my best to see that no one gets killed."

As the four of us came down the platform, the gargoyles parted to either side of us. If stone statues could look mildly amused at our presence, this was the right crowd for it. Every last one of them towered over us and it took all of my courage not to feel trapped in the middle of them.

As we approached the dais, we caught the Butcher's

attention and he smiled at us, his evil grin all the more chilling coming from the carved stone angel he was.

"Nathaniel Crane," I said as I went. "Or should I just call you the Butcher of the Bowery?"

"That, or Robert Patrick Dorman will suffice," the Butcher said. "Nathaniel Crane was the name of that gargoyle I had just killed when you and your gargoyle stumbled across me."

"And why did he have to die?" I asked. "What was his crime?"

"I asked him into my flock here and he refused," he said. "I have no truck with those who oppose me."

"Your crimes against the arcane community and your own stone kind are far worse than anything that gargoyle did, I assure you."

"You've clearly done your homework since we last met," he said. "Still, it's a pity those sheep at Union Square didn't take care of you the other night."

"You preach to those people like you're a god," I said, pointing up at the collection of Titans behind him on the platform. "You stride among them like one, and they worship you for simply existing. And what do you offer them in return? You lure people here under the promise of the Life Eternal and then use them for your rituals. And worse, you're using blood magic to do it."

"Well, you *did* tell my servants you were not going to help us, Ms. Belarus," the Butcher said.

"Haven't you already helped yourself enough already?" I asked. "Forming your little cult, stealing the Cagliostro Medallion . . ."

The Butcher cocked his head at us. "You know about that, do you?"

"We saw what happened at the cemetery," Caleb said. "And to my friend Fletcher."

The Butcher gave a deep laugh. "I attempted to return to the cemetery in the park, hoping to give the O'Shea family crypt a more thorough search for the medallion. Your friend died because he tried to bar my way. Although his blood did prove useful in attempting to discover the medallion's true location. And yet for all my efforts, the Cagliostro Medallion is not in my possession."

"I saw the way you tore oh so thoroughly through the O'Sheas' family plot the first time," I said.

"But despite my thoroughness that time and my last, that which I sought out was *not* there."

"So you killed Fletcher just to aid you in your search," Caleb said, not holding his contempt back

"It will be mine," he said, spreading his stone-feathery wings. "Do you know how long I spent without form or function before I was given this stone vessel?"

"I imagine for a notorious hedonist like yourself, it must kill you to not be able to take a human form," Marshall said as sharp as ever.

"No," the Butcher said. "I don't think you people *can* imagine my desire."

"I don't give a crap about your desires, gargoyle or otherwise," I said. "Let these people go. Now."

The angel looked genuinely surprised and amused.

"You come and make this stand before me, and just expect me to do your bidding?" he asked with a laugh. "You *did* look around you, yes?"

"Let these people go," I repeated. I kept my eyes on him, refusing to look at the vast number surrounding us. "If these two humans are guilty of anything, they're guilty of being too trusting, or perhaps they need the kind of help that *you* can't provide."

"Or they're stupid," Caleb whispered.

"Not helping," Marshall said, slapping his hand over Caleb's mouth.

The Butcher looked unconvinced. "And you think we will just hand them over to you?" he asked.

"Pretty much, yeah," I said, the conviction of my words as unwavering as my grip on the spell book.

"And why would I ever do that?" The joy in his voice at how little a threat he perceived us as drove me over the edge and I snapped.

"Because you forget where you are and who you are talking to," I said, straightening as I opened the spell book. "This station was constructed by Alexander Belarus, and you are dealing with the last Spellmason. My last visit here I was run out, but now that I've had the time for greater focus on my true calling? Well, let's just say I don't run anymore."

"You ran from here?" The Butcher chuckled. "What made you run?"

"That's on me," Marshall said, raising his hand and stepping forward. "I triggered something. Kind of a defiling-the-temple kind of thing." He pointed to the statues all around the platform, ending up at the towering Medusa behind the Butcher. "Made a few enemies in the process."

"But what once were enemies," I said, reading from the book and snapping my will out to all corners of the station, "are now allies."

The stone soldiers lining the walls came to life at my command. Behind the Butcher, the Titans on the platform writhed into motion and stepped out from behind the decorative wall that separated them. With a singular thought, I set all of the stone creatures to converge on the mass of gargoyles, whose wings unfurled as they took to the air or ran at the advancing stone soldiers.

"Holy crap," Marshall said. "Are you controlling *all* of them?"

"Yes and no," I said, checking the spell book, figuring it out as I went along. "Alexander set *some* protective parameters on them centuries ago. Like attacking you when you retrieved one of Stanis's soul gems for us. All these statues . . . they're not soulful in the same way *grotesques* are, but they understand my intent." The Medusa on the platform swung her snake tail, snapping one of the gargoyles in half, tumbling it off the platform onto the tracks. "And boy, do they pack a punch."

The Butcher himself was preoccupied with the Titan of Atlas, who had sprung to life right behind him. While it took several gargoyles to deal with one soldier at a time, the Butcher seemed fine going at it one-on-one with creatures at least three times his height. Atlas reached down to pick the Butcher up by his wings, but the gargoyle raked his hands down the creature's arms. Deep gouges appeared and, grabbing on, the Butcher gave a twist of his wrists, snapping off Atlas's entire forearm.

"Jesus," Marshall said from directly behind me out of harm's way. "Someone's been eating his Wheaties."

"We need a plan, Marshall," I shouted out to him. "Now!"

I knew Marshall to be a tactician and a planner, which was what I needed. With all the stonework in my control, it was hard to concentrate on much else going on in the subway station.

"Are we looking to win this fight?" he asked. "Not sure how great the odds are on that."

"Get us and those people out of here," I said, and set several of the stone sentinels to swatting some of the flyers out of the air. Broken gargoyles tumbled out of the sky, crashing into walls or back down onto the platform where they shattered on impact.

Marshall stepped out from behind me and ran forward through the crowd.

"Rory, Caleb!" he shouted out through cupped hands to our friends who were already locked in combat. "I need you to free those people!"

"On it," Rory called out. She slid her pole arm between the legs of the gargoyle she was locked in combat with, and twisted, tripping him. As soon as he was down, Rory ran for the horizontal pillar where the two people were chained down.

Caleb ducked under the swing of another gargoyle and ran past it in the same direction, vials already flashing out of his pockets.

Rory made her way down the platform with her dancer's grace, dodging the uncontrolled lashing of gargoyle wings, twirling out of claws' harm as she went. When she got to the pillar, Rory brought the blade of her pole arm down hard on the chains binding the man's hands. The weapon's blade cut through the links with ease.

Caleb simultaneously poured two of his concoctions together and spread it over the chains binding the legs of the female. The metal fizzed and hissed as gray smoke shot up from the reaction and the woman's legs came free.

The two of them set to work freeing the other ends of the

restraints. I turned away from them, needing to focus on the Butcher, who had just finished taking down his second of the Titans single-handedly.

"Hey, Robbie!" I shouted, hoping to taunt him. "Think fast!"

The Butcher twisted around, ignoring the other Titans converging on him. I whipped my mind out to the fallen pillar-turned-altar, sliding it out from under the two freed humans and shooting it toward the Butcher. His wings flew open and he leapt into the air as the pillar slid through the now-empty space.

"Not so fast," I said, pressing one end up and the other down, launching the piece end over end into the air, hoisting the weight of it with my will, driving a mental spike into the center of my brain.

The Butcher shot straight up to avoid it, but I was just a hair faster and the tumbling pillar caught his legs. It sent the gargoyle into an uncontrolled spin that drove him into the station's wall off to my left. He fell hard onto the subway tracks, but with a flap of his wings he stood once again in seconds. He leapt up onto the platform in a flash and I braced myself for his charge, but it never came.

Instead, the Butcher ignored me where I stood and ran off across the platform in the opposite direction. I started after him as he ran toward one of the still-standing support pillars.

No, not toward. *Through*.

The gargoyle threw his shoulder into the pillar at a full run, cracking its foundation. His momentum carried him forward, the base of the pillar breaking apart as the rest of the column reaching the ceiling high overhead showered down on the platform. I stopped in my tracks, which saved me from one of the heavy pieces crushing me. The others landed hard on the platform, bits of dust and broken, jagged pieces of rock showering down from the ceiling above.

As I crawled over the broken pillar, the Butcher was already running off in a different direction across the platform, going for another one of the support pillars.

I lashed my power out at the base of the pillar, holding it

steady in place, and when the Butcher struck it, it didn't budge. The gargoyle seemed to sense the resistance and instead drove his claws into the pillar itself. As he twisted his hands within it, much of it began to crumble away. While I was able to maintain control over some of the pieces, the damage became too extensive for me to hold on to. The weight of the column above it was too much, and the whole pillar collapsed in sections down to the platform.

Over the sounds of fighting all around me, the greater crackle and crunch of the station's ceiling giving way filled my ears. A quick look around the platform had me assessing the situation as fast as I could. Caleb and Rory were hobbling halfway down it with their two rescue victims in tow. Even fighting one-handed with a pole arm as she held the blond girl up, Rory was still able to parry away any attacks that came at her while Caleb drove other gargoyles back with concoction after concoction flying out of his jacket. Nearby, Marshall was dodging his way toward me.

"Go help Rory and Caleb!" I shouted to him. "We need those people out of here, now! Not sure I can keep this place together."

What little color remained in Marshall's face drained away, but he nodded, reversed direction, and chased after them.

I released the pillars from my power. At this point they were a lost cause and I had larger issues to deal with.

Huge chunks of the ceiling began to fall away. Despite my grandfather's superior stonework, the place simply could not withstand such an assault. Dirt and rubble poured down after the stonework had fallen away, and as if some sort of subterranean clouds had parted, there were suddenly lights shining down on me. Above, I could see the sign for Macy's hanging on a building as the ever-widening hold collapsed in to reveal it.

The cries of people above and the honking of horns filled the air.

There were no parting words. No villainous cackle. No "I'll get you next time, Gadget!" The Butcher simply signaled to his men and shot up and out through the collapsing ceiling of the station. Within seconds, he was gone and the rest of his people moved to follow.

Through the chaos of their departure, I realized I had a bigger problem. The flurry of wings and debris above gave way to the sight of innocent passersby falling as the sidewalk above crumbled away beneath their feet. With swift reaction, I called to the Titans and stone soldiers alike to catch them, working hard to finesse the creatures so nobody got crushed in my rush to action.

I was feeling really good about how it was going—the soldiers catching and then setting down the people out of harm's way—until the sound of two cars colliding took my attention away from it. The lights of a vehicle flashed into the now-massive sinkhole, and my heart fell. None of my soldiers would make it over to it in time.

"Caleb!" I shouted to the only person I thought capable of helping right now.

He turned, caught sight of the falling vehicle, and shoved the woman he was carrying in Marshall's direction. Without hesitation, he quick-drew a potion out of his coat, chugged it down with a wince, then leapt in the air like Superman bounding over a tall building toward the falling vehicle.

His body rose at a lightning rate, and for reasons that were about to become clear, he strangely spread his body out wide like he was a flying squirrel. My heart pounded in my chest to watch as he impacted with the front end of the car, but I had forgotten his indestructible nature.

The front end of the car crumpled, but thanks to Caleb's spread-out pose the damage wasn't concentrated on any one area of the hood, spreading evenly to prevent damage to those within the vehicle. More important, the momentum of the car's fall was minimized by the force of Caleb's leap, which meant the car came down onto the platform at a much slower speed. In the end, the people in the vehicle looked stunned, but thankfully alive.

Caleb, however, ended up entirely underneath the vehicle.

I ran over to him. "You okay?" I asked, only able to see one arm and just the top of his head poking out from beneath the vehicle.

Caleb managed a quick, "Mm-hmm."

I pulled open the car door, and motioned the family inside it toward the empty tracks. "Go. Hurry!"

They sat stunned for a moment; then the woman at the wheel undid her seat belt and grabbed one of her kids to get them in motion. As the husband grabbed the other, I took Caleb's hand in mine and pulled as hard as I could to drag him out from underneath the car.

He moaned and groaned until I had finished clearing him out from under it.

"Quiet, you," I said. "You're indestructible, remember?"

"Still hurts," he said, sitting up slowly. He held his hand out to me so I could help him up, but I made no move to do so. "Umm, Lexi . . . ?"

"Hold on," I said.

My eyes darted around the emptying platform.

"You're indestructible," I repeated, the word triggering in my brain, "but the Butcher *won't* be, *if* I can recover his bones . . . which he would have been keeping close after taking them from the cemetery. Just hold on!"

A chunk of debris smashed down on the car, crushing in a small section of its roof. "I don't think we have time to hold on," Caleb said.

"This is important," I said. "Stay here."

As I ran off toward the Butcher's throne area, Caleb called out after me.

"Lexi, I don't have the time to stay here," he said as he slowly tried to work his way up to standing.

"This is the Butcher's place," I shouted back to him, searching around the raised dais. "His inner sanctum. They *have* to be around here somewhere."

"The medallion?" he asked. "Lex, I think I believed him when he said he didn't have it. Why would he lie, especially since he felt like he clearly had the upper hand here?"

"I'm not talking about the medallion," I said, taking to the top of the dais. I scanned around me in a 360, my eyes stopping when they came to the short retaining wall that the Titans had been showcased behind. I leapt from the platform, running over to it.

"What *are* you talking about, then?" he asked, trying to avoid the still-falling ceiling and street above.

"This," I said as my eyes caught what I was looking for on the other side of the wall. I reached down and grabbed the withered skeleton lying there, its remaining skin feeling like a dog's dried chew toy against my skin. "Robert Patrick Dorman's bones."

Caleb gave me a grim smile. "Can we go now?" he asked.

I started toward him, cradling the corpse and trying not to throw up. Above, the camera lights of cell phones lit the rim of the sinkhole.

"Absolutely," I said, heading for the protection of the empty tracks at the side of the platform. "Given the numbers of stone-winged baddies we saw here tonight, I think we should put in some time with a friendlier sort of gargoyle."

Caleb—still recovering from having a car dropped on him—made no effort to help me with the body, which was fine. It was light enough, all things considered. He jumped down onto the tracks and helped me down.

As we joined Marshall, Rory, and the two people we had rescued, Caleb shook his head and let out the kind of laugh that only comes from surviving chaotic mayhem.

"You okay?" I asked.

"Fine," he said, leading us down the tracks, "but we're all going to have a sit-down when we get out of here and have a serious discussion about the definition of reconnaissance."

"Fair enough," I said.

Twenty-six

☽

Stanis

Trinity Church was far more impressive than the humble one that housed Sanctuary, but it was a stellar place to perch myself as I sat among my fellow *grotesques* awaiting my visitors. Word had come down to me from several of my comrades that my human friends were en route, which pleased me. With all of us working in synergy, my fellow *grotesques* were beginning to show a marked improvement in their communications, which I supposed was a step toward uniting our community. Leadership, I had discovered, proved difficult, especially when trying to avoid the mistakes of my father.

A large yellow vehicle pulled up in front of Sanctuary. Caleb emerged from the front of it as Alexandra handed its driver some of their currency. Aurora and Marshall emerged from the back. The trunk opened, and Alexandra went to it, producing a large blue bag with white cloth handles.

"Gargoyle Central," she said as I watched them, setting down the duffel bag onto the sidewalk as the yellow vehicle pulled away. Her eyes went up to the front of the abandoned-looking church that functioned as Sanctuary.

"At least the non-malevolent version of it," Aurora added.

"Non-malevolent gargoyles would be a nice change," Marshall said to his friends far below.

Caleb stepped next to Alexandra, taking up the bag from the sidewalk. "You ready?"

Alexandra nodded and started up the stairs to the boarded-over front of Sanctuary.

To other humans passing by, the building looked deserted, its entrance hidden cleverly among the mismatched slats of wood. Alexandra, of course, knew better and pulled the one loose board that triggered the secret door to open. When she encountered the angelic form of Jonathan directly behind it, she jumped back from the door.

I stayed where I was perched, watching.

The monk-turned-*grotesque* bowed his head in greeting. "It is good to see you again," he said.

"Jonathan, right?" Alexandra asked, stepping forward.

"Yes," I called out before he could answer. The four humans turned as I stood up from the Trinity Church steeple I was on. I spread my wings fully and glided down to street level. "I thought it fitting that a former man of the cloth should prove a good caretaker here at Sanctuary."

I gestured the humans into Sanctuary and Jonathan as well, waiting for them to enter before going in myself and sealing the door shut.

"I make sure everyone is taken care of, monitor this scanner of yours," Jonathan said as he moved across the foyer. "It keeps me busy, and I find the church a restful place to spend my time."

"Sorry about the last time we met," Aurora offered. "The whole hog-tying-you thing and all that."

Jonathan smiled. "It is all right," he said. "I now understand the necessity."

Alexandra raised an eyebrow at him. "You do?"

He nodded. "Yes, I have learned much in my short time here helping to organize those who seek out Sanctuary. It has turned out to be . . ." He looked to me. "What was your phrase for it again?"

"It is like herding cats," I said, and Alexandra laughed. "Did I not say it right?"

"No, it's perfect," she said. "Where did you pick *that* up?"

"Aurora taught it to me," I said, giving my blue-haired friend a smile.

She smiled back. "I'm a giver," Aurora said, then looked out into the church. "Is Emily around?"

"What does your visit have to do with her?" I asked.

"I'm not entirely sure," Alexandra said. "That's why we'd like to see her."

"As you wish," I said with a nod of my head and turned, heading down the stairs into the old church. "Come."

Emily sat by the cages that held our latest newcomers, reciting to them her litany of welcoming. These new ones had come in warier than most, no doubt thanks to unfortunate interactions with the Butcher's men out on the streets of Manhattan. When she saw the humans with me, she smiled, and I waved her over to join us at the large stone table at the center of the aisle.

"Welcome to Sanctuary," she said as she approached.

Alexandra set her bag upon the table. "Thank you," she said, shrugging off her backpack next. "I wish this were just a social call."

"When are things *ever* these days?" Emily asked with a smile.

"True," Alexandra said.

Now that we were all close and standing still, I had a chance to better look over the humans. Their clothes were dirty and torn, their hair and faces caked in a thick layer of dust. Scratches and blood were evident on all of them.

"You are injured," I said.

Alexandra nodded. "All things considered," she said, "we're not that bad off."

"What happened?"

"The Butcher happened," Aurora said. "We found where he and his people have been hiding out."

My wings twitched uncontrolled with agitation. "You took him on without thinking to bring in me or my people?"

"We weren't looking for a fight," Alexandra said, coming back at me just as angry. "But we found one nonetheless.

There were people among them that they were going to kill.
I couldn't let that happen."

"Don't worry," Marshall added, leaning back against the
edge of the table. "There will be plenty more for you to fight.
The Butcher's been building his army, and many of them got
away."

"I didn't come here to fight," Alexandra said, calming herself down. She laid a hand on top of the bag she had brought.

Although I was not pleased with her news, I, too, attempted
to let go of my anger. "What did you come here for, then?" I
asked.

Alexandra unzipped the bag and pulled it open. Emily
leaned in first, but recoiled. I stepped closer to the table and
looked in the bag myself. Skin the color of dirt was stretched
over bones that filled the long bag, the body adorned in the
tattered remains of what looked like arcane vestments.

"That is a body," I said.

"You don't miss anything, do you?" Caleb added.

Ignoring him, I looked to Alexandra. "Who is this?"

"These are the bones of Robert Patrick Dorman," Alexandra said. "The Butcher of the Bowery."

Emily stepped closer to me, the tips of her wings shivering
with nerves. "Oh," she said quietly as if in attendance at a
funeral. "And what will you be doing with them?"

"We plan on sageing and salting them," Caleb said.

"For what purpose?" I asked.

"If we destroy his body," Alexandra said, "all of its mortal
attachment to this plane will be severed."

Emily looked with caution into the bag once more. "Once
you destroy *this*, he'll be gone?"

Alexandra shook her head. "Not quite," she said. "We still
have to destroy his current form, the angelic stone one. Without
his old body tethering him to our world, he should pass on.
This is all theoretical, mind you. I'm just going on a combina-
tion of what Warren said about the Butcher wanting to secure
his bones and what Fletcher told us . . . before he was killed."

Alexandra closed the bag and zipped it shut.

"But first," she added, "I need to ask Emily a favor."

"Me?" Emily asked, sounding startled at the request.

"Yes," Alexandra said. "After hearing about how your human form died, I believe the same thing recently happened to a friend of Caleb and mine. There was a ritual that was performed, but I'm not sure exactly what the ritual was used for. In order to figure out the purpose of that ritual, I'd need to know the specifics of what happened to your body."

"She does not remember what happened to her," I said. "And after discussing it with Detectives Rowland and Maron, they are laying the blame for her death at the feet of the Career Girl murderer."

"There is another way to find out," Alexandra said.

"How?" Emily asked.

"You can't recall them, but you *do* have memories of that night," she said. "Your body may have died but your spirit was still there for whatever ritual was done to you. I think I can unlock those memories, if you'll let me try."

Emily looked over to me, her eyes nervous and seeking guidance. Or it was quite possible that perhaps she had changed her mind about wanting to find out such things since Detective Rowland had shown us the grisly photos.

"It is your choice," I said to her. "But I will be here for you either way you choose."

"Actually," Alexandra said, "I'm going to need both of you for what I need to do."

I turned to the Spellmason. "What is it exactly that you have in mind?"

"Remember when you didn't know anything about your own past?" she asked me.

"Of course," I said. I turned to Emily. "Alexander had split who I was into arcane pieces of memory and hid them away, both for his safety and mine."

"Which I restored for him," Alexandra said as she pulled her notebook out of the pocket of her coat. "Those gemstones hidden in your chest. I think I can access them and use them as a spell focus to draw out Emily's own memories. It's a sort of sympathy magic."

"Will that hurt Stanis?" Emily asked.

"You need not concern yourself with that," I told her. "I have withstood a greater pain watching you not know your past. The greater question is do you still wish to know?"

"I don't know if this will hurt," Alexandra said. "I wish I had a better answer, but I just don't know. I've never attempted anything like this. I'm mixing some of my notes, Alexander's knowledge, and some alchemy I'm borrowing from Caleb and Marshall. I just do not know."

We stood in silence, all of us waiting for Emily to decide. The majesty of so holy a space had a calming effect, which I took solace in until Emily spoke again a moment later.

"Very well," she said. "I was not sure if I truly wished to have these memories, but they *are* part of my past, a part of me. I think I will be better for the knowing. And if it can help you deal with this abomination of a *grotesque*, so be it."

Alexandra placed her hand on Emily's shoulder and eased her onto the table, helping her lie down. Caleb went through the contents of his jacket, checking vials as he prepared them for the ritual that lay ahead. The Spellmason pulled her great-great-grandfather's spell book from the bag she took off her back and laid it out on the table, willing it from stone into a real tome. From the pocket of her coat she took her own notebook, and flipped through several pages she studied for a long moment before looking up at me as she let out a long, slow sigh, focusing herself.

Alexandra placed her hand on the center of my chest, the skin cool against me.

"Are you ready?" she asked.

"You think you will be able to get what you need?" I asked her back.

Alexandra smiled.

"Hey, I was able to fish out several hundred years of your entire past," she said. "I think I can manage stirring up some memories from 1963."

I went to smile back, but it died on my lips as the arcane snap of power to Alexandra hit me. Caught off guard, I staggered back before digging my claws into the stone of the floor, steadying myself.

It had been some time since I had felt true pain thanks to my stone form, but my chest felt as if it were on fire as it tore open. The smooth stone of it erupted into a series of snakelike patterns that twisted and turned at Alexandra's touch. One by one the four gemstones came to the surface as their stone settings worked their way out. My mind filled with a clarity I did not normally possess, swimming with the touch points of my past all at once.

"You still with me?" Alexandra asked, flipping through her spell notes with her free hand.

I tried to answer, but found myself unable to form words and merely nodded.

"Marshall!" she called out. "Hold this open for me. I don't want to screw this up, and I need both hands free."

"On it!" Marshall said and ran around the table and my inert form to take control of the book.

Alexandra then nodded to Caleb, who poured a vial into her mouth. She choked down whatever had been in it, coughing out a glowing purple mist before slamming her free hand down onto the prone form of Emily.

Her dragonlike wings twitched wide, but thanks to where Alexandra had positioned me, none of my friends was knocked away from the blow, my body absorbing it. Alexandra continued on with her spell, whispering her words of power, and as the last one left her lips, my mind flooded with foreign images.

Although the images were not mine, I recognized the time period they came from. The vehicles, the clothes of the people on the streets of Manhattan, the looks of the very buildings themselves—all of it screamed 1960s. Everything I saw was through Emily's eyes, but my perception was still partly my own. The images came and went with ferocity, none lasting more than a few seconds as Alexandra searched through Emily's memories. It reminded me of watching the fleeting images that appeared on the large screens in Times Square.

My world went black. In one moment, I was within the confines of a modest apartment, and the next there was nothingness.

"This has to be the part of Emily's mind that she doesn't have access to," Alexandra said. "Stanis, we *need* to break through."

Over the centuries I had assessed the boundaries of what I could and could not do, always testing the limits and lengths of my power. One thing rarely failed me when I needed to overcome an obstacle. I did what I did best.

I attacked the darkness, imagining it a tangible foe when in reality I could see no actual nemesis to contend with. I imagined my wings flaring wide, thrashing back and forth with each strike of my claws against a black wall.

"It's working," Alexandra said through the strain of her efforts, which sounded heavy judging by the pained hiss of her words.

The darkness crumbled in piece after slow piece, falling away as my mind filled with glimpses of an image that was slow to reveal itself.

A darkened apartment came to light, its furnishings sparse but feminine, and of a time long past. A woman lay tied on the couch of the living space, but it was not the face of Emily that I had seen in the photographs. This was the face of the other human who had died at her side.

This was Emily's view upon entering her apartment, finding the light switch unresponsive, but even as she closed the door behind her, she had not processed the whole of what she was seeing. The bound woman screamed out through the gag in her mouth, and as Emily ran to her, a strange figure darted out from the corner of her eye. The burn of rope caught on her wrists as total confusion set in and she fell to the floor.

I had known violence in my life. From my own death through that which I had caused over the centuries in my protection of the Belarus family, but nothing had prepared me for the brutality of this knife attack. The photos of it were nothing compared to the raw pain of experiencing Emily's death.

When it was done, the face of her attacker came into focus.

I had seen the face of human addiction before, humans wasting away, some through drink and others by the prick of needles. It reminded me of a dark alchemy of sorts, and this young man's eyes held the desperation of a man crippled by his addiction. What fueled it, I did not know, but it did not matter. All that mattered was that Emily did not expect to find this man in her apartment; nor did she expect the knife in his hand and her roommate already tied up.

A burglary. She had simply been the victim of a desperate man's attempt to rob her apartment, and for that she and her roommate lost their lives to stroke after vicious stroke of the blade, more than sixty in total. Pain, surprise, panic . . . all these emotions flowed through Emily, but even when the worst was over and her soul lingered in a room now vacant of all life, the crime scene bothered me, but for reasons beyond those I already thought it would.

Emily Hoffert was of course dead, but not in the way the crime scene photos had depicted. Her attacker left, but there was no ritualistic laying out of her body, no symbols written in her blood. None of what the photos had shown me was evident here, although the location was the same as in the pictures.

Emily's soul remained in the room, that of her roommate nowhere to be found. Judging by the movement of light streaming in from outside the building, time was passing, but before long the door to the apartment opened. To my surprise, a white-marbled gargoyle with a feminine mix of angelic and demonic features ducked its way through the doorframe. She look displeased to see the bodies lying on the floor, but the gargoyle did not seem surprised as she moved to Emily and kneeled down next to her.

"You poor thing," its voice said. It was unfamiliar to me, but not to the Spellmason.

"Laurien," Alexandra said, drawing a piece of my mind back to the anchor of reality.

"What about Laurien?" Caleb asked.

"She's there," Alexandra said. "Only she's a lot more marble-textured and winged than she looked at the Convocation."

"I'm sorry," Marshall said. "Did you just say Laurien is a *gargoyle*?"

Alexandra nodded.

"How?" Aurora asked, unable to hold back the disbelief in her voice.

"What the hell is she doing there?" Caleb asked.

"Everyone be quiet and let me find out," Alexandra said and fell silent as she adjusted her hand on Emily's chest as if feeling around for the memories.

In my mind's eyes, this Laurien pulled out a book of her own from a leather satchel she wore over her shoulder. She laid it next to the body, carefully beginning to move and arrange it in such a way that I began to see the patterns that would become the arcane ritual I knew from the photographs. Emily's soul watched on with a morbid fascination at the gargoyle as she finished laying things out in the way we had both seen in the photograph.

"She is preparing a spell of some kind," I said.

The gargoyle touched her hands to the outer ring of blood she had formed and incanted words that were foreign to me. Emily's soul reacted. Her strange curiosity about the circumstances of her human form melted immediately away, replaced by one all-consuming word.

Find.

Before I could even wonder as to what it meant to seek, the answer came from Laurien's lips.

"Cagliostro," she whispered in the quiet apartment.

The results were like watching the crime scene where the Butcher had killed Fletcher to enact the same blood-magic ritual. At the word, Emily's soul shot from the room through the walls of the building, and my perspective flew off with it across the city. I was used to flying fast over the city, but this pace was hard for me to follow although I thought we were headed across the island of Manhattan. I confirmed it seconds later as Emily's soul flashed into Central Park, the trees and pathways blurring by.

Neither the pathway leading to the clearing known as Strawberry Fields nor the memorial itself existed yet, but I recognized the area of the park nonetheless as Emily shot deep into the woods there. Seconds later her soul met some sort of invisible resistance, slowing as it forced itself through it to suddenly find itself within a vast cemetery. Rolling hills of gravestones flew by, the journey ending only when Emily entered a massive tomb with the name *O'SHEA* on it, coming to rest on one of the raised sarcophagi within.

Anne Elizabeth O'Shea, its marker read.

"The gargoyle Laurien found the location of the medallion in the mausoleum," Alexandra said. "I think she took it from the grave of one of the O'Sheas. Decades before the Butcher tried to seek it out."

Alexandra released the spell and my mind's eyes closed as if the image of the graveyard was receding down a tunnel. As I came back to reality the world around me returned. I collapsed to my knees, releasing a tension I had not realized had accumulated during Alexandra's manipulation of me. My chest burned as the gemstones slid back beneath the surface on their knot work of tracks, smoothing over to its unmarred state once more.

Alexandra dropped down beside me, her one hand remaining on Emily's prone figure. "You okay?" she asked, grabbing my hand with her other as if she could lift me.

I took a moment, composed myself, and nodded, using the stone table to steady me as I lifted myself back up. Emily stirred on the table but with eyes closed made no move to rise.

"Is she . . . ?"

Alexandra checked the spell book Marshall was still holding open, and muttered a foreign phrase, adjusting her hand on Emily. "She's fine," she said, "but I think she's going to need a moment to recover."

"You mentioned Laurien," Caleb said. "What did our grand high witchy-poo have to do with Emily's death? You know, I've never trusted her."

"Hey!" Marshall said, taking offense. "She's a good customer."

Caleb shook his head at him. "Oh, sure," he said. "When she's not killing our friends . . ."

"Laurien did not kill Emily," I said, which stopped the two men's bickering.

"It's true," Emily said, attempting to sit up on the table. I took her hand and helped her. She swung her legs over the side of the table and stretched her wings out from under her. "Laurien was there, but I was . . ." She hesitated to say the words as I watched her process the images. "I was already dead."

"Laurien only used her for a ritual," Alexandra said. "The same one the Butcher used on our friend Fletcher."

"Cagliostro," Emily said. "Laurien spoke the word."

"She was seeking out this medallion you told us of," I said to Alexandra.

"But why?" Caleb asked.

"Because that gargoyle version of her wanted to be flesh and blood," I said, "and because people in power always seek out more power. My father did so, and so goes it with the head of the Convocation."

"When Warren finds out that it was Laurien who took his family's medallion, he's going to go ballistic," Caleb said. "And he's going to have trouble on his hands if he tries to take it back from her."

"No, he's not," Alexandra said.

Caleb laughed at that. "He's *not*?"

Alexandra shook her head. "Because we're going to help him," she added.

"Awesome," Caleb said, but it did not sound as if he meant the word. "And how will we do that exactly?"

"We're going to call for a Convocation," she said.

"That's not going to happen," Caleb said.

Alexandra gave him a look more full of stone than any I could have.

"I'm not being a dick," he said. "You saw what an explosion-filled meeting that was, and that was one that was planned out for months. You're on trial before them at this juncture, so you don't get to call the shots. I can't make that happen. I'm sorry, but I can't."

"Fine," she said, and her face filled with defeat, but not for long. "Then call Warren. Tell him I want a meeting with him *and* just Laurien."

"I'm not sure I can make that fly, either," he said.

Alexandra walked up to him and took his face in her hands. "I have faith in you," she said. "I'm not asking for the entire witching and wizarding community here. I just need to meet with the two of them. I'll even make it easy. I'll host it at my home on Saint Mark's. They don't even have to plan a thing other than to hear me out."

There was an intimacy to their conversation that filled me with discomfort, and I instead focused on helping Emily down from the table, making sure she was not too rattled from what she had seen.

"I'll see what I can do," Caleb said after a minute. "I can't promise anything."

When I looked back over, Alexandra had picked up the bag of bones and was already making her way back to the front door of Sanctuary, Aurora and Marshall hurrying to follow.

"I need better than a promise," she said as she headed up the stairs leading to the door out to Trinity Place.

"What about us?" Emily called out after her.

Alexandra turned at the top of the stairs. "You know how you died now," she said. "Now it's time to figure out how you want to live. How you *all* want to live."

"What do you mean by that?" I asked.

"There will soon come a time when the *grotesques* of Manhattan must make a stand," Alexandra said. "It is up to you for them to be ready."

I had many a question, but Alexandra did not wait to hear any of them. Instead, she turned back around and got all the way to the door before spinning to face us once more, her eyes landing on Caleb, who had not moved.

She lifted the bag, shaking it to the point that it rattled the bones within.

"Don't forget to get Laurien to my place," she said, throwing open the door. "Tell her I have a bone—several, in fact— to pick with her. Plus I'd like to talk to her woman to woman about the kind of jewelry she likes to wear."

Caleb, Marshall, and Aurora followed after her, leaving Emily and me alone in the middle of the church.

"I fear there are unpleasant times to come," I said, then turned to her. "How do you feel after what you saw?"

"As horrific as it was?" she said. "Strangely at peace."

"That must be of some comfort," I said.

Emily nodded. "More than you can imagine," she said. "There is a strange and welcome closure in my mind knowing how I died."

"May that bring you peace," I said, embracing her.

She returned the gesture, but fell silent for a long time.

"Only . . ." Emily pulled herself away from me and looked up at me. "I don't think I can stay here."

"What?" I asked, feeling as if she had struck me. "Emily, why?"

"I remember it *all*," she said. "My life before that night. I had come to this city wide-eyed and hopeful. My time here was cut all too short, but . . . there was the family I left behind. It broke my heart to leave them in Edina, Minnesota, and my murder must have destroyed them. I can't stay here . . . I need to go. I need to find them."

"What about your life here?" I asked. "What about Sanctuary? What about . . . me?"

Emily managed a smile and took my hands in hers. "I think I have done my work here," she said. "I have laid out a path for those who come to Sanctuary seeking answers. Jonathan is a quick study. It will be fine." Emily let go of my hands. "As for you, I have seen the great care and affection you have for me."

"Then how can you leave?" I asked, confusion filling my mind as I fought to process what she was saying.

"You are a good person, Stanis Ruthenia," she said. "But do not confuse your desire to help me reclaim who I was with actual desire."

"It is more than a desire to help you," I countered, but Emily shook her head.

"No," she said. "It's not. I know you think it is, but my mind is clear now. I see the way you are with Alexandra. There is something there that you and I can never have. I would not wish to be in the way of that. My heart lies elsewhere."

"And where is that?" I asked, unable to hide a bit of anger

over her trying to assess whom I did and did not care for. There might be truth to it, but in the moment all I wanted was answers from her.

"Edina, Minnesota," she said. "You spent centuries watching over the Belarus family. I wish to seek mine out and do the same. I need to reclaim that part of my humanity. I need it more than anything."

I fell silent, lowering my head at her with eyes shut. There was no arguing with her, not about her desire to watch over her family or where she thought my secret heart lay. I kept my questions to myself, but there was only one that I needed to answer.

Was my heart truly bound to another?

Twenty-seven

Alexandra

It wasn't every day I had unfamiliar company at my place on Saint Mark's, and frankly having a witch and a warlock at my door was about as welcome as someone preaching the word of Insert the God of Your Choice Here. Nonetheless, I smiled and held my front door open to the two of them.

"Thanks for coming," I said, gesturing Warren and Laurien inside. The warlock had a natural curiosity in his eyes as he entered and looked around, but Laurien hesitated, looking less than thrilled to be here. In fact, she looked downright put out by it, but after a moment entered.

"You wished to speak with me?" she asked as I shut the door behind her, clearly not wanting to be here a moment longer than she had to.

"This will be worth it," I said, moving to the steps leading down to the library. "Promise."

"Let us hope so," she said. "Warren had to call in a few favors to get me here. I hope this is not a waste of his time as well as mine."

I hit the bottom of the stairs, waiting for them to join me

among the heavy wooden shelves and lush seating before continuing farther back into my building.

"Impressive library," Warren said as they followed me.

"It's about to get more impressive," I said, stepping to one of the bookcases. I reached behind a copy of *The Hunchback of Notre Dame* on the top shelf, activating the pressure plate against the back wall. The mechanism clicked and the bookcase swiveled free, revealing the stone door behind it. I whispered my words of power to the massive door, willing it open. I stepped through the opening behind it, finding the familiar comfort of my great-great-grandfather's guildhall.

Caleb, Rory, and Marshall stood assembled at the large stone table I had formed at the room's center, one end of it draped over with cloth and the other holding the bag of bones I had taken from the Butcher's secret court.

Warren came through the door into the guildhall, marveling at the height of the large circular space and its stonework. Laurien entered last, pausing for a moment when she saw all my friends there. Once it was clear none of us had any intention of hostility toward her, her eyes left my group and looked around the hall as she and Warren moved to where we were in the center.

"You recognize this place, don't you?" I asked her.

Warren raised an eyebrow and gave her a sidelong look, his ring-covered hands folded together in front of him.

Laurien didn't notice him, but continued looking around the room, her eyes coming to rest on the large glass cabinets full of alchemical mixes along one wall.

"I don't believe so, no," she said, then looked back to me, her eyes filled with a strange mix of nerves and anger. "Should I?"

"Oh, most definitely, I think," I said, not looking away from her, keeping my gaze fixed on her.

Laurien looked over at Warren, and her eyes narrowed to the point that he actually stepped back from her. "You were a fool to bring me here," she said with a heavy sigh.

Agitated, she turned to leave, but I reached out my will to the door, slamming it shut. The stone door disappeared, its seams fading into the texture of the wall.

Laurien spun around to me. "How dare you! You are dealing with the head of the Convocation here."

I unzipped the bag and, with little reverence for its contents, upended it. The bones within poured out onto the stone table, clicking and clacking together like bits of dry wood.

"I thought you might like to see this," I said, grabbing the large box of salt off the table, liberally pouring it over the pile of bones.

"Is that who I think it is?" Warren asked.

"Depends on who you think it is," I said, waving Marshall over.

He walked to me as I crumpled a bushel of sage over the remains. When I was done, he slid two different vials into my hand.

"The Butcher," Laurien said. "The remains of Robert Patrick Dorman."

"You see?" I said with a smile. "It *is* who you think it is."

Warren moved closer to the table, looking down at them. "How did you finally come by them?" he asked.

"We got the drop on him," Caleb said, then lowered his voice to a whisper, "even if it was a bit of an accident."

I shot him a look, then turned back to Warren and Laurien. "I forced him to leave his secret court a bit more hastily than he expected," I said. "And now there's one less thing for you to worry about, Warren."

I unstopped the two vials and poured them together over the bones. The pile erupted into a cold eldritch flame, burning the salt black and consuming the bones until all that was left was a charred pile of ash and the warm smell of sage in the air.

"That doesn't kill him," Laurien said, as if angrily correcting a child she thought was being foolish.

"I know," I said, "but it *is* one step closer to finishing him off."

Warren could not take his eyes from the pile, looking less relieved than I thought he would. "But no medallion," he said.

"No, not yet," I said. "But that's why I asked you two here."

I moved to the back end of the table, which was still draped with cloth, and pulled it away. The sight of a second set of bones—the petrified body I had found in our walls—caused the anger to fall out of Laurien, her eyes widening at the corpse.

"Alexander Belarus hid the details of his apprentice well among his books and books of notes, but he *did* still write about an apprentice," I said. "He even went as far as to hide the name of that apprentice in his notes. This is you, isn't it?"

The head witch stared at the body for a long moment before slowly nodding. "I've certainly looked better," she said with no humor in the words.

"I think you'd better explain yourself, Laurien . . . before I sage this body and salt it as well."

"I suppose you leave me little choice in the matter," she said with little fight in her, but then she met my eyes, a dark power radiating from them. Her demeanor shifted to pure bravado and threat. "Or I could invoke my power and reduce the lot of you to cinders."

Marshall looked flustered at her response, dropping two of his vials, watching them roll across the stone floor of the chamber. Rory's posture changed, going from casual with her hands in her back pockets to hands on her hips, more aggressive. Caleb simply remained stone-faced, waiting to see how I was going to handle it. Personally, I wasn't sure how I was going to handle it. All I knew was that Laurien had touched a raw nerve with me and I was livid.

"Do you think I'm honestly afraid of you anymore?" I asked her as I walked up to her, each step slow and full of purpose. "In the past year, I've been threatened by cultists, stone monstrosities, the police, people within your Convocation. All I wanted was to practice art. Not arcane art, mind you. Sculpture, painting . . . these were my passions. You know what I end up doing? Trying to keep the cops from shooting me and my friends. Hopefully figuring out the good *grotesques* from the bad ones, usually finding out by seeing if they swing their claws at me once I'm up close. Peeling entanglement vines from warlocks intent on capturing me. So you get to herd the cats that are the witching and warlocking community. Big hairy deal. You want to fight me—fight *us*—instead of giving me an answer? Fine. You could take that chance, but then you'd be trapped in here. Sure, you *might* be able to power your way out of my great-great-grandfather's guildhall, but then again, you might not be up to that task. This stone is strong."

"I *know* how strong it is," she said.

"Do you?"

The vibe coming off the woman was still intimidating, no doubt amplified by the power lurking just behind her eyes, but I did not move.

"What *do* you know about this place?" I asked her. "What do you know about the Spellmasons?"

"I knew Alexander Belarus," she said, dropping her anger and hanging her head. "Centuries ago. I was young, ambitious, and seeking power. I thought Alexander a fool. He had such power at his disposal, but what did he choose to do with it? Hide quietly in his secret hall with his singular stone construct."

"How did you come to know him?" I asked.

"He had heard of our community here in New York after coming here, and approached our Convocation," she said. "We had heard rumors of his gargoyle, some even claiming to have seen it, but none had met him until he approached *us*. To tell the truth, I think it was to alleviate his loneliness more than anything."

"He had just escaped to this country fearing the tyranny and reprisal of Kejetan Ruthenia," I said. "He had only his wife and had lost his first son, replacing him with an eternal one in Stanis. Of course he would want to seek out others with whom he shared the same passion for the arcane."

"I was an initiate within the Convocation back then," she said, "but I craved the knowledge and Alexander was all too willing to share . . . at first, anyway."

"You were his apprentice," I said. "There is mention of you in his notes, although there is very little said. I mean, he built this guildhall with the clear intention of sharing knowledge. Why would he stop after taking an apprentice?"

"I was the *first* of his students," she said. "And I would turn out to be his last. Remember, I was young, vain, and wanting for power. Your great-great-grandfather, however, was a man of caution."

"Of course he was," I said. "He had already watched the

last person he taught back in the old country die. That's how Stanis was born."

"He was so cautious that he would not even let me see the creature Stanis," she said, a bit of bitterness returning to her voice. "I studied alone, and the longer I studied, the more I desired to see the creature, to see the results of his work. But no."

"You wanted the secrets of his power," I said. "You wanted to create a golem of your own."

"And I did," Laurien said. "Against Alexander's wishes. 'Too fast,' he said, his words only burning away against the fire of my ambition."

"You needed a soul to complete the work on it, though," I said. "To animate its form."

"And what better one than my own?" she asked, sadness in the question. "I would be more powerful than any other. I performed the Spellmasonry myself here in this very chamber. Alexander found me here once I had become a *grotesque*, my new form unconscious from my arcane efforts. He was furious that I had betrayed his wishes, but even more furious with himself for failing me."

"Wait, wait, wait," Marshall interjected. "How exactly did *he* fail *you*?"

"I understand it," Caleb said to him. "It's like when I started showing you how alchemy worked. You were *my* student. If you did well, it reflects on me. If you fail, it also reflects on me." He turned to Laurien. "Is that about right?"

"Exactly so," she said. "I fled from this place and never saw the man again. I had achieved immortality, but in doing so I lost more than a master. I lost everything. The Convocation frowned upon my transformation, ostracizing me, leaving me alone in this world."

"Hold on, now," Rory said. "You're looking fit and spry and entirely not made of stone right now. Don't tell me you just made a full recovery."

"Of course not," I said, meeting Laurien's eyes. "You care to show them what we're talking about? Why you needed Emily . . ."

Laurien went to the collar of her shirt, drawing it open. A

golden necklace lay against her skin, a heavy charm carved with runes of red hanging at the center of it.

"The Cagliostro Medallion," I said, but even before the words were out of my mouth, the woman before me had begun to transform.

She doubled over with a muffled cry, her skin going a veiny marble white. The back of her shirt tore open. Large batlike wings grew out of her, unfolding. Her frame bulked up in size while somehow managing to keep its femininity, and while she stood taller than me now, it was now in a mix of demonic and angelic forms that had the carving style of my great-great-grandfather's work.

She rose to her full height and let her wings work back and forth behind her.

"It has been a while," she said. "I spent years in this form in solitude, all the while regretting what I had done to myself in my selfish quest for greater power. It had removed me from the people I cared about. It had removed me from my kind—from the Convocation. It was many years later that I discovered there was hope."

"My family?" Warren asked, raising an eyebrow. "We had tried to keep arcane knowledge out of the mainstream, but the O'Sheas have always had a propensity for being a bit larger than life, grandiose."

"You don't say," Rory said with a smile.

Warren ignored her, but Laurien nodded.

"When I heard of the Cagliostro Medallion, I knew I must seek it out," she said. "The only arcane knowledge I knew for divining its true location was through a dark ritual."

"Blood magic," I said. "I watched you do it. You used Emily for it. The same way the Butcher used it to try to seek out the medallion now by using the blood power of our friend Fletcher. I saw his vision, too. Dorman's spell to find the medallion showed him the Convocation, but it could not actually pinpoint a source for the piece."

"I am thankful, then, for all the arcane confusion that can be generated at one of our events," she said. "But yes, I used blood magic. It was something I had studied in my quest for more power, but I found I could not take the life of an innocent. I trailed the worst of humanity from high above in the sky, hoping to come across the consequences of one of their acts of desperation. In a city like Manhattan, it did not take long. The screams of Emily Hoffert drew me to her then-lifeless body, and I used the remaining energy of her death to fuel my divination."

"Which led you to my family's crypt," Warren said. "The Butcher tried the same thing, but came up empty-handed, but not before desecrating our mausoleum."

"I am sorry for that," Laurien said. "For my initial theft, and for what the Butcher did." She turned to me. "It took some time—months and months, in fact—to learn how to control the power of the medallion. Once I could consistently obtain and hold a human form, I returned to the Convocation, all the wiser for my years of foolishness. No one remembered my disappearance long ago, and I have spent the last half a century bound to protecting my people in any way that I can. If I seem harsh or cruel at times in my ruling, it has only been in service to the betterment of my kind."

"Then we have something in common," I said. "Even though you don't consider any of us one of your kind yet, we *all* want the same thing."

"The death of Robert Patrick Dorman," she said.

"We want the safety of our people," I said. "Of your people. Of this city's people. And if it takes his death to do it, then so be it."

"Forgive my lies and deception," she said after considering what I had said for a moment longer. "When we met and you told me of the Butcher seeking the medallion, I feared for my own secrets . . . and my life. To have the kin of the arcane teacher show up at the same time as the greatest threat to all I had worked to hide and make up for . . . I fought for reasons to keep you away from us. I panicked. I had hoped telling you that your great-great-grandfather was a murderer shunned by the Convocation would buy me time to figure out a plan for my safety, but I see now that perhaps I have lost sight of what I have been struggling for all along."

"The safety of your people," I said.

Laurien nodded. "Taking down the Butcher will be no easy feat," she said. "And you've made him more desperate than ever. Dorman has no body to return to, no ties to the mortal plane should he be driven from his stone form. He's got more to lose now than ever."

"That's great," Caleb said, "but where are we going to find the guy? We drove him out of his hiding place under the city. He's not going to return to that sinkhole we created by Macy's."

"Don't worry about that," I said, "because *he's* going to come to *us* next time."

Laurien raised a demonic eyebrow, and I almost had to laugh. Same attitude from the woman, but in a wholly different body. "And why would he ever do that?" she asked.

"Because we're going to give him what he wants," I said. "We're going to give him the medallion."

"Are we, now?" Laurien asked, her clawed hand reaching up to her neck.

"Yes," I said with conviction. "We are."

Everyone remained silent while we all waited to see whether Laurien was going to challenge me on this or not. In the end, however, the gargoyle sighed and folded her wings close against her back. She held up her arms as if striking a pose like a model.

"Very well, then," she said, "but I don't suppose you have something I could borrow to wear? I hadn't exactly planned on doing this and as you can see this transformation wreaks havoc on my clothing."

"Not a problem," I said, and added a trip up to my closet to my ever-growing list of things I needed to get done. I slipped it in right before where I planned to call the detectives but after taking the time to breathe a sigh of relief that Laurien had chosen not to go toe-to-toe with me and my friends. There was just one more thing that I needed to know.

"Tell me how it works."

"Lexi," Rory said with warning in her voice. "I don't think we have months to learn how to master its use like Laurien did."

"Actually," I said with a dark smile, "that's what I'm counting on."

Twenty-eight

———— ☾ ————

Alexandra

"Do you think he'll show?" Marshall asked from the top of the tourist-filled Red Stairs that stood atop the TKTS booth in Times Square. He pulled the hood he had made for both me and Rory up over my head to hide my features. He then reached over and did the same for Rory, whose face magically disappeared into the shadows of it.

Tourists intermingled with our mix of witches, warlocks, and detectives as well as my friends, unaware there was anything unusual about our gathered crowd.

"How can he not?" I said, adjusting my hood for a better fit. "I'm dangling the one carrot he really wants."

"Lovely," Laurien said, once more in her human form, her hand tucking the medallion within the collar of her coat. "So I am a carrot now."

"What about his stone cronies?" Caleb asked, checking the skies above.

"He knows better than to show up alone," I said.

"I do not think he will expect so many of us joined together," Laurien added. "Even though my people spread rumors far and wide that the medallion would be here, he will surely not expect

gargoyles and our arcane brothers and sisters working together."
Laurien looked out into the crowd where the familiar faces of
the Convocation were spread out among it.

I looked up at the surrounding buildings all around the
large open space of Times Square. The shadows of our winged
troops moved against the skyline, leaving me to wonder where
Stanis was among them. Emily's leaving had shaken him, but
I prayed his focus was with him and his *grotesques* could be
counted on tonight.

"Don't forget us humans," Detective Rowland added.

At her side, Detective Maron checked his watch. "How
much time are we working with now?"

"We've got about forty-five minutes give or take," I said. "I
figured it would be best to be early, for coordination's sake. I
only hope your people responded to your call."

"Well, we're going to look like assholes if your winged
buddies are a no-show," Rowland said.

"Don't worry about that," I said. "Just make sure your
people clear the area."

Marshall dropped his notebook, scrambling down onto his
knees to recover it, nervousness filling his eyes.

I knelt down next to him and handed him a few pages that
had come free. "You okay?" I asked.

He nodded and we both stood.

"I'm not used to being this exposed while we work," he
said. "I've never coordinated anything on this scale before."

"It'll be fine," I said, doing my best to hide my own nerves
as I reassured him. "I have faith in you, Dungeon Master."

Marshall smiled at that. "At least you got the terminology
right," he said. "At least it happened once before we die,
right?"

"We're *not* going to die," Rory said, lifting the twin hammers she held in both of her hands. "It's hammer time!"

"How do they feel?" Marshall asked.

"Good," she said, dropping them back to her side. "Certainly
more discreet in Times Square than my usual pole arm. Of
course it would have been nice if I had had a chance to test
them out on *a* gargoyle before, you know, *all* the gargoyles.

The balance is nice. I just hope they do what they're supposed to and make with the smashy smashy."

"The enchantments I put on them will work just fine," he said with a confident smile. "Don't worry. I've got your back."

Unexpectedly, Rory threw her arms around Marshall and hugged him hard. "I know," she said. "Thank you."

Marshall looked as surprised as I did by the gesture, but returned the embrace. Such intimacy only made the estranged coldness between Caleb and me all the more awkward. Luckily, I didn't have to break it up as Laurien cleared her throat next to me.

"This is all very touching," she said, "but perhaps we should focus on—"

Laurien didn't get a chance to finish her sentence.

One second Rory was hugging Marshall and the next she was pushing him into a crowd of tourists sitting on the Red Stairs. The glass rail and several of the stairs behind her exploded apart, barely giving her time to dive in the other direction to safety.

The stone form of the Butcher shot through the spot where she and Marshall had just stood, but they had not been his intended target. They had simply been in the way of the straightest line from a subway exit to the madman's intended target—Laurien.

Before the rest of us could even react, the gargoyle's claws tore into the fabric of the coat Laurien wore, and with a flap of his feathered stone wings, he flew off with her into the sky above.

"Stanis!" I shouted up into the night sky, my voice feeling so tiny against the screams and shouts of the crowd around us.

Above, the sky erupted with activity. Gargoyles shot into Times Square from every direction, but they were not all our own. Ours took off from their posts in response, and several dropped down into the streets nearby, including Stanis and Jonathan, who both came up the stairs at us as people fled out of their way.

"I wasn't sure where you were," I said to him.

"Forgive my lateness," he said, looking down at me. "My

organizational skills among my people leave much to be desired, but I believe them ready, even though this attack seems premature."

"Marshall!" I shouted. "Keep this thing coordinated."

"On it!" he said as he stood himself up and turned to the detectives. "Maron! Rowland! I need your people to get the bystanders back."

Both detectives barked orders into their walkie-talkies, and all around Times Square the side streets lit up with a wash of alternating red and blue flashers. Apparently the detectives *had* gotten their fellow officers to believe that the paranormal threat to Manhattan was a real thing, as if a sky full of gargoyles wasn't enough evidence. Officers poured out of the side streets, driving the stunned crowds of tourists away from the erupting chaos all around us.

Most people in the crowd were in a state of panic, making it easier to spot the witches and warlocks standing among them.

Marshall looked out over them. "Convocation!" he shouted. "For Laurien, fight!"

Some of the crowd took to the air to engage with the gargoyles; others simply erupted into sprays of fire, explosions, and a whole host of things my brain could barely process. *This is what an acid trip must feel like,* I thought.

I closed my eyes for a second, blocking it all out, and turned my focus back to Stanis and Jonathan.

"Can you get us up there?" I asked, pulling Caleb over to them.

Stanis scooped me up without hesitation while Caleb wrapped his arms around Jonathan's neck.

"As you wish," Stanis said, and with a mighty leap, we shot up into the sky.

My stomach dropped from the sensation, the cool night air whipping against my face, but our target was in sight still.

Laurien's attempts to struggle out of the Butcher's grasp had helped slow him, allowing Stanis and me to catch up, Caleb and Jonathan not far behind.

"Please tell me you have more of a plan than this," the

Butcher said, unable to resist laughing in my face, which only made me want to drop an entire building on him.

"Me?" I asked. "I don't have a plan. *We* have a plan."

"The four of you chasing me is hardly much of a threat," he said.

"Let her go," Caleb shouted at him from Jonathan's back.

"From up here?" the Butcher asked, his face a twisted mask of delight. "Gladly. But first . . ."

Although Laurien had been struggling, she still looked dazed from the midair tackle down on the Red Stairs seconds ago. Some of the life came back into her face as she regained her focus. The Butcher's hand went to her throat, the claws seeking purchase on the medallion hanging from it. Laurien twisted and turned, the continued struggle keeping it just out of his reach.

"Get us in close," I told Stanis, and he did so to the point we were wing to wing with the two of them.

I pressed my will into the stone of the Butcher. There was no way I could gain control over so purposeful a creature, but I hoped to delay him in his efforts to relieve Laurien of the medallion. His hand sought out the object, but with every ounce of what I had, I willed him to keep him from taking it from her.

Laurien started to transform. Her skin shifted to the pale white of her marble form, her wings struggling to burst free from her coat. Seeing it only angered the Butcher further, and I felt his will struggling against mine even harder, but I refused to let his hand close on the medallion's chain.

No doubt sensing my presence within the stone of his body, he looked to me, his focus shifting. My focus was pressed so hard into resisting his strength pressing *toward* Laurien that I did not expect it to reverse and I found my own power adding to his momentum as he swung his clawed hand out at me instead.

Stanis was quick to react and pulled back, but with my added weight it was simply not enough. I braced myself for the blow.

"No!" Laurien cried out, and swung herself into harm's

way, deflecting the intended strike. The Butcher's claws tore into one of her half-formed wings, sticking there.

He let go of Laurien, leaving her to shift and dangle from her torn, trapped wing. As she swayed back and forth, he plucked the chain from around her neck with his other hand and jerked it free. His fingers closed around the medallion as he raised his clawed feet and pressed them against Laurien until the stone around her torn wing crumbled somewhere between stone and flesh, knocking her free.

Laurien fell, shouting her own words of power, which I did not understand, but nothing followed. She simply continued falling. I had to act fast.

I looked into Stanis's face as he held me. "Please get her," I said. "I'll deal with the Butcher." Trusting he would indulge my request, I shoved myself free of his arms and out into the open air. I landed on the Butcher, struggling to wrap my arms around his neck before I could slide off. I joined my hands together, holding myself in place, and swung around to his back.

Stanis hesitated, surprise on his face, which unfortunately gave the Butcher an opening. His clawed feet shot out at Stanis, catching one of his wings. The blow forced him into an uncontrollable spin, one that also sent him careening into Jonathan and Caleb nearby.

Caleb scrambled to get out from the middle of the two stone men colliding, and as Stanis knocked Jonathan from his holding pattern, there was little choice but for the alchemist to leap toward me midair.

I grabbed for him with one hand, catching his wrist and swinging him around to the front of the Butcher. Caleb fought for some kind of hold as he slid down the Butcher's body, pressing his feet off of the Butcher's legs and securing himself around the arm that held the medallion.

With our additional weight, the Butcher fought to stay airborne. There was little else he could do with the two of us attached to him, and I felt a small bit of triumph until the sound of Laurien hitting the street below filled our ears.

The dull *thunk* echoed over and over among the concrete

canyons of Manhattan, mixing with the sounds of battle that rose up all around us from the massive conflict. The sound shoved me into action and I met Caleb's eyes.

"Get the medallion," I shouted to him.

Keeping one arm wrapped around the Butcher's, Caleb fumbled the medallion free from the gargoyle's claws, all of us struggling not to fall. The alchemist shoved his hands against mine, and I grabbed it, pulling it around the Butcher's neck.

I secured its clasp in place and let the medallion fall against his chest.

The Butcher laughed in triumph.

"I wouldn't celebrate just yet," I said. "You don't know how this works exactly, do you?"

"It's thought-controlled," he said. "By me. By *my* thoughts."

"Exactly," I said. "Let's hope a century of being a free, roaming spirit of ill will and six months of occupying one of my great-great-grandfather's forms has left you a little rusty."

The Butcher's face became a mask of confusion. "What do you mean?" he shouted.

Was that actual panic I heard creeping into his voice?

"I've studied you," I said. "According to Warren, isn't returning to flesh what your corrupt little heart desires most in this world? It took months for Laurien to master control of the medallion. Let's see how well you fare this high up trying to do the same. Give in to your heart's desire."

At my suggestion, the gargoyle winced with a sudden jerk of surprise, the features on his face shifting from their dark angelic form to something that looked more akin to human.

"Not here," he growled, trying to fight it. "Not now!"

"Too late!" Caleb said, still clutching the side of his face. "I dare you not to think about that which you most crave— your humanity. Give in to it."

Much like telling someone not to think about a pink elephant, the Butcher could not fight against his longest and deepest desire. His body of stone began to transform against his will. The chiseled smoothness of his angelic figure fluctuated back and forth from flesh to stone midair, the three of us starting to fall as he tried to fight his ever-changing form.

I held tight around his neck, pressed between his wings as I awaited an opportunity to strike. If I didn't act soon, however, either I was going to be shaken free or the three of us would crash to the ground far below together.

I fought the image of Laurien's fate, focusing in as the stone of the Butcher's body shifted partially back to the flesh.

"Time to clip your wings," I said, grabbing fistfuls of the transforming material of the angel's now-flesh-colored feathers.

I tore away at them, huge chunks of flesh coming out, immediately turning to gray stone and crumbling between my fingers. It felt like tearing a chicken apart with my bare hands and I fought the urge to vomit, but I kept on pulling at them over and over.

Immediately, we went from falling to plummeting. I looked up into the night sky above. Stanis had finally corrected his flight and was diving down after us.

"Catch us," I cried out.

"Catch *her*," Caleb said as he held on tight to the falling figure of the Butcher.

"What?!"

"I'll be fine," Caleb said, taking one of my hands and pressing me away from the broken angel so Stanis could get a better grip on me.

Once Stanis held me in his arms, Caleb let go of both me and the frantically flapping Butcher, pulling a vial from within his coat. He fell away, my stomach dropping with him. His body relaxed as he plummeted, the only movement coming from raising the vial to his lips and drinking. His body hit the pavement in the middle of Broadway not far from the broken form of Laurien, but upon impact it seemed to stretch and distort like a water-filled balloon hitting the ground but not breaking.

The Butcher crashed down onto the street with a thunderous *crack*, a monstrous crater appearing in the pavement. The sound reverberated throughout Times Square, but it was not enough to stop the fighting that raged both on the ground and in the air. Wizards, warlocks, and gargoyles fought against the Butcher's men on both fronts, and the battle looked far from over.

"To Marshall!" I shouted.

"As you wish," Stanis said, and brought me back to the Red Stairs where Marshall was holding his ground.

Any gargoyle that dared to mount the stairs heading for him had apparently been facing the wrath of Rory's hammers and losing, judging by the pile of broken stone pieces that littered the area. When Stanis and I landed, she swung around, hammers bearing down on us.

Stanis wrapped his wings around me in a protective cocoon.

"Whoa, whoa, whoa," I said, holding up my hands from within. "It's us!"

She caught herself and lowered her weapons.

"Sorry," she said. "I saw stone and reacted. It's a little crazy."

"That's the understatement of the year," Marshall added, then barked into his phone. "Rowland! I need those tourists off of Forty-ninth Street, like, five minutes ago."

"If I wanted people yelling at me, I'd go back to traffic duty," she called back through the speaker. "But, yes, sir! Right away, sir!"

"Please and thank you," Marshall said, and within seconds there was a wave of New York's Finest flooding that area, escorting people to safety.

"Well, hopefully downing the Butcher will take some of the fight out of his people," I said.

Another gargoyle landed on the stairs and Rory leapt at him, bringing the twin hammers down hard. A large section of its shoulder fell away with the first of her blows.

"Let's hope so," Rory said as she took out one of the creature's legs. "My arms are getting tired."

"Umm, guys," Marshall said, drawing my attention. "I wouldn't speak too soon about the Butcher being down."

I spun around to find the tatter-winged figure of the Butcher pulling himself up and out of the impact crater in the middle of Broadway. Although he looked worse for the wear, he still managed to heft up a nearby police car and toss it in our direction.

Several wizards managed to dissolve it with a blast of eldritch-colored energy, leaving only a surviving tire to bounce up the stairs harmlessly toward us.

"To me!" the Butcher cried out. The area around and above him swarmed with the pulsing wings of his gargoyles, the streets also filling with those humans who had no doubt been camping at Union Square hoping for the Life Eternal.

"Please tell me you have notes on this," I said to Marshall.

The frantic flipping of pages came from behind me as I watched the remaining witches and warlocks attack the herd of rogue gargoyles.

"Working on it," he said, then after what felt like far too long a pause: "Got it!"

Rory and I both turned to him, but his face was still buried in his notes.

"Well?" I asked.

"Oh, sorry," he said, looking up and pointing to the Butcher. "He's not flying anywhere with those wings, right?"

"Doubtful," I said.

"You know the expression 'Pick on someone your own size'?" he said, not waiting for an answer. "Well, screw that. With him grounded, I say we give him something several stories tall to pick on."

"Like when we escaped Union Square and you blocked the street with that wave of pavement!" Rory said.

"Nice thought," I said, "but I nearly split my head in two doing that. I don't think I can muster something big enough to go against this assembly."

"Let me worry about that," Marshall said. He slapped his notebook shut and ran down the stairs past me. "Don't think of a wave or wall. Think more of Bricksley . . . times a million."

Rory went back to defending the stairs as I pulled out my great-great-grandfather's tome and set about in preparation. Arcane gestures and the Slavic words from the language of the old country filled my mouth, and I focused my energy into the streets at the center of Times Square. My will pressed into the pavement, spreading as wide as my mind could go without bursting, and I called the golem into being.

Cars and debris from the battle fell away as the stone pulled itself from the ground, slowly forming a hulking figure that stood a little over a story tall. I was impressed with my effort, but against the scale of Times Square, my creation looked like a toy.

Several of the gargoyles rushed it, tearing chunks out of its legs with their sharp little claws, and it was all I could do to hold my creation together, managing the occasional swipe at its foes. But for everyone I knocked away, another fell into place to continue its work of chipping away at my creature.

Marshall stumbled back out of the crowd all around us, dragging a familiar figure behind him. The heat of battle made the warlock in his tow look more wild-haired than ever, his fists aglow from the rings he wore on every finger.

"Warren!" I shouted. "Right about now would be a great time for a boost."

The rings on Warren's hands lit up like a Christmas tree, and when he spoke his voice came out like he was speaking through a loudspeaker.

"Convocation!" he shouted. "Concentrate your energy on me."

Flashes of light in every color of the spectrum shot out across Times Square. Almost every witch and warlock lit up as the beams came at Warren. Somehow his body managed to absorb it, although it looked as if it might tear him apart at any moment. Fighting to control himself, he slowly raised his hands out toward me, spreading his fingers wide. A pure white blast of light shot from them out to me, and when it hit, I barely held my spell of the pavement golem.

I gave in to the power channeling through me, adding it to my own, allowing it to amplify my will. The story-tall figure of stone grew at my command as I pulled more of the streets of New York into its form until it stood a good ten stories high.

"Now we've got a fair fight!" I shouted.

Much of the battle continued on around me in all

directions, but I trusted my allies to hold their own and focused on the main group that had come to make their stand with the Butcher.

Driven by my wrath—my hatred of everything this monster and his people had brought upon me and my city these past few months—I unleashed the giant golem, leading it into battle against them.

The gargoyles fought hard to defend their master, but this time it was of little use. Giant fists, feet, and limbs crashed down on them, smashing the creatures into broken piles of stone that flew in all directions across Times Square. They were simply no match against my amplified aggression.

"This is for Laurien," I said, driving a blow down on him, taking off one of his wings. "For Fletcher." Another blow, and the entire left side of the Butcher broke free, crumbling to the ground. "But most of all, this is for making me destroy the work of Alexander Belarus." I could no longer hold myself in check, raining blow after blow down upon the Butcher, his form shattering until all that was left was a pile of stone dust that was already disappearing on the wind as I let up on my attack.

I collapsed my creation down, its component parts spreading out in great piles on the streets of Times Square. Despite the boost of power I had been given, I still felt drained and fell to all fours, trying to calm myself. My friends came to me, but I pushed them off, crawling over to where Laurien's broken human body lay.

"I'm sorry," I said, touching her face. "I tried."

The witch twitched at my touch and I drew my hand away in surprise.

"She's alive!" I shouted out, looking to the gathered witches and warlocks. "Somebody do something!"

Laurien shook her head and coughed. "Nothing arcane can save me now, I'm afraid," she said.

"Why did you do that up there?" I asked, wanting to shout in frustration. "You got in the way of the Butcher's blow. It should be me lying here."

She shook her head and gave me a pained smile. "Have you learned so little of me?" she asked. "All the times you found me to be short with you, it was all for the defense of the Convocation. Years ago I struggled to regain my human form so I could better serve my community, witch and warlock alike. I dedicated my life to defending my people. So how, then, could I let you come into harm's way up there? You have proven that you *are* my people, Alexandra. Make no mistake about that."

There were no words I could say, no comfort I could give, and in the end, Laurien seemed at peace with meeting her death. There was no pleading, no last gasp for life or begging for more time. Her eyes slid shut, her presence a sudden absence in my arms, and she was gone.

Silence filled Times Square all around us, the strangest thing to experience in the heart of my city. I gave Laurien over to a group of her people as they gathered in around her, and I stepped away to join my friends, stone and human alike.

Every last part of me felt drained to the core, and I could do nothing more than stand there silently among those of us who had survived until the sound of Marshall clearing his throat drew my attention.

Stanis, Caleb, Warren, Rory, and I all looked at him.

"I don't want to alarm anyone," Marshall said, "but the *world* is watching."

I laughed, mostly to keep from crying, the kind of cry that I knew might never stop. I could process everything that had just happened—the insanity of arcana at this scale, that we had probably saved thousands of lives here in Times Square tonight, let alone those the Butcher and his people would have harmed had we not stopped him. All of that seemed like a relatively easy task compared to what we were about to face.

How do you take on the world?

Twenty-nine

Stanis

More humans than I had ever experienced at once were coming into Times Square. All around us, faces pressed against the glass of all the buildings as people took their phones out and pointed them down at us.

"Shit," Detective Rowland said. "I don't think our brothers and sisters in blue will be able to hold them back much longer."

"Plus there's probably a whole precinct or two that would like a word with us, and the lot of you," Maron added.

"We should probably take this somewhere a little more private," Alexandra said.

I looked around the rapidly filling streets in every direction. "Where would you suggest?" I asked.

"Up above the giant television monitor," she said. "You know, where they drop the ball on New Year's Eve?"

This I did know, never quite understanding the ritual, but now was not the time to inquire about it. Instead, I scooped Alexandra up in my arms and brought her up to the top of the building while Jonathan and a few other of my *grotesques* lent a hand transporting the rest of our group there. Several trips later, my people had gathered Detectives Rowland and Maron, Aurora, Warren, Caleb, and several other witches and warlocks that they pointed out.

"So what now?" Detective Maron asked, brushing himself off.

"Listen up," Alexandra said. "All of you. This is our one chance to get this right."

Detective Rowland laughed. "I thought we got it right when we kicked the Butcher's ass," she said.

I shook my head. "The end is just the beginning, is it not?" I asked.

Alexandra smiled. "Exactly," she said. "From this point forward our three factions—humans, *grotesques*, and arcanists—we all know of each other now. All of us assembled up here . . . What we do here today *matters*. What we *decide* here today matters. We set the tone not just for our future, but for the future of the world."

Marshall gave an uneasy laugh. "No pressure or anything," he said.

"That's a pretty big task," Rowland said. "Where do you see us fitting into this? I can tell you right now that the NYPD is going to take what just happened down there as a sign of gargoyle aggression."

"Even though my people fought against them?" I asked.

Rowland nodded. "New York's Finest are a little slow-moving against profiling. It's going to take some time before they run up and hug a gargoyle. Sorry, but it's true."

Alexandra fell silent as she contemplated the detective's question. The longer it went, the more I felt compelled to speak.

"While I can only speak for those *grotesques* who fall within my dominion, I shall try to keep a continued peace among them," I said. "However, I will admit to a need for a more public presence for policing them to put at ease the common man. My father's dungeons were used to house the worst of humankind back in Kobryn. Could we not institute some sort of facility here that would hold the worst of my kind?"

"A super prison?" Marshall asked, his eyes lighting up.

The excitement in his voice caused all of us to turn to him. "Sorry. We have these things in the comics I read."

"We could convert the old subway station my great-great-grandfather built to our purposes," Alexandra suggested as she carefully thought it through. "The stone there—while a bit beat up from our battle with the Butcher—is still rich in arcane magic, and I'm sure I could reinforce it."

"You," Caleb started, then stopped. "*We* should probably make it strong enough to house witches and warlocks, too."

"Hold on, now," Warren said, taking offense. "Are you suggesting we are criminals?"

"Without giving up anyone under my strict policy of client-freelancer privilege," Caleb said, "let's just say I've worked for the best and worst among you and leave it at that. Maybe the fear of jail time for the worst offenders out there might solve some of the issues that take up so much time when your Convocation meets."

Warren paused to consider it.

"A fair and thought-provoking point," he said, then turned to his murmuring assemblage of people.

"We must discuss this further among ourselves," a blond woman with them said.

Warren remained with us, but the rest of the witches and warlocks moved off to the far side of the roof, conferring among themselves.

"I'm not sure the mayor's office will go for that," Rowland said.

"Then we make them," Maron said. "Chloe, we just went from being mocked by the department to suddenly handling the largest shift in law enforcement history *ever*. They're going to want answers, and fast, before we have a citywide panic. Presenting them with a solution that helps police the situation is a step in the right direction."

"And who exactly is going to police it?" Rowland asked.

"I can help with that," Aurora said, stepping forward. "I would expect the police to eventually take over such a task, but in the meantime, I have no problem with keeping the peace, and using force on those who would break it."

Aurora held up her twin hammers. Rowland looked at her, skepticism in her eyes.

"Despite the blue hair and glasses," I said, "Aurora is more than a formidable fighter . . . in case you missed it down below."

"I can vouch for her," Detective Maron said with a smile. "She managed to save me down there, probably more than once."

Aurora smiled back at him, her face turning a bright crimson hue. "It's what I do," she said with a shrug.

Marshall walked to the edge of the roof and stared down into Times Square far below. "With that many cameras, maybe I should have worn a T-shirt with my store's name on it."

"Don't worry," Aurora said, turning away from the detective. She clapped Marshall on the shoulder, then put her arm around him. "After what you helped pull off here tonight, I think you'll more than expand your client base among the witches and warlocks alone."

"Let's hope I can make some of them gamers," he said.

Aurora gave him a compassionate squeeze, and to my surprise did not mock him for his answer. Instead she kept her arm around him as they stared out over the city in silence.

I turned to the warlock Warren. "I am sorry about Laurien," I said.

He smiled, but it was a grim one. "Thank you," he said.

"She died protecting her people," Alexandra said.

"It is the way I am sure she wished to go out," he said, then looked over to the witches and warlocks he had asked me to bring up with us. "If you will excuse me, I should probably join the others of my kind, for there is much for me to discuss concerning her passing."

Alexandra and I both nodded our approval, and Warren walked off across the roof to his people.

For a moment it was just Alexandra and me alone where we stood, the rest of our friends and detectives conferring with one another a short distance away. I looked over the edge of the building, at the people below and the *grotesques* that filled the open air. Alexandra rested her hands on my arms, her skin cool against my rough stone.

"You okay?" she asked.

I thought for a long moment before answering. "I suppose I will be, yes," I said.

"You don't sound so certain," she said.

"I thought with the creation of Sanctuary, I would finally make up for the sins of my father," I said. "That I would be a better leader."

"You *are* a better leader," she insisted.

"No," I said. "I am a less harmful one, less damaging, but I am no leader yet. And even if I were, I would be an incomplete one. I need someone by my side. If I am to be a king to my people, then I wish you to be my queen."

Alexandra stepped back, her arms dropping to her side.

"I cannot rule alone," I said.

One moment her face held a smile and the next it was a mask of bewilderment. "Would you be saying that if Emily was still here?" Alexandra asked.

I fell silent as I thought about it for a moment. "I do not think it is something she ever truly desired," I said. "It was enough for her to find out who she was. She has her own family to look after."

It was hard to read Alexandra's face, but I detected the hint of a smile at the corner of her mouth, which did my heart good.

"And what about you?" Alexandra asked. "What about *your* family?"

"I am among my own . . . both *grotesque* and humankind, but as I said, I cannot rule alone. My father did so by his will and his alone, and it was not conducive to leading well. I need a partner in this."

Alexandra smiled as Warren came back over to us from his crowd. Aurora, Marshall, and the detectives walked over to us as well.

"I would understand if you did not wish to commit your life to ruling over creatures of stone," I said. "You have your art, these witches and warlocks to contend with, not to mention these detectives and the people of Manhattan, who are all more aware of my kind than ever."

Alexandra shook her head. "Laurien said I was one of her people," Alexandra said. "But I'm one of *your* people, too. Through arcana, I am a witch—a Spellmason—but it also makes your *grotesques* my people as well." She looked to Warren, who gave her a nod, then back at me. "Ruling at your side will help bridge the gap between all of us."

"Perhaps," Warren said with a shrug, "but do not look to me for your answer on that."

"Well, who should I be looking at?" she asked as she searched the crowd of witches and warlocks.

"Ask Caleb," he said.

All of us turned to Caleb, who had not seemed to register what Warren had said.

When he noticed all of us staring, his face changed and he turned to Warren. "Excuse me . . . ?"

"Our kind spend much of our time deliberating," Warren said.

"I had not noticed," I said. "Even among my kind, who find the passage of a decade short, you take forever."

"And that is why we came to our decision so quickly," Warren said. "As you've experienced, there is much infighting among our various factions. Everyone was nominating this one and that one in their own self-interests, but there was only one person we agreed on who never took sides: Caleb."

"But he is an outsider," Marshall said. "A *freelancer.*"

"It's not a dirty word, you know," Caleb shot back.

"You do things for money," I said.

"Exactly," Warren said. "And that's his strong point. Everyone in our community has worked with Caleb, and for reasons I barely understand, they *all* like him."

I stared at the alchemist, who gave me a smug smile back. "How could they like you so much?" I asked.

"Don't be so shocked," he said. "It's easy. I don't take sides. I keep the peace because, yes, not choosing sides has helped me make a fair share of bank working for these people. That, apparently, holds a great value with them."

"So you will head our Convocation?" Warren asked, nervously adjusting the rings on his fingers.

Caleb nodded without hesitation. "There had better be some perks," he said.

"Unlimited power over every magical being in the city enough for you?" Warren asked.

Caleb looked to Alexandra as if seeking her approval, but she would not meet his eye. He went to her. "Well?" he asked.

"Take it," she said. "It's what you've always wanted from those you worked with—power and acceptance from your own kind."

"I'm sorry," he said with utter sincerity in his words, looking from her to me. "For everything I've done." He turned back to Alexandra. "I promise to be a better ally than I was a boyfriend."

"Let's hope so," she said.

"It would be a shame to have to start another gargoyle war if you do not," I added.

Caleb gave me a grim smile, then turned back to Warren and nodded.

"It is so, then," Warren said, and gestured him toward the other witches and warlocks waiting nearby.

Caleb started off, then stopped. "One last thing," Caleb said, and turned to Alexandra and me. He reached into the lining of his jacket. "You called me an opportunist earlier . . ."

When neither of us tried to argue against him, Caleb laughed.

"Fair enough," he said, "it's true. I'm fine with it. It's who I am, at heart. But I'd like to think maybe I've learned a bit about opportunity from being around such kind hearts as yours, and I'd like to think I know when to *give* an opportunity, too."

Caleb's hand came out of his coat, the long chain and stone of the Cagliostro Medallion clasped in his fist. He walked up to me and held it out in front of him.

"Take it," he said, looking me straight in the eye.

I looked to Alexandra at his side, but it was clear that this was between Caleb and myself. I met his eyes as I grabbed the stone at the end of the chain and held it in my hand.

"You would wish me to have this?" I asked. "Why?"

Caleb did not look away as he spoke. "I know you and I have not been the best of friends," he said, "but there is a bond we share."

"Alexandra," I said.

"Exactly," he said. "Last year, when you and I were on Kejetan's floating barge kingdom, I told you that it would be best if she were with me. "

"You told me I had little to offer her," I reminded him, bitter at the memory of that night. "That she should be with someone who could be there for her, to be with her night and day."

"I said she should be with someone human," he corrected. Caleb looked down at the medallion hanging from his hand to mine. "I was wrong. I was being selfish. I've tried to make things work with her—mandatory date nights, even—but no matter what, there's always one thing in the way that I can't control. And that's you, Stanis. I promised Lexi I'd give it and I truly want you to have this. Wear it with my blessing."

Caleb released the chain and the medallion slid into my clawed hand. All I could do for several seconds was stare at it. Finally, I looked up at him. "I do not know what to say," I said.

"You don't need to say anything," he said, sliding his hands into the pockets of his jeans. "You've more than earned it." He turned to Alexandra. "And you deserve it."

She wrapped her arms around him and hugged him, and after a moment of reluctance he hugged her back.

"Thank you," she said when she released him from the embrace. "For doing the right thing."

"Yes," I said. "Thank you."

"We may make an altruist out of you yet," Alexandra said

"Don't hold your breath," Caleb said as he walked off with Warren toward the other witches and warlocks. "The blow is softened a bit by being given the reins of the whole Convocation."

As he walked away, I handed the medallion to Alexandra.

She stood on the tips of her toes to fasten the medallion around my neck, the metallic scrape of it sounding out against the stone of my skin as she clasped it shut.

"Ready?"

"I believe so," I said, wondering just how I was supposed to make this thing work. "What do I—"

I did not have a chance to finish my question. Apparently the very thought of the transition willed it into action. I doubled forward, falling to my knees and cracking the rooftop below me.

"Stanis!" Alexandra called out, kneeling down in front of me, reaching out to grab my shoulders, but the second her hands touched me, she pulled away.

My body was on fire. Not with a visible flame, but every last part of me screamed out with the act of transformation. My head arched to the heavens as I let out a silent scream, my wings stretched as wide as they went.

To my shock and surprise, they were *shrinking* from my sight. My weight shifted as the wings disappeared against my back, my clawed hands and feet becoming less pointed and more soft and rounded . . . more human.

The usual dark gray of my skin changed, fading to a pale white in the moonlight. I tried to stand, but my center of balance was off and I stumbled forward. While normally a fall forward would have crushed anything or anyone in my way, Alexandra's hands slid under my shoulders and her arms wrapped around me.

"You . . . caught me," I said.

Alexandra laughed. "I know, right? You don't weigh several tons now."

With her help, I stood and steadied myself, but it would be some time no doubt before I would get used to the change in my center of balance. I turned to the reflective surface of the large glass ball, catching sight of myself.

A young man—the shoulder-length blond hair and face from a distant memory—stared back at me with a wide-eyed, foolish look and wild-faced grin. The clothes—the ones Alexander Belarus had long ago carved for me—barely covered my body, the torn outfit blowing in the wind.

"I had forgotten that person," I said, watching his mouth move in time with mine. "For so long in all my recollections of my past, I have pictured my *grotesque*."

I turned back to Alexandra, seeing her for what felt like the first time with these human eyes of mine.

"We're going to have to get you something more modern to wear," she said with a smile.

I lifted my hand and pressed it to the side of her face, her hair brushing against the softness of my now-human skin. "You mean nineteenth-century European is not all the rage these days?"

"Not quite," she said, her hand rising to touch my face back. "Ready for your first sunrise this millennium?"

"More than ready," I said, pulling her close to me. "Care to rule by my side?"

Her eyes widened but her face was uncertain. "Are you sure?"

"More than I have ever been about anything," I said, feeling the weight of the medallion around my neck. "I have known you all your life, Alexandra Belarus. With you at my side, all things are possible. I see that now."

Alexandra nodded and pulled herself even closer to me.

Time would tell what path our rule would take or how our lives would entwine themselves together, but I had never been afraid of time, and there was also this newfound sensation in me—hope.

The future was full of hope, even if always uncertain, but I gave myself over to the moment, loving the sensation of Alexandra's skin touching mine, of our lips finally meeting, an impossibility of my most secret desire made real.

And in that moment, the world around us fell away.

About the Author

ANTON STROUT was born in the Berkshire Hills mere miles from writing heavyweights Nathaniel Hawthorne and Herman Melville. He currently lives outside New York City in the haunted corn maze that is New Jersey (where nothing paranormal ever really happens, he assures you).

His writing has appeared in several DAW anthologies—some of which feature Simon Canderous tie-in stories—including: *The Dimension Next Door*, *Spells of the City*, and *Zombie Raccoons & Killer Bunnies*.

In his scant spare time, he is an always writer, sometimes actor, sometimes musician, occasional RPGer, and the world's most casual and controller-smashing video gamer. He now works in the exciting world of publishing, and yes, it is as glamorous as it sounds.

He is currently hard at work on his next book and can be found lurking the darkened hallways of antonstrout.com.

Don't miss

Stonecast

BOOK TWO OF
The Spellmason Chronicles

BY
ANTON STROUT

☾

Alexandra Belarus, the last practicing Spellmason, doesn't know what has become of Stanis, her gargoyle protector. Hidden forces are watching and threatening her, but she's worried for her stone-hearted friend—who may no longer be so friendly...

PRAISE FOR THE SPELLMASON CHRONICLES

"The magical elements will keep you riveted, and I guarantee you'll be begging for more."
—*Night Owl Reviews*

"Excellent character development."
—*Nerdist*

antonstrout.com
twitter.com/AntonStrout
facebook.com/ProjectParanormalBooks
penguin.com

M1503T0514

PRAISE FOR THE SPELLMASON CHRONICLES

Stonecast

"One of the more unique premises that I've encountered in the urban fantasy genre, and there is plenty of action and mystery to keep a person occupied."   —*All Things Urban Fantasy*

"*Stonecast* reads like an episode of television: high stakes, high tension, stark contrasts, well-rounded cast, and dialogue complete with quips and banter."   —*Urban Fantasy Land*

"Thrilling . . . Skillful characterization enriches a story that is filled with peril, loss, treachery, and sacrifice. Great stuff!"
                                                               —*RT Book Reviews*

"A fantastic sequel in this unique and exciting fantasy series. Full of suspense, intrigue, magic, and humor—gargoyles have never been this fun. The story ends with a climactic and satisfying conclusion . . . Don't miss this fast-paced urban fantasy."   —*SciFiChick.com*

Alchemystic

"Loved *Alchemystic*. Every girl needs her own Stanis!"
                        —Jeanne C. Stein, national bestselling author of *Blood Bond*

"Like being strapped to a wrecking ball of urban fantasy fun. Hang on and enjoy the mayhem."
                                —Mario Acevedo, author of *Werewolf Smackdown*

"Just when I thought Mr. Strout couldn't do any better than his Simon Canderous series, I was proven wrong! I couldn't put *Alchemystic* down. It was nonstop action and tension, a bit of romance but not overdone, and all sorts of twists and turns . . . The magical elements will keep you riveted, and I guarantee you'll be begging for more."   —*Night Owl Reviews*

continued . . .

"This is a heartfelt look into the human nature that is intertwined with magical elements. Metaphysics, romance, humanity, compassion, action, and humor all meshed into a wonderful masterpiece of writing splendor." —*Earth's Book Nook*

"The magic behind *Alchemystic* was incredibly intriguing . . . All in all, *Alchemystic* was a very solid start to a new series that will definitely be on my radar for future releases." —*A Book Obsession*

"Strout has come up with an even more fantastic story than before. *Alchemystic* is a fun and exciting start to a promising new urban fantasy series. With plenty of adventure, mystery, suspense, and magic, this was impossible to put down. Fast-paced, fresh, and surprising, there is never a dull moment. Urban fantasy fans will definitely want to check out this new series (as well as Strout's previous Simon Canderous series)." —*SciFiChick.com*

"*Alchemystic* has a unique story with delightful characters and plenty of mystery to keep you interested." —*Rabid Reads*

"*Alchemystic* is thrilling, funny, and eerie—all the elements that make Strout books such irreverent fun!" —*RT Book Reviews*

"Excellent character development. The ending leaves this whole world open in a great way . . . My favorite part of this is the use of magic . . . It feels organic and interesting." —*Nerdist*

PRAISE FOR ANTON STROUT AND HIS SIMON CANDEROUS NOVELS

Dead Matter

"Great sense of humor, combined with vivid characters, a complex mystery, and plenty of danger . . . a fantastic read. Urban fantasy fans should not miss this exciting series." —*SciFiChick.com*

"[Strout's] skillful blending of the creepy and the wacky gives his series an original appeal. Don't miss out!" —*RT Book Reviews* (top pick)

Deader Still

"Take the New York of *Men in Black* and *Ghostbusters*, inject the same pop-culture awareness and irreverence of *Buffy the Vampire Slayer* or *The Middleman*, toss in a little *Thomas Crown Affair*, shake and stir, and you've got something fairly close to this book."
—*The Green Man Review*

"It has a *Men in Black* flavor mixed with *NYPD Blue*'s more gritty realism."
—*SFRevu*

"A fun read . . . If you liked *Dead to Me*, it's a safe bet you'll like this one even more."
—Jim C. Hines, author of *Codex Born*

"Unique from a lot of the urban fantasy genre. This is a fantastic series."
—*Bitten by Books* (5 tombstones)

Dead to Me

"Following Simon's adventures is like being the pinball in an especially antic game, but it's well worth the wear and tear."
—Charlaine Harris, #1 *New York Times* bestselling author of *Midnight Crossroad*

"Part *Ghostbusters*, part *Men in Black*, Strout's debut is both dark and funny, with quirky characters, an eminently likable protagonist, and the comfortable, familiar voice of a close friend."
—Rachel Vincent, *New York Times* bestselling author of *Oath Bound*

"Urban fantasy with a wink and a nod . . . A genuinely fun book with a fresh and firmly tongue-in-cheek take on the idea of paranormal police."
—Kelly McCullough, author of *Blade Reforged*

"Clever, fast-paced, and a refreshing change in the genre of urban fantasy."
—*SFRevu*

"Strout's inventive story line raises the genre's bar with his collection of oddly mismatched, entertaining characters and not-so-secret organizations."
—*Monsters and Critics*